TALES OF THE JOURNEY

WHO IS GEM MARIE

By

Stacey Allanda Brown

Dear Reader,

Welcome to *Tales of The Scotney (Who Is Gem Marie)*, a novel born from a character introduced in my previous work, *8830*. This story is a blend of my deep love for history, a vivid imagination, and fragments of my own life experiences woven into the narrative. As you immerse yourself in the world of Gem Marie, my hope is that the journey provokes something within you be it wonder, intrigue, or even discomfort. If, at any moment, the story stirs your emotions and rattles your thinking pattern, whether good or bad, then I've succeeded in my goal. Which is to take you along as my guest into one of the greatest wonders of the world the human imagination.

I want to thank you for sharing one of your most valuable commodities with me, your time. I hope this book offers you an experience that lingers and resonates long after you've turned the final page.

Enjoy the adventure, and thank you again.

Warmly,

Stacey Allanda Brown

Table of Contents

Chapter: 1

The Making of Jean Paul

Jean Paul Heritage emerged into the world within the embrace of humble beginnings, his birth was woven into existence by Baptiste Heritage and Camille Vitello. As their courtship blossomed, they stole moments together beneath the shade of ancient oak trees, whispering sweet nothings amidst the rustle of leaves. Yet, their love was not without its trials. Baptiste's family, wary of Camille's modest means, forbade their union, fearing it would bring shame upon their name. Likewise, Camille's parents, mindful of Baptiste's uncertain future with their daughter, urged her to seek a more suitable equal match. Ignoring all advice about their union, fueled only by the fiery fervor of youthful love the two ran off. Holding their bond together, the two flourished amidst the unforgiving landscape of poverty and the absence of formal education. Now in the shadows of hardship, they found solace in each other, their dreams intermingling with the struggles of daily life. Through the lens of their shared journey, Jean Paul's story unfolds, the power of his unwavering spirit that defies adversity. "His father Baptiste's mastery in handling livestock was truly remarkable; he possessed an extraordinary ability to rescue and nurture animals, ensuring their well-being and fostering the production of the healthiest stock. There's was a sincerity in his dedication that's evident in the countless lives he manage to touch. Notably, he once skillfully stitched a gash on a young colt, tending to it with such precision and care that it healed to absolute perfection. His commitment to the highest standards of care for the animals and the relationship between his fellow man was a constant showcase, his ability to treat animals as if he could feel their illness was remarkable. It was this blend of skills that truly intrigued and inspired fellow countrymen and acquaintances. Those who frequently sought guidance from Baptiste often proclaimed, "Turn to Heritage,' for he is an equitable man." His words carried a profound sense of clarity and sincerity. Despite their youthfulness, Baptiste, and Camille's affection for each other was held in high regard, demonstrated through a maturity and commitment akin to that of a devoted married couple. Their union not only brought forth Jean Paul but also his sister, Elenor.

Together they made ends meet in a modest dwelling, the result of Baptiste's labor as a farmer. Initially he was cautioned about the rough terrain of the land and was warned that it might not yield much return for many years to come. Despite this, he purchased the land at a modest price, determined to make it thrive. Impressively, the impoverished young farmer's diligent efforts transformed the land, resulting in bountiful crops that surpassed expectations. The couple's reputation preceded them without their awareness. Rumors had spread throughout Paris about a young, impoverished couple whose wisdom, seemingly inherited from their elders, had transformed barren lands into fertile fields teeming with crops and greenery. Their youthful presence, along with the authentic love they shared became the subject of discussion among both young and old alike. The two created memorable occasions without trying, one particular incident solidified their reputation. During an unexpected rain downpour in town, Baptiste, and Camille, who were out trading and shopping, left their horse and buggy at a distant hitching post. Instead of seeking temporary shelter from nearby shops, like the other local Parisians. Baptiste gallantly lifted Camille as she sheltered them with her parasol as they braved the pouring rain. While he lifted her, Camille's dress shifted and revealed a flash of red, along with two bright red bows adorning the tops of her boots that were hidden by her dress. Surprised by the unexpected adornments, Baptiste's smile widened, and he impulsively kissed Camille, causing her to startle and inadvertently led them both to tumble to the muddy ground. Completely soaked and sitting in a puddle, the two couldn't help but laugh at their predicament. This charming scene didn't go unnoticed, onlookers whispered from storefront windows, while the local intellectuals that had gathered at the coffeehouse on the hill, observed in fascination. The incident even sparked a great debate and lengthy discussions among them, pondering the significance of Camille's choice of wearing red beneath her dress. "A color typically known and associated with wealth and opulence," one onlooker stated. Their family life seemed to be picture perfect, the joyous anticipation of welcoming their third child into the world, tragedy descended upon the couple like an uninvited storm. Camille, radiant with the glow of impending motherhood, was unexpectedly snatched away from them, leaving behind a void that seemed insurmountable. The heartbreaking twist of fate struck even harder as Camille, in her final moments, cradled the stillborn child in her arms, while tenderly whispering "Bonne Nuit," as if bidding farewell to the fragile soul before succumbing to an eternal slumber herself. It was as if she had orchestrated her own poetic departure, leaving behind a haunting echo of her love and tenderness. The stillness that followed Camille's passing was evident, enveloping the family in a shroud of grief and disbelief. With the words "Good Night" as a poignant reminder of what could have been, Jean Paul and his sister Elenor found themselves thrusted into a world where the warmth of maternal care was abruptly extinguished. Only leaving them to navigate the treacherous waters of childhood motherless. Yet, amidst the darkness, whispers of mystery lingered. Baptiste questioned what unseen forces had woven such a tragic tapestry of fate for this once happy family? Baptiste, unaccustomed to the dual responsibilities of parenting and maintaining the household, sought solace in the advice of obtaining a new wife. There was an open invite for young fifteen-year-old girl named Lauren Chereche L'or. Raised by her mother, a woman known as a widow, though rumors swirled that her true story was far more complex. Some whispered of a passionate liaison with a famed half-Native American fur trader, shrouded in the mists of secrecy. Lauren's mother wove a tale of loss and heroism, claiming her daughter's father was a valiant soldier in the Continental Army, and fallen in battle. She presented a weathered musket, claiming it as his, a tangible relic of his valor. Yet, Lauren herself had never known the touch of her father's hand. Despite this enigmatic background, Lauren possessed an exotic allure, a beauty her mother insisted she inherited from her elusive father. Lauren stepped into the role of stepmother with a stern demeanor. Her presence cast an enigmatic shadow over the household, her beauty a captivating veil, masking her true intentions. With a gaze as sharp as her wit, she commanded both respect and fear from those around her. Yet, beneath her stern exterior lay a complexity that intrigued even Baptiste, who found himself caught in her young web of mystery and allure. Despite her insistence on being addressed as sister Lauren instead of mother, there was an air of authority that transcended familial boundaries, leaving those under her rule with little choice but to obey. As the days passed, whispers of her past circulated, adding fuel to the intrigue surrounding this enigmatic figure who had woven herself into the fabric of Baptiste's heart. Amidst the daily tasks of running the household, she boldly rejected the idea of becoming a mother, a decision that went against the subtle expectations imposed by her own mother. Despite her mother's nudges towards Baptiste, her marriage remained devoid of maternal aspirations.

Instead, guided by her mother's counsel, she meticulously molded herself after Baptiste's late wife, Camille, learning her likes and dislikes. It was Lauren's mother who confirmed the ownership of the land beneath Baptiste's modest abode, urging swift organization within its walls. Under Lauren's reign, the household transformed into a realm of strict order and unwavering servitude. She demanded opulent gifts and indulgences, stretching Baptiste's modest earnings to their limits. With each passing day, the weight of providing for the family bore down heavily upon Baptiste's weary shoulders, until a debilitating illness struck him down, leaving Jean Paul to assume the mantle of manhood prematurely, burdened with responsibilities far beyond his tender years. Despite his youth, Jean Paul possessed a remarkable physical stature, he was often mistaken for someone older. His towering presence drew the attention of many women including the affluent businessman Monsieur Gracieux's daughter, Madame Lady Fleur. Madame Fleur found herself captivated by his charisma and his handsome chiseled features. As fate would have it, Jean Paul's encounter with Madam Fleur would alter the course of his destiny. Little did he know that his journey was about to take an unexpected turn in the opulent Parisian lifestyles of the aristocratic quarter. In the air that carried whispers of privilege and refinement, Jean Paul was considered an anomaly. Although quiet and diligent, his stark contrast to the dashing, well-refined, educated youths who frequented Madam Fleur courtship circle left her intrigued. His presence, though unassuming, caught the eye of the wealthy Madam Fleur Dior Gracieux again one fateful afternoon as she peered through the gilded window of a dress shop. Madam Fleur on her eighteenth birthday, accustomed to having her desires fulfilled with the swiftness of a conjured spell, wasted no time with submitting her request to satisfy her newfound desire. She notified her father and insisted on having Jean Paul with the same intensity she would use to request a custom-made gown or a prized ornament. Just as easily as her whims were indulged, so too was her wish for Jean Paul to be hers. Baptiste Heritage, still frail, ill, and unable to advocate fully for his son, remained oblivious to the intricacies of the arrangement that had been made. Lauren, his wife, had agreed to the indentured servant sale of Jean Paul. She carefully spun a tale of Jean Paul's departure for work and helping the family, omitting the truth that she had sold him to become a pawn in Madam Fleur's romantic pursuits. Jean Paul, unwittingly consigned to a fate, assuming that his work for the affluent family would help his loved ones he would leave

4

behind. Beyond his imagination, he was whisked away to the imposing Gracieux mansion, where amidst the grandeur and the dictates of high society, he was molded into the image of a proper gentleman. His humble meager past was obscured by the veneer of refinement. Yet beneath the facade, secrets simmered, waiting to unravel the carefully crafted tapestry of aristocratic intrigue. In the realm of high society, Jean Paul found himself thrust into a whirlwind of mock balls and grand events, each meticulously crafted to groom him for his newfound life. Despite the ache for his father and distant family, there was an undeniable allure to this extravagant lifestyle that had grown to ensnared him. As Jean Paul blossomed into his fifteenth year, a fateful union transpired, the merging of two distinct worlds. Their nuptials ignited fervent chatter amongst the elite echelons of Paris, spinning tales of a young man of modest origins stealing the heart of Madam Fleur with his charismatic charm. The wedding was destined to be nothing short of extravagant, an opulent affair and a lavish feast spanning an entire week. With his captivating allure and a charm capable of melting the most steadfast hearts, Jean Paul emerged as the very embodiment of desire for Madam Fleur who adored him unreservedly. Their love story unfolded like a masterpiece, inspiring local artists to weave intricate tales of their courtship onto the canvas of admiration. Each brushstroke captured the essence of their intertwined destinies, painting a portrait of passion and devotion that ignited the imagination of all who beheld it. Among their portrait masterpieces, one stands out for its daring portrayal, a depiction of the two entwined in a garden, stripped of all pretenses, reminiscent of Adam and Eve in their raw vulnerability. Invitations flooded their lavish mansion, each beseeching their presence at the grandest soirées and most prestigious gatherings. They became synonymous with Parisian social grace, their absence from any event deemed a grievous oversight, a void in the tapestry of the city's elite gatherings. Thus, Jean Paul and Madam Fleur Dior forged an indomitable legacy as the quintessential couple of the Parisian aristocracy, their lives intertwined in a dance of opulence and adoration. Amidst the whispers of high society, there stood Jean Paul, a figure of fascination and intrigue. By the tender age of twenty, his demeanor exuded the refinement of generations past, earning him the admiration of all who crossed his path. Yet, his union with Madam Fleur, long anticipated by society's eager tongues, became the canvas upon which unfavorable rumors painted their strokes. They spoke of Madam Fleur Dor's unwavering devotion, a love that withstood the tempests of Jean Paul's infidelities. Some whispered truths, others spun tales beyond reality, but all agreed on one thing: the bond between Jean Paul and Madam Fleur was a subject ripe for gossip. However, the tides of conversation shifted dramatically when Lady Priscilla entered the scene. With the grace of a porcelain figurine, she captivated hearts effortlessly. Hailing from a prestigious lineage of jewelers whose family had relocated to Paris from England. Her beauty was matched only by her family's renown. At the age of sixteen Lady Priscilla's infatuation with Jean Paul led to them being frequent companions, their presence a spectacle at every soirée and gala. Yet, it was a grand event that would etch their names into the tombstones of scandal. Rumor had it that Lady Priscilla, with her ethereal charm, brought along a newly adopted French poodle to the affair. However, the pure pedigree vanished into the labyrinthine gardens, evading the searching gazes of attendees. It took her and Jean Paul alone over two hours to finally locate the animal within the mazed garden. The talk of their disappearance became so demeaning that Lady Priscilla, as a poor diversion, started taking interest in a very esteem young architecture by the name of Colbert Hansbury. Burdened by the constraints of society, she found herself ensnared in a web of gossip and deceit. Seeking refuge from the constant cutting remarks, she continued the sudden courtship of architect Colbert Hansberry. Their frequent luncheons kept the rumors down, or so everyone thought. Until one evening she eagerly accompanied Colbert to a much-awaited extravagant ball. She was draped in the finest fabric. Unfortunately, the beautiful unique gown she wore made matters worse the scandal surrounding the woman who created the gown and Lady Priscilla's reputation took a devastating turn. When the news surfaced that Colbert had abandoned her in favor of the humble seamstress the very one responsible for designing her exquisite gowns. Lady Priscilla once again became the topic of the lady's social clubs. The poor seamstress by the name of Clara was more enamored with her craft than with monetary gain, captured Colbert's attention. This dealt a severe blow to Lady Priscilla's pride with each whispered rumor that sliced deeper into her wounded heart. Left her reeling from the betrayal, in addition to the bitter irony, Lady Priscilla inadvertently facilitated Colbert's pursuit of the seamstress. By providing him with her name and location she unknowingly guided him towards his newfound obsession. It was during a request for monogrammed handkerchiefs, similar to the meticulous workmanship of the seamstress's gowns, that Colbert's fascination with the dress maker's talents became apparent. He longed to meet the woman whose craftsmanship mirrored that of an esteemed architect. Upon first laying eyes on the petit seamstress, Colbert and she became entwined in a passionate love affair, in the dressmaker's shop. After sealing their bond, Colbert swiftly whisked Clara away to America, leaving her shop in the care of her youngest niece. Rumors swirled that the couple started a family, blessed with two sets of twin boys. The heartbreak and humiliation drove Lady Priscilla right back into the arms of Jean Paul. After their reunion, they continued to see each other secretly, now taking great care to avoid being seen together. Despite their efforts, rumors persisted about their affair and speculation arose that Jean Paul might leave his marriage. However, everything changed when Madame Fleur gave birth to her first child, a boy name Philip Adam Heritage. He bore a striking resemblance to Jean Paul. Throughout her pregnancy, Madame Fleur's growing belly served as a poignant reminder of their shared bond. However, the faithful evening of Philip's birth brought the reality of their created life to fruition. Philip's features as an infant were reminiscent of aristocracy, captivating the community and social elites who showered him with unique gifts. As Philip grew, his mannerisms mirrored those of his father, further reinforcing their undeniable connection. With the arrival of their son, the marriage between Jean Paul and Madame Fleur seemed to strengthen. Jean Paul's infatuation with Lady Priscilla appeared to diminish as his attention shifted swiftly to Philip almost bordering on obsession. One afternoon Madam Fleur overheard him confess to the young Philip that he would not allow him to be taken away as he himself had been done as a youth. He swore on his life as he whispered in Philip's ear that he would watch over him closely just as his own father Baptiste had done before he grew ill. Jean Paul's behavior now mirrored the two men one that loved him dearly and had watched over him, the other that had grown to love him but was responsible for him being taken away without notice. Although Jean Paul grew to love Madam Fleur, he still harbored some small resentment for being misled about why he was brought to the estate. There were times he longed for his family he had once knew but was not allowed to speak of. Now he dedicated his spare time to overseeing Philip's education and various musical lessons. Jean Paul's bond with Monsieur Gracieux had grown exceedingly stronger during this time. As the grooming that once initially was intended for Jean Paul was now being used for the rearing of young Philip. Jean Paul and Monsieur Gracieux frequently sat together while they watched young Philip emerging into this great being. Engaging in conversation while observing Philip's skillful performance on the violin or his recital of the literature and math lessons he had skillfully retained. One evening, Monsieur Gracieux shared the tale of how he had inherited and cultivated the empire he now oversaw. With no male heir of his own to mentor, he confided in Jean Paul that he would one day impart upon him all the necessary knowledge. Meanwhile, Madam Fleur found herself in high spirits, her days now filled with admiration for the three beloved men in her life. Their companionship brought her immense joy and fulfillment. Societal luncheons were often spent celebrating her maternal instincts, and she was encouraged to expand her family, thus bestowing society with the gift of their exceptional lineage. One winter when young Philip was just five years old, his grandfather, Monsieur Gracieux, fell seriously ill. Concealing the decline in his health, Monsieur Gracieux's health took a sharp turn one bitter evening after winter, his persistent cough breaking the silence of young Philip's recital. Seated nearby, Jean Paul discreetly handed him a handkerchief, attempting to muffle the fit and maintain decorum. When Jean Paul later retrieved the handkerchief left behind on the chair, his heart sank, streaks of blood confirmed his worst fears. Monsieur Gracieux's time with the family was drawing to a close. Sensing the inevitable, Jean Paul quietly began preparing Madam Fleur and young Philip for the looming loss. He would subtly pose hypothetical questions about life without certain comforts, carefully framing them to soften the blow. Madame Fleur often dismissed these exercises, not realizing their true intent. It wasn't long before Monsieur Gracieux slipped away in the stillness of a spring morning, passing peacefully with the very handkerchief clasped to his chest. In the aftermath, Jean Paul took charge of the family's affairs, his attention increasingly pulled away to business matters. As he traveled frequently between Paris, Italy and England, Madame Fleur was left to navigate her grief alone. The loss of her father hit her hardest in the quiet moments, when his comforting words and steady presence were most missed. Rumors about Jean Paul's dealings swirled through their social circles, casting a shadow over their lives. Although he brushed them off, assuring her it was nothing more than envy of their financial standing, Madame Fleur struggled to keep her composure. Without her father's protective guidance, and with Jean Paul more distant than ever, her only anchor in the storm was young Philip, whom she poured her heart into caring for. Yet even this, at times, felt like an impossible task with the weight of sorrow pressing down on her. Jean Paul gained control and took charge of the two banking institutions and the two hundred acres of flourishing farmland left behind by Madame Fleur's father, managing the transition seamlessly. His adept handling of affairs earned him praise even from relatives and close friends. Although some of whom were former The constituents of Monsieur Gracieux attempted to belittle him one day at a social club, their aim solely to discredit his work. They asserted the importance of proper education over having success handed to someone. Jean Paul, who quietly observed their conversation without their knowledge, responded not with words but with action. He meticulously monitored the financial accounts of those gossiping men and promptly increased their fees when their loan payments were even a day overdue. During Monsieur Gracieux's lifetime, he refrained from using the leverage of his business to retaliate, even in the face of gossip about his daughter or son-in-law. Now, Jean Paul, having gained access to nearly everyone's financial records, began noticing a pattern: those who often spoke loudly were the ones most in need of his assistance. With a strategic adjustment to the fee structure and removing the previously generous grace period, he began to acquire several estates near and abroad. Jean Paul immediate compliance both verbal and financial was swiftly achieved by all parties involved. He earned such a high level of respect that everyone was exceedingly cautious about what they said whenever the family name was mentioned. Even well after Lady Priscilla had married another man and severed all ties with Jean Paul, people remained guarded in their conversations about her. Jean Paul, once a subject of relentless gossip, had since risen to a position of great power. He was now entrusted with overseeing the arrangements and agreements that had once fallen under his father-in-law's view, a responsibility he approached with unyielding resolve. Determined not to be lenient on matters of money or ownership, Jean Paul ensured that personal friendships would never cloud his business decisions. His primary focus, however, was young Philip, who exhibited remarkable intelligence and was growing into a true gentleman. With his grace and cultured manner, Philip became the talk of many social circles. Yet, when Philip turned fourteen, an unsettling rumor began to surface, one that threatened to overshadow Jean Paul's careful reputation: whispers suggested that Lady Priscilla's eldest daughter, Bella, might also be Jean Paul's child. The implications of such a rumor could unravel years of calculated control and discretion, leaving Jean Paul teetering on the edge of a scandal that could change everything. With both Philip and Bella bearing a striking resemblance to Jean Paul and only four months apart the speculations heightened. Yet, with Jean Paul overseeing nearly everyone's finances, discussion of the matter was limited to hushed tones behind closed doors and at private gatherings. There was an incident where someone overheard Jean Paul reprimanding Lady Priscilla along a secluded cherry blossom trail for allowing Bella to be taken by her current husband's relatives. Although Jean Paul had no authority over Bella, his perceived overprotectiveness towards Philip suggested that his lack of control over Bella's life led him to ensure Philip's well-being. However, the persistent rumors about Bella being Jean Paul's child also tormented Madam Fleur, who despite her advancing age, had been unable to bear another child for Jean Paul. Madam Fleur rarely touched the subject of Bella unless under the influence of wine and often during the quiet aftermath of one of their elaborate parties at the mansion. She would vent her frustrations about the illegitimate child, while sobbing and recounting some lonesome nights, when Jean Paul could not be found. To which Jean Paul would loudly deny any accusations and profess his undying love for her and Philip only. Madam Fleur consistently found solace in Jean Paul's denials, despite harboring an awareness of his deceit. She derived comfort from the belief that he would forsake even his own kin for her. However, one late spring evening his love would be tested, Lady Priscilla dispatched an urgent messenger to the mansion to deliver the distressing news that Bella had tragically fallen from a small boat into the deep waters of the lake. Panic-stricken, her petticoat became entangled in the weeds, ensnaring her limbs. By the time assistance arrived, Bella had already ingested a fatal amount of water. It took an arduous hour of searching before a fieldmen finally located her lifeless body. Bella's delicate figure floated face down amidst a rare cluster of water lilies. Upon learning of the devastating incident, Jean Paul, who became overwhelmed with grief, secluded himself in a room, abstaining from food and contact for three days. Rumors swirled that it was on that sorrowful day that Madam Fleur had finally received undeniable confirmation of Bella's true parentage. Immediately following Bella's burial, Lady Priscilla and her husband made the decision to relocate to Italy and never returned. Now left with Philip as his only air, Jean Paul kept him under even more watchful eye. The relentless pressure exerted by Jean Paul had placed an immense strain on his relationship with his son

Philip. Always in a state of hypothetical tragedies Philip was shielded from anything that could cause potential harm. At the tender age of twenty, Philip made arrangements to embark on a journey to Italy with friends. However, his father's pervasive anxieties instilled such trepidation in him that he recoiled from the opportunity. Instead, Philip redirected his focus towards the meticulous cultivation of their family's farmland, tethering himself to the estate and eschewing travel. As Philip matured, his parents harbored lofty aspirations for his prosperous future, united in their vision. Jean Paul remained a steadfast presence, adamantly overseeing what he perceived to be Philip's promising trajectory. Matters escalated to the extent that one evening, during a formal dinner engagement, it was Philip's mother who interceded on his behalf. Madam Fleur, adorned in elegance, had spent the evening gracefully mingling with the guests, her glass of wine a constant companion. The occasion coincided closely with the anniversary of Bella's passing, a poignant reminder of grief lingering in the air. Madam Fleur's demeanor, however, belied a fervent fixation she harbored towards a particular guest, a young widower recently bereaved of his spouse. Jean Paul noticing the unusual behavior made his move towards his wife quickly. In hopes of putting an end to her advances towards the gentleman. Once aware of his action Madam fleur made a loud intoxicating comment about Jean Paul's habit of stifling a person. Her cynical tone towards Jean Paul in regard to his need to oversee everything that Philip did solely stemmed from his guilt for not providing his unclaimed Bella with swimming lessons. She went on to say that Philip may meet the same fate but not due to water but by the overbearing nature of Jean Paul's need to control his every move. The vibrant room, that once buzzed with lively chatter and a festive ambiance, now hung heavy with an oppressive silence, all thanks to Madame Fleur's cutting remark, "Where do you disappear to at night? Perhaps lost in the botanical hedges in search for fallen women's mongrel mutt." In the suffocating embrace of silence, Madame Fleur found herself engulfed by disbelief. The weight of her words hung heavily in the air, a verbal low blow delivered with a force she hadn't intended. Waves of guilt and a tumult of emotions crashed over her, threatening to drown her in remorse as onlookers witnessing eyes thirst for more secrets. In her vulnerable state, she crumbled, her resolve shattered into fragments of regret. It was Jean Paul, steadfast and unwavering, who came to her aid. Despite the sting of her venomous words, he embraced her tenderly, offering solace as he gently guided her upstairs to bed. As Madame Fleur succumbed to the turmoil within, the room bore witness to the raw intensity of the moment. Shock reverberated through the silent space, a definite echo of the emotional upheaval that had unfolded. Slowly, some of those who were present began to disperse, leaving behind a lingering sense of unease and unanswered questions. Surrounded by the deafening silence and disbelief. Madame fleur was now aware of the verbal low blow she had just struck. Too consumed with guilt and emotions, she broke down to the point where she now needed Philip to assist in coaxing her to sleep. Philip, unaffected by her abrasive words, just cuddled her as he sat at her bedside consoling her. Downstairs in the dining room, the dramatic novelty finally wearing off prompted the final guest to slowly departed as Jean Paul thanked them for their attendance. It was the late of spring after his mother's passing that young Philip now took serious heed to one of his mother's last suggestions. She often warned him not to spent so much time with work. She advised him to seek love and that it may come in unusual packages. She teased him about wanting to see her grandchildren before she moved on into the after world. Philip, who would often remind her she was still vibrant and lovely, refused to heed her warnings in between her playful banter. He also refuse to accept her physical deterioration and symptoms, which plague her. He made excuses for her longer hours in the bed in relation to her just needing more rest and sleep. That coming spring Madam fleur took her usual stroll through her garden admiring various collections of English Blue Bells. She stopped at the large gazebo to rest, with her servant at her side now pruning roses at her request, she sat with a large locket in hand that held a painted picture of Jean Paul and Philip together. She with contentment staring off into the distance at the estate the walk had taken a slight toll on her she told the servant that she would like a dozen of red roses, she slowly closed her eyes in the shaded comfortable armchair that sat under the gazebo and let out her last breath. When the servant inquired if her selection of roses were pleasing to madame Fleur. She noticed that she sat with her eyes closed and did not answer. She let out a scream as a gentle tap on Madam Fleur's shoulder caused her head to drop to one side. She quickly ran to the mansion and into the parlor and notified everyone that Madam fleur had fallen into one of her deep sleeps again and could not be awaken. Jean Paul and Philip swiftly gathered and strolled towards the gazebo, contemplating the type of floral arrangement they would need to carry back with them today after Madam's

12

long selection of various flowers. Philip, accustomed to assisting his mother back to the mansion once fatigue overwhelmed her, remained focused on his father, who briskly led the way. As they approached the shaded area of the gazebo, Philip observed his father's unusual movements, noticing him falter then dropping to his knees upon seeing his mother. With tears streaming down Jean Paul's face, his grief consumed him, reducing him to the resemblance of a weeping child. Philip, frozen in place, stood silently behind his father, his eyes fixed on his mother's serene, pale blue face. She held a locket in her right hand, her eyes closed in peaceful repose, almost as if she were smiling. In anguish, Jean Paul cried out, "Did you love him so deeply that you forgot about your love for me, my love?" After the passing of Madam Fleur Jean Paul scarcely spoke, communicating only with Philip every other day, imparting to him the duties of managing the banks and the estate. It seemed as if Jean Paul's grief knew no bounds, enveloping him entirely. Though Jean Paul sought reassurance that Philip was fully prepared to assume control of the business before he could depart to join his wife. Sadley on a warm summer afternoon, Jean Paul, in a rare moment of better spirits, made an unusual request. He asked Philip, who hadn't touched his violin in years, to play some Vivaldi, Philip hesitated at first but in an effort to brighten the day, he decided to play one of Jean Paul's favorite pieces. Jean Paul settled into a high-backed chair, his gaze drifting toward the garden beyond the window. Sunlight poured into the room, casting a soft glow that seemed to blend with the music. Outside, a robin perched delicately on a branch, its presence enhancing the tranquil scene. As Philip's violin gently swelled into a crescendo, Jean Paul felt something stir deep within him. He smiled, not outwardly, but within a peaceful smile that held more than contentment. It was the smile of someone who knew that, when the final note of the melody faded, he would soon reunite with his beloved wife. The music played on, flowing like time itself, but all moments come to an end. Eventually, Jean Paul and his wife were laid to rest, side by side, in mausoleums that mirrored one another. Their tombstones were crafted in the shape of oversized lockets, intricate and timeless. When placed together, the engravings on these marble headstone treasures aligned to reveal the words: "A love beyond life." The legacy of their love, like Philip's haunting melody, lingered in the air a testament to the bond that not even death could sever.

Chapter: 2

Monsieur Philip Adam Heritage'

Philip Heritage often found solace in the quiet company of his parents' graves, particularly during the early stages of their passing. Whispers circulated among the locals that if one lingered nearby, they might catch the echo of his sorrowful sobs or the murmur of heartfelt conversations with his departed loved ones. For countless evenings, Philip devoted himself to this ritual, balancing his daytime obligations with these poignant moments of reflection amidst the solemn serenity of the cemetery. There you could find him pouring tea for his mother and discussing politics while drinking wine with his father. Amidst this emotional landscape one evening, an intriguing figure emerged the aging butler, Sirsea. Weathered by time yet still possessed of a vibrant spirit, Sirsea had faithfully served the Gracieux family for generations. His connection to Monsieur Gracieux, and Philip's father, Jean Paul, ran deep, having spent considerable time at both the Paris estate and the storied grounds of The Scotney. With an astute eye and meticulous record-keeping, Sirsea bore witness to the ebb and flow of life within the family, offering a wealth of insights whenever called upon. Sirsea sensed an opportunity for Philip to reconnect with his Aunt Elenor, unburdened by past constraints and suited for a fresh beginning. In a quiet yet significant gesture, Sirsea penned a letter to Philip's aunt Elenor, requesting her presence at the Scotney. It was a subtle nudge, a gentle suggestion that perhaps Philip could find solace and support in the company of his extended family. When Philip Heritage arrived at the Scotney he graciously declined Sirsea's usual services, opting instead for his retirement, it became clear to the astute butler that a new chapter was unfolding. With Monsieur Gracieux no longer present to hinder familial reunions, the bonding between Philip and his aunt Elenor soon came to past and flourished. After she received the letter from Sirsea she agreed to travel to the Scotney to get acquainted with her nephew Philip. Following her arrival there were countless evenings were the two exchanged family memories. Aunt Elenor reminisced about a peculiar day from her childhood, a time spent in town with her stepmother, Lauren. The air was thick with the scent of secrets, as an old friend of her father's delved into Lauren's world with probing questions about Baptiste's health and the rumored sale of Jean Paul to a wealthy family. Lauren, with a practiced poise, danced around the inquiries, painting a picture of Jean Paul's enchanted journey abroad, his heart captured by love, all with Baptiste's silent blessing, as he lay confined to his bed. It wasn't until Elenor reached her later years that the veils of secrecy began to unravel the tangled threads of deception. Monsieur Gracieux, the silent benefactor, had been discreetly channeling funds to Lauren twice yearly, a revelation that dawned upon Eleanor during a visit to the bank in pursuit of a travel loan. Astonishingly, it was disclosed that Monsieur Gracieux had orchestrated a discrete deposit of a portion of the funds to be set aside in safekeeping until Elenor was a competent adult. He had instructed the bank. "When she is old enough to walk in here alone, she is to be given her money." The revelation, like a whisper in the wind, hinted at Monsieur Gracieux's benevolence, a generosity shielded from the naive gaze of her distant brother Jean Paul, who remained ensconced in his sheltered existence, oblivious to the truth that lingered just beyond his grasp. Aunt Elenor encouraged Philip to explore the world without fear, advocating for a fresh life beyond the confines of the estate. Proudly recounting her own adventures in England, which began as a means to escape her stepmother Elenor, she emphasized the importance of seizing opportunities, echoing the aspirations his father had explored. Moreover, she advised him to consider marriage to ensure the perpetuation of the esteemed Heritage lineage. Despite numerous suitors competing for his attention, Philip instead developed remarkable skill with a dagger and fencing through relentless practice and discipline, transforming himself into a marksman of deadly precision. His skill with a dagger became so sharp that he could strike moving targets with pinpoint accuracy, a talent that became both a personal passion and a formidable defense. Beyond his skill with weapons, Philip channeled his intense drive into his family's business, applying the same focus and discipline to finance and strategy. By the age of twenty-five, his expertise in business not only earned him immense wealth but also elevated his family's reputation. His combination of martial prowess and business shrewdness transformed him into a respected and sometimes feared figure in both professional and personal spheres. Yet, as success left him restless, he heeded his Aunt Elenor's counsel and embarked on a temporary relocation to the family's English estate. Nestled within its grounds stood a castle once owned by his parents, frequented in their time but unfamiliar to Philip. Meticulously overseen by a distant relative from his maternal lineage and a devoted cadre of servants, the estate offered a tantalizing glimpse into his family's rich heritage. Yet, with the passing of the last relative that occupied the castle the Scotney now laid dormant, its halls echoing with emptiness save for the faithful attendants left to tend its grandeur. Upon learning of this vacancy, Philip felt a stirring determination. He resolved to breathe life back into the estate, just as he had done with the Parisian property. As soon as he arrived at the Scotney, Philip wasted no time in setting his plans into swift motion. Accompanied by a select few staff members from France, he meticulously trained the remaining servants to meet his exacting standards, retaining only those he found to be truly reliable. At the heart of Philip's approach was a philosophy deeply rooted in Jean Paul's wisdom, "Those of you who oversee this castle and craft the meals let me remind you that you should inspire unwavering loyalty and dedication." Guided by this principle, the Scotney flourished under Philip's direction. Its grounds were transformed into a breathtaking panorama of meticulously manicured gardens, while its staff operated with seamless precision, embodying a spirit of unwavering dedication. As a year passed, Philip found his connections to France gradually waning. With the abundance of loyal servants and distant relatives tending to the Paris estate, Philip harbored no doubts about its upkeep. Thus, he wholeheartedly embraced his newfound life in England. However, propelled by an insatiable thirst for knowledge of the family's banking ties in Italy, he felt drawn to venturing into the heart of Tuscany. He became deeply engrossed in the region's renowned industries of textiles, banking, and agriculture, eagerly absorbing their wealth of expertise during his two-month vacation. Amidst his stay, Philip encountered a local woman who approached him daily persistently, speaking only in her native tongue. Though unable to comprehend her words, Philip consistently extended gestures of goodwill, offering her clothing or food, to which she responded with appreciative nods before departing. This mysterious encounter left Philip intrigued, pondering over the significance of their brief interactions amidst the backdrop of Tuscany's enchanting allure. However, on the eve of his departure, the woman appeared once more, this time accompanied by a young child. With tears streaming down the woman's face she urgently conversed in the ancient dialect. Then without a moment's hesitation, she thrust the child, wearing a cloak and clutching a small satchel, into Philip's bewildered arms. Her frantic demeanor hinted there may be trouble near. Philip, taken aback and unaware of the gravity of the situation, instinctively began to search his pockets for something to offer the distressed woman. As he fumbled for coins, he gingerly placed the child down at his side while continuing to search his pockets. Intent on extending his customary gesture of assistance to the woman who always appeared to be in dire straits, he finally retrieved two shiny coins at the tips of his fingertips. Just as he looked up to hand them to the woman, she disappeared. Unable to fathom where the woman could have gone so quickly, Philip scanned through the maze of people feverishly for the woman who had been draped in black with a scarf wrapped around her head. Staring into the sea of crowd cloaked in the common garb anxiety now hovered over him as the woman was nowhere to be found. Philip finally finding relief as he laid eyes on a familiar sight. One of the men a former privateer who had been aboard the ship with Philip, walked towards him after noticing his frantic look of concern. Many locals knew him as a seasoned seaman from Italy who had spent most of his life sailing the Mediterranean Sea and had acquired various knowledge on the many cultures. Philip, now relieved, showed him the child and explained what had transpired. The seaman pointed to the small bag the woman had left along with the child. Inside was a homemade doll made of hay and old rags, one small dress worn and filthy. The seaman explained that it was not uncommon for women without husbands to leave their children with someone they trusted to care for them. Philip found himself facing a dilemma as the morning drew near, torn between his imminent departure for England and the pressing need to ensure the safety of a lost child and reunite her with her mother. Complicating matters further, the woman who seemed to be the child's caregiver spoke an unfamiliar language, adding layers of difficulty to the already challenging task ahead. Standing resolute in the fading light, Philip couldn't shake the belief that the woman would return for the child. But as darkness enveloped the scene and the chill of the night set in, hope waned with each passing moment. Contemplating alternatives, he briefly entertained the idea of enlisting the help of another woman, perhaps with monetary incentive, to care for the child temporarily and aid in locating her mother. Yet, almost as quickly as the thought emerged, he dismissed it. Hours stretched on, with no sign of the woman's return. With a heavy heart, Philip reluctantly arranged for a carriage to transport him to his lodgings, where he resolved to wait. He

17

cradled the sleeping child in his arms the entire way wondering why would any mother walk away from her child. As Philip settled into his suite, he tenderly lifted the hooded cloak that veiled the child's face, revealing the hidden beauty beneath layers of grime and neglect. Despite her worn appearance, there was an undeniable allure to her delicate features, her ebony hair along with light brown streaks cascading around her like a dark waterfall. The stark contrast between her dirt layered skin and the warmth of the well-lit room accentuated her vulnerability. Moved by an overwhelming surge of compassion, Philip wasted no time in seeking aid from the head of the household staff, a woman of refined demeanor. With careful instructions, he implored her to attend to the child's immediate needs, taking note to her sensitivity to the sun and distinctly instructing her to find the largest bonnet for the child. Generously, he provided funds for clean clothing and toys, determined to offer solace and care to the girl in her hour of need. Upon instructing the woman to retain the remaining funds for herself, she eagerly accepted the gesture, her heart touched by Philip's generosity. Taking the small, soiled hand of the child into her own, she led her away, a beacon of hope amidst the darkness of neglect. As the genteel woman eagerly ushered the girl to the door, the child cast a poignant glance back at Philip, her expression laden with an impending sense of sorrow. Despite himself, Philip felt a surge of empathy for the girl who seemed to require extra care, resolving to search for her mother once more. If she failed to appear again the following day, he vowed to depart immediately, taking the child back to England with him. Philip reasoned with himself on the fact that the woman walked away without a moments regret. Seated at a modest writing desk, Philip's thoughts drifted to his father, Jean Paul, and how protective he was of him. Losing a child without warning had been his father's greatest fear, and now, what was left before was a small, fragile girl, deliberately abandoned by her mother. Doodling absentmindedly, Philip, who possessed a latent artistic talent, sketched the girl standing alone in a bustling marketplace, her bonnet drawn down protectively over her. Through his sketches, he narrated a silent tale of discovery and rescue, envisioning how he would bring her back to England. Once finished with his visual storytelling, Philip settled in to wait patiently for the woman's return with the child. As minutes stretched into an hour, Philip couldn't shake the gnawing anxiety for the small girl's return. His mind, ever prone to wandering, conjured up unsettling scenarios. Had the woman vanished with the girl? Maybe she sold the child off, perhaps? With a furrowed brow, Philip ventured into the hallway, scanning for any sign of the woman's whereabouts. His pulse quickened with each passing moment, until finally, a wave of relief washed over him as the woman reappeared, the girl in tow. Clean and smartly dressed, the child stood before him, a small bag clutched in her hands. With the grime washed away, her true complexion emerged a delicate, slender frame with brown chestnut eyes that shimmered with innocence. With a mix of curiosity and concern, Philip reached out to the child, questioning her name in English, French, and Italian. Yet, she remained silent, her response a mere smile as she toyed with the ribbons adorning her hair beneath a large bonnet. Holding her gaze, Philip found himself captivated by the enigma before him, her silence only deepening the mystery. The woman witnessing the unfolding scene, whispered to Philip, "She's merely three or four, if that. Her words, if any, are foreign Etruscan, Italy perhaps. Look at her, she's unable to speak, not even a whimper." Now with his patience waning, Philip nodded in comprehension and thanked the woman, gently guiding her towards the exit. Seating the child at the table, Philip offered nourishment, which the small, enigmatic girl eagerly consumed, her gaze fixed on him with a curious innocence. Mimicking Philip's every move, she ate with enthusiasm, a radiant smile adorning her face. When Philip tenderly presented her with the worn doll retrieved from her bag, she accepted it eagerly, delicately feeding it morsels of food. With a practiced touch, she then used the edge of her napkin to wipe the doll's mouth, a gesture of care and tenderness emulated from Philip that spoke volumes. As she continued to replicate Philip's earlier actions, by unfolding the napkin onto her lap and dabbing at the corners of her mouth, Philip found himself captivated by the child's innocent play. In that moment, a realization dawned upon him as he thought to himself, "This child is now mine. Her mother shall have no second chances, she belongs to me." In the dim light of dawn, with the ship poised for departure, Philip meticulously gathered his belongings, including those of the little girl, and made his way to the vessel bound for England. As they stepped aboard, the attention of the other passengers was drawn to the tiny girl as she removed her bonnet, emitting curious grunts. Unfazed by the stares and glares, Philip silently instructed her to keep the bonnet on to shield her from the chilly sea breeze, speaking to her in gentle French. With a quick smile, she complied, refraining from touching the bonnet again. He had provisioned abundantly for the thirty-day voyage, ensuring they had ample food and supplies. Throughout the journey, he engaged the girl in lessons, teaching her the alphabet, numbers, and colors. Despite her inability to speak, her knack for identifying new objects fascinated Philip. Their days fell into a rhythm of play; she would awaken first, reaching out for Philip's hands, as though beckoning him to applaud her morning rise. One day, while strolling the upper deck, they encountered a young boy slumbering beside a storage tank, clearly out of place in his attire. He was rudely roused by an older crewman, whose sudden clapping of his hands and a swift kick to the boy's legs startled the sleeping boy awake. His abrupt awakening amused the small crowd that had gathered, eliciting laughter from the petite girl who, seizing Philip's hand, mimicked clapping in a playful gesture. Philip, now disturbed, scooped up the girl, cradling her gently, and inquired about her brief but undoubtedly eventful life. His mind was troubled by the notion of this little girl being awaken by some brutish man rudely clapping in her face. Swiftly, he whisked her away, back to the shelter of their cabin. Once inside, he wasted no time in laying out pencils and paper. Determination etched on his face, he resolved to impart the gift of language to the child during their thirty-to-forty-day voyage. Philip simply couldn't fathom the idea of her unable to articulate the whirlwind of thoughts in her young mind. Summoning every ounce of patience, he patiently covered all the basics, catering to her budding curiosity and thirst for knowledge. As the ship finally docked in England, the girl, who still remained nameless, was reciting her letters, identifying animals, and confidently counting to a hundred. It was a testament to Philip's unwavering commitment and the girl's innate resilience. Yet, amidst the triumph, lingered the question: what unseen adventures lay ahead for this newfound scholar?When the ship finally docked on England's shores, they were escorted home by carriage. As they arrived at the doorstep of the grand Scotney Castle, the entire staff greeted them with a mix of shock and surprise, yet all warmly welcomed the tiny new addition. The head butler made the announcement Monsieur Philip Heritage, has returned home." With an air of authority, Monsieur Heritage introduced the child, declaring, "She is my daughter, and her mother's whereabouts are not to be questioned or discussed. Failure to abide by this rule will result in swift punishment without leniency. She is to be cared for and only provided the best of her heart's desire." The staff's response was complete silence, no one questioned how he came about the child, nor did they discuss it amongst themselves. The castle itself was a magnificent sight, adorned with the finest silk and linen, its opulent appearance left visitors breathless. However, despite its grandeur, it often bore an air of quiet loneliness and draftiness. Yet, with the arrival of the mysterious little girl that was full of life, the once melancholic shadows that cloaked the castle walls seemed to dissipate. Her echoing laughter and the pitter patters of her tiny footsteps brought life to every corner and hall. The castle's draftiness was replaced with warmth and coziness, spurred by the mere sound of her tiny sneeze. Monsieur Heritage ordered an abundance of wood to be chopped to fuel continuous fires throughout the winter months and chilly summer nights. The child was placed on a rigorous schedule mirroring that of Monsieur Heritage's upbringing, designed by his father, Jean Paul. Mornings began with etiquette lessons followed by sessions in music, languages, arithmetic, literature, and science. After her studies, she was free to indulge in play, particularly enjoying private tea parties and concerts with porcelain dolls and Monsieur Heritage. It was almost a year before one of the servants, who was overheard murmuring and questioning why Monsieur Heritage had not chosen a name for the adorable little girl. While everyone referred to her with endearing terms like "little one," "darling," or "princess," her true name remained a mystery. Monsieur Heritage refrained from bestowing a name upon her, for when he discovered her, she couldn't disclose her own name. He had convinced himself that the idea of arbitrarily assigning her a name was akin to labeling a mere possession of an animal. The child undoubtedly had a name; it simply eluded his knowledge. To dub her without true understanding of her name or its origin seemed unjust. Yet, the notion of her existence devoid of an identity, both on paper and in life, occasionally struck him as absurd. It wasn't until Aunt Eleanor's unexpected visit that Philip seriously contemplated the matter. She was provided the news from Sirsea of an unusual adoption involving Monsieur Heritage. Though he cherished Aunt Eleanor, Philip treasured his privacy and was unsettled by her intrusion. Aging and without a husband, she now roamed, reconnecting with distant kin. During one of her impromptu visits to the Scotney, Aunt Eleanor probed Philip about the child's origin and upbringing, pointing out the peculiarity of her namelessness. As servants discreetly cleaned nearby, awaiting Philip's response, the sound of tiny footsteps heralded. The beautiful petite girl dressed in lavender and white rushed into Philip's embrace, it was if she instinctively sensed his unease. With a tender smile, Philip cradled her, declaring, "You are my little Gem; they overlook your true name, Gem Marie Heritage, due to their inattention." Gem Marie, eager to assist, promptly affirmed, "I am Gem Marie," stunning the onlookers with her clarity. Startled by the vividness of her response, a servant dropped a dish, shattering the silence and startling Gem Marie. Sensing the opportunity to retreat, Philip excused himself, tenderly carrying the excited child away from the commotion. He strolled purposefully into the expansive library, guiding Gem Marie to the exquisite custom-made harp awaiting her delicate touch. Crafted precisely for her petite frame, the instrument allowed Gem Marie to wield its strings with effortless grace. As she settled onto the yellow satin bench, her slender fingers poised, anticipation filled the room. With precision, she embarked on Beethoven's Moonlight Sonata, the first movement resonating through the air with haunting magnificence. Monsieur Heritage wore a contented smile, a silent tribute to Gem Marie's undeniable talent as she performed. Enthralled, Aunt Eleanor and the household staff gathered in the doorway, drawn into the enchanting melody woven by Gem Marie's skillful hands. As the final notes drifted, applause erupted from Monsieur Heritage, echoed by Gem Marie's gleeful squeal of delight. In her jubilation, she leaped from the bench, rushing towards Monsieur Heritage, her small hand seeking comfort in his warmth. Yet, beneath the surface of this joyous scene, a subtle tension lingered. Aunt Eleanor, though impressed by Gem Marie's abilities, dared to broach the subject of Gem Marie's background and the prospect of her exploring life beyond the Scotney estate. However, Philip swiftly intervened, sternly reprimanding her for such notions, resolute in his determination to safeguard Gem Marie and uphold the boundaries of the Heritage legacy. Yet, beneath Philip's ostensibly benevolent facade, signs of his father's controlling tendencies began to emerge. Material indulgence abounded for Gem Marie, yet her world remained circumscribed, devoid of companionship beyond the estate's confines. Any semblance of curiosity regarding her lineage or maternal figure was swiftly squashed, relegated to the realms of taboo. In her later years an incident, wherein a compassionate servant attempted to offer Gem Marie clarity regarding her mother, resulted in immediate dismissal. Witnessing the servant's departure, Gem Marie's heart swelled with compassion, beseeching Monsieur Heritage for leniency on her behalf. Reluctantly, he relented, allowing the woman to remain, yet sealing the fate of any further discussion on the matter. Nestled within the walls of the

Heritage estate, a pervasive silence veiled the mystery of Gem Marie's origins, a mystery that echoed. The lack of resemblance to Monsieur Heritage she often vocalized remained obscured within the shadows of history. Whenever Gem Marie dared to inquire about her dissimilarities, questioning why her eyes were brown while Monsieur Heritage's were green, her queries were met with hushed responses from servants: "He is a man, you are a girl; fret not over such matters and go play." Thus, the subject would swiftly be dismissed, leaving Gem Marie to seek solace in new hobbies to quell her curiosity. As Gem Marie matured in her solitary existence within the castle grounds, she embarked on a journey of exploration, delving into various pursuits. If ever she stumbled upon something intriguing in a book, Monsieur Heritage would procure the finest materials or summon a specialist to assist her in her endeavors. During one particular year, Gem Marie became utterly consumed by her passion for the sport cricket. She orchestrated a grand spectacle, enlisting all the castle staff, including Monsieur Heritage, to join her in the game. Even the venerable Madam Henry was enlisted to keep score, her advanced age preventing her from running about. Gem Marie's enthusiasm knew no bounds, sparing no one from her fervent requests. Monsieur Heritage, committed to catering to her every whim within the castle's confines, ensured her desires were met. Determine to create an oasis within the Scotney his ability to keep Gem Marie content was an easy task. Her upbringing was a rich tapestry, marked by the mastery of four languages, participation in various instruments, and even self-taught ballet from the pages of books. Save for the annual visits from delivery personnel bringing cattle and provisions, the outside world remained a distant notion. Restricted to the castle grounds, Gem Marie's longing to explore beyond the walls often weighed heavily upon her in silence. Unaware of her secret desire Monsieur Heritage was adept at assuaging her melancholy, consistently conjuring diversions to captivate her. A menagerie of animals provided solace and companionship, offering a semblance of the wider world she so yearned to experience. It was the audacious daughter of a long-serving servant, Madam Henry, who finally dared to break the silence surrounding Gem Marie's isolation. Greta, as bold as she was stunning and quiet, summoned the courage to confront Monsieur Heritage, stirring the stagnant air of the castle with her bold inquiry. The twenty-five-year-old, Greta was striking, with golden brown hair that caught the sun as she spent most of her days tending to the gardens. She found solace among the flowers and the earth, especially her beloved English bluebells, which she cared for beneath the open sky. It was during one of these tranquil afternoons, while she knelt in the soil, that Monsieur Heritage appeared, taking his usual evening stroll. But this time, something was different. His face, often stern but composed, was clouded with a look of deep worry a look Greta recognized all too well. Her mother had worn that same expression many times over the years. Though Greta knew well the invisible line between servant and master, something in her stirred. There was an unease in Monsieur Heritage's eyes that could no longer be ignored. Mustering her courage, despite the undeniable risk, Greta decided it was time to confront Philip with the question that had weighed on her mind for so long. With a steady voice, she asked, "Monsieur Heritage, what kind of future do you envision for Gem Marie now that she is growing into a young woman?" At once, Philip's expression darkened. His eyes narrowed, and a storm of fury overtook him. "How dare you speak to me in such a manner? You have no right to ask a question like that." he thundered, his voice laced with menace. He threatened to dismiss her on the spot, his temper flaring in ways she hadn't expected. Greta, taken aback but determined, quickly begged for his forgiveness. "I didn't mean to offend, but... why does the question anger you so?" she pressed, her curiosity now tinged with something deeper fear and intrigue. In response, Greta's hand trembled slightly as she reached into her pocket, retrieving a delicate silver locket. She opened it slowly, revealing the portrait of a man inside. The image showed a distinguished figure, his complexion a warm olive, dressed in a fine suit. With a somber air, Greta whispered, "This man... he is my father." Monsieur Heritage anger faltered, confusion replacing it. Greta, her voice growing steadier as the weight of her secret spilled forth, revealed the hidden truth of her life. "My mother kept me hidden for years, working tirelessly beside her. She never spoke much of him, nor did she let me venture beyond the confines of the Scotney. I'm twenty-five years old, Monsieur, and I've never seen the world beyond these walls. My mother's control... it's like an invisible prison that I accept because of my role. "Monsieur Heritage, now fully grasping the gravity of her words, responded softly but firmly. "You have the power to free yourself from her, Greta. You are not bound to her choices, nor her past. Whatever your mother did before I arrived it has nothing to do with me." Greta's gaze dropped to the floor, her voice barely a whisper. "But you don't understand. The bonds a mother weaves around her child... they aren't made of chains or ropes. They're far more insidious. They're unseen, but they're still there." Philip watched her closely, seeing the tears brimming in her eyes. His own emotions swirled in confusion with mental questions, was he meant to react with anger at her defiance or with compassion for the life she had endured? For the first time in a long while, Philip found himself at a loss, torn between the shadows of his own feelings and the painful truth Greta had unveiled. In that moment, emotions surged, filling the air with tension. Greta, taken aback by Monsieur Heritage's unexpected display of affection, wrestled with conflicting emotions. Uncertain whether his words were meant to comfort or wound, Greta withdrew in silence, returning to her task of pruning. Yet, that brief exchange ignited a quiet yet undeniable connection between the two. From that moment on, there were additional dialogs some requesting opinions on the proper colors for certain rooms in the house. The talks became so frequent that Philip and Greta began to steal secret moments together in the secluded corners of the castle's garden, often meeting near the moat where the ancient stones of the fortress whispered of forgotten tales. Philip would regale her with stories of distant lands and the mysterious origin of Gem Marie, his words like the breeze that carried the scent of English bluebells. Greta fascinated with literature often sat in the garden while Philip read to her. With each shared secret, their bond deepened. A trust forged in the quiet of night and bound by a vow of silence. Greta honored that vow, never once revealing their connection, not even to her mother. But the pain of their separation grew unbearable. Under the cover of darkness, Greta began sneaking to Philip's room, moving silently through the castle's stone corridors while the household lay in slumber. They sought refuge in a room no one would dare enter without just cause, the one place within the castle where they could be free. By daylight, Philip found excuses to linger near the old garden, where the English bluebells bloomed, a spot rarely visited by the servants who stayed near the main house. There, amid the crumbling stones, they reveled in stolen moments of joy, their societal roles of master and servant erased as they stood in each other's company. In those brief interludes, Greta felt like more than just a servant she became Philip's queen. Together, they prepared a hidden room, one filled with elegant garments and fine jewelry that Philip had gifted her. Among the treasures was a necklace, a symbol of their love, locked away behind a stone in the wall a secret within a secret. Their lives, though separated by birth and status, became intertwined in those hidden hours, a love existing in two worlds at once. For a time, their forbidden love flourished unnoticed, thriving in the shadow of the castle's walls, where propriety held no sway, and the weight of their secret love hung like a soft, invisible veil over all they shared.

Chapter: 3

Unborn Child

In the late summer of 1855, Greta began noticing a gradual weight gain that ignited a series of undercover actions. One evening, under the cloak of twilight, she vanished into the distant shadows toward an abandoned barn, leaving Monsieur Heritage absorbed in his habitual routine of issuing commands to the household staff in the parlor. Greta, strategically, subtly orchestrated her movements to fuel curiosity and speculation of a secret love affair. By carefully choosing moments coinciding with rapid deliveries to the estate, she let slip the tantalizing suggestion that she was meeting a mysterious admirer. Her deliberate timing, vanishing while Monsieur was occupied with staff, ensured that he was excluded from suspicion as a possible suitor. But beneath the layers of intrigue, Greta uncovered a revelation of her own: she carried within her the most precious secret, she was pregnant with Monsieur Heritage's child and loved it. Shielding the truth from prying eyes, she balanced on a knife's edge between exhilaration and fear. The joy of impending motherhood filled her with awe, a silent affirmation of the hidden love she and Monsieur Heritage had shared. Yet, with each passing day, the weight of their secret became harder to bear. The fear of discovery loomed ever larger, intensified by the rigid social divide that separated them. Greta now found herself at the center of a delicate dance, one of deception, desire, and the relentless pull of a truth that could unravel everything. Monsieur Heritage was an enigmatic figure of influence, though he never demanded the title of "master." Yet, in the grand estate of the Scotney, it was undeniable he ruled. His standing in England's upper echelons was not just a matter of pride; it was his safeguard, the very foundation of his sanctuary and the privacy he fiercely guarded. Any breach of that privacy would not merely be scandalous, it would be ruinous. The mere whisper of an illicit relationship could shatter the carefully constructed walls of his reputation. For Monsieur Heritage, the consequences of such a revelation were unthinkable. As heir to Monsieur Gracieux, he could not allow the bloodline to be tainted by the birth of his firstborn to a servant slave. Greta, though a steadfast and loyal servant, held no sway in the world that mattered. She was powerless, invisible in the eyes of society, should the truth of her condition come to light, she would not just lose her position within the castle; she would be cast into the merciless streets, alone and disgraced. She had been taught by her mother the ways of the world. Desperate to protect herself and the unborn child growing within her Greta concealed her pregnancy beneath layers of modest clothing. In public, she became a ghost, avoiding Monsieur Heritage's gaze, playing the part of the obedient servant. Their once-passionate love, kindled within the castle's walls, was now imprisoned within its labyrinth of shadowed corridors, where every glance could betray them. The very sanctuary that had cradled their affair had turned into a cage. As her belly swelled with life, so did her dread. Greta knew the truth would eventually betray her, yet the idea of facing it filled her with terror. Sleepless nights haunted her, as did vivid dreams where hope and fear danced a cruel waltz. She longed for a world where she could openly love the man who had captured her heart, where their child would be free to exist without shame. But that world was far from her grasp, and the reality of her situation pressed upon her with unbearable weight. And so, in the shadows of Scotney Castle, amid its sprawling picturesque estate, Greta's battle continued a delicate balance between love and despair, hope and tragedy, with no clear end in sight. The secret they shared clung to her like a heavy veil, threatening to suffocate her with every passing day. The secrecy of their love story became a burden that she carried, threatening to unravel the delicate threads of their intertwined lives. As she navigated the challenges of her pregnancy and the impending storm of revelation, Greta clung to the hope that one day, their love could be set free from the confines of secrecy. Allowing her and Monsieur Heritage' to face the world together, unafraid, and unashamed. Her mother, who noticed her weight gain now viewed her with suspecting eyes. She began to question her daughter incessantly, demanding to know identity and whereabouts of the father. She even tried a reverse psychology imploring Greta that one of the delivery men were a good catch. Her mother, utterly unaware that Monsieur Heritage could be the father, instead she turned to him in desperation as a last resort to force Greta to reveal the father's identity. Distraught and pleading for help, she beseeched him to investigate all the butlers and groundmen for any possible involvement. Monsieur Heritage, taken aback but intrigued, informed Madam Henry that without Greta's cooperation and her unwillingness to divulge the father's identity there was little that he could do. He then cautioned her against discussing such sensitive matters in the presence of the other servants, warning that any inquiries could imply Greta's ignorance of the father's identity. He concluded that such gossip could tarnish her reputation and cast a shameful stain over the Scotney estate to which Madam Henry agree to remain quiet about the matter. Monsieur Heritage conveyed his intention to approach Greta privately, urging Madam Henry not to press the issue should Greta protest. Later that evening, Monsieur Heritage met with Greta, delicately broaching the topic, and revealing her mother's request of their earlier conversation. When he questioned how long had she been carrying the child Greta's response was subdued, offering only her vow of silence and reassurance that she would not divulge a word. As Monsieur Heritage inquired again about the timeline of her realization, Greta's uncertainty surfaced, tempered by her mother's recent suspicions regarding her condition. In a poignant moment, Greta reached out, gently guiding Monsieur Heritage's hand to her stomach, silently conveying the weight and movement of their shared secret. The anticipation hung thick in the air as the couple stood there, waiting with bated breath for their unborn child to stir once more. When the baby made a sudden, lively movement, Monsieur Heritage chuckled warmly and gently continued to caress Greta's stomach, reassuring her with his touch. He whispered words of comfort, promising to handle everything with her mother, ensuring her worries were controlled. With conviction, he declared that their child would be raised at Scotney, nowhere else. A serene smile graced Greta's lips as she nodded in agreement, expressing her need to return before her mother noticed her absence. Agreeing to meet again in the covert setting of their encounter the following evening, Monsieur Heritage cautioned Greta against divulging their meeting to Greta's mother. With a solemn nod, Greta hastened her departure, disappearing into the shadows, leaving behind the weight of their secret. The revelation of impending fatherhood pulsed within Monsieur Heritage, a fire of excitement burning within him. Yet, amidst his elation, a sobering realization took hold. Should news of his paternity with Greta leak, the delicate fabric of his carefully constructed arrangements with conservative investors in the banking and trading sectors could unravel. Thus, he bore the burden of their secret, knowing the consequences of its exposure could be dire. Monsieur Heritage, a man who reveled in the solitude and power he commanded at the Scotney, now basked in the acknowledgment of his self-imposed dominion. Within the estate's confines, he orchestrated his own realm, shielded from external disturbances. To him, every challenge seemed conquerable within Scotney's grounds. If disputes among the staff and servants arose, they were swiftly brought before Monsieur Heritage for resolution, his authority unquestioned. In their clandestine rendezvous, Greta proposed a delicate ploy to Monsieur Heritage. She urged him to convey to Gem Marie the notion that her mother, like Greta herself, once cradled her in her womb. However, unable to care for her, Gem Marie was entrusted to the best possible guardian. Though he listened attentively, Monsieur Heritage remained adamant that Gem Marie need not be burdened with the knowledge of her abandonment in a bustling marketplace. He also questioned Greta why was it important that Gem Marie know the details of her origin. To which he noticed the query brought an unsettling look to Greta's face. Needless he continued pleading his case, emphasizing the potential emotional scars of feeling unwanted, arguing that he was never endowed with Gem Marie's or her mother's name, much less a loving moment for him to recollect. A truth and a revelation that could cruelly unsettle a tender heart. Greta, however, countered, asserting that Gem Marie was yet unaware of the distinctions between herself and the animals of the estate. She divulged that Gem Marie once compared herself to being hatched like a chicken, her understanding of her origins shrouded in innocent naivety. Monsieur Heritage found himself enveloped in an uncomfortable silence, grappling with the weight of truth. With measured words, he instructed Greta not to reveal to Gem Marie the unsettling tale of her mother's departure into the unknown. Instead, he crafted a narrative of compassion and tragedy: Gem Marie's mother, he explained, was a woman of modest means, her kindness matched only by her unfortunate illness. Unable to care for her daughter any longer, she entrusted Gem Marie to Monsieur's protection before succumbing to her affliction. Greta, with a solemn nod, agreed to uphold this fabricated history should Gem Marie ever inquire about her origins again. Yet, she cautioned Monsieur Heritage about the dangers lurking beyond the sanctuary of the Scotney Castle. In a world where status and lineage held sway, the presence of an unknown child might invite scrutiny and scorn from the elite and society in general. Monsieur Heritage, however, dismissed these concerns, viewing himself merely as a custodian of wealth rather than a member of the aristocracy. Yet, Greta challenged his narrow perspective, reminding him that within the walls of the Scotney, he wielded influence beyond mere monetary transactions. She painted a stark picture of the challenges awaiting a child without lineage in a world dictated by blue blood. Undeterred, Monsieur Heritage asserted his dominance over the Scotney's domain, declaring himself the sovereign ruler whose authority brooked no challenge. But Greta, her voice tinged with urgency, sought to shake his confidence. "Monsieur Heritage," she implored, "The outside world is a realm beyond our control. Its depths harbor darkness far beyond our imagination and Gem Marie grows older day by day." Caught off guard by Greta's boldness, Monsieur Heritage countered, asserting his command over those who dared trespass upon his land. Yet, as the exchange unfolded, it became evident that Greta's words had planted a seed of doubt in his mind. For in the face of the unknown, even the self-proclaimed ruler of the Scotney Castle could not shield himself from the uncertainties that lay beyond its walls. As Monsieur Heritage took steps away from Greta, pondering on the worst-case scenarios of ignorant outsiders, he walked to a nearby sword that he kept hanging above a mantel. The sword had been given to his grandfather and passed to him before the death of his father. He rubbed his finger very softly against the blade that had not been sharpen in years, yet still it manage to create a small stream of blood on his index finger. As he watched the small stream of blood roll down his finger, he wiped the blood away with a handkerchief as he spoke aloud with conviction. "Let it be known that any who dares trespass upon the lands of the Scotney castle shall face the gravest consequences and the most severe punishment. This is soil that has been cultivated by my beliefs and rules and no man nor woman shall come against thee while I stand upon my own refuge. Trespassers will be met with unwavering justice, ensuring that they regret their actions for the remainder of their days." Greta listened attentively, nodded, and replied, "Yes Master Heritage."

Chapter: 4

The Newspaper

As Gem Marie approached her fourteenth birthday, her curiosity surged, spiraling into a whirlwind of relentless questions that knew no limits. She explored every hidden corner of her home and even delved into the minds of the delivery men who frequently passed through the castle ground. Their responses were as varied as the men themselves some offered amused smiles, while others turned away, their laughter trailing behind like an unsolved riddle. Monsieur Heritage, once captivated by her inquisitiveness, had grown increasingly distant, consumed by Greta's impending motherhood. His attention now anchored to the household's future, Gem Marie found herself adrift in the complexities of adolescence, left to navigate this confusing chapter on her own. In his absence, a subtle but growing disrespect began to settle in. The deliverymen, once polite, now met her questions with impatience, their manners fraying as though the rules of decorum no longer applied. Gem Marie, with a resilience far beyond her years, attributed their behavior to a lack of proper upbringing. She dismissed their impoliteness with the same maturity Monsieur Heritage had instilled in her, he often reminded her of the importance of etiquette, a lesson that had taken deep root in her character. One afternoon, as Gem Marie danced among the animals in the barn, her laughter rising like a melody amid the soft rustle of hay, she found herself abruptly pulled into a confrontation she hadn't anticipated. The air, once filled with the innocent joy of youth, shifted, and in that moment, her curiosity would lead her down a path of discovery she was not yet prepared for. The deliverymen, dropping off sacks of feed, caught sight of her and, with a callousness that pierced the innocence of the moment, one of the men remarked upon Monsieur Heritage's penchant for extravagance. In a thinly veiled insult, he suggested that Monsieur Heritage not only lavished attention on his barns but also on his house pets, insinuating that Gem Marie herself was akin to one of his well-groomed animals. The jab as cutting as it was unexpected, Gem Marie was taken aback when the men referred to her clothing and her annoyance of many questions. One commented on her ability to speak without pause and hinted at her potential connection to the neighboring chickens and their hatchlings. With her curiosity piqued, she questioned them about their knowledge of her mother. Their response was unexpected: a collective exchange of knowing glances followed by hearty laughter. But the joviality swiftly turned sour as one of the men began to mock Gem Marie's speech, hurling insults she had never encountered before. Though unfamiliar, their malicious intent was unmistakable. Watching his lips curl with disdain as he spat out the words, Gem Marie's frustration boiled over, and she retaliated with a string of profanities in French and German, languages she had picked up from Rudolf, a former sailor turned groundman. The men, stunned by her outburst, erupted into laughter once more before hastily completing their delivery and departing. Sometime later, Gem Marie crossed paths with Rudolf again. Recalling her encounter with the delivery men, she repeated the offensive phrases she had learned from him. Rudolf's reaction was one of shock and dismay, as he implored her, nearly in tears, never to utter those words to Monsieur Heritage. With a solemn nod, Gem Marie reassured Rudolf with echoing words of comfort that Greta had once offered her in moments of distress. She vowed never to betray Rudolf's trust by repeating those words to Monsieur Heritage or ever again. Now armed with her newfound words and ready for her impending encounter with the delivery men, Gem Marie stood firm. Two weeks later when the trio of men returned once more, accompanied this time by a fourth, notably younger than the rest. Their banter commenced anew, filled with jest and taunts. With a smirk, one of the men compared Gem Marie to a particularly attractive monkey he had once kept aboard a ship for entertainment. Their collective laughter echoed, reverberating through the air. Gem Marie, whose childhood readings had often painted pirates as the keepers of monkeys, simmered with indignation. In a swift retort, she rebuked them in English, accusing them of lacking refinement and belonging where animals roamed freely. When one of the men, seemingly amused and simultaneously indulging in an apple from his pocket, Gem Marie's response was swift and cutting, "You old nag you dare eat that apple without a trough, when your done make haste and throw the core to your piglet friends." The men, taken aback by Gem Marie's linguistic prowess and the precision of her insults, fell into stunned silence. Their once-confident demeanors now wavered, subdued by her verbal onslaught. Their silence, a stark contrast to their earlier bravado, unnerved Gem Marie. Sensing victory in her ability to silence them weighed more than its appearance, she bolted towards the safety of the house, with the intent on informing Monsieur Heritage of the crude exchange of the men. As she fled, the distant voice of one of the men called out to her in French, but Gem Marie paid it no heed, her focus fixed on reaching Monsieur Heritage. With each stride, she replied the insults hurled at her, determined to use them as ammunition in her defense. Finally reaching the castle's entrance, she collided with Monsieur Heritage, her breathless urgency mirroring the turmoil of her emotions. Monsieur Heritage immediately noticed the distress imprinted on her face as she approached him, her pace hurried and breaths shallow. Deep concern now etched his features as he inquired why she seemed so distraught and rushed. Gem Marie, fearing interruption from the men, hastened to relay the unfolding events to Monsieur, her words tumbling out in a haste. "They know about me," she blurted out anxiously. Monsieur Heritage arched a curious brow, prompting her to elaborate. With a deep breath, Gem Marie composed herself and began to speak more slowly, the weight of her words hanging heavy in the air. "They know how you taught me to speak," she explained, her voice trembling slightly. "They ridiculed me, likening me to a pet monkey, dressed up at your request" She repeated a word one of them had used, its meaning lost to her, with total obliviousness adding to her distress. At the mention of the one word, Monsieur's countenance darkened with anger, transforming him into a different man entirely. Without a word, he strode past Gem Marie, his hand instinctively reaching for a walking stick combined with cherry oak and ivory tusk adorned with twenty-four karats of gold at its handle symbol of fondness rather than necessity, mainly reserved for his strolls on unleveled ground. Gem Marie, fearing the repercussions of her behavior being exposed, trailed behind him, pleading in French, confessing to her use of foul language only in response to the ridicule. "J'ai seulement dit de très mauvais mots parce qu'ils me taquinaient!" Monsieur Heritage halted abruptly, his gaze piercing as he commanded her to return to the safety of the castle. Before she could offer further explanation, he gestured sternly with his cane, indicating her immediate retreat towards the castle. With a racing heart and eyes wide with fear, Gem Marie obeyed, hastening back towards the sanctuary of the castle walls. Once closer, she encountered Greta, emerging from the garden, to whom she relayed the tumultuous encounter with Monsieur Heritage and the troubling revelations. Greta, sensing the urgency in the situation, moved

34

swiftly to calm Gem Marie, realizing that Monsieur's solitary trek to the seldom-visited stable area signaled trouble. With each step, Greta's pace slowed, her advancing pregnancy weighing upon her. They navigated halfway to the barn when they spotted Monsieur Heritage already there, his demeanor ablaze with anger as he stood near the feed area. In a thunderous voice, he rebuked them, forbidding any vulgarity on his land and reminding them of their purpose: to work, not to speak. The men, stunned into silence by his ferocity, stood as if frozen until Monsieur Heritage erupted again, defending a child of his from perceived disrespect. The youngest man among them inexperienced and bewildered, dared to question Monsieur's claim. With a mixture of incredulity and amusement, he asked, "Your child?" Monsieur, offering no response, strode over and delivered a swift blow with his walking stick, sending the young man crashing to the ground in agonized screams. The older men, seized by fear, fumbled in nervous French, apologizing for the young man's ignorance, and attributing it to his inexperience. But Monsieur Heritage, still consumed by rage, dismissed their apologies, asserting his dominion over all that inhabited Scotney land, insisting on respect for everything under his purview. In a final decree, he declared Scotney soil a bastion against the vulgarity of the outside world, a sanctuary where decency and respect reigned supreme. The other men pleaded and apologized profusely. Meanwhile, the young man writhed in agony, both from the pain shooting through his knee and the sting to his pride. Summoning his last shreds of dignity, he managed to utter, "Monsieur, that child is not yours." Monsieur Heritage, a formidable figure, approached him slowly. As the young man lay sprawled in the dirt, Monsieur prodded his injured leg with the gold-tipped cane, eliciting a cry of excruciating pain. With a menacing intent, he raised his walking stick once more, poised for another strike. However, before he could deliver the punishing blow, Greta's piercing scream pierced the air, halting him in his tracks. Frozen in place, Monsieur Heritage surveyed the scene, taking notes of the fear imprinted into every onlooker's face. With a disdainful flick of his hand, he tossed a handful of coins onto the ground near the injured young man. He commanded them to take their wages and leave, never to return. Furthermore, he issued a chilling warning: if any of them dared to breathe a word of this incident, he would ensure they lost their homes and livelihoods forever. Hastily, the two older men gathered the coins and carried their battered companion away in their carriage. Left alone in the barn,

Monsieur Heritage watched as Gem Marie wept in Greta's comforting embrace. Amidst the turmoil, he reaffirmed his resolve to protect them at all costs. The trio made their way back to the castle, Greta supported between them for balance. In the doorway, Madam Henry observed their return, her thoughts swirling with newfound understanding. "I must know the identity of her child's father," she mused silently. Upon reaching the threshold, Monsieur Heritage instructed Madam Henry to find new deliverymen for the feed and to enlist Rudolf, the groundman, to assist her. Greta exchanged a meaningful glance with her mother, silently conveying her plea not to inquire further. With the situation settled and semblance of normalcy restored, Gem Marie retreated to her room, finding solace in the pages of the newspaper she often perused. Her interest lingered particularly on articles and stories that held secrets yet untold. She couldn't help but notice the unsettling trend certain articles consistently were removed from the newspaper's pages. Monsieur Heritage, the enigmatic caretaker, offered a cryptic explanation only hinting that the omitted pieces were deemed unsuitable for young minds, harboring disturbing narratives. Gem Marie, though initially dubious, found her skepticism shaken and challenged when one particular article manage to slip through. The oversighted article told an eerie tale recounting the tragic demise of a London mother who horrifically ended the lives of her three children as they slept. The story left Gem Marie haunted, her nights besieged by ghostly apparitions of a white glowing figure gliding through her window, relentlessly pursuing her through the shadows of her chamber. Terrified, she bore her nightly torment in silence, each sip of water a futile attempt to calm her rising fear. Come morning, she took matters into her own hands, by taking care to exclude any disturbing article that bore any dark undertones. Instead she focused on articles with a narrative extolling the virtues of the elite, one in particular by the name of Christian Pierre, a philanthropic tycoon renowned for his benevolent deeds and societal influence. Enthralled by his multilingual fluency, Gem Marie found herself spellbound by the mystique surrounding Christian Pierre. Tales of his journeys across continents stirred and ignited her imagination, particularly about the lush landscapes of America's southern territories. A French of considerable wealth, he had amassed his fortune through shrewd dealings, including the lucrative trade of livestock. With each passing day, Gem Marie's fascination with Christian Pierre deepened, now envisioning him as a gallant and daring figure capable of liberating her from the confines of the Scotney. Gem Marie yearned to experience the world beyond her provincial town, a world she had only ever glimpsed in literature. Determined, she concocted a daring scheme to seek out the man who had captured her heart, despite their never having met in person. Obsessed with the idea of meeting him, Gem Marie scoured newspapers and magazines daily for any mention of his name, her longing intensifying with each passing moment. Only one more article hinted at his departure from England, suggesting he would soon be heading back home. Gem Marie, absorbed in the pages of her geography book, meticulously mapped out the swiftest routes to both America and France. Driven by an unwavering resolve to chart her own destiny, she embarked on a clandestine mission to plan her escape. Amidst the ceaseless bustle of the castle's deliveries of supplies, Gem Marie stealthily explored the labyrinthine confines of the barns, her mind swirling with schemes and hideouts. After meticulous examination, she unearthed her optimal refuge nestled underneath the carriage, a dim enclave where she could vanish without a trace. With nothing but the weathered wooden beams for support, she realized the daunting task ahead. Tethering herself to these beams with whatever makeshift materials she could find to use and make the proper length of rope. She braced herself for the arduous feat. The prospect of clinging on for an uncertain duration, perhaps an hour or more, loomed before her. Gem Marie understood all too well that her escape hinged on her possessing superior upper body strength. To fortify herself for the impending challenge, she devised a rigorous training regimen akin to crafting a lesson plan. Each night, under the cover of darkness when all were sleeping, Gem Marie retreated beneath her large sized bed. There she transformed the confined space into her covert training ground. With determination etched in her mind, she methodically executed her exercises, lifting herself inch by inch using only her arms. This clandestine routine honed her upper body prowess, preparing her for the Herculean task that lay ahead. In her meticulous preparation for escape, Gem Marie wielded a lengthy piece of cloth with practiced precision. One end nestled securely in her mouth while the other was firmly gripped in her hand. With deft movements, she wound the fabric around the bed's sturdy boards, crafting a makeshift loop into which she slid her wrist. The resultant knot, reminiscent of a slip knot, served as her tether, ensuring her wrist remained firmly in place. With her wrist securely nestled in the cloth's embrace, she clung onto the bed's supportive frame, finding stability and an anchor amidst the impending chaos. Wedging her feet between the wooden slots, she braced herself for the test ahead. Her objective was to endure the hanging for as long as humanly possible before the inevitable tremors of fatigue set in. To gauge the duration of her endurance, she placed an hourglass sand timer within her line of sight. Each grain of sand's descent became a tangible marker of her resilience, a testament to her unyielding determination. Yet, as the sand trickled downwards, there came a pivotal moment. A threshold where the agony of her suspended state threatened to overwhelm her resolve. She closed her eyes, transporting herself into the embrace of Christian Pierre, relishing in the warmth of his presence and the joy in his eyes upon seeing her. In that suspended moment, amidst her reverie, the familiar melody of raindrops serenaded her senses. Yet, as she opened her eyes, reality flooded back, revealing the stark evidence of her relentless efforts. The droplets of sweat that slid off her brow painting a testament to her determination upon the floor below. Counting each bead of perspiration became her ritual, a diversion from the ache that pulsed through her body, a gauge of her endurance. With each passing night, she hung beneath the bedstead, measuring her strength against the relentless march of time. When every grain of sand had cascaded through the hourglass and a bit more, she knew the threshold of her resilience had been crossed. Her silent signal and confirmation of her physical readiness for her daring escape. For a month, this nocturnal routine became her lifeline, a symphony of perseverance echoing in the solitude of her confinement. And then, one fateful day, her newfound strength manifested itself beyond the confines of her hidden chamber. In the presence of Monsieur Heritage and his stable of animals, Gem Marie effortlessly harnessed her power, pulling a cow with a grace that left them astounded, her metamorphosis from captive to conqueror etched in every sinew of her being. Monsieur called to her and asked, "How have you grown to pull that cow in that manner?" Gem Marie, now aware that the strength of her arms had surpassed her knowledge of her own strength, she quickly replied. "This cow is old Monsieur and very tame she will go wherever one guides her." Now, deeply concerned about Gem Marie's lapse in etiquette, Monsieur Heritage took it upon himself to address the matter during dinner that very evening. With a gentle yet firm tone, he reminded her of the paramount importance of maintaining her grace and poise at all times, emphasizing that true ladies refrain from engaging in such undignified activities as pulling cows. Despite the seriousness of the reprimand, Gem Marie couldn't help but stifle a giggle, earning herself a sharper chastisement from Monsieur Heritage, who promptly informed her that she would be enrolled in charm lessons the following morning. Gem Marie agreed without protest, her spirits undampened. Swiftly finishing her meal, she bestowed a quick kiss on Monsieur Heritage's cheek before darting off to her beloved harp. There, she dedicated herself to practicing a new composition she had composed, envisioning herself adorned in an exquisite gown, captivating an audience eagerly awaiting her performance. In her mind's eye, she saw Christian Pierre among the spectators, his eyes alight with wonder as her fingers danced across the strings with fervor. Throughout the day, Gem Marie found herself lost in reverie, her thoughts consumed by various scenarios featuring her and Christian together, each culminating in her being lauded for her impassioned rendition of the piece. That evening after everyone was asleep, Gem Marie retired early, settling into a grand white and gold armchair nestled in the corner of her room. Her gaze fixated on the bed before her, transforming it into a portal, a gateway to realms beyond Scotney. This night marked her trial, a test of her true strength. With deliberate precision, she shed her garments, layer by layer, only to meticulously re-attire herself, each piece carefully secured. Purses and bags adorned around her form, concealed beneath layers of makeshift clothing fashioned from aged linen, all the way down to her undergarments. Every pocket and pouch was filled with items collected from her room, each serving a purpose in her clandestine endeavor. Locking her bedroom door behind her, she grasped her hourglass and slipped beneath the bed. Methodically, she ascended to the wooden beams that traversed her mattress, securing herself with slip knots tied using only her mouth. Suspended across the expanse of her queen-sized bed, she awaited, her determination unwavering, her gaze fixed upon the dwindling sands of time. With each grain of sand that cascaded through the hourglass, she counted down, each moment drawing her nearer to Christian Pierre. The weight of her layered clothing grew burdensome, yet she persisted. This was her dress rehearsal, each garment worn in preparation for her eventual escape. As the final grains of sand trickled through the hourglass, a small pool of sweat collected before her. Fatigue gnawed at her limbs, her body trembling with exertion. Despite the strain, she maintained her crucifix position, refusing to release herself until the appointed time. For she knew the stronger her arms, more closer to victory she would be. Humming a tune and moving her fingers as if she were plucking her harp, Gem Marie endured hanging beneath her bed it was only when the morning sun cast its golden rays through the Victorian windows did, she relent, freeing herself from the confines of her bed. It was then she realized she had succumbed to a deep sleep, still bound by her self-imposed restraints. Emerging slowly from beneath the bed's shadowy refuge, Gem Marie stood upright, peeling away layers of clothing saturated with perspiration. Her limbs aching, stiff from hours of confinement. Bruises and marks adorned her wrists, souvenirs of desperate attempts at restraint. Her ankles throbbed, each step a reminder of her mounting exhaustion as she swayed precariously, teetering on the brink of collapse. Seated at the basin, Gem Marie splashed cool water over her face, the chill offering a fleeting moment of relief from the turmoil brewing within her. As she wiped her skin dry, the inevitability of the servants' arrival weighed heavily on her mind. A quiet resolve settled in her bones. "No more practice," she whispered under her breath, her voice barely audible in the stillness. "It's time for the great escape." That day, everything changed. Gone were her usual playful distractions and aimless strolls through the estate. Instead, she moved with methodical precision, silently pacing the familiar halls as she collected small bottles and filled them with vital provisions: water, wine, oil. Each step felt like part of a ritual. Back in her chamber, she meticulously sewed hidden pouches into the folds of her underskirt, securing her makeshift supplies with care. The fabric would hide the evidence of her intent, but her heart still raced at the thought of what was to come. With the essentials gathered, she found solace in a shadowed corner behind a dresser, out of sight from prying eyes. There, beneath the layers of silk and secrecy, she penned the date of her departure on a delicate slip of paper. Next to it, she placed a tattered newspaper clipping an article about the enigmatic Christian Pierre, a name whispered in certain circles, always linked with her desire to leave the Scotney. She folded the scrap of paper carefully, sliding both the date and the article into a hidden jewelry box stashed under the silk-draped bench. "One week," Gem Marie murmured, her fingers tracing the edges of the hidden box. "In one week, I will be free." The vow echoed in her mind like a solemn promise, but the weight of her plan lingered heavily in the air. Each detail had been set in motion. Now, all that remained was to wait for the moment to strike, for her courage to hold fast, and for freedom to finally be within her grasp.

Chapter: 5

This Is My Family

In the dim, chilly hours of February 28, 1856, Greta Henry writhed in the throes of labor within her small, candlelit quarters. The air was thick with tension as her mother, Madame Henry, and two trusted servants-turned-midwives hovered near, their hands trembling as they prepared for the birth. Outside the room, the old house creaked under the weight of a long night, every sound amplified by the urgency within. Sensing time was slipping away, Madame Henry, her face etched with worry, called upon a male servant by the name of Livingston, to fetch Monsieur Heritage, the household patriarch. But to her shock, Livingston recoiled. His lips tightened as he muttered the words she could scarcely believe: "I won't wake the master of the house for the birth of a bastard child. Have you forgotten Madam your daughter's refusal to name the father." The venom in his voice hung in the air, and the room seemed to grow colder. For a moment, Madame Henry stood frozen, disbelief flooding her. Livingston's defiance his audacity to utter such disrespect sent a tremor through her. She was a woman of calm reserve, used to maintaining her dignity in silence, but something inside her unleashed itself. Her eyes darkened with a primal rage, and without hesitation, she moved swiftly, driven by a fierce instinct to protect her daughter and the life struggling to come into the world. Madame Henry's rage was evident, a force uncontainable, shifting the dynamic in that small room. Grabbing a pair of scissors from a nearby sewing basket she poised them at Livingston's throat, while delivering a stern warning in her native French, asserting the honor and lineage of her daughter. In a daring display of maternal protection, she silenced Livingston's insolence, threatening dire consequences should he disparage her daughter again. Her resolve unyielding, Madam Henry swiftly entrusted a wet towel to a female servant, tasking her with Greta's care while she ventured to awaken Monsieur Heritage. Ascending the grand staircase to the opulent chambers above, Madam Henry's heart weighed heavy with doubt. The servant's words lingered, casting doubt upon Greta's honor and the paternity of the child. Had Greta, like her mother before her, succumbed to the folly of a mismatched

41

liaison? Entering the hushed sanctum of Monsieur Heritage, Madam Henry's knuckles rapped softly against the imposing French doors. Yet, beneath her composed exterior, turmoil raged within her. Uncertainty gnawed at her resolve as she grappled with the internal implications of her daughter's predicament. For in all her observations, she had never witnessed any meaningful interaction between Greta and Monsieur Heritage, leaving her to question the truth behind her mind's fleeting accusations. There was one single instance that she watched Monsieur assist Greta with such care. The same care that Greta's father had once done with Madam Henry after he impregnated her. Greta, unbeknownst to her, was the daughter of an American slave owner not the French one she was led to believe by her mother. A truth concealed by her mother, which has never been spoken. Madam Henry now recalling the evening, she was ordered to retreat to the cellar beneath the American plantation house, she sensed the impending danger to her life as she crawled into the hay filled cot covered in leftover fabric scraps of materials. Across from two other servants, she remained awake, her back turned to them with her eyes fixated on the stone wall before her. She listened and witnessed the verbal turmoil that had erupted on the floor above her head. Master Ridley and his wife Prudence Ridley, affectionately known as Dearest Prudence. Within the tumult of their argument, amidst cries and accusations of fathering many slaves, one particular remark from Prudence pierced the air like a venomous arrow. Madam Henry laid on the cot frighten and ashamed as Prudence's voice rattled the house, "Don't you walk away from me Bartholomew Ridley, It's not enough that you've deemed yourself the appropriate facilitator to expand the population of our livestock. But now you've seem to grow accustomed to one in particular nag. Lord knows half of these 'darkies' run around here resemble you, why two of them even have the nerve to have green eyes like yours. And while you spend your days sipping mint Julep with your constituents and lavishing extra care on that French slave. I am here faced with the weight of running this home, All the while trying to uphold the dignified reputation and good name of the Ridley. And I must tell you it has not been an easy task. I saw you Bartholomew Ridley, I saw how you assisted that French darkie with the cotton the other day. Your hands wander, in broad daylight your hands wander like they have a life of their own with no compass. I only wonder if they will ever find their way back to this vessel, the one you made a vow with before God. I am your wife Bartholomew, or did you forget that, well let me be clear: if that French darkie's baby comes out with so much of a glimmer of emerald eyes, I'm demanding that both her and that pickaninee be sold and sent off to Slaytter brothers. And you won't have to worry about counting the fingers and toes as you so love to do whenever there is a new arrival. Because as sure as my name is Prudence Ridley I will be the one to count the fingers and toes on that one." Madame Henry, who held her stomach the entire time listened as the venomous words poured into the stale air of the cellar. The left-over aroma of the early morning breakfast and late supper permeated within cool cellar stone walls that caused hunger pangs along with nervous twitching in her stomach. She adjusted herself on her side so that her fingernail could reach the stone wall. She dug her nail into the stone were she placed marks in order to keep track of the days she was pregnant. When one stone was filled with marks she went on to the next being slightly educated from her former master she knew how to count a hundred. When she first arrived at Master Ridley's plantation she thought she had been fortunate when she was brought to work in the main house and not out in the fields. Master Ridley had been invited to Europe to discuss the dynamics of the slave trades in America in Maryland. During his visit Master Ridley became enamored with the refinement of European slaves. So impressed with their mannerism and refinement that he pulled out twenty thousand dollars at the dining table and insisted that his host Maître Francois Bordeaux sell him some of his own refined, bilingual slaves. In an attempt to persuade Master Ridley to reconsider his crude proposal, Maître Francois Bordeaux informed Ridley that twenty thousand dollars would barely be sufficient to purchase merely two slaves and that was his base price. Ridley's gesture was viewed as distasteful, especially during dinner while in the presence of invited guest. Master Ridley impulsively countered the offer with thirty thousand dollars for ten slaves. Maître Francois Bordeaux, pride mow stung by the insult, sought to swiftly conclude the distasteful bout of crass bargaining retorted, "Thirty thousand dollars would only secure two of my high-end slaves for you. These servants speak multiple language they are in the best of health for we do not believe in damaging our property." Driven by his ego and embarrassment, Master Ridley pointed towards Madame Henry, resplendent in her exquisite attire, and declared, "I believe I'll hand-pick my own then. That young 'brown one' in the gown, what is she called?" Reluctantly, Maître Francois Bordeaux identified her as Madame Daphne Henry. He then added a male slave by the name of

Sirsea to list of the exchange in hopes that he would watch over Madam Henry. Thus, the two accompanied Master Ridley's ship ride back to his plantation in America. Remembering her naivety Madame Henry lay still, pretending to sleep, through half-closed eyes, she listened to two other slaves resting across from her, their whispered conversations laced with a cruel sense of superiority. They hinted at the possibility of her being traded or sold if the child she carried bore any resemblance to Master Ridley. It was a grim reality known to all: when a female slave bore a child by the master of the house, her fate hung in the precarious balance of the wife. If the master were easily swayed by his wife, any slave could be dispensed in order to maintain peace. Once a pregnant female slave was sold, she faced myriads of abuses. Firstly, she became a perceived threat to her new master's wife, a target for the desires of other masters or overseers with an appetite for women of her kind. Secondly, she endured the scorn of fellow male slaves, labeled as tainted, a woman defiled by the slave master's touch, often referred to as spoiled and rancid. As Madam Henry made the daring decision to escape to the harbor before her baby's arrival, the mere thought of being sold to the Slaytter brothers was enough for her to take the risk for Paris. The only person she dared to share her escape plans with was Sirsea. She confided in him about the conversation she had overheard with Master Ridley and his wife Prudence. She instructed Sirsea that if questioned about having any knowledge of her escape, he should mention only to Master Ridley or his wife only. He was to describe Madam Henry's peculiar behavior before entering the shop for sugar and flour. Sirsea was to stress that Madam Henry inquired about how to keep a baby's eyes shut. He was to make it clear that he did not understand her meaning of keeping the child's eyes shut. He then insinuated that she may have gone mad may have wanted to kill the baby. She assured Sirsea speaking in this manner would keep him out of any trouble. Additionally, she made a solemn pact with Sirsea: should fate ever separate them, they would reunite in Paris some way. Setting sail on a ship loaded with tea, sugar, and tobacco, Madame Henry embarked on a journey filled with uncertainty and resolve. Arriving in town under the guise of a routine errands, Madam Henry, accompanied by the castle's coachman, slipped aboard the bustling vessel bound for Europe. With only scant provisions and some meager coins intended for supplies, Madam inconspicuously navigated through crowded bustling decks by attaching her unchained self to lines of slave cargo. Her presence unnoticed amidst the large commotion as she kept her head down. When given the opportunity she quickly hid down in the belly of the ship with the food cargo. Her voyage was one of solitude, only for occasional visits from the crew to ensure the ship's integrity and to safeguard its cargo. Amidst the solitude, she found solace in the company of a frail, stray cat. Utilizing her maternal instinct and resourcefulness, she tenderly coaxed milk from her full breasts, nurturing both herself and the weak feline companion in an old tin cup. This small act of kindness forged a bond, as the cat, bolstered by the unexpected sustenance, bravely defended their shared sanctuary from any rodent bold enough to intrude. In the midst of the cargo's provisions was barrels of ale, dried pork, beef, and sugar. The goods surrounded her as she navigated her hunger cautiously, mindful not to disrupt the weight balance that might draw attention. When the ship finally docked in England the air filled with the recitation of manifestos, a chorus of uncertainty echoing through her mind as she struggled to discern ownership amidst the chaos. Finally, a seaman's warning pierced the commotion like a life jacket, "Take care with that cargo bound for the Scotney or Monsieur Gracieux will deduct any damage from our wages. He's a fare man and he always pays generously, and I want no follies with his goods." Madame Henry, catching wind of this, discreetly ascended to the upper deck, her senses heightened by the gravity of the situation. As she prepared to depart with a group bound for the Scotney, a privateer intercepted her path, inquiring about her origins. "Where did you come from? And where do you think you're going?" With a reflex honed by servitude at the lavish balls of Master Francois Bordeaux, Madame Henry gracefully replied, "From the Scotney Sir," punctuating her response with a deferential curtsy and long sentence in French about Monsieur Gracieux. Amusement danced in the privateer's eyes as he leaned in, pressing further, "I didn't inquire where you're headed, but where you hail from." His fingers traced the strands of her hair that sat on her face, a gesture that sent shivers down her spine. "I don't believe I've seen you before where did you come from? You're a very pretty one aren't you." he inquired, his tone tinged with curiosity. With a tremor in her voice, Madame Henry repeated, "The Scotney, I am cargo." her gaze darting nervously between the privateer and the loud vigilant seaman nearby, who boisterously reiterated the consequences of mishandling any goods bound for the enigmatic Scotney castle. "Monsieur Gracieux' will not pay if his cargo is damaged in any way." Without further

45

ado, the privateer quickly seized her arm, ushering her into a small group of individuals garbed in finer attire but marred by filth, leaving Madame Henry to ponder her uncertain fate among these unlikely companions. As Madam Henry stood amidst the group, her attention was drawn to a woman adorned in a breathtaking dress, its elegance covered by the traces of travel etched in dirt, resembling a lavish gown. Despite her disheveled appearance, there was an air of refinement about her. Sensing the woman's apprehension, Madam Henry turned away as their eyes met. She then felt a gentle touch as the stranger tenderly wiped away dirt from her face with a torn piece of cloth. In hushed tones and rapid French, the woman imparted a cryptic message: "Remember, always be courteous and speak only when spoken to." With a cautious glance around to ensure no prying ears were nearby, she introduced herself as Mademoiselle Claire. Her words carried the weight of a once-coveted status, now overshadowed by the harsh realities of her journey, handpicked by an overseer of the Scotney she was on her way to the high-ranking castle. A flicker of understanding passed between them as Madam Henry's smile softened the tension in the air. With a subtle gesture, Mademoiselle Claire offered a shawl, a modest veil to conceal the swell of Madam Henry's belly, a secret they now kept from their fellow travelers. "Keep your shoulders back and stand up straight. Remember always keep moving while working polish and shine everything whether it needs it or not. Be seen and never heard." The older woman's words of advice rang in Madam Henry's ears. When they arrived at the Scotney they were all lined up and told the owners of the Scotney live in France and comes to visit regularly. They were instructed, the castle is to be well organized and without flaws. if not, there will be consequences. Madam Henry stood in stunned silence. Scotney was magnificent, with its elaborate décor and historic architecture, a place in a class of its own. The independence granted to her as an enslaved person on the estate was both a relief and a burden. The relief came from fewer interactions with overseers or a plantation master, but the burden lay in the knowledge that she would never be allowed to step beyond its grounds. There was no outside life to anticipate; life was confined to what one could make of it on the Scotney Estate. Family life was rare unless you were fortunate enough to have started one before arriving. The ratio of enslaved people was unequal, with many older, a few young, and women outnumbering men. Most had been there for years. With no master living on-site to increase the population, the enslaved community remained small and isolated. The estate owner, a widowed man who preferred his life in Paris with his daughter and son-in-law, seldom visited. Throughout her years of service under four separate masters of Scotney, Madam Henry had endured only three instances of physical punishment, all inflicted by an overseer who had long since passed. His indulgence in wine and bar wenches had finally caught up with him. And now, here she was, pulled back into the present moment, standing in the castle where she had once given birth. There she stood alone facing the daunting task of knocking on Monsieur Heritage's chamber door. As she hesitated, contemplating the weight of her purpose, she gently rapped on the door, the sound echoing faintly down the candlelit corridor. Receiving no immediate response, she began to retreat, only to find Monsieur Heritage emerging from his chambers, his demeanor stern and questioning. "Madam Henry, why are you here?" he demanded, his tone sharp with curiosity to her back as she walked away. Madam Henry's voice trembled as she offered her explanation, her words tentative yet sincere. She spoke of her daughter Greta, on the cusp of bringing new life into the world, and her desire to shield Monsieur Heritage from any potential disturbance or alarm caused by the inevitable sounds of childbirth. Monsieur Heritage, initially caught off guard, swiftly regained his composure, his initial excitement tempered by the gravity of the situation. "And who is attending to the birth?" he inquired, his concern evident in his tone. Madam Henry informed him that she will bringing forth the child, but she is slightly wary use to the other servant inexperience with birth she reminded him that there were only few births at the Scotney and Greta being one of them. Just then the reality of the event flooded monsieur Heritage he was about to be a father he quickly turned and asked why was she still standing there. He told Madam Henry that he would be down in a moment to make sure everything was in order. Madam Henry who thanked him profusely hurried back to Greta, smiling and elated because she had just been given another confirmation that Monsieur Heritage' held her and Greta in high regards. Monsieur Heritage, upon returning to his room momentarily, tried not to appear overly eager. Despite the excitement bubbling within him, he was determined to maintain composure. With measured steps, he descended into the cellar. As he approached, the echoing moans and cries of Greta reached his ears, stirring a concern and creating a disturbance within him. Particularly, one cry caught his attention, prompting him to quicken his pace with urgency.

Along the hallway, other male servants observed Monsieur Heritage's demeanor from their doorways, with a mixture of curiosity and apprehension evident on their faces. An older servant, his expression reflecting astonishment of Monsieur presence, retreated into his room, closing the door behind him. Meanwhile, another, by the name of Manuel, summoned enough courage to ventured closer to Monsieur Heritage and inquired if he required assistance. Monsieur, perhaps unaware of the transparency of his emotions, responded hastily, "I tire of the incessant cries of the woman." Startled by yet another of Greta's yells, the two men slowly approached the closed door together. Just as Monsieur Heritage was about to knock, a faint cry of a baby pierced through the air, halting his movements. Amidst the hushed ambiance, a woman's jubilant squeal pierced the air, prompting her swift dash to the door, anticipation etched on her face, expecting the arrival of other servants. However, her exuberance faltered upon beholding Monsieur Heritage standing in stoic silence. Caught off guard, a mixture of nerves and surprise gripped her as she paused and uttered, "Pardon Moi, Monsieur Heritage, but Miss Greta has just welcomed a baby boy! Manuel why do you stand there so? Go fetch clean water for the child." Concealing his delight at the news of a boy, Monsieur Heritage, with a stern countenance, sidestepped the nervous servant and entered the room. Joy surged within him as he approached Madam Henry, who had just finished cleaning and tending to the newborn. She wrapped the infant in a pristine white blanket she meticulously had woven and prepared in secrecy for this very moment. Catching sight of Monsieur Heritage, Madam Henry noticed a longing in his eyes wrapped in nervousness, veiled beneath a façade of composure. Madam Henry turned to him and softly said, "Please forgive the disturbance, Monsieur. Although it's late, the child is healthy. I understand your need as master of the Scotney to inspect him, as he is the newest addition to the castle." Without waiting for Monsieur Heritage to respond, she gently inquired, "Would you like to examine him, sir?" Monsieur Heritage, rendered speechless, eagerly nodded, his demeanor reminiscent of a child's anticipation. With delicate care, Madam Henry placed the newborn in his arms, and as Monsieur Heritage gazed upon the precious life before him, barely able to open its eyes, a profound connection seemed to spark between them. With meticulous care, Monsieur examined the delicate hands and toes of the newborn, counting each one with precision. As he scrutinized the infant's features, familiar echoes of his own and his father's visage reverberated through his mind. Turning to the exhausted yet content Greta, he leaned in towards Madam Henry, his voice barely a whisper as he inquired about the chosen name. Madam Henry confessed that Greta had not yet decided on a name for the child, lacking inspiration for either a girl or a boy. The servants gathered, their curiosity now piqued, they awaited eagerly for a decision. Madam Henry caught sight of the male servant Livingston who had once referred to the unborn child as a bastard, and with a glance towards Monsieur Heritage, she sought his input, acknowledging his authority as the ruler and master of the Scotney. Without hesitation, Monsieur Heritage asserted his dominion, his voice carrying the weight of authority as he declared, "This child, born on my estate, under my auspices, shall bear the name Philip." Shock rippled through the servants at this proclamation, while Madam Henry's pride shone brightly. With a triumphant smile, she strutted off, leaving the servants to contemplate the significance of Monsieur Heritage's decree. With the grace of a peacock, she eagerly attended to Greta, placing a cool cloth on her forehead with the delicate precision of a ballerina. She watched Monsieur lost in the newfound life that had entered the Scotney. Monsieur Heritage who was oblivious to the hushed tension that enveloped the room, continued to hold the child in his arms. Knowing the complete value of the present day he dare not forsake the moment of fatherhood. The next day brought a flurry of activity and lively chatter as the household buzzed with the arrival of the newest family member. Gem Marie, who had yet to set eyes on the newborn, approached Monsieur Heritage with a proposition. She suggested they pay a visit to Greta's chamber to meet the latest addition to the family. Monsieur Heritage, although he had already caught a glimpse of the baby, reluctantly agreed, his resistance softened by Gem Marie's persuasive charm. Gem Marie, skilled in the art of swaying Monsieur Heritage to her wishes, gently took hold of his hands and began to playfully maneuver them, as if conducting a silent symphony. It was a tactic she had mastered over time, one that never failed to weaken Monsieur Heritage's resolve a subtle reminder of their shared history. Seeing Gem Marie's hands in action, Monsieur Heritage was transported back to a moment from their past, where he had cradled the tiny hands of a four-year-old girl aboard a ship. With a smile, he relented to Gem Marie's request, "Alright, as you wish let's go and visit the new baby." With eager anticipation, Gem Marie interjected, "It's a baby boy, Monsieur! What is his name?" Monsieur Heritage, brimming with pride, invited her to guess, teasing, "What's the best name in all the world?" Gem Marie's eyes lit up with excitement as she ventured, "Christian?" Monsieur Heritage gently corrected her, "No, try again." Undeterred, Gem Marie's gaze sparkled as she thought for a moment before proposing, "Philip!" Confirming her intuition, Monsieur Heritage affirmed, "Yes, you are correct." As the two made their way through the grand hallway, their footsteps echoing against the walls, they headed towards the kitchen area and descended into the cellar, their shared anticipation very evident in the air. Upon their arrival, one signal servant stood sentinel over Greta, who lay in peaceful slumber, her breath still slightly labored. The room was shrouded in dim light, a faint ray of sunlight piercing through a clouded cellar window. The air was a bit chilling and damp, Monsieur Heritage, his brow knit with concern, turned to the servant, and inquired sharply, "What afflicts her? Why does she sleep so deeply?" The servant, speaking in hushed tones, replied, " Begging your pardon Monsieur Heritage, it is the aftermath of her bleeding. It has just subsided, but with time and rest, she will regain her strength." Now filled with concern for Greta, the servant quickly placed a cool cloth on Greta's forehead before departing to fetch fresh water. As she closed the door behind her, she paused briefly to eavesdrop. Upon hearing Gem Marie ask Monsieur Heritage if she could hold the baby, she felt reassured and left. Monsieur Heritage consented, and with the utmost care, he lifted the newborn into his arms, mirroring the delicate technique Madam Henry had taught him. In the daylight it appeared that baby Philip had acquired more of his features overnight. Monsieur Heritage then passed the infant to Gem Marie, guiding her in the same careful manner he had been guided. With a gentle transition before releasing his hold, he cautioned Gem Marie to handle the baby with care. Gem Marie, cradling the baby with ease, moved towards a small area where sunlight streamed in through the cellar window, casting a warm glow upon them both. She stood there and spoke to the baby and called him Mon petit Philip. She stared at him and marveled at how tiny his hands and feet were she turned and faced Monsieur Heritage' and said, "Regarde comme ses mains sont petites, look how small his hands are." When the baby yawned and opened his mouth wide, both Gem Marie and Monsieur Heritage laughed. Gem Marie then addressed the baby, saying, "Regarde-toi, you have a man's chin just like Monsieur Heritage. You are definitely a boy, not a girl." Gem Marie, filled with joy, laughed again. Monsieur Heritage, upon hearing Gem Marie's reasoning for why baby Philip resembled him, immediately turned to Greta, who was still sleeping. He then settled into the chair beside her bed. While Gem Marie had her back turned, engrossed in little Philip, he carefully took hold of Greta's hand and leaned forward to kiss it. He quickly withdrew when he sensed Gem Marie might be turning around. Greta, who opened her eyes slowly regained her focus and recognized Monsieur Heritage' she smiled and began to speak. Before she could complete her sentence he smiled and pointed to Gem Marie who was holding and singing to the baby. Greta watched her interacting with her child her eyes slowly glanced over Monsieur Heritage who was also watching carefully, then amidst her gaze she heard Gem Marie voice speak, "Welcome Mon Petit Philip welcome to the Scotney." Greta, who was in shock, looked at Monsieur Heritage' who smiled and whispered, "Yes, because he is my son." Greta, who was now overtaken by her emotions, eyes began to well up with tears. Just then Madam Henry entered the room, surprised by the presence of Gem Marie and Monsieur Heritage' she quickly tried to excuse herself and began backing out of the room. Monsieur Heritage sprang from his seat with urgency, his voice carrying concern as he addressed Madam Henry. "No need to depart just yet, Madam Henry, we were just leaving. But it seems Greta is unwell, suffering from bleeding and stricken with pain," he explained." If Gem Marie had not insisted I accompany her to see the child, I would have never known of her sickness." Expressing his wishes firmly, Monsieur Heritage directed that Greta and the infant be relocated to the main level bedroom at the rear of the house. He assured Madam Henry that he would provide all necessary materials and supplies for a proper bassinet, emphasizing the importance of cleanliness and comfort for both mother and child he ordered, "Under no circumstances will there be any fatalities at the Scotney, I want the room prepared immediately." Madam Henry, taken aback by the sudden turn of events, diligently noted Monsieur Heritage's instructions. She promptly summoned another female servant and briefed her on the required changes. Together, they hurried upstairs to prepare the designated room for Greta and baby Philip's arrival. Quickly with precision a new bassinet, which was meticulously crafted with skilled carpentry, was set aside in the bedroom awaiting the newborn's arrival. Lined with exquisite silk imported from China and Türkiye, it exuded luxury and care. Every detail was attended to with precision: linens were changed, floors meticulously washed, and drapes and rugs meticulously cleaned. By the time

Greta and her baby were settled into their new quarters, the room gleamed with immaculate cleanliness. With fresh water and food and medicine that was rode in by messenger. Monsieur Heritage's decisive actions and attention to detail had ensured that Greta and her child were provided with the utmost comfort and care, setting a standard of care by him. He strategically added extra chores onto every servant's duty giving the excuse that he needed the land and the animals to produce more of everything. He also stated that the garden had been suffering since Greta was ill and it will not be tolerated. He insisted that every servant step up and do their additional work in order to bring the Scotney back up to its high standards. Monsieur Heritage' knew that by providing more work he would have more time alone without disturbance with Greta and the baby. Having Greta out of the cellar gave him comfort in knowing they were only one level below him. Now a set visiting time had been established for Gem Marie's sake. Reminding Monsieur of their departure time for their daily visit, she would often enter Greta's room with Monsieur Heritage quietly and stand over the sleeping baby. Every day it was as if baby Philip could sense they were there because he would awaken on his own. One he would yawned and opened his eyes wide, both Gem Marie and Monsieur Heritage would laugh. Gem Marie promptly address baby Philip by saying, "Regarde-toi, you have a man's chin just like Monsieur Heritage. I can see you are definitely a boy and not a girl." Gem Marie, filled with joy, laughed again. Monsieur Heritage, upon hearing Gem Marie's reasoning for why little Philip resembled him, turned to Greta, who had never awaken. He settled back into the chair beside her bed, while Gem Marie with her back turned, deeply engrossed herself in play time with little Philip. Monsieur Heritage took hold of Greta's hand and studied the limp movement of it he tried leaning it to lay a kiss on it, but quickly withdrew his attempt when Gem Marie turned around. He nestled back into the chair and observed the room in all its splendor and thought to himself, "This is my family. I have created my own world with my own family of choice." Monsieur Heritage began to frequent Greta's room at his leisure mainly when all staff was out of the castle in the fields One crisp afternoon, while tenderly engaging with his son, he expressed to Greta his firm resolve that Philip would receive a proper education, destined not for servitude but to blossom into a well-rounded gentleman drenched in culture. As these words settled upon Greta's ears, she couldn't help but voice her concerns about societal perceptions and the hurdles

Philip might face. Monsieur Heritage paused, then lifted the child to his own face, asserting confidently, "Look at him, he is the very reflection of me. No one would dare question his lineage." In that moment, Greta confronted the reality of her son's future, recognizing the stark dissimilarity between him and herself, much like her own departure from her mother's likeness. In the serene confines of the Scotney, Greta's connection to the estate, coupled with her mother's status as Madam Henry, shielded her identity from scrutiny. Yet, beneath this facade lay a reality fraught with complexity. Greta understood all too well that if her son diverged from Monsieur Heritage's prescribed path, he would face a perilous journey. As she reclined on the bed, a veil of silence enveloped her thoughts. As she watched Monsieur Heritage tenderly cradle baby Philip, a flood of emotions stirred within her. She had spent years longing for a different life one filled with love and the fulfillment of dreams that now, finally, seemed within reach. But as she looked on, an unsettling realization crept in. The happiness she had so desperately sought had come at an unforeseen cost. She hadn't imagined that her newfound joy might demand such a sacrifice perhaps even the delicate bond with her firstborn child, now hanging in the balance. As Monsieur Heritage continued to engage with Philip, the infant's cries shattered the tranquility. With swift grace, he placed the baby upon Greta's chest and uttered in French, "Tu as faim, mon fils" ("You are hungry, my son.") Greta, now immersed in the French language under the tutelage of Gem Marie and Monsieur, recognized the sentiment. With a determined resolve, she sat upright, tenderly guiding her newborn to her breast, nourishing him with a mother's instinct and a heart heavy with unspoken truths. As Monsieur Heritage watched Greta's gentle nature as his son was being fed, he leaned in with a sincere curiosity and asked, "Is it truly akin to cow's milk? What does it taste like?" Greta, taken aback by the unexpected query, hesitated before responding, "I don't know, I don't query such things." her gaze drifting out the window. Monsieur Heritage, exuding his hierarchy persisted, convinced out of curiosity Greta must have tasted it at least once. Greta, bewildered by the unusual implication, replied, "I haven't, how could I? A mother's milk is not for herself." Growing increasingly playful but agitated, Monsieur Heritage accused her of dishonesty. "Do you not wonder what is it that nourishes and delights your own child?" Embarrassed by the accusation, Greta reiterated her truthfulness, "But how could I?" Monsieur Heritage, consumed by frustration, abruptly pulled aside her cotton shirt, "Simply Like this," and thrusted her free breast into his mouth and commence the suckling motions. Speechless and stunned, Greta could only watch in disbelief as the man she loved and her precious son both were latched onto her. Greta, who was now speechless and in shock, could not say anything as she looked down and watched her child and the father both nursing off her body's milk. As Monsieur Heritage observed his son being fed simultaneously his curiosity piqued, prompting him to stop for a moment and lean in towards Greta's mouth and kiss her gently, leaving traces of her own milk upon her lips. He then leaned closer into her ear and whispered softly, "Is it not reminiscent of cow's milk? How would you describe its taste?" Greta, caught off guard by the unexpected question, hesitated momentarily, her gaze wandering out of the window before she replied, "I'm not entirely certain." "Monsieur Heritage persisted, his conviction unwavering as he insisted that she must have savored it at least once before. Greta, taken aback by the implication, cradled their now sleeping son, responded with bewilderment, "I assure you, I haven't. like I said before it is not for me how could I?" As tension mounted, Monsieur Heritage's agitation grew evident as he leveled accusations of dishonesty against her. Feeling deeply embarrassed by the unfounded accusation, Greta reaffirmed her honesty with a resolute, "But why would I, It is the child that needs it's nourishment" Monsieur Heritage, consumed by intrigue and frustration noted, "Something comes out of your body that you give to our child to which he saviors it so to a point he cries for it, and you never pondered on what its taste may resemble." Monsieur pulled his chair closer to her bedside and without breaking eye contact abruptly pulled aside her cotton shirt and thrusted her breast into his mouth once again. This time with deliberate force he suctioned the milk from her nipples. Speechless and stunned, Greta could only watch in disbelief as the man she loved aggressively suckled milk off of her. Greta now with her eyes fixated on Monsieur, watched his motions grow harder and more frequently as he closed his eyes, his breathing began to increase. Unable to control the wave of sensations that had consumed her she found herself aroused by the new tabu of events. Unable to suppress her silence any longer she too closed her eyes and let out a soft moan. The two completely lost and now immersed in the forbidden act sole focus was on the sensation that consumed them. Lost in their unsighted bliss the two were oblivious to their surroundings. Madam Henry, on her way from the garden, had chamber door slowly without warning she had carefully entered the room quietly all the while staring at the floor her mind focused mainly on maintaining the needed silence its resting occupants sake. Careful not to disturb Baby Philip, she peered to the side of the large room where his bassinet sat. She tipped toed softly deeper into the room while carrying a small basket filled with berries and fresh cut flowers. Her gaze still not clear to the act taking place on the large bed in her distance. It was nearly halfway into the bedroom, when she gained an understanding of the erotic event that was taking place. Her eyes now focused on Greta and Monsieur Heritage produced a wave of overwhelming shock. Acting quickly she quietly backed out of the room while watching the two deeply immersed in eroticism with their eyes shut. Once she stood safely outside of the door she cupped her mouth with her hand in horror. Fighting to hold back her anger and embarrassment for the two, she quickly gained her composure and wiped away her tears and waited a moment before she purposely made some rustling sounds as she reapproached the door. Set on making her presence known from behind the door she hummed a tune as she gently knocked on the door. Deliberately knocking again she called out Greta's name while slowly opening the door. Upon hearing Greta's response of, "Yes, mother," Madam Henry hastened her pace, entering the room with a smile. This time the depiction of the room showed Greta laying under the covers, while Monsieur Heritage sat in the chair cradling baby Philip while the two slept peacefully. Playing along with the masquerade, Madam Henry approached Monsieur Heritage and gently woke him. While taking the authentic sleeping baby from his arms, she remarked that he must get his rest also and graciously offered to relieve him of his duties. With a nod of gratitude, Monsieur Heritage surrendered the baby and quickly rose to his feet and explained, "I heard the baby's cries through the corridors and, upon arrival Greta was immersed in a deep slumber, taking pity on her weary state I decided to try and comfort the child myself. Not sure of the proper measures I sat down in the chair, and to my surprise I must have done well because I not only put the child to sleep but myself as well." Madam Henry chuckled appreciatively, thanking him, and apologizing for the additional burden the baby had placed on him. She gently scolded Greta for sleeping so heavily and not attending to her own child, reminding her of the impending return to her garden duties. Greta nodded in agreement, expressing her gratitude to Monsieur Heritage, and assuring him that it wouldn't happen again. Then with a brief farewell, Monsieur Heritage swiftly exited the room.

Greta, now trying to keep up the act, began talking about feeling fatigue and how grateful she was that Monsieur Heritage' had heard Philip crying. Madam Henry listened as she settled baby Philip back into his basinet. She slowly walked over to Greta who was still laying on the bed trying to speak casually. Greta watched her mother's movement as she moved closer to the bed and stood in front of her silent. Her conversation went on about returning to the garden and being grateful for the extra time she was given by Monsieur to rest. Madam Henry with a scornful face listened while Greta spoke, she adjusted Greta's pillow behind her carefully propping her head up for more comfort. Greta now looking into her mother's darting eyes paused for a moment in between thoughts. Madam Henry unable to control her emotions bent down quickly called out, "Whore!" Then in one quick motion she struck Greta across the face. She then proceeded to tell her how for years at the hands of her father she was violated without warning and with nowhere to go. With pain she told her that whenever he laid within her, it was never on a large bed upon fine cotton sheets. The torment that raced through her veins traveled in one flush to her throat so that now her voice, revealed that she was ashamed to call Greta her daughter. Confessing to Greta that the filthy act she witnessed her commit with Monsieur Heritage was unspeakable. She asked Greta how could she permit Monsieur Heritage' to suckle off her along with her fatherless son. Greta, who was crying uncontrollably, pleaded and insisted, "But mother, it was Monsieur Heritage' who began the unspeakable act upon me. What could I have done when he demanded and questioned me about the taste of my own milk." Madam Henry infuriated shouted in rage , "Fool!" and struck Greta again with a forceful thunderous slap. The echoing sound frightened baby Philip who began to whimper slightly. Greta, who was holding her face, could feel the raises of her skin taking on the form of her mother's hand. The forceful blow had jolted and removed any slumber that was left within her. she quickly maneuvered herself from under the covers and sat sideways on the edge of the large bed. The tips of her toes barely touching the cold floor, her blouse still unfastened from the double feeding showed milk stains on the white cotton. Her breast slightly exposed as she sat staring down at the floor while watching her toes make a desperate attempt to touch the floor. Madam Henry, disgusted with the site of her own daughter glanced at her half-exposed breast that had caused a wet yellow stains on her white nightgown, "Whore!" she shouted again as she positioned herself to strike the other side of Greta's face as she sat. Reacting instinctively to the pain, Greta quickly moved into a defensive stance and grabbed her mother's wrist. With a heavy mix of hurt and shame from the recent physical and verbal blows, Greta tightened her grip on her mother's hand. "Greta's grip on her mother's wrist remained firm as anger surged through her. She couldn't believe Madam Henry had spoken to her that way so cruelly and unjustly. Overwhelmed by the sting of betrayal, Greta, her voice shaking with emotion, insisted she didn't deserve such treatment before finally releasing her mother's hand."

"My master is no married man, and I am no mistress. I do not steal away in the dead of night from empty barns and desolate cellars to lie upon a bed of hay, surrendering my precious gift to a man who craves me while his wife sleeps, oblivious." Greta released her mother's hand, her gaze unwavering. In that moment, she had revealed her mother's hidden story, and she did so without regret. The shocking truth of Greta's real father left Madam Henry speechless. For the first time, Greta grasped the full extent of her mother's suffering a past of repeated assaults that had gradually reshaped her mother's mistress role into one of quiet compliance. Her mother could never understand the love she shared with Monsieur. Feeling her confidence swell, Greta rose to her feet, standing resolute before her mother. "It is not my fault that the man I gave my purity to has given me a son. My willingness awakened a longing in him, and his desire to know every part of me has created a hunger we now both share," she declared. "You wish to know who fathered my son? He is the ruler of the Scotney Castle." Madam Henry, who had long harbored suspicions, now shuddered at the confirmation. Greta, noticing her mother's shock, spoke again, "Mother, Monsieur Heritage cherishes his heir. This is why, even now, my son rests on silk sheets, carrying his father's name." She reminded her mother of a lifetime spent instilling fear, obedience, and silence in her to follow orders, to speak only when spoken to. "So when Monsieur called upon me, I did not refuse him for I love him." Greta's voice softened yet held firm. "I will no longer allow you to make me feel fear or shame over the man I love. I am glad he is the father of my child, and I believe he loves me, too." Greta sauntered over to baby Philip's bassinet and lifted him gently, holding him close to her heart as she softly rocked him. Slowly, she walked back to Madam Henry, who watched her every move in silence. Greta tenderly pressed her bruised cheek against Philip's tiny head, as if the touch might somehow bring healing. She moved and stood directly in front of her mother, meeting her gaze as she carefully placed baby Philip into her arms. With a calm smile, Greta spoke, her eyes never leaving her mother's. "There is your grandson, Madam Henry, and I am your daughter. Please, learn to love us, for the ruler of the Scotney, Monsieur Heritage, your master loves us both." Madam Henry, speechless and stunned, could no longer doubt the truth: Monsieur Heritage was the father of her daughter's child. Her thoughts simmered as she held baby Philip, her gaze drifting around the room she had been ordered to scrub, clean, and prepare for her own daughter all at Monsieur Heritage's command. Quietly, with a smirk, she thought, *Yes, my daughter, Monsieur Heritage loves you now. Your son lies on silk, and you sleep in a bed fit for royalty. But wait until he needs a legitimate heir not one from a slave girl. When he takes a wife, you'll see my foolish daughter.* Greta, interpreting her mother's silence as acceptance, walked over to her basin behind the wardrobe and gently cleansed her face.

She removed her sleep wear and stood in front of the mirror and admired herself, she thought about what Monsieur Heritage' had done to her. Now curious of why he was determined to perform such an act, she deliberately stood to the side out of her mother's sight. She caressed and coupled her breast until they were becoming engorged with milk, then timidly almost as if she were afraid of her own breast, she squeezed out a small amount of milk into her hand and then tasted it. The substance had no taste she could compare it to, and it left her with no desire to seek more. She couldn't understand why Monsieur Heritage would want it again, but she knew he enjoyed it, and the feeling it brought her was unlike anything she had ever experienced. She told herself that if he requested it again, she would secure the lock on the door and would not object. Greta made a silent vow to herself she would continue to please him, no matter the cost, for the sake of little Philip's future. Greta with her eyes focused on a small drop of milk that ran down her breast reached for a gown out of the wardrobe and placed it on. She pulled her long hair up into a bun and left two cascading curls down at both sides of her face. She walked over and reached for the basket of wild berries and flowers her mother had placed on the dresser. She mashed one of the berries in an old cloth and pressed the juices against her lips until it left a reddish stain on her lips. She then took a small bottle of water that was filled with lavender and rose pedals and rubbed it on her neck. She then walked back over to her mother and gently removed Little Philip from her arms. She instructed her to go to the cellar and make

58

sure that the servants were preparing the meals for the day. Madam Henry who was astounded watched her daughter now take on the mannerism as the lady of the house. She said nothing but "Yes daughter" as she exited the room. Now left alone with the baby Philip, Greta sat down in a chair and properly fed her son. She hummed the melody that she heard Gem Marie play often on her harp. She held him close and looked down into his freshly awaken eyes, "My dear precious son, you must never ever forget that I am your mother."

Chapter: 6

Gem Marie

It was almost six months since little Philip had been born and Gem Marie had almost been distracted by his new arrival. Instead of being jealous or feeling slighted by Monsieur Heritage' whose full focus on Philip and Greta had become the talk of the castle. Gem Marie welcomed his new fixation because it gave her more free time to plan her perfect escape. The delivery men were scheduled to come any day to deliver the feed and Gem Marie knew their early arrival meant that she would have to prepare herself to hide beneath the carriage before they would pull off. She knew that once the carriages and wagons were loaded, they would sometimes linger and talk and double check items before they started their journey off of the Scotney. She had her layers of clothing, and her supplies already prepared. She had calculated the time it would take her to get dress and then leave so she decided once she saw the men's arrival. She would dress lightly and remove her clothing quickly and quietly, slipping through the house under the cover of early dawn. The barn was her sanctuary, where she could move freely, away from prying eyes. She stashed her garments there, she would have to change swiftly before the men returned. In the dim light, she prepared the cloths and items she'd use to suspend herself beneath the wagon, her escape hinging on their strength. With a steady hand, she took long, thick strips of cloth, cutting them into narrow lengths before braiding them tightly. The resulting cord was thick and sturdy plus strong enough, she hoped to hold her weight. Every twist of the braid was done with precision, as if her very life might depended on it. The hardest part was yet to come waiting, hidden away until the precise moment to act. When the time came, she would slip beneath the carriage, her heart pounding in her chest as she thought about it. If she had to endure more than an hour in that precarious position, she told herself she would, just as she had the night she hid under her bed, fighting the ache in her limbs until sleep overtook her. She had endured pain before, and she would again. But this time, her survival depended on it and Christian Pierre was her sole motivation. She needed an idea of when the men would arrive, but she did not want to ask Monsieur

Heritage' or Madam Henry so she decided to visit Greta and little Philip. When Gem Marie arrived at Greta's room, she was sewing a quilt while baby Philip was resting peacefully in his basinet. Gem Marie, who was watching Greta sew, took a seat, and admired her hair and eyes for a moment. She took note and watched her hand movement very closely, then asked if she could try. Greta eagerly handed the needle and thread to Gem Marie and guided her hand along the stitching. Gem Marie, quick to grasp the pattern, began steering the conversation towards a more personal topic. With curiosity sparkling in her eyes, she asked Greta, "What does it feel like to love someone who isn't your father or mother?" Greta paused, surprised by the question's depth. "Why do you think I would have knowledge on such things? "she replied smiling, a touch of amusement in her voice. "Well," Gem Marie responded thoughtfully, "because you had Philip, and he was born from love, wasn't he?" Greta, who had begun her day at the crack of dawn, hadn't expected to be reflecting on matters of the heart, let alone her relationship with Monsieur Heritage. Her mind raced, searching for the right words. "Love isn't something you can hold in your hand, like this needle," Greta finally said, holding it up for emphasis. "It's a feeling a deep knowing that the person you've chosen is *the* one, the one who is meant for you. They'll remind you of everything you've ever cherished. And because the emotions they stir are so unique, so rare, it'll feel as though you're searching for something in your life to compare it to, though nothing will quite match. Because this love is so unlike anything you have ever felt you may search your heart to find one other thing like it. But when you look around you and you will not find anything else like them." Greta had spoken from her heart and now, with the undeniable proof she knew the truth. This new feeling, so tender and profound, could only be one thing, a love that had quietly taken root in her heart, sparked by Monsieur Heritage. Overwhelmed by this revelation, Greta rose to her feet, her emotions teetering on the edge. To hide her streaming tears from Gem Marie, she gently picked up baby Philip and used him as a distraction. Gem Marie sat nearby, her hands busy with embroidering but her thoughts wandered, echoing Greta's words. She too thought of Monsieur Heritage, and then her mind drifted to Christian Pierre the feeling was not the same. Her heart ached in confusion. She loved them both, but with Christian, the feeling was different indescribable, yet undeniable. Perhaps, she mused, this was the sign that Greta's confession had been right. Could it be that what she felt for Christian Pierre was true love, even though she did not know him? Her heart whispered yes, convincing her that this deep and genuine affection was real. Gem Marie, on the verge of sharing her thoughts about Christian Pierre with Greta, abruptly stood up, her words caught in her throat. Something held her back, a quiet hesitation. Instead, she casually mentioned her desire to check on one of her horses but only if there were no deliveries today. Her tone was light, but she couldn't conceal the underlying unease. She had always felt uncomfortable around the men in the barn since the day Monsieur Heritage had brought his wrath down. Greta, still tender from her own emotional admission, warned her that deliveries were indeed scheduled for today and advised against her going. "Even though there are all new delivery men, it's best to wait until they're gone. Or perhaps, it would be better to visit the barn tomorrow," she suggested with a knowing glance. Gem Marie nodded, grateful for the information but a flicker of tension lingered in the air as the secrets she held within. Once Gem Marie heard that the deliveries were coming in the evening her heart skipped a beat. Then a burst of energy rushed through her. Now it felt like she was moving one step closer to her love Christian. She quickly put down the needle and quilt and told Greta she just remembered she had some studies and Harp lessons to complete. Gem Marie leaned in, pressing a gentle kiss on baby Philip's forehead. She then wrapped her arms around Greta in a tight embrace, catching her off guard with the sudden display of affection. Greta, momentarily startled, softened and returned the sentiment with a tender kiss on the top of Gem Marie's head. "Go on, now," Greta murmured, her voice warm but firm, "finish your studies." With a nod, Gem Marie hurried down the long corridor, her heart pounding harder with every step. Reaching her room upstairs, she locked the door behind her and moved swiftly to the window. Her eyes scanned the horizon, anxiously searching the farmlands for any sign of the delivery men approaching. But the landscape remained empty, the silence almost taunting. Relieved yet unsettled, Gem Marie turned away from the window. She crossed the room to her secret hiding place, a narrow space beneath the floorboards, carefully lifting the loose plank. Inside was her escape plan a set of worn, practical clothes meant for running. She placed them down methodically, her mind racing through the steps of what was to come. The time was drawing near. She then opened the silk bench and removed a couple of the newspaper articles she had hidden about Christian Pierre, she folded them and pushed it into one of the small bags that she had pinned on the inside of her traveling clothing. She grabbed the sack of items and peered out her large window again. It was then she noticed a wagon going towards the farm area she quickly picked up the sack and peered into the hallways. Gem Marie, whose hands were shaking, looked out for anyone who could spot her. Once she confirmed the hallways and corridors were empty, she ran swiftly towards the back stairs of the castle that lead her to the back way of the farmland. Gem Marie moved with quiet precision, making sure to avoid any path where the servants might catch sight of her. Once she slipped into the garden area, she paused, to catch her breath. The large sack she carried was growing heavier by the minute, its weight slowing her down. She leaned against a tree, briefly wondering if she had overpacked. But time was running short. Gritting her teeth, she slung the sack over her back once more and broke into a run. Her eyes locked on the distant barn, the critical checkpoint in her daring escape. If she could just reach it and hide the contents, she'd be halfway to freedom. The rest would depend on her timing waiting for the wagons to be loaded and then strapping herself to the underside of it, just as she had carefully plotted. The barn loomed closer. Her legs burned slightly from the effort, but she forced herself to move faster. Once inside, she heaved the sack behind the bales of hay, which were set aside for the horses. After a quick glance around to make sure she was alone, she darted to the far side of the barn. Pressing her back against the rough wooden wall, she finally allowed herself a moment to breathe. Her heart pounded, but she was one step closer to escaping. Suddenly she heard some unfamiliar voices when she peeked through the cracks of the barn, she saw some men unloading the freight wagon's feed then re loaded them with wheat. Gem Marie watched the men going back and forth, they were working feverishly as if they had a deadline. Seeing the men's tempo, she became worried that she may not have enough time to slip on her travel clothes and tie herself properly underneath the wagon. While she stood there waiting for the men to complete their task, she heard a bird crow in the distance towards the castle. Instantly she began to think about everyone inside and how she will miss them dearly, this prompted a mental note to write everyone as soon as she and Christian Pierre were well acquainted. With her breathing returning to normal she watched how the English Blue Bells swayed in the wind against the gentle breeze. She canvased the Scotney and for the first time she truly saw how magnificent it was. She thought about going back and saying goodbye to Monsieur Heritage' with a last hug or smile maybe. Just then she heard one of the men confirmed that the last bag of feed has been loaded. Once the men had finished their task, they exchanged a few words before one of them remarked, "We'll need to settle accounts with Monsieur Heritage approval." With that, they began walking toward the castle's garden, their shadows stretching long in the fading light. As soon as they were out of sight, Gem Marie darted into the barn. Her heart raced as she quickly stripped off the dress she had been wearing. She tore open the sack, her fingers trembling slightly, and began layering the new garments piece by piece with precise care. Each item had its place, each layer secured with deliberate attention. She then took the long strips of cloth and wrapped them tightly around her, pulling them snug as though the very fabric could shield her from what was to come. Now fully concealed in her disguise, she slid beneath the wagon. To her astonishment, its massive size loomed far larger than she had imagined easily dwarfing the queen-sized bed she knew so well. She carefully selected the braided pieces of cloth, tying two of them at the bottom of the wagon, each one secured across from the other. The remaining two pieces were fastened near the head of the wagon on its axle, mirroring the arrangement at the bottom of the wagon. She left enough slack in each cloth to ensure there was just enough room to slip her wrists and feet through the loop. With meticulous precision, she turn over onto her stomach then slid each of her feet into a cloth loops, securing them snugly around the bars. Her boots remained untied, deliberately loose, giving her an edge if she needed to remove them quickly. Once her feet were anchored, she laid flat on the palms of her hands pressed into the ground beneath the wagon. Her legs anchored behind her, resting along the wagon's wooden beam, the position gave her just enough freedom to maneuver. She then proceeded to slip her left hand through the braided cloth hanging from around the axle beam. She tightened the ends just enough to leave room for her wrist to move if needed. The final step required more dexterity: she repeated the process with her right hand, this time using her mouth to pull the cloth tightly, now ensuring both wrists were secured but not immobile, she hung there. Hanging with her arms and legs spread wide a surge of tension filled her body and the air. The preparation wasn't just about survival it was a game of precision and timing. Every knot, every twist of the cloth, had to be perfect. Any slip could mean the difference between life and death. Gem Marie was hoisted beneath the freight wagon, suspended across the wooden axle beams like a human bridge. With her arms stretched wide almost in a spread-eagle position she maneuvered her hands and wrist, so they were tightly secured upon the rectangular piece of wood. She practiced gripping the rough timber, the coarse texture of the wood bit into her fingertips, and a sharp sting told her a splinter had pierced her skin. Wincing, she shifted her weight, loosening her grip just enough to ease the strain on her back. With her back no longer held rigid she let her body sag. Slightly lowering herself closer to the ground she settled into a concave position. It was a calculated move, meant to conserve her strength for the journey ahead. Once the carriage lurched into motion, she would have no choice but to hold herself aloft, while maintaining a straight posture to avoid being dragged against the unforgiving terrain below. Every moment hanging here was a battle between endurance and pain, but Gem Marie knew she had no other option if she wanted to survive the rough road that awaited her. Now becoming nervous, she drew her attention on the ground below her. She watched how the insects that crawled effortlessly across the dirt and rocks, moving small pieces of leaves and tiny bits of feed. There was a group of ants that were moving as if they were running an assembly line. Gem Marie became captivated with how the small ants carried pieces of feed three times their weight. She watched and admired how they assisted one another on their journey and never became tired. As she watched the ants and insect's marvelous feat, she heard voices from the distance growing closer. The men returned, pacing back and forth along the wagon, carefully checking that the wheat was properly secured. From her hidden spot, Gem Marie could only see their worn shoes and the frayed hems of their trousers. One man's boots caught her attention thick with mud, a clump on the heel stained an unusual purplish-blue. Her heart skipped. Bluebells. He had been trampling in the garden. Gem Marie held her breath, willing herself to stay perfectly still, her pulse quickening as she feared that even the slightest sound would betray her hiding place. There was a small breeze that blew and raised the loose dirt from under the wagon. The small dirt particles tickled her nose almost causing her to sneeze unable to scratch it she wiggled it instead. She continued holding on now using her all her body strength to keep still, with doubt beginning to creep in she thought to herself, "I will be tired before the wagon leaves." Finally, the unmistakable thud of boots clambering aboard the wagon reverberated through Gem Marie's body. She strained to listen, and moments later, heard one of the men call out a command for the horses. The crack of the reins echoed in the cool air, and with a jolt, the wagon lurched forward. Glancing quickly to her left and right, she saw the wheels slowly creaking to life. Her pulse quickened as the uneven, rocky path of Scotney's farm came into view, the wagon rattling with each bump. Gem Marie's knuckles whitened as she clung on to the wooden beam, her body jostled and tossed side to side. The rough road caused her fingers to slip which let the weight of her arm added pressure of her wrist hang from her makeshift rope. Panic surged through her, but she quickly grasped the beam again, this time feeling the sharp sting of splinters digging into her skin. The pain barely registered as the wagon approached a steep hill, picking up speed. With a sudden jolt, her body was thrust forward, head and shoulders pitched as if she were about to dive headlong into the blur of earth speeding beneath her. She pressed her ankles hard against the wood, desperate to steady herself. But the driver's sharp crack of the reins sent the horses into a frenzied gallop, the wind now whipping past her. Gem Marie squeezed her eyes shut, her breath caught in her chest, as the world spun in a dizzying rush around her. Now she could no longer see but she could hear the horses galloping hooves. The wheels of the wagon made a rumbling crashing noise every time they road over a large stone. The belly of the wagon would lift up and then instantly send her crash towards the dirt road which caused dust and small rocks to pelt her body. With every bump, Gem Marie learned to recognize the landscape they traversed by the frequency of the debris that pelted her. One particular stretch seemed softer, more forgiving, as mud slapped her face with the sting of tiny bee bites. curious by this sudden sensation, she opened her eyes to pinpoint the source of the intermittent attacks only to be met with a sharp stone that struck her forehead with a brutal thud. A flash of white specks danced before her eyes like dying stars as pain surged through her. She instinctively opened her mouth to release a low, desperate moan, but as her cries echoed into the dust-laden air, dirt and tiny fragments flew down her throat. She swallowed instinctively, attempting to clear her throat, but was met only by a harsh soreness that now gripped the back of her throat, leaving her gasping for relief amid the chaos. She pressed her lips together and closed her eyes, tuning her ears to the rhythmic pounding of horse hooves and the creaking of the wagon wheel. She listened intently to the rolling sounds, punctuated by the occasional crash of the wheels against the uneven ground. Opening her eyes for just a fleeting moment, she lifted her head, desperate to glimpse the world beyond the galloping legs of the horses.

Sunlight flickered through the gaps, casting playful shadows that danced with each powerful stride. As the wagon took a sharp turn, a long ray of sunlight pierced through, momentarily blinding her. In that instant, a sharp stone struck her mouth, causing her to wince. Gem Marie quickly squeezed her eyes shut again and lowered her head, instinctively shielding herself from the propelling stones surrounding her. She felt warmth pooling under her nose and on her lips. With a sudden realization, she sucked her lip into her mouth, using her tongue to explore the source of the moisture. To her shock, she discovered it was her own blood. The taste was metallic and warm, and she held her lip in place, allowing the fluid to gather beneath her tongue for a heartbeat before swallowing. The mingling of blood and saliva provided a strange solace, coating her throat and easing its passageway, as if offering a momentary reprieve from the tumult around her. With the sandpaper-like sensation now faded, Gem Marie turned her attention to the sensations in her arms. She sensed their growing weakness, but she couldn't tell if it was due to the relentless blows she had endured or simply the creeping fatigue of time. She tightened her grip again, focusing intently on her arms and shoulders, desperately trying to gauge whether an hour had passed. As lightheadedness washed over her, Gem Marie took a deep breath through her nose and exhaled slowly through her mouth. Turning her head to the right, she scanned her surroundings for anything that could help her keep track of time. What felt like mere minutes seemed to stretch into hours, each tick dragging on relentlessly. Now the wagon had entered a stretch of muddy, slippery terrain. The wet soil clung to everything it touched, swallowing up small stones and debris. For a brief moment, this reprieve spared her from the onslaught of stones pelting her skin. She turned her gaze forward, watching the horses' hooves trample the earth, their rhythmic pounding a cruel reminder of her captivity. In a moment of despair, she let out a cry of hopelessness, but it was muffled by the relentless creaking of the wagon wheels and the low, oppressive sounds of the journey. Unable to control her hysteria, she let out a piercing cry, uncaring whether the men heard her desperate plea. This final scream was her last attempt to be released from the merciless belly of the wagon. Yet, it was met only with a cloud of horse manure mixed with dirt that choked her throat, stifling her voice. Suddenly, Gem Marie felt her body lifted, as if she had levitated and was suspended in air, before crashing down into an abyss of darkness. When the world around her faded, she found herself in a dimly lit room, her harp standing defiantly under a solitary spotlight. Instinctively, she began to play the song she had been rehearsing for Christian Pierre. Mesmerized, she watched her fingers dance gracefully over the strings, each note resonating with the echo of her despair and longing. She glanced around, her mind swirling with confusion as she played, pondering how she had ended up in this strange place. Suddenly, a violent gagging jolted her from her thoughts, and she found herself heaving, the bitter taste of vomit erupting from her mouth. The acrid liquid splattered onto her face and clothing. The cold substance hitting her shocked her and snapped her back to reality. As she struggled to comprehend her surroundings, Gem Marie, who could no longer endure the afflictions of the devilish wagon, decided she would release herself from its grips. she lifted one leg, wiggling her toes and ankles until her boot dangled precariously from her foot. With a final, determined wiggle, the boot tumbled away. She repeated the action with her opposite foot, each movement infused with a fierce resolve. Once both boots lay abandoned, she skillfully untangled her feet from the strips of cloth that bound her to the wooden beam. Locking her legs together, she prepared to lay them flat against the rough surface beneath her. With a surge of adrenaline, she wiggled her wrists free from the now worn braided ties, freed from the restraints that once held them captive against the front beam, a rush of cool air flowed over her skin as the bindings fell away. Now, relying solely on her own upper body strength she tightened her grip on the wagon's axle, bracing herself for what lay ahead. With a powerful move, she dropped her legs from the axle beams, her toes scraping against the coarse earth below. A fiery sting ignited in her feet as they were dragged across the jagged ground, but she pressed on, fueled by the burning desire for freedom. Gem Marie counted silently in her head, timing her release perfectly. She let go of the wooden beam, crossing her arms in an X over her face. With a sharp inhale, she pressed her elbows and torso firmly into the damp soil beneath her, bracing for impact. The ground came up fast, but she remained motionless, her face buried in her cupped hands, stiff as a board. Every muscle was tense, focused on one thing preventing her body from rolling as the wagon rumbled past. She lay there, still as the earth beneath her, not daring to move until the sound of the wheels faded into the distance. Then, in the quiet that followed, she cautiously rolled onto her back. The world felt calm, untouched by the danger that had just passed. Looking up at the sky, she let the warmth of the sun pour over her. Gem Marie laid there, her chest rising and falling as she replayed what she had just done. The weight of it all sank in, steady and relentless, like a slow-moving tide. She tried to sit up, pressing herself onto her elbows as the sun's warmth tingled at her toes. Then she noticed the blood. Her heart jolted at the sight one of her toenails had been torn clean off, leaving raw skin beneath. Wincing, she forced herself to stand, her bruised and battered limbs shaking from the relentless jostling of the brutal wagon ride. The air seemed to thicken around her as she began the long, agonizing walk back in search of her boots. With each step, she counted to distract herself from the searing pain in her feet. "Eighty-seven... eighty-eight..." The number thrummed in her mind like a drumbeat. By the time she reached one hundred and ten, her eyes caught sight of one boot, half-buried in the grass, filled with dirt and small stones, but otherwise unharmed. She tugged it free, but instead of relief, a sharp pain shot through her, reminding her that the other boot was still missing. Gem pressed on, her feet now nearly numb, her stockings shredded beyond recognition, dragging her soles across the rough, unforgiving terrain. She found the second boot lying defiantly in the middle of the road, as if mocking her struggle. She cast a quick glance around, scanning for any sign of danger. She look towards the wooded area and saw a very large rock. She walked over to the large flat rock that almost resemble a table and unpacked her items that were pinned and tied to her. She began to remove first layer of clothing that was muddy and covered in filth, she placed them in a large cloth bag that she had made out of some old sheets. She then began removing her items, first she pulled out a small bottle of wine, then a small bottle of water, lastly some torn pieces of cloth. Then she pulled out the only pair of stockings she had left. She sat down on the rock and poured wine on her feet. The deep red wine made her toes burn. She quickly pour some water on both feet then wrapped them with the torn cloth. She then placed her clean stockings over the cloths on her feet. She took off another layer of clean clothes and placed them in a separate bag. She hurriedly packed everything away, but not before wiping her face with water and a torn piece of cloth, which she discarded carelessly. Settling on the large rock, she pondered which direction she should headfirst in her frantic rush, she had forgotten her compass and would now have to rely on her memory and the position of the sun for directions. As she sat there gathering her thoughts, the distant sound of horses reached her ears. Without hesitation, she sprang to the opposite side of the rock and flattened herself against the ground, hidden from view. The massive boulder shielded her from the road on her right, while dense woods to her left provided no clear path for escape. She lay motionless, listening to the pounding hooves draw nearer. Gem Marie's heart thundered in her chest, so loud it seemed to echo in her ears. She held her breath, willing the drumming in her head to stop, desperate to remain undetected. The ground beneath her felt cold and unforgiving, her body pressed against a layer of dried leaves and loose soil. Her eyes were fixed on the rock, now looming inches from her face. She remained still, her senses heightened, waiting for the danger to pass. At last, the galloping hooves began to fade, their rhythmic beats growing fainter until they disappeared into silence. Gem Marie exhaled softly, her body trembling as she waited just a moment longer to be sure she was truly alone. As she laid there facing the large rock, the only thing she heard was the humming of the insects around her then all of a sudden there was a loud thump close to her left ear. Now terribly afraid to turn her head, she continued to lay still with her head facing the large rock. Her attention and focus was broken when a large white neck vulture landed on the large flat rock above. It peered down at Gem Marie with its elongated white neck then expanded its eight feet wide wings above her. Now petrified in terror she slowly turned her head to the left away from the large bird only to find herself now staring into the eyes of a large dead possum. With its mouth wide open and dripping with blood and one of the eyes had small maggots wiggling out of it. The vulture had dropped his kill beside her believing she may have been dead also. Gem Marie jumped to her feet and took off running, she ran through the wooded area nonstop without looking back or forward. With everything appearing to be one big blur she used her hands to shield her face as she swatted tree limbs and anything in her way. She only came to a complete stop when she fell into a small hole hidden under a small pile of leaves. Now with the adrenaline coursing through her veins she could no longer feel any pain in her feet. She quickly rose to her feet again and began running. She only slowed her momentum when she came to a small stream of water. She paused and quickly took out a piece of cloth and wiped her face and hands. As she kneeled on the ground to catch her breath, she canvased the area. She found a large log resting on the edge of the stream and sank down onto it, exhausted. Her shoes and stockings were soaked in blood. Grimacing, she peeled them off and dipped her aching feet into the cool, rushing water. The coldness brought immediate relief, soothing the throbbing pain. As she sat there, the quiet of the woods surrounding her, she rinsed her stockings and laid them across the log to dry. Pulling out a bundle of dirty clothes from a separate bag, she scrubbed them in the stream, then laid them out alongside the rest. For a moment, she was alone in the stillness, the sound of the water trickling around her. Examining her feet again, she saw they were red and bruised, she thought to herself, "At least the bleeding has stopped." Leaving them bare and exposed to the fresh air, she let nature take its course. The woods were quiet, but her senses remained sharp, scanning for any sign of danger in the stillness. Now paying better attention to her surroundings, she look off into the distance and saw just trees. She decided to follow the stream to wherever it ends. Now feeling a little rested she wrapped her feet with the damp clean cloth and pulled her stockings over them. She found a long thick tree branch and use it for support. After walking several miles to the end of the stream, Gem Marie came upon an old, abandoned shack with its door slightly ajar. She hesitated for a moment before stepping closer, her eyes scanning the dilapidated structure. Inside, the place was barren just a small stool, a cot, a fireplace, and two tiny windows that barely let in the waning daylight. With evening fast approaching and the threat of being caught in the darkness looming, she decided to make camp there for the night. Settling herself in the center of the shack's creaky wooden floor, Gem carefully unpacked a small tin of John Walker's friction matches. She struck one against the rough surface, the flame flickering to life in the dim space. She found an old, half-melted wax candle, its wick frayed and brittle, likely left behind by a previous traveler. As the candle's soft glow filled the room, it cast shadows that danced along the weathered walls, adding an eerie yet comforting warmth to her makeshift shelter. he candle flickered, casting ghostly shadows that danced across the walls. Gem Marie glanced around the small, dusty shack, doubt creeping into her mind. Had she made the right decision in running away? The world outside the castle walls felt far different from the adventures she had imagined far colder and lonelier than the stories in schoolbooks or newspapers had led her to believe. Freedom came with inconvenience, and nothing was as thrilling as she had once dreamed. Here, there were no servants to bring her a warm blanket or a soothing cup of tea. For the first time, she missed the comforts of home, even Monsieur Heritage, whom she had started holding resentment for keeping the secrets of love and life from her. She sighed, laying out her damp clothes to dry, then gathered her few belongings into a bundle to serve as a makeshift pillow. The hard, leaf-filled cot was nothing like the soft, feather-stuffed bed she was accustomed to. Gem Marie closed her eyes and listened to the eerie sounds of the woods outside, where the wind whistled through the cracks in the cabin's walls and windows. Suddenly, a strong gust blew the door open with a bang, sending a jolt of fear through her. She rushed to prop a worn stool against the door, hoping it would hold, then crept back to the cot. This time, she forced her mind away from the unease. She imagined herself back at the castle, playing her harp. The sweet, tender notes floated through her thoughts, calming her. In her mind's eye, she saw baby Philip reaching out for the strings, his tiny hands grasping at the sound. She held onto that comforting vision, replaying it over and over until, at last, sleep claimed her. When Gem Marie awoke the next morning, the sun was shining through the trees and through the small windows of the shack. Gem Marie sat and ate a piece of bread and a small piece of cheese she had wrapped in a cloth. All her items that were laid out the night before were now dry, she packed them into her bag and got ready to head out back into the woods. Gem Marie opened the shack door and took one step out and was immediately hit with something heavy and hard. It knocked her off her feet and sent her into a dream state where she was back in the castle in her room playing the piano. She turned and looked at a man that was standing next to her, but he had no face. She called out for Monsieur Heritage' but the faceless man kept walking away from her. Then there was a tap on her shoulders, it was Greta telling her to wake up and open her eyes. Greta kept shaking her until Gem Marie opened her eyes and saw a strange woman staring down at her. "Where is Greta, what happened?"

Chapter: 7

English, French, Italian and German

Gem Marie found herself with her head in a strange woman's lap the woman whispered, "Don't talk anymore and don't go to sleep you talk in your sleep. You been out cold for a while." Gem Marie, now frighten removed her head from the woman's lap and sat up. That's when she realized she was on the back of a large wagon with some other people. Some were young and old, some were sleeping and awake, but all were strangers to her. She turned back to the woman and whispered, "Where are we going?" "To town" the woman replied "Don't talk" the woman whispered. "It will only make them mad." Once the wagon stopped moving everyone was told to get out and move to another area. The men who drove the wagon walked over to a group of other men that were counting bags of feed and began talking. Everyone was lined up, the men separated from the women. Gem Marie stood silently, watching as one of the women was violently grabbed and thrown aside. Two men approached the woman, demanding to know where she had come from. At first, she refused to answer, sobbing uncontrollably, but after several harsh blows, she finally cried out, "I'm lost." The taller of the two men then turned his attention to Gem Marie, his eyes narrowing as he strode towards her. "Where did you come from?" he asked, his voice cold and commanding. Gem Marie, now regretting every decision that led her to this moment especially the one about Christian Pierre quickly responded, "I'm from the Scotney estate, with Monsieur Héritage." The man stepped back, scrutinizing her clothes, which were noticeably in better condition than those of the others. Suspicious, he called over another man, who limped as he approached. As the limping man came closer, Gem Marie's stomach sank. She recognized him instantly the young delivery boy whom Monsieur Héritage had beaten with his walking stick not long ago. The boy's eyes, burning with resentment, locked onto hers. His lips curled into a smirk. The tall man barked at him, "You used to deliver to the Scotney! Do you recognize this girl?" The boy, filled with revenge, limped closer, his gaze sweeping over Gem Marie. After a long, tense moment, he spoke: "No, I don't know her. I know everyone from the Scotney, even the slaves and servants. I've never seen her there before." The tallest man turned back to Gem Marie, his face darkening. Without warning, he grabbed a fistful of her hair, jerking her head back. "Liar," he snarled. "Tell me where you really came from, or I'll make sure you regret it." Terror surged through her, and though her voice trembled, she repeated, "The Scotney... I'm from the Scotney." The tall man struck Gem Marie hard across the face, his voice low and menacing. "If you don't tell the truth," he warned, "Or you'll feel the back of my hand." Gem Marie, trembling and unsure of what to say, blurted out, "I came from Christian Pierre. I'm looking for him." The men fell silent for a moment, then burst into laughter. The tall man, still smirking, asked, "Why didn't you say that from the start? The Pierre cargo will be leaving in the morning. You'd better make proper sure your on it." His eyes narrowed. "Get over here, how did you get away?" Gem Marie's hands shook, but she said nothing. Her silence didn't go unnoticed. Another man swiftly grabbed her arm, leading her away to yet another wagon. As she was hoisted onto the back, she glanced at a young man with a limp, standing nearby. His expression had changed he now looked just as terrified as she felt. He knew all too well what would happen if Monsieur Heritage ever came looking for Gem Marie and found out he had lied. The memory of his last punishment still haunted him, and he was too afraid to confess now. Instead, he stood frozen, watching the wagon pull away with Gem Marie aboard, his fear deepening with each turn of the wheels. Before the wagon disappeared completely, the woman who had warned Gem Marie to remain silent was tossed in beside her, their shared fate now sealed. Once they were secured on the wagon and it began to move, the woman slid closer to Gem Marie and whispered, "Is Christian Pierre a good man?" Gem Marie, feeling withdrawn and reluctant to engage, remained silent. The woman continued, sharing her story. "I ran away from my home and lost my way. Then I ended up on a ship that sailed to England, but I'm determined to return back home." Gem Marie turned to meet her gaze, her curiosity piqued. "Me too," she replied, the shared longing for home igniting a flicker of connection between them. The woman told Gem Marie her name was Claudette. "Gem Marie," she replied, "I'm the daughter of Monsieur Heritage of the Scotney." The surprise flickered across Claudette's face as she quickly covered Gem Marie's mouth, her eyes wide with urgency. "Never say that again." Confusion washed over Gem Marie. Why did mentioning Monsieur Heritage bring such trouble? "Where are we going?" she asked, her voice trembling. "To the boat, so we can go to America," Claudette replied, a mixture of excitement and apprehension in her tone. The reality of her situation hit Gem Marie like a cold wave, and she instantly began to cry. There was no turning back now; she was heading to a place she knew nothing about, completely unprotected. In that moment, she understood why Monsieur Heritage had kept her so well guarded. Helplessness enveloped her. Noticing the tears streaming down Gem Marie's face, Claudette's expression softened. "What's wrong?" she asked gently. "I am from the Scotney I live in the Scotney castle," Gem Marie explained, her voice choked with emotion. "The young man lied. My father Monsieur Heritage beat him with a walking stick, for speaking ill to me, that's how he received the limp." Claudette listened attentively, then glanced at Gem Marie's clothes. They were slightly dirty, but the fabric suggested a higher quality than what most wore. "Why did you choose to run away?" Claudette inquired, her curiosity piqued. Gem Marie took a deep breath, wiping her tears. "I saw Christian Pierre in the newspaper," she confessed. "I wanted to meet him because I'm in love with him." Claudette's eyes widened in shock. What did this young girl know about love and why would she run away from such a lavish home." Claudette sensed that Gem Marie must be younger than she appeared or had been kept hidden away for far too long and had no understanding of the words she was using. Intrigued, she probed, "How old are you?" "I'll be Fifteen, very soon," Gem Marie replied. Just then, the wagon lurched to a stop, and the two girls were ushered off and led toward the bustling docks. They were met by groups of people boarding the ship, some moving willingly while others were being forced. The man who had brought them leaned in and warned, "If anyone asks, tell them you're with Christian Pierre then keep your mouth shut." Suddenly, a man approached with a clipboard and asked one of the men if these were the two girls to be added to Christian Pierre's count. As they stood waiting to board the ship, Gem Marie's attention was drawn to a little girl in a beautiful dress, who was with her mother and father. The little girl stared at Gem Marie and then spoke to her in French. Surprised, Gem Marie responded, and the little girl burst into laughter. "Animals cannot speak in French," she repeated, still chuckling. The woman overheard their conversation and turned to Gem Marie with wide eyes. " What is your name and who taught you to speak French?" she asked, astonished. "Monsieur Heritage, and my name is Gem Marie" she replied. The woman spoke in French again, then boldly approached the two men discussing the Christian Pierre cargo. "Where is this young girl headed?" she demanded. "America," the man answered tersely. The woman insisted, "I want her to stay with me and my family for the duration of the trip." I need her to keep my daughter company, I promise to return her before departing in Maryland." The men exchanged glances and retorted, "She is bound for Louisiana with Christian Pierre's cargo, and he is very particular about his property," one of them clarified. Unfazed, the woman replied, "I'll be departing in Maryland and can return her the night before we leave." Tension crackled in the air as the men hesitated, caught between their duty and the unexpected plea of the woman who seemed determined to take Gem Marie under her wing. As the woman reached into her purse, she pulled out two coins and handed them to the men and reaffirmed, "I will return Gem Marie before the ship lands," she'll be back in the galleys a day early. The men, visibly satisfied with their payment, nodded and walked away, taking Claudette with them. Gem Marie, bewildered by the unfolding events, turned back to Francine and began chatting with her again. The woman and her husband exchanged astonished glances. Mr. Chardon now intrigued asked, "What other languages do you speak?" With a spark of pride, Gem Marie replied, "Italian, German, and English!" The husband raised an eyebrow in surprise. "Who taught you so many languages?" Before Gem Marie could respond, his wife interjected, "She has a vivid imagination! She says Monsieur Heritage taught her." The husband chuckled, "Ah, yes! A big imagination indeed. I didn't realize Monsieur Heritage was aboard to give French lessons." Just as Gem Marie was about to reveal that she was his daughter, she hesitated, recalling Claudette's warning to stay quiet. Memories of their earlier conversation echoed in her mind, reminding her that she needed to be cautious about how often she mentioned his name. After boarding the ship, she followed the couple and their daughter to their cabin. Gem Marie was made to wait outside the cabin door while the woman instructed her to get cleaned and prepared to watch over her daughter. Gem Marie nodded then slipped into a small supply room across from the couple's quarters. There was a large basin awaited her, its surface glistening with remnants of countless washes. The room, spacious enough to allow her it offered her some privacy to shed a layer of her clothing. She quickly rinsed out her clothing then hung it on a makeshift line to dry. Carefully, she stored a small bag, pinned beneath her petticoat, in a corner of the room, ensuring it was out of sight. Then, with the zeal of someone reclaiming their dignity, she scrubbed her face, hands, legs, and feet with a bar of soap she fetched from the storage shelves. She dampened her hair, twisting it into a tidy bun, then she surveyed the cuts adorning her face and feet that seemed to be fading. To her relief, they had begun to heal, and the bleeding had ceased. With a struck of luck she found a small worn sheet, she tore off a piece of the cloth, and with expert precision she wrapped her feet before slipping on her stockings and boots. With a few final touches, she doctored her injured lips, which had nearly healed completely, before gathering her belongings and stashing them beneath some cleaning supplies. Taking a deep breath, she slowly peeked out of the supply room, ensuring no one was around, and stepped into the corridor. Gem Marie stood before the couple's door, her heart pounding in anticipation. Finally, the door swung open, and Madame Chardon slightly startled at the sight of Gem Marie, now freshly cleaned and waiting spoke. "Good you are ready." In a hushed voice, Gem Marie asked the woman how should she address them.. "We are Monsieur and Madame Chardon," the wife quickly replied, her tone a blend of curiosity and caution. Madame Chardon instructed Gem Marie to take care of their daughter, Francine, "You must keep her company. She's only six years old," Madame Chardon warned, her eyes narrowing slightly, "So be careful not to upset her." With this charge hanging in the air, Gem Marie felt the weight of her new role settle upon her, brimming with uncertainty and hope, she was not sure but had a feeling that being with the couple was better than going with the two men. The men smelled of ale and perspiration and one of the men with a cruel demeanor stared at her wickedly. She accompanied the couple wherever they went for the entire trip to America. They even gave Gem Marie their left over after they were done eating. Once they returned back to their room., they would hand to Gem Marie in a napkin everything they had not eaten. Gem Marie, who was now recognized as their servant, would wait outside their room, or hide away somewhere until the couple returned from dinner. Then she would take the leftover scraps into the supply room and eat them before bed. On the day of her fifteenth birthday she was surprised to find a small piece of chocolate cake that was wrapped in the napkin. It made her think of the many birthdays she had spent at the Scotney now the cake that had once been a joyous surprise caused her to weep. The soak-filled cake now had a sweet and salty taste that she ate slowly that night of her birthday. When the day finally arrived for Gem Marie to leave and return to the gallows little Francine hugged her and whimpered. Just as instructed the night before the ship was set to dock the couple met up with one of the men and handed off Gem Marie. She was taken to the galley and thrown into a far corner and made to sit. She had grabbed her items out of the storage room and hidden them under her petti coat in a bag she tied around her waist. The man who had received the money from the couple was standing in front and staring at Gem Marie. One of the men finally spoke and asked what's so special about her. Gem Marie responded in French that she had no time to speak to hateful fools. The man just stood there not saying a word. Gem Marie knew he didn't speak French, and she was enjoying that she could say what she wanted without him knowing. He finally answered and said, "That's the reason she speaks different languages." He then walked away leaving her to sit alone in a small corner, where she listened to moans and cries all night. There was a very frail woman who appeared to had lost her child. She sat alone and held an imaginary baby in her arms that she rocked to sleep. Every now and then she would speak to the imaginary child ever so gently, then without a moment's notice she would burst into tears. It was like she was reliving the birth of the child, then suddenly robbed of the joyous moments by its death. Gem Marie watched the woman so closely the whole night that she began to see the entire events of what had taken place. She saw the woman endure a difficult childbirth then the relief of its arrival as she laid the newborn on her bosom. Only after an hour she was robbed of the gift, the child must have stop breathing in her arms. Gem Marie could no longer bear to watch the woman's pantomime of grief, so she shifted her focus to a man sitting partially in shadow. Though his body was cloaked in darkness, he kept his hands and arms illuminated, reaching out as if grasping for something unseen. He never spoke, only moved in periodic attempts to retrieve whatever eluded him, each reach quick but careful, pulling it gently back toward his chest, as though coaxing a reluctant companion. Later, Gem Marie would learn that it was his own soul he was trying to reclaim. The brutal journey on the ship the relentless waves, the scarce food had left him fragile and exhausted, and now his soul seemed ready to abandon him. But he wasn't ready for its departure; whenever he paused his reaching it drifted away but he summoned it back, trapping it within him once more. As Gem Marie continued to watch the unceasing displays of sorrow and torment around her, she felt herself nearing the edge of madness. She closed her eyes tightly, squeezing them shut until the specks of white floating behind her eyelids blended into the familiar shape of her harp. In her mind, she could see it clearly, so she began to play, her fingers moving in the air, strumming invisible strings, while she mimicked the pitch of each chord with her voice. She became so lost in the illusion that it wasn't until she opened her eyes midway through the song that she noticed the attention of everyone around her. They had all paused to listen, even the frail woman mourning her phantom child, had silenced her cries. The old man too ceased at the act of collecting his soul, now stepping into the light and clutching his chest he listened he listen to the sound that gave him solace. Gem Marie, who was grateful for the peace that her imaginative harp had brought over the environment, moved her fingers with even more precision for her newfound audience. She played until all had fallen asleep and all she felt was the rocking and the swaying of the ship. In the early hours of the morning Gem Marie was awoken by Claudette, who shook her and handed her a large bonnet. She told Gem Marie, "You could pass for me we both will wear these and remember to keep your head down." Gem Marie asked her "Why?" Claudette said, "Because ,we are in Baltimore, and we are going to run. Christian Pierre is in Louisiana, and we are not going there." Before Gem Marie could ask why again the same man that had thrown her into the corner had returned. He now had a stick that he walked around with, poking various people that either looked weak or dead. If they moved or made a sound, he left them alone and walked over to the next person. If they did not move, he wrote something down then called for two other men who then moved the bodies and placed them in a corner away from the living. Gem Marie grew frightened because there was a man that had been lifted to be taken away but minutes later, he started coughing and was quickly dropped. Gem Marie and Claudette sat in a corner with their heads down making sure to cough to inform the stick carrying man that they were alive. When the boat had finally docked, and it was no longer rocking from side to side as it had before, this was a signal for Claudette to take Gem Marie's hand and lead her to the stairs. Silently, they crept up the steps, unnoticed, as everyone's attention was on moving the dead that was wrapped in cloth. Once they reached the halfway point, the two broke into a run, racing to the top deck. Claudette whispered for Gem Marie to keep her head down and move quickly, blending into the throng of paying passenger people disembarking. For a moment, Gem Marie glanced up and spotted the couple with the young

Francine she had been assigned to watch over. Then out of nowhere, a man stepped directly in front of Claudette, blocking her path and demanding to know where she was going. Before Claudette could respond, Gem Marie released her hand and dashed toward the couple with the young girl. Switching to French, she quickly explained to the woman that she and her sister were being detained because the authorities doubted their relation, as they hadn't been seen together. Gem Marie pleaded with the woman and her husband to tell the man she was with them and had broken no rules and she had been with them while caring for little Francine. The couple approached the man with Gem Marie, positioning themselves strategically between Claudette and the man gripping her arm. The man startled by their bold appearance, let go of Claudette's arm as Monsieur Chardon stepped forward and began to speak about Gem Marie. Visibly perplexed, the overseer glanced between the Chardons, evidently unsure why the couple had intervened. When he instructed them to slow down, and informed them that he couldn't make sense of their thick French accents as they spoke over one another. Monsieur Chardon's patience evaporated instantly he launched into a flurry of rapid French, his voice rising. Gem Marie seized this moment, with a gleam of satisfaction flashing across her face. She quickly grabbed Claudette's hand, and together they bolted for the ship's exit, their footsteps echoing in the narrow passageway as they disappeared. The pair slipped skillfully past the line of people anxiously waiting to have their papers verified, weaving between distracted guards and tense travelers. Their sprint didn't slow until they felt the firm solid ground underfoot. Up ahead, a small patch of grass and thick, towering bushes offered cover. Without hesitation the two continued never looking back, they darted into the greenery, crouching low and disappearing into the shadows of the leaves. They stayed there, breaths held, as they scanned the area, while uncertainty gnawed at them. The two in a simultaneous mental quandary, "Where can we go next? Suddenly, a rhythmic, thunderous beat broke the silence, pounding drums the sound was close and insistent, pulsing from somewhere behind them, now drawing them in like a whispered command. Trading a wary glance, the two began to rise slowly from their leafy shelter, curiosity overpowering caution. In clear view, Gem Marie watched an unexpected scene unfolding a bustling crowd herding hundreds of pigs down the main street, all seeming to celebrate the swine in a lively, boisterous spectacle. Gem Marie had never seen anything like it, venturing further, she spotted a horse-drawn wagon loaded with vibrant fruits and vegetables off to the side. A basket in front brimming with shiny red apples made her mouth water. Just as she reached out to take one, a slender young man appeared out of nowhere, grabbing her hand to stop her. He released her quickly, glancing around as though wary of being seen. "Are they not for everyone? Are they free?" Gem Marie asked, her curiosity piqued. The man's expression shifted to irritation as he pulled her aside, into the shadow of a large tree. "There ain't nothing free for a nigger," he muttered, his voice laced with bitterness. Gem Marie froze, startled by his words, what is its meaning she thought. She'd heard that word before usually tinged with contempt. It had been spoken by others, even on the ship, yet when Monsieur Heritage overheard it he was, visibly displeased. "Such a word has no place among civilized company," he'd mutter that day in the barn. Now, hearing it again, sharp and unfiltered, she felt a knot of confusion rise within her. She studied the young man before her, questions forming in her mind. *"What language birthed this word, this weapon that angers monsieur? Why does it seem to slice through the air with such force, cutting as deep as any blade?"* Claudette finally caught up with Gem Marie and immediately noticed the look of distress on her friend's face. Turning to the slender man beside them, she asked him sharply, "What did you say to her?" The young man shrugged and retorted, "Nothing much, she was about to grab an apple off that white man's wagon. All I said was, 'There ain't nothing free for a nigger." Claudette, stunned, took hold of Gem Marie and shook her gently. "You stealing girl? Answer me now because I can't be running with you if you gon be stealing all the time." Gem Marie, now looking utterly baffled, asked, "What is a 'nigger?" Claudette, who tried to stifle her laughter, assumed the question was some attempt to try and make light of her stealing habits. She laughed along with the young man who shook his head. But as Claudette looked closer at Gem Marie's face, and her humor faded. The laughter stopped abruptly. "Wait," she said, a trace of suspicion creeping into her voice. "Your serious, you really don't know what that means. Where did you *really* come from?" "The castle. I'm from the Scotney Castle," Gem Marie replied. She continued explaining that she'd never once left the grounds and had never been allowed to ride into town with Monsieur Heritage. She told them she had ever seen or spoke to any outside people except for servants and delivery men. Claudette stopped her abruptly, "That can't be right. That cripple back in England said he'd never laid eyes on

81

you before remember?" "Lies! He lies," Gem Marie insisted, a defiant glint in her eyes. "Monsieur Heritage, my father, gave him that limp, he struck him with his walking stick, after he used that same word nigger. But he never told me why it made him so angry. " Gem Marie glanced at the slender young man, "That word is forbidden at the Scotney, I heard Monsieur tell the cripple that no one uses it in his presence." The slender young man, now visibly rattled, narrowed his eyes. "Did you two just come off that ship?" he muttered to Claudette. "Yes," she answered, glancing around warily. "We were headed for a Louisiana plantation, but we ran." The man leaned in close, dropping his voice to a hush. "You two need to stay clear of this area, the Slaytter brothers got a mean bunch that's good at sniffing out folks like you two. They don't take kindly to runaways. You got a good chance on getting away seein it's a busy day today. Well it's been nice talking to you two. I'll be on my way." He gave her a quick, meaningful look. "And remember, "don't touch nothing and we all gon be free soon." Gem Marie tilted her head, her confusion deepening. "What do you mean?" she asked stopping the slender man in his tracks. "I thought everyone outside the castle walls were already free. I thought they were the true free ones." Gem Marie Studied the slim man's face, she had never met a male close to her age before. He was much taller than her that he had to bend down slightly just to asked her what was her name. He looked at her again now studying her closely and asked, "How old are you gal?" Quickly Gem Marie spat, "I will be fifteen and my name is Gem Marie Heritage." The slender young man looked at Gem Marie with a glint of pride. "Well my name is Otis Washington Baltimore named after thee Lord Baltimore himself." Gem Marie arched an eyebrow, unconvinced. "Lord Baltimore?" she asked, with a touch of doubt. "Do you really have a lord or knight in the family? "Her mind drifted to her own brother, Baby Philip, named after Monsieur Heritage his father and hers. She bore the Heritage name too, an inheritance carrying more mystery than pride. Meanwhile, Claudette stepped forward, her voice steady. "I'm Claudette Harrington. I'm seventeen." Otis acknowledged her introduction with a quick nod, then asked, "So, do you two have any family or friends here in Maryland because you gonna need a place stay to figure out where you're going. Two women outch here can be rough and you two bout as green as grass." They shook their heads, and watched his demeanor change, "Then follow me," Otis said, suddenly serious. "Don't talk or touch anyone or anything. Do exactly as I do." Otis turned and set off, his pace quick and determined. Gem Marie and Claudette fell in line, following Otis through winding streets until the landscape changed. Soon, they were moving past open-air pens, where pigs wandered freely, and into a crowded, mixed neighborhood where faces of all shades intermingled. It was the home of the railroad workers the men who spent the majority of their days building the railroads. Some people where covered in grease, dirt and black oil it was hard to tell who was really white and who wasn't. The children were diverse and fast moving they often popped out of cubby holes from the streets, then disappeared into nearby shacks. A woman ran out of a shop with a wooden spoon and grabbed a random man that she forced to taste something, when the man swallowed and then smiled the woman quickly ran back into the shop. Claudette taking in the whole atmosphere leaned in toward Otis, glancing around with wide eyes and whispered, "What kind of place is this?" Otis looked back, his voice low. "They call it B&O, Pig town. it's the one place the pigs get to run wild... right up to the slaughterhouse. Come on, watch your step now!" Before they could react, Otis darted across a large street, heading toward a worn building that looked like a barn house. He stood at a side door, waving them over. Gem Marie and Claudette followed, stepping into the dimly lit interior, where every shadow seemed to hold a story waiting to be told. There were several large doors that sat in a foyer area once they entered the dark building that only had one large window that sat high above the main entrance door. Otis walked through one of the doors for a moment then came back and walked Gem Marie and Claudette through the large door into a room that had a wood burning stove and a small table in a corner. There was a small sitting room with a cot in it and one bedroom that was filled with four beds and children. Gem Marie stood in the middle of the room glancing around the small, crowded space, astonished that it could hold so many people. She couldn't help but compare it to her bedroom, which was bigger than this entire house. "How could they live like this? "she thought, puzzled, "Didn't they have a father who took care of things?" Otis continued weaving through the tiny home until they reached a door that led to the backyard area, where tree stumps were lined up like makeshift chairs. With a casual air, Otis climbed onto one of the stumps, plucked two apples from a low branch, and rubbed them clean on his shirt. Then, he pulled out a small knife, slicing the apples into neat pieces before handing them to Gem Marie and Claudette. A woman from a top window yelled into the backyard, "Otis Baltimore! don't you pick on that tree you get em off the ground!" then she disappeared from the window. Gem Marie removed the bag that had been attached to her petite coat and dug into it, pulling out a small bottle with a hint of wine still sloshing at the bottom. Handing it to Otis, she watched as he uncorked it, sniffed the aroma, and raised a brow. "Did you steal this?" he asked with a half-smile, his tone half-joking, half-curious. She lifted her chin with pride. "That wine belongs to my father. It came from his vineyard. As for the bottle," she added with a smirk, "that belongs to me." Otis, intrigued by her refined accent and boldness, asked, "So, what's your father's name?" "Monsieur Philip Héritage," she replied, a hint of pride in her voice. "He taught me languages, gave me the best schooling. I can speak English, French, Italian, and German." Otis stared, shocked. He glanced around nervously and lowered his voice. "Listen here, what's your name? Gem Marie. Don't you *ever* let white folks hear you say that. You hear me? And don't go around telling people you can read or write, unless you looking to swing from one of these apple trees." Gem Marie blinked, confused. "White folks?" She tilted her head, genuinely puzzled. "Are they French, German, or Italian? And why should I hide my schooling from them? What family crest does this *white folk* clan bear? Are they some sort of army in America?" Otis stepped back, stunned. *How could she not know?* he wondered, staring at her like she was a rare bird. He suddenly noticed the faint bruise near her mouth and gestured toward it. "That mark on your face," he asked, his tone softening, "how'd that happen?" Gem Marie raised a hand right above her lip as if just now remembering the bruise. She'd almost forgotten about the rocks thrown at her from under the wagon, her skin accustomed by now to the throb that came and went like an uninvited guest. Once she had been captured, she had forgotten all about it but since he had reminded her it seemed like the pain came back. "A rock flew from a wagon I was on and struck me hard." Otis examined it closely then told her, "Just don't tell anyone not a soul that you can read or speak other languages. Some white folks will kill you for that. Don't you know that's the white man's law. You must have learned about it some. Did you ever go outside of that castle?" Gem Marie paused now having to confess that she was never allow pass the castle's mote told Otis, "No, I have never been off castle grounds and that's one of the reasons why I ran away. I wanted to be free to see the outside world and to find Christian Pierre. Then she pulled out the small newspaper article and showed both Claudette and Otis. The two looked at the article, not being able to read, they stared at the picture of the refined looking man and took Gem Marie's word for it. Gem Marie spoke with a newfound resolve, explaining why she finally understood Monsieur Heritage's stern warnings and his insistence that she remain within the castle grounds. "The world beyond the castle walls," she told them, "is vast and yet so very small. It is rich and poor, ugly and beautiful, but above all it is frightening." Her recent experiences had unveiled the harshness of poverty in ways she had never imagined. Growing up, Gem Marie had often overheard her Aunt Elenor speak of the poor with a tone that suggested they were almost otherworldly people best kept at a distance. Aunt Elenor's voice would turn steely, recounting how they were always hungry, cold, or inclined toward wrongdoing, as if being impoverished somehow stripped people of their goodness. Gem Marie now saw things differently, and it unsettled her. Poverty, she realized, was not just a lack of comfort; it was a weight, a trap, and, at times, a punishment. She felt Monsieur Heritage had tried to shield her from this truth, but perhaps he had only delayed the inevitable. Claudette, a mixture of disbelief and outrage etched across her face, leaned in close to Otis, her voice lowered to a tense whisper. "You mean to tell me that Gem Marie ain't ever set foot off the Scotney?" she asked, her gaze darting over to where the young woman crouched nearby, idly scratching in the dirt with a stick. "It ain't natural, Otis," Claudette continued, shaking her head. "Locked up her whole life in that big ole' castle, surrounded by servants, with no real notion of what she is or what she ain't. That girl doesn't even know she's a negro, nor does she think she's white. Far as she's concerned, her name's the only thing she's got. Have you noticed? She hasn't mentioned her mama even once. Whatever she's mixed with, it's got her tangled up for sure." Otis sat quietly on a stump, absorbing Claudette's words, while his eyes lingered on Gem Marie, who was now tracing something in the dirt with a long, slender stick. Claudette's reasoning struck him as sound, yet Gem Marie's story felt genuine in its own strange way. His gut told him she was being honest, her innocence was too raw, too unguarded to be anything else but real. Feeling the weight of unanswered questions, he walked over and stood over her where she knelt. Casting a shadow over her small, hunched figure he asked, "What're you doing there, gal?" he asked, his tone curious but cautious. Gem Marie looked up, her face breaking into a soft, almost shy smile. "Just writing my name," she replied, her fingers dancing as they moved the stick through the dirt with practiced ease. Otis glanced down at the shapes she was drawing and felt his stomach lurch with sudden dread. Those markings weren't just any scratches. They were letters, like the ones he'd seen on the front page of a newspaper once. "Didn't I tell you!" he burst out, panic coloring his voice. "Ain't no reading or writing, Do you hear me! Didn't I tell you that! You'll get us all in a world of trouble if anybody finds out." Without another thought, he snatched the stick from her hand and snapped it clean in half over his knee, the pieces falling in the dust between them. Gem Marie's eyes widened, the shock mingling with a flicker of hurt, and Otis's heart wavered, caught between fear for their safety and the stirring sense that this girl was something more than what either of them had imagined. In the dim glow of evening, Gem Marie sat silently, struggling to stifle the fear building within her. She had grown up untouched by the truths of the world outside of the castle, raised with a fierce love from her father whose attempts to protect her perhaps left her unprepared for life. The words escaped her almost desperately, a stubborn reflection of what she believed to be true, "There are no slaves at the Scotney, only servants. There is no black or white, just me, Monsieur Heritage, the servants, the workmen, and sometimes Aunt Eleanor when she visits. Otis your world is foolish and makes no sense. Look at me, I am Gem Marie made without your world's rules. I am beautiful and smart as my father professed to me many times. What need I fear." Otis, now reflecting on himself as a boy not much older than Gem Marie, shook his head, bewildered. "Then why did you run off, Gem Marie?" Otis questioned with irritation, "Why didn't you ask your father Monsieur Heritage to take you with him one day instead of running away? Why didn't you just go with him?" Claudette cut in sharply, her eyes narrowing. "Can't you see? Monsieur Heritage is white he can't walk her around with him. Look at her skin sure she's light, but her mother might have been from somewhere else. To white folks she looks mulatto, but we know she got something else in her. That child was kept away for a reason. But one thing I know for sure is that man is looking for her." Gem Marie listening to them speak as if she weren't there shot back, her voice wavering but fierce, "My mother may have been what! Answer me! All my life, nobody would speak of her." Gem Marie now moving closer to Claudette demanded, "Tell me what you know! I am no chicken; I did not hatch!" Otis exchanged a worried look with Claudette, uncertain whether to reveal what they all sensed. Gem Marie had grown up without understanding how babies were born or the sharp lines drawn between black and white, lines so deep they tore lives apart.

She knew colors as something found on a canvas, people as faces, voices, and the languages they spoke. But the world was not so simple. Claudette took Gem Marie's hand, her voice softening. "Your father wanted to protect you, child, but he may have done more harm than he knew by hiding these things from you. Out here, people see your skin color first." Claudette now holding and pointing to Gem Marie's arm, "Everything is separated by color and money. Black is poor, but white can be rich or poor. And even the poor whites they can be mistreated too." Otis nodded, finally adding, "That's right. You see the white children playing out here with us? They're poor, same as us, some worse off. And that's why they can play with blacks. But there are mean whites, that will just as soon kill them for playing with blacks. There are kind ones and mean ones. You keep away from the mean ones. But always remember this, rich or poor mean or nice niggers always come last." Gem Marie, who had lived her whole life free from thoughts of color or division, felt a chill settle over her entire body, the confusion within the separation she could barely understand, much less articulate. The world as she had known it was breaking away, and what lay beneath unsettled her more than she'd ever dreamed. Gem Marie felt a surge of emotions flooding her mind, wondering how Monsieur Heritage could possess such knowledge yet withhold it from her. Wasn't there a book or a lesson she could have studied, a truth to be whispered to her through dusty pages? In a world, where Black hands were barred from books and their tongues clipped from asking too many questions, people like her were relegated to cramped quarters that looked more like barns. Breakfast was scavenged from the ground apples that had fallen too soon, and walnuts not quite ripened. Dinner was an exercise in survival, pieced together from several scraps. As these realizations sank in, Gem Marie grew certain: she had to find her way back to the Scotney. The promises of freedom and adventure in lands beyond the castle walls were illusions painted on fragile glass. Books and newspapers had sold her fantasies of dashing businessmen in fine suits and women gliding through debutante balls. But Monsieur Heritage, with his careful fingers, had scissored away the uglier truths from those pages, leaving only visions of allure reserved for white folks. The world outside was not one of beauty or liberation. It was a jagged, dark place where rage lashed at the defenseless, where women cradled their rancid grief like ghostly infants and old men starved as they clung to life, willing their souls to stay within their vessels for one more night. And in this bitter market of humanity, people were sold off when the moment was ripe, fetching whatever price could be wrung from the highest bidder. Gem Marie's heart pulled her back towards England, but the road home lay beyond her reach. Her nautical lessons were but fragments, and a boat was as distant to her as the stars. She sat trembling in a crowded, unfamiliar yard, the hard reality sinking in a creeping chill that made her teeth rattle like the frigid nights of winter. The grim possibility that she might never see her home again wrapped around her like an iron chain, each link forged from the ache of knowing, and not knowing, the way forward. She thought about her harp and how it always brought her comfort. Desperately, she turned to Otis and asked, "Where do the children go for music? Where do they learn to play the harp or violin?" Otis, now even more shocked, turned to Claudette and shook his head, and laughed. "I don't know, I suppose something as fancy as a harp or a violin might be found at the Canterberry, but that's for white folks' children only." The Canterberry?" Gem Marie's eyes sparkled with curiosity as she spoke, her voice barely a whisper. "I want to go there soon." Otis, his curiosity piqued but cautious, replied, "It's not as simple as walking in. The Canterberry's no place for wandering people; you need a reason to be there. You have to know someone in there." He paused, then gave her a speculative glance. "You say you can play instruments and speak in different tongues." Otis's gaze shifted to Gem Marie, sizing her up, though a glint of doubt lingered in his eyes. Without another word, he strolled over to a huddle of children at play, pretending to be horses. Dressed in potato sacks, they kicked up their heels in the dirt, dust swirling around them. One particularly tall boy, his face smudged with grime, tore pants flapping at his ankles, pulled a half-eaten licorice stick from his pocket and began chewing it thoughtfully. "Fetch the old fiddle," Otis commanded, eyeing the boy. Without hesitation, the lanky lad darted to the corner of the yard, clambering onto an old stump before stretching to reach the eaves of the house. He grasped a bundle wrapped in a stained cloth and handed it reverently to Otis, who returned to Gem Marie, trailed by the curious crowd of children. They formed a tight circle around her, whispering and jostling as Otis unwrapped the fiddle with a slow, almost ceremonious care. Revealed in the fading light was a tattered instrument, its bow frayed, and its wood cracked with age. Gem Marie, who had only ever laid hands on a pristine Stradivarius, stared at the worn fiddle as though it were a relic from a time lost to legend. The tall boy smirked, amusement lighting up his dirt-streaked face.

"Bet you a stick of licorice she can't play it," he taunted, his voice brimming with skepticism. Otis glanced at Gem Marie, his own doubt growing as he saw her eyes widen, searching the fiddle's battered form. Claudette stepped forward protectively, meeting each child's gaze in defiance. "She's my friend, and she ain't no storyteller!" she declared, before leaning close to Gem Marie's ear and whispering, "Listen here, don't you worry bout them none. You go on and play, like your daddy taught you." Gem Marie raised the fiddle to her chin, its rough wood biting into her skin, a splinter pricking her cheek. She let out a small gasp, drawing laughter from the children that rose in cruel, mocking waves. Claudette, eyes blazing, shot back, "I'll bet two sticks of licorice she can play!" The tall boy's eyes gleamed, a challenge glinting in his stare. "Deal," he quickly replied. Claudette with a smile and a nod of her head locked eyes with Gem Marie. Glancing around, her heart pounding as the children's laughter faded into a watchful silence, Gem Marie now holding back her tears, tightened her grip on the bow and prepared to play. knowing that this moment held more weight than any she'd faced before, with trembling hands Gem Marie lifted the fiddle once more. Her gaze now quickly darting through a gap in the circle of children, leading to the old apple tree. Her focus settled on a single apple, blushing red and green, large enough to see a small hole where a worm had burrowed in. She waited, transfixed, almost daring the worm to reappear. As her hand moved instinctively, she drew the bow across the fiddle's frail strings. Despite the missing string and the wood's splintered age, the instrument released a haunting melody, raw and otherworldly. A hush instantly fell over the yard, the laughter stilled, the breeze quieted, even the birds in the trees paused mid-chirp. Otis stared, transfixed, as the melancholy strains poured from the instrument. Pride mingled with unease as he glanced around at the other children, their wide-eyed faces locked in rapt attention, their laughter forgotten, their breathing hushed, as if time itself had paused to listen. Then, a prickle of fear rose in Otis's chest as he noticed a shadow in the doorway. There stood a man a figure unfamiliar, cloaked in darkness, his eyes fixed on Gem Marie with an intensity that sent chills down Otis's spine. Breaking free from the musical spell, Otis rushed to Gem Marie, his voice low and urgent. "That's enough of that," he murmured, gently but firmly lowering the fiddle. The crowd of eyes blinked and shifted, as though waking from a dream. Claudette seized the moment, striding up to the tall boy with a victorious grin. "I believe you owe me two licorice sticks," she announced. "Pay up." As the children murmured, Otis stole one last glance at the shadow in the doorway, that now had disappeared. From that day forward, Gem Marie would play her fiddle in secret, offering melodies to the children as a special treat whenever the adults were out of earshot. Word spread quickly among them: her music, it was said, could mend a scraped knee or soothe a frightened child, lifting their spirits like solace. Soon, her melodies became a cherished remedy, and whenever one of them was ill or troubled, a small voice would pipe up, calling for "Gem Marie's healing tune." Otis, however, grew uneasy as he noticed the lengths to which the children would go to reach the fiddle, stacking tree stumps or bits of wood to reclaim the instrument from its hiding place. He became vigilant, watchful of the doors and windows whenever Gem Marie played, his gaze lingering on the adults who passed nearby. Finally, he pulled her aside, his expression grave. "Don't play if any grown-ups are around," he warned in a low voice. Gem Marie, perplexed, looked up at him. "But why?" she asked, her innocent curiosity piercing through his fear. He hesitated, choosing his words carefully. "You're in a place where people don't take kindly to those who are... different. They like to understand what makes a person different, and sometimes," he added, lowering his voice even more, "That means you have to take a trip to the good doctor, and you don't want that." The warning hung heavy in the air, and to make sure she understood, Otis leaned closer, eyes intent. "It's against the law," Gem Marie, whispered, Otis confirmed with a slow nod. From that day on, she played only in hidden corners and quiet moments, her music a secret gift, sheltered from prying eyes and from whatever fate lay beyond them.

Chapter: 8

The Search

It had been two months since Gem Marie came up missing and Monsieur Heritage' now filled with rage and bitterness was the person everyone avoided. His only moments of peace were watching and interacting with little Philip. The day that Gem Marie went missing he rode out feverishly in his horse alone with a bag of money in search of her. He looked high and low on the land and across the wooded area for her and even into the blacken night, but he could find nothing. Finally, after one day of searching and giving one of the town's low-level workers a silver coin. Monsieur Heritage' was informed by the man that although, did not actually see Gem Marie, he knew for certain that there were runaways and some women being stolen in order to be sold to wealthy social lights in America that preferred refine servants and field workers. The demand was not that high because the price for them were dear and any damage to the cargo could result in death. After informing Monsieur Heritage' that Gem Marie could be anywhere in America and that locating her would be exceedingly difficult and useless especially if she could not read. Once informed of the possibility that she could be alive and maybe clever enough to find her way back home, he suddenly boosted his confidence. The small glimmer of hope gave him comfort because he himself had provided Gem Marie with the finest education and had taught her how to read from age four. Monsieur Heritage' instantly believed that Gem Marie had to be alive somewhere, the unique, talented, and energetic child would have to be smart enough to find a way to defend her life. Although he also knew that along her travels she could be even killed if the wrong people found out she could read and write and was highly educated. Now evaluating the circumstance from the outside world's angle, he began to torment himself about keeping her totally secluded from the reality of the vicious world's circumstances may have caused her to flee from the Scotney. He raised her in an environment that had no boundaries, only the castle walls that he used to shield her from all the ugly torments of the outside world. He raised her with so much freedom that she believed that she could fall in love with any man no matter who he was or where he was from. Monsieur Heritage' was now face to face with his delusional methods of raising the little girl that was left in his arms without warning. The same child that for years hung on to his legs as he sat and wrote. Although beautiful, smart, and innocent, for the outside world these qualities would not be enough to spare her life. The outside world would not see her true inner beauty they would see her as an underserving outsider that had been trained and dressed up like a primate. They would determine if she needed to be broken or killed. These were the kinds of thoughts that were now haunting him since he had been told about people being stolen and shipped to America. Early one morning while the castle stood silent in its slumber, Monsieur Heritage' had gone into the large parlour and sat at Gem Marie's harp, he strummed one note and listened as the note lingered in the air. He then turned his attention to the custom-made harp he had made when she was four years old. The small harp perfectly sized for her petit frame was beautiful and crafted from mahogany and rosewood. He sat down and imagined that Gem Marie was playing beautifully all the while wearing a white and pink satin dress he had purchased in Paris. His mine shifted to the last time he heard her playing; he could now hear the melancholy in the song that she had last practiced before she went missing. The sound now vibrating in his ears traveled to his brain then to his heart that traveled back to his head which brought a tear to his eyes. He stared at the harp and saw Gem Marie's little four-year-old hands playing, moving so quickly and gracefully. It was like she was right there in front of him and once she finished playing, she grabbed his hands and put them together in a clapping motion. Overwhelmed by the haunting memory and the harp's piercing echo in his mind, Monsieur Heritage let out a strangled cry. He turned abruptly and made his way to her bedroom, his steps heavy with purpose. Entering the darkened room, he was struck by its musty stillness, a faint, stale scent lingering in the air. He moved to the window, pulling the drapes back and opening it wide, allowing a fresh breeze to sweep in and breathe life into the stagnant space. His gaze drifted over her room filled with rows of dolls lined on shelves. Delicate statues poised in corners, haunting dresses hanging like ghosts in the dim light. On the dresser, a collection of tiny trinkets and bottles of fragrance water gleamed faintly. He picked up a bottle, curious, as he uncorked it, the stopper slipped from his fingers, tumbling under the dresser. Cursing softly, Monsieur Heritage knelt down and reached beneath, feeling his way along the floor. As he lay flat, peering beneath the dresser, his hand brushed against something unexpected: a small, hidden compartment between the floorboards. His pulse quickened as he pried it open, revealing a tiny jewelry box nestled inside. Inside, he found an assortment of carefully folded papers and a few personal mementos. Unfolding the slips of paper, he discovered written prayers, each word painstakingly inked, along with a worn article about a man named Christian Pierre. He read the article twice, then returned to the prayers. One was different Gem Marie had written a plea, asking to be shown the way to find him. The discovery sent a chill down his spine. Heart racing, he hastily gathered the papers and left the room, heading to his study. There, he snatched up a stack of documents and a few essential books, his movements hurried and precise. Calling out for the servants, he ordered his horse to be saddled, his eyes shadowed with newfound determination and the hint of a revelation that left no room for delay. Before departing he stepped into Greta's room, with a stern face, he informed her that he was setting out once more to search for Gem Marie. His tone was clipped as he revealed the papers he'd uncovered in Gem Marie's chambers. Hinting she may have vanished in search of a man named Christian Pierre. With a fixed sharp gaze on Greta, he demanded, "Have you ever heard her speak of this name?" Greta hesitated, her hands wringing as she confessed, "No, sir, I have not heard of him. But on the day she disappeared, Gem Marie asked me questions about love." Greta paused, glancing up nervously. "She wanted to know how one knows they're in love, and she said I must know about it because she believed baby Philip was conceived from love." Monsieur Heritage's eyes narrowed, his surprise quickly twisting into fury. "And you chose to keep such thoughts from me?" His voice grew cold as he chastised her, warning of the consequences of hiding secrets under his roof. Greta shrank back, trembling under his glare. Without another word, he stormed from the room, gathering his things with barely restrained anger. Moments later, he mounted his stallion, spurring it into a gallop that echoed across the castle grounds. The wind stung his face as he raced toward town, his mind seething with a fierce resolve to find anyone who knew of Christian Pierre and whether he had left England. Monsieur Heritage's gaze was fixed on the path ahead, his determination to make a sharp blade slicing through the night as he pushed onward, undeterred, with questions that demanded answers. Upon arriving in town, Monsieur Heritage made his first stop at the local farrier to replace his horse's worn shoes. As the work began, he strolled down the streets, his gaze scanning the faces of the townspeople, assessing each expression for even a flicker of recognition. He wondered if any of them had seen Gem Marie and, more importantly, if they'd dare tell him the truth if they had. Near the old mill, where a group of men labored in the mid-morning sun, Monsieur Heritage approached quietly, standing just at the edge of their huddle, listening without announcing himself. After a moment, he reached into his coat pocket and drew out a small portrait of Gem Marie on her tenth birthday. Though years had passed, the portrait still held her likeness with a striking, unmistakable clarity. Taking a deep breath, he stepped forward, holding the portrait where they could see. The men, sensing his presence, fell silent and turned to greet him with respectful nods. Monsieur Heritage singled out an older man who seemed to command the group with his firm tone and steady gaze. "Have you seen this girl?" he asked, voice edged with tension. The elder looked at the portrait, and responded guarded. "No, sir, no lost children around here." But then he barked an order to the others: "If any of you have seen her, speak now." The men shook their heads, one after the other, muttering that they hadn't seen any young girl in recent memory. But as the painting passed before them, one man a grizzled figure with nervous eyes shifted uncomfortably and took a step back, his gaze darting to the ground. Monsieur Heritage's eyes narrowed, sensing a crack in the silence, and he turned his full attention to the man, prepared to press for the answers he'd traveled so far to find. Monsieur Heritage, keenly observing every expression and gesture, immediately caught the man's unease. He ordered the man to come forward and explain his sudden shift in demeanor. The man, now visibly unsettled and with a quivering voice, cast his eyes to the ground and began to speak in a near whisper. The group's leader sternly intervened, urging him to raise his voice and not waste Monsieur Heritage's time. Under pressure, the man stammered out that a lame cripple who had once worked at the Scotney claimed the girl wasn't local when asked by overseers to confirm her identity right before she was taken away. He insisted that the portrait matched the girl who was sent off on an American-bound ship. As the onlookers pressed him for more details, the man found himself encircled by a mob, their stern warnings echoing around him to ensure his account was truthful. It wasn't until he shouted, "It was the same child, taken only after the dressmaker's cripple denied knowing her!" that the crowd, now awash in murmurs, parted to let him step forward. Now, with more space and a bit more confidence, he revealed to Monsieur Heritage that several runaways had been rounded up and dispatched to various wealthy Americans. Monsieur Heritage felt a bitter sting of reality Gem Marie was no longer in England, likely bound for America, where she'd be bought and sold. He bit his lip hard enough to draw blood, the sharp pain grounding him, momentarily staving off the wave of grief swelling within. Determined to hide any hint of weakness from the other men, he redirected his anger, his gaze settling on the cripple, whom he now saw as the probable culprit in Gem Marie's disappearance. Fury surged within him as he imagined someone sneaking around, disguised as one of his own workers. The thought alone threatened to drive him to his breaking point. Consumed with emotion, he approached the older man and seized him by the throat, causing the man to stumble and lose his footing. Now, suspended by Monsieur Heritage's tightening grip, he kept his precarious balance with only the tips of his shoes scraping the ground. The older man's gaze locked on Monsieur Heritage's lips, which had taken on an unsettling, blood-red tint in the dim light. Each word Heritage spoke vibrated through the stillness of the night, his voice a deep, chilling baritone. "Who is this *cripple* you keep mentioning?" he growled slowly. "I have no cripple in my employ!" The man's voice failed him; his face turned ashen, unable to muster the words to explain. Desperately, he raised a trembling finger, pointing across the walkway, a silent plea for mercy mingling with the darkness. With his hands still trembling and shaking he pointed his index finger across to the small dressmaker's shop which looked to be empty. Now with his attention immersed in the small shop's window, Monsieur Heritage' released the fear inflicted man, who once his feet was reunited with the soil again, quickly ran and led the way across the path. Like a blood hound dog towards the dress shop, all the men immediately followed and rushed across the road to the front door. They flung open the unlocked door and were immediately greeted by a petite woman, the shop owner. The interior was dimly lit, adorned with a few dresses left behind by her grandmother and great aunt who had relocated years ago. Seated amidst the garments, a young woman meticulously beaded a gown, following the techniques passed down by her great aunt. The elderly man approached her, his tone kind, inquiring about her nephew's whereabouts. Startled by the sudden influx of men into her small dress shop, she reluctantly gestured towards the backdoor, revealing that he was outside, cutting wood. The group swiftly made their way past her and through the back door, where they found a young man seated on a stool, wielding a small axe to chop wood. Although he still possessed some movement in his legs, the injury he had endured had slowed him down, necessitating the use of crutches. As Monsieur Heritage pushed through the crowd to get a clearer view of the young man, he recognized him instantly. Memories instantly flooded back to the day Gem Marie had returned to the castle from the barn with tears in her eyes, upset by a delivery man who had spoken harshly to her, using a forbidden words on his land. "It is you!" Monsieur Heritage bellowed. Startled by the sound of his voice, the young man dropped the axe, hastily reaching for his crutches as he slowly rose to his feet. Now backing away, his retreat was halted by a small cutting table in the yard, upon which he leaned on for support. Monsieur, upon receiving confirmation of Gem Marie's capture, erupted into a violent rage. His mind raced with visions of the potential horrors Gem Marie might endure. Without hesitation, he lunged toward the young man, who was now sobbing uncontrollably. Gripping him tightly, Monsieur Heritage shook him and struck him, the force of his powerful blows caused the cutting table to shatter beneath them. As they crashed to the ground and with all his weight bearing down he relentlessly battered the young man's frail form against the cold earth. Amidst the chaos, his voice strained with anguish, he vowed vengeance, each word punctuated by the sickening thud of the young man's head striking the ground. "I will have your life this time with no question or interference!" The words echoed into the still night air that formed a chill on everyone's neck. The only sounds came from the movements of Monsieur Heritage's body and fist that pummeled the young man's face. As the young man's head repeatedly hit the dirt pieces of splinters and wood became lodge in his scalp and hair from the shattered table. There were occasional gasps from the crowd of men as the sounds of fractured bones popped and cracked in the still night air. One man unable withstand the scene that was unfolding, looked away in disgust, struggling to contain the urge to regurgitate. They all stood watching in horror, while pleading with Monsieur Heritage to cease his gruesome display of intense, channeled hatred. The unconscious young man moved like a lifeless rag doll, eliciting distress from the onlookers. In a futile attempt to halt the slow murder, one man grabbed Monsieur Heritage's arm and begged for him to release the lifeless body. However, Monsieur Heritage's powerful thrashing continued, sending the brave man tumbling into the crowd of petrified spectators as Monsieur drew back his fist once more. It was only the piercing, blood-curdling scream of the young seamstress that was able to break Monsieur Heritage's violent trance. Standing in the doorway, with horror widened eyes watching her nephew's lifeless body, being repeatedly struck, she rushed forward, only to be restrained by one of the men. At last, Monsieur Heritage snapped out of his fury, releasing his grip on the young man and collapsing beside him with a low, anguished moan. His voice, thick with despair, called out, "Gem Marie," like a child crying for its mother. The men around him stood frozen, stunned and silent, unable to process the nightmare unfolding before them. The seamstress knelt beside her battered nephew, his head resting in her lap as she wept over him, her sobs mingling with the heavy silence in the room. Tenderly, she stroked his hair, assuring him he would be alright. After meticulously removing splinters from his head for several minutes, she turned to one of the men nearby and requested water from the well nestled in the corner of the yard. Using scraps of cloth, she gently wiped his face and head clean before retrieving a thick black thread from a pocket in her sewing apron. With practiced ease, she extracted a needle from a scarf draped around her neck, effortlessly threading it. With the precision of an artist, she began to stitch the large gash on the side of her nephew's head, the once bloody wound now yielding to her careful ministrations. All eyes were fixed on her as she meticulously mended the injury to a neat stitch. Once she had wiped away any remaining blood from the young man's face, she carefully poured water down his throat and tenderly rubbed his forehead. With a harsh cough, followed by a deep breath, the young man stirred, eliciting sighs of relief from the onlookers. Moments before, they had feared the seamstress's efforts were in vain, believing the man beyond saving. The older man who had initially led the crowd looked heavenward, with clasp hands as he moved quickly to assist, he approached Monsieur Heritage and extended his hand. To which Monsieur grasped it firmly, and rose to his feet. Away from the crowd, Monsieur Heritage now stood alone with the older man, who wiped away the sweat, dirt, and blood from his face with a monogrammed handkerchief, his movements steady and precise. Monsieur asked the old man about the ships, inquiring how long they would be at sea and where they might make port. The old man replied that he wasn't certain but promised to find out and send word as soon as possible. With a grave expression, he warned Monsieur Heritage that if he wished to obtain information on Gem Marie, he would have to refer to her as "cargo" and "property." He added, "Should I return with documents using such language, please understand it is simply the terminology needed to complete the task." Monsieur Heritage looked taken aback by the old man's forthrightness. Just then, his eyes fell upon the young man he had struck moments before, and a wave of shame and regret began to rise within him. He turned back to the old man, who waited with a steady gaze, subtly revealing the harsh reality of the world they lived in. Slowly, Monsieur Heritage nodded, acknowledging the gentle warning in the old man's words. He swiftly handed the old man a few pieces of silver, instructing him to uncover everything he could about the ship *Gem Marie* and its last known location. The old man, eyes gleaming with assurance, promised to leave no stone unturned and vowed to send word to the Scotney once he gathered all possible information. Monsieur Heritage, now passing by the young seamstress who was cradling her battered nephew's head, felt a pang of remorse. Inconspicuously slipping several silver coins from his pocket, he knelt just enough to place them on her gown that was spread like a blanket over the cold ground. As he completed the gesture two coins slipped through his fingers, which caused a faint chime similar to a bell. The woman drawn to the sound shifted her gaze onto Monsieur. Her eyes traced over his sharp features while lingering on the quiet intensity of his expression. Her stare still intense drifted down to his attire, it was as if she were seeking answers within his ensemble. Her eyes rolled over the front of his embroidered blood-filled shirt and tailcoat. She followed the stitching in his trousers then marveled at the polished buttons and the intricate detailing that lined his clothing, and although fully soiled with blood and dirt they still held their social stratum. Now focused on his shoes and the brass buckles that adorn the toes, her eyes now caught a glance of the silver coins that he had laid on her dark velvet dress. Looking at the coins and then at her nephew's battered body, she let out a cry and turned away from Monsieur Heritage' in disgust. The coins reminded her that the man standing before her wearing some of the finest clothing and bearing the posture of a gentlemen had just behaved like an uncivilized barbarian. Monsieur Heritage' who had also watched the admiration leave the woman's face walked away towards the dress shop's back door. As he was leaving, he could hear one man stating that the cripple aided in his daughter being sold off. Monsieur slammed the shop's front door behind him as he exited then immediately mounted his stallion and rode off into the darkness. Under the pale glow of the moon, he guided his horse back to the Scotney, the memory of his brutal attack on the young cripple lingering like a dark shadow in his mind. Mixed with those memories was a haunting vision of Gem Marie, torn from his grasp, beaten and bound on some distant ship. Greta's warning echoed through his thoughts how she had urged him to stop shielding Gem Marie from the world's cruelty. Now, with exhaustion clinging to his bones, he yearned to return to Scotney soil. Each mile weighed heavier, his arms sore from the merciless blows he'd dealt to the frail young man, only the familiar earth beneath his feet could cure his guilt filled fatigue. With every stride, his mind drifted to his land the Scotney, a private haven where he could enforce his own rules, where order and obedience always reigned. Thoughts of Greta and baby Philip, his only anchors to sanity left, their fragile scaffolding keeping him from slipping into the abyss of his own rage and regret. As he rode, each step of his horse echoed the simmering turmoil within him, pulling him closer and away from the sanctity he craved and the self-inflicted torment he could not escape. And yet, even as his mind wrestled with the shadows of vengeance and regret, the memory of Greta's steadfast gaze tempered his fury, pulling him back from the edge a quiet reminder that, somehow, he must find his way home to her."

"Greta had not left her room since the moment Monsieur Heritage departed. She lay in bed with baby Philip beside her, her mind swirling with anxiety over what Monsieur Heritage might uncover in town while searching for Gem Marie. The thought of him crossing paths with the wrong person, leading to unforeseen dangers, filled her with dread. She cradled her sleeping son, watching his peaceful breathing, struck by how each gentle rise and fall of his chest mirrored his father's features. The candlelight flickered on the walls, casting dancing shadows that slowly faded as the candle burned lower. After a moment, a sense of calm washed over Greta. She rose from the bed and gently placed baby Philip into his beautifully hand-crafted bassinet, lined with silk, satin, and filled with down feathers, it was a luxurious cradle for her precious child. She laid him atop a crochet blanket, then covered him snugly with two more, ensuring he was warm and safe. The familiar scent of peppermint and lemon lingered through the room, rising from the pot of boiling water nestled in the fireplace. She moved toward it, mesmerized by the swirling leaves and lemon peels drifting in circles, their rhythmic motion oddly soothing. Wrapping thick cloths around the handle, she lifted the heavy pot with care, feeling its warmth seep through the fabric as she carried it to the waiting tub. With a steady hand, she poured the steaming contents into the bath, watching as clouds of fragrant steam billowed up from the oversized copper basin. Greta stood before her closed bedroom door, her eyes shimmering with unshed tears. Each passing moment without Monsieur Heritage felt like an eternity, her mind racing through the worst scenarios that might explain his delay. A whispered plea for forgiveness slipped from her lips as the thought of his potential absence cast a heavy shadow over her heart, filling her with profound sorrow. The mere idea of him never returning sent waves of overwhelming grief crashing through her very core. On this night, Greta grappled with an undeniable truth: she had fallen deeply and hopelessly in love with a man far beyond her station. A mere servant, a slave bound by circumstance, she carried his child in secret. A love that flourished only in stolen moments and whispered shadows, never to be openly acknowledged. Many nights, she dreamt of a future spent growing old at his side, only to awaken alone, lost in dreams woven from the threads of longing that could never emerge into reality. She understood she could never be Madame Heritage, yet the hope of his presence tonight held a significance that transcended words. If he returned to her, it would be the affirmation she longed for, the confirmation that they were kindred spirits, destined to defy the rigid boundaries imposed by society. In that singular act, a simple return, lay the promise of a love that dared to exist despite the constraints that sought to separate them. The two nurturing a love that would remain untouched by reality, living instead as cherished illusions on Scotney soil. As she stood before the imposing oak door, the full moon cast its cold gaze upon her, as if questioning her resolve to endure such a forbidden love. Greta trembled, yet did not turn back. Her silent pledge of devotion bound her, heart and soul, to Monsieur Heritage. She thought to herself, "He will come to me." Her feet now frozen to the floor, she continued to watch the brass doorknob until it began turning. The door creaked open at last, and Greta's heart raced as her wish appeared in the flesh. Monsieur Heritage stepped in, his face etched with exhaustion. He took two deliberate steps, halting mere inches before her, both of them rooted as if frozen in time. Greta searched his eyes, seeking the unspoken answer she so desperately needed. His gaze was intense, his breath uneven as he looked upon her. He had returned to the Scotney, drawn straight to her with neither thought nor hesitation, as if an invisible force had pulled him into this very moment. Their statuesque stillness shattered as baby Philip released a soft, shuddering sigh. Monsieur Heritage turned his weary gaze toward his son, and tears welled in his eyes, an expression caught somewhere between admiration and despair. Greta said nothing, but a sorrowful understanding passed between them. Gently, she took his rough, bloodstained hand and kissed his fingertips, tasting the bitter residue of earth and blood filth clinging to him as if a shadow from some dreadful encounter. Her eyes traveled over his shirt, its fabric marred with dark, rusty stains. She traced the splotches with a tentative finger, noticing how the color deepened in a grim circle over his heart. A chill coiled around her curiosity, yet she resisted the impulse to ask whose blood now marked him or what unholy events had turned his clothes into a dark canvas of suffering. Instead, with delicate resolve, she began to strip away his garments, piece by piece, unveiling the weary figure beneath. Only one relic remained a single ring on his right hand, a silent witness to whatever haunted his past and held him here in this moment, bound yet breaking. As Monsieur Heritage' stood there naked in silence, Greta took inventory of his body in a way she could have never done before. She watched every vein, freckle, and bruise that covered his body. She watched how the muscles protruded out of his chest and arms and then mentally etched it in her mind. This being the only time she had ever seen a naked man this close for this long without contact. She was fascinated by his total anatomy she told herself to cherish the moment now when she looked up into his eyes, she could see his vulnerable state. It was as if he allowed her to see him without anything to masked his true form. She took his hand as one might guide a child, and led him to the bath she had prepared with quiet care. Monsieur Heritage stepped into the warm water and the sharp scents of peppermint and lemon jolting him from his sullen daze. Stirred, he turned to Greta, his gaze lingering on the intricate specks of brown and green in her hazel eyes. Each fleck a mystery he hadn't thought to explore until now. The warm bath, which acted as a baptism was what his weary soul craved and needed. He let his arms rest on the tub's rim, while watching entranced as rivulets of reddish water slipped from his body and curled along the bath as a ghostly reminder of the battles left behind. Greta took the opportunity to tend to him, her hands moving with gentle precision. She knelt behind him, carefully wiping his shoulders down to his fingers before moving to his neck and chest, scrubbing away dried specks of blood and dirt with a practiced touch. When she squeezed the cloth, it released tiny pink circles in the water, faint but telling. Monsieur Heritage, who watched the ripple reddish pink circles fade in the water, opened his mouth as if to explain the reason for the blood, and was quickly intercepted by Greta. Sensing his hesitation, quietly silenced him with a deliberate soft, stroke along the back of his head. She moved to face, her expression unreadable but tender and with the same care she used to clean baby Philip, she wiped away any remnants of the night from his face and mouth. Her touch deliberate and soft, almost maternal, yet weighted with something more silent understanding shared in the flickering light. Greta captured one of the peppermint leaves in a warm cloth, then began to move it in a gentle, circular motion across Monsieur's chest. The minty scent mingled with the steam, and as the warmth seeped into his skin, he sank back deeper into the tub, sighing. "This bath smells delightful," he murmured with a satisfied smile. "You're just what every king needs." Greta, momentarily taken aback by his praise and the unexpected power it hinted at, hesitated before turning to the dresser. She picked up a small bottle of olive oil, letting a few drops slide onto her palms. She rubbed her hands together and then laid them on his shoulders, working the oil into his skin in slow, steady strokes. Her hands, slick and fragrant, moved more confidently over his neck and shoulders, a touch both invigorating and calming. Monsieur closed his eyes, the day's tensions melting as the warmth and scent of peppermint filled the room. Any thought of his recent dealings with the cripple faded, replaced by the languid tranquility that Greta's unexpected ritual stirred in him. He wondered, as her hands continued their rhythmic massage, if this was a ritual she reserved only for herself yet now, somehow, it felt like it had always been meant for him. The thought gripped him with an almost tangible force as he pictured her, bare and glistening with oil, droplets tracing their delicate paths down her skin to the cool stone floor. A quiet intensity stirred within him as he watched her rise slowly, an unreadable look shadowing her features. Greta felt an unexplainable pull, a quiet ache coursing through her as she crossed the room with measured steps. Reaching an old wardrobe, she opened it carefully and took out a man's sleeping gown, a relic left behind by a previous occupant of the room. She laid it upon the armchair deliberately, her movements calculated, aware of Monsieur Heritage's silent gaze lingering on her. Yet she did not turn to meet his eyes. With a composed swiftness, she climbed into the bed, pulling the heavy quilts and blankets tightly around her. She turned toward the window, letting her gaze settle on the bright, indifferent moon outside, willing its cold light to steady her thoughts. As Greta lay still, feigning sleep, she listened intently to the sounds of Monsieur Heritage moving in the bath. She caught each subtle splash and, with closed eyes, could almost see him mirroring her ritual—the delicate wringing of the cloth, the water cascading down over his face, tracing his lips and jaw. The thought stirred something deep within her, an aching throb she tried to ignore. Replaying her own sensual ritual in her mind, she imagined that he, too, would soon finish and quietly return to his quarters. Eyes shut tightly, she willed herself to sleep, though her heart betrayed her, pounding against the restraint she placed on her desire. She was afraid, almost unbearably so, to meet his gaze to see in his eyes a truth she wasn't sure she could bear. With the dim candlelight casting long shadows across the room, Greta lay motionless, her body tense beneath the covers as she willed herself to silence. She bit back the tears that threatened to betray her, fearing that even a single sound would shatter the fragile, invisible barrier between herself and Monsieur Héritage. She sensed him rise from the bed, felt the shift of the bed as he moved away from her, and the cool draft that swept in as he dressed. Monsieur Héritage stood by the bedside, watching her with a gaze that she dared not meet. *Was she disgusted by him too?* The thought lingered like a dark cloud as he noted the dried blood on his own hands and clothes, crusted remnants of a violence he hadn't spoken of, and she hadn't questioned. He wondered if she, like the others who witness his confrontation with the cripple, found his brutal ways abhorrent. Still, she lay facing away, the warm reflection of her skin of her back stark in the dimness, as though she turned away in silent judgment. Quietly, he collected his belongings, slipping each item into his blood-stained coat with a peculiar delicacy, as though his movements might disturb the tension hovering in the room. Before leaving, he stole one last glance at her lingering gaze upon her slender form as her body rose and fell in a slow, rhythmic breath. Greta's steady breathing deceived him; she remained entirely aware, listening, forcing each breath to be even and deep, each heartbeat steady. In the corner of the room, baby Philip's crib sat cloaked in shadows, and Monsieur Héritage crossed the floor softly, leaning over the boy. He pressed a brief kiss upon Philip's forehead, the faintest hint of tenderness hidden beneath the hardened edge of his gaze. Greta listened intently to this wordless interaction, every nerve taut as she heard him turn and finally exit the room, closing the door softly behind him. The silence that followed pressed in around her like a weight, and the ache she'd held so tightly within her burst forth, spilling over as tears dampened her pillow. Greta's heart ached with a hopeless question: *Was there love beneath his coldness? Could he care for her, as much as he seemed to care for their child?* The bitter truth twisted inside her, as sharp as any blade. Monsieur Heritage's affection, reserved for their son, was a distance she could neither cross nor conquer. She lay there, wracked with silent sobs, the hollow ache of unanswered love carving deep into her. The candle by her bedside flickered low, casting one last shuddering glow before succumbing to darkness, much like the fragile glimmer of hope fading within her heart. And as sleep finally claimed her, one thought lingered Monsieur Héritage had left her with nothing but questions, and an emptiness that would haunt her long into the night.

Chapter: 9

Do Not Speak

Otis rose with the sun one crisp morning, rousing Gem Marie from her slumber with urgency. He instructed her to tidy herself and prepare herself for the day, for he had plans to introduce her to someone who might aid in her quest to return home. With a tone of reassurance, he revealed his connection with a scientist nestled amidst the bustle of a well-known street called, "Medicine Row," Dr. Hertz who was well known by locals and the medical community occasionally engaged Otis in the task of retrieving lost or injured animals for mending. Otis emphasized the importance of Gem Marie keeping silent during their visit, insisting that he alone would handle all interactions and dialog. "Now when we get in there don't you say one word, you hear me. I got a plan, and it won't work if you start talking, do you understand. Where we are about to go, we got to go through some places that if they know you with me, it could be trouble." Gem Marie now looking at Otis inquisitively nodded her head and answered, "Yes I understand." Gem Marie, feeling the weight of her predicament, now found solace in Otis as her beacon of hope. As they readied to depart, Otis guided her to the rear of their rooming house, where a sizeable bush concealed a curious sight: a wheelbarrow draped in a pristine white cloth bearing the inscription "Laboratory Property." Sensing Gem Marie's curiosity, Otis elaborated on its origin, recounting proudly how it came into his possession after capturing particularly odorous creatures, earning him favor with Dr. Hertz. Dr. Hertz not only had bestowed the wheelbarrow but also provided a black coat emblazoned with "White Wing" in bold letters on the back of it. He also provided Otis with a written letter to carry at all times to fend off prying eyes and inquiries. With pride, Otis brandished the letter, imbuing it with a significance akin to a badge of honor, and shared its contents with Gem Marie. The note, bearing Dr. Hertz's credentials, bore a stern warning against anyone's interference, citing the sanctity of medical procedures and patient confidentiality. At its conclusion, a directive urged immediate contact with any queries, cementing Otis's authority in their undertaking. Otis now standing with his chest out spoke with confidence, "See that there paper has medical information on it written by Dr. Hertz himself that letter and this here wheelbarrow, is what has kept me from being taken by the Slaytter brothers plenty of times. Now when folks see me coming they move. I mean they really move out my way even white folks." Gem Marie nodded, absorbing the gravity of their mission as she quickly read the letter provided by Otis. Still wanting to keep him unaware of her true intelligence she pretended not to understand the letter as she handed it back to him as he continued talking. "People around here have grown accustomed to me wheeling dead animals back and forth. They don't bother me none cause they know what I got under my sheet ain't pretty." His presence became a sort of local fixture, an oddity embraced by the community. Otis earned the right to roam freely through an incident that became a cautionary tale among the locals. One day, a skeptical man challenged Otis, tearing off the covers of his wheelbarrow to reveal its grisly contents. Among the deceased was a trapped animal, its paw ensnared in the cruel jaws of the device. In a desperate bid for freedom, the creature had chewed at its own limb until half death, leaving a grotesque scene of maggots swarming around the decaying flesh and mouth. The sight was so harrowing that the man who uncovered it was haunted by the image for weeks, unable to shake off the horror. He rushed home to his wife, his mind plagued by the macabre tableau he had witnessed. Once Dr. Hertz had learned about the incident, he contacted the Slaytter brothers and officials and warned them of possible contamination if the contents of the wheel barrel were tampered with and the detriment if any of their personal items or cargo ever came in contact with the medical animals. From that moment on, the locals dubbed them, the Good Doctor and Otis the scientist, perhaps as a dark jest, and to avoided interfering with him or the enigmatic doctor again. As for Otis, he strolled alongside Gem Marie towards an area known as Medicine Row. The name was fitting, for it boasted an array of houses and buildings where all manner of medical professionals could be found. Some were legitimate doctors, while others were of a more dubious nature. It was a chance you took, especially if you were poor and didn't know anyone from there. Before heading there Otis stopped by a wooded area where he kept some animal traps, when he arrived there was an exceptionally large racoon caught in a square wired metal box. Otis had designed it so that once any animal climbed into the trap for food then tried to escape by sticking their head out first. The trap would lock around their neck leaving their body in the cage and their head sticking out. The racoon, tired but still squealing and fighting to get free, made an attempt to bite Otis, so he took some string out of his pocket and wrapped it around its mouth into a knot. He then added more string and wrapped it around until it's jaws were locked and secured in place. It wiggled it's legs and arms in the cage but grew tired and just laid there breathing heavily. Once placed in the wheelbarrow with the cloth over it became silent. Gem Marie looked at Otis and wondered if he was aware that he was just providing the animals so they could be experimented upon and cut apart. She had often read about it in the medical books Monsieur kept in his library that was how cures were found. She didn't have the heart to tell Otis that the animals weren't sick they were just used to test medicine as she had read in one of her schoolbooks about J. Hunter, an elite scientific doctor. He would collect samples of sores from people and animals and then infect a healthy animal to see the effects of the disease. Once they arrived at the back entrance of the building situated along Medicine Row, Otis discreetly passed the note to a guard who appeared to be new to his post. The guard, scanning the contents of the letter, inquired about Gem Marie's presence and her destination. Otis, assuming an air of feigned ignorance, explained to the guard that Gem Marie, afflicted with mutism from birth, was being brought in for examination by a doctor who claimed he could restore her ability to speak. The guard glanced at Gem Marie skeptically, then relented, opening the door to admit them. Navigating through the expansive building, Otis and Gem Marie traversed a lengthy corridor until they reached the farthest office. Upon entering, Otis proudly wheeled in the raccoon, informing Dr. Hertz that this specimen was particularly robust and had put up a good struggle. Dr. Hertz, with a smile playing at the corners of his lips, approached the cage where Otis had secured the raccoon's mouth. With a skillful hand, he dampened a small piece of cloth with a liquid from a nearby bottle and placed it over the raccoon's snout, inducing instant slumber. Swiftly, he whisked the creature behind a curtain and secured it in place. Returning to Otis's side, Dr. Hertz quizzically inquired about Gem Marie's identity. Otis, weaving a tale on the spot, portrayed her as a distant cousin who, although mute, possessed a captivating penchant for communicating through intricate hand movements akin to playing a melodic composition. Otis eagerly approached the doctor, his eyes gleaming with anticipation. "Doctor, I think she may know something by the way she moves her hands. Do you think your brother at the Canterberry could take a look at her?" Otis asked, nodding toward Gem Marie. "I have a feeling in my bones she might be able to play music, and I was thinking sir your brother could run some tests, like you do with the animals, to see if she can really play." Dr. Hertz shifted his gaze from Otis to Gem Marie, who was lost in watching the bustling activity outside the window. Assessing Gem Marie's distant expression, Dr. Hertz turned back to Otis. "I'm skeptical about her musical abilities," he remarked. "She does seems to have some hearing and speech impairments. She appears slow and mute." Gem Marie's attention snapped back to the conversation upon hearing herself being referred to as "Dumb." She strained to listen closely, realizing that Otis hadn't presented a compelling case for her. Recalling her promise to Otis to remain silent, she felt torn. However, the opportunity to return to the Scotney was too precious to let slip away. With silent resolve, Gem Marie glanced around and noticed a few loose sheets of paper scattered by the windowsill. She stepped over, delicately picking one up, and with nimble fingers, folded and rolled it into a makeshift flute. This small act stirred memories from her childhood, where every object held musical potential. She recalled her imaginary concerts, held with her beloved dolls as the rapt audience. One memory surfaced most vividly Monsieur Heritage, crafting a paper flute at her request. It was before he had insisted she dedicate herself solely to the violin. "You'll thank me one day, Gem Marie, for guiding you to the violin," he'd said sternly, sure of his direction. But even then, her heart longed for more than one melody, more than a single instrument. Growing weary of Monsieur's rigid tutelage, Gem Marie had once rebelled by picking up that paper flute, playing it with fervor, desperate to prove she was more than his model violinist. Now, standing in Dr. Hertz's office, her fate resting in Otis's unreadable hands, the memory came rushing back, and she felt a renewed defiance. It was as if, in this moment, she could no longer remain silent. Gem Marie lifted her hands and began to mime a violin solo, her fingers speeding through an imagined melody with practiced grace. Then, silently, she raised the paper flute to her lips, letting the memory take over. She closed her eyes and surrendered to the melody only she could hear, her mind conjuring Monsieur's face, stern but proud, watching her. She played as if he were before her, her spirit weaving through each note, yearning and full of pride. Lost in her music, her fingers trembling with emotion, she reached out as if to touch the vision, only to be pulled back by the sudden flutter of the paper flute slipping from her grasp.

She blinked, bending down to retrieve it, but as she straightened, her gaze met the piercing eyes of Dr. Hertz and the guarded expression of Otis. The room felt as though it held its breath, her private world shattered by their scrutiny. Dr. Hertz approached, his eyes narrowing with a calculating intensity, each step resonating with a heavy silence that filled the room. "Quite the performance," he murmured, his voice low, almost threatening. "But tell me, Miss Marie…does your heart lie in playing *for* us, or is it simply that you play for yourself?" Gem Marie's heart pounded as the meaning behind his words lingered in the air, heavy and laden with unspoken implications. Her future felt like it teetered on the edge, as fragile as the paper flute in her hands. And yet, with a glance toward Otis, she sensed he held a secret, something that bound him to her fate And in that lingering moment, with Dr. Hertz's cold eyes on her and Otis silently watching, Gem Marie understood and remained silent her fate, her future, was already being written just not by her hand. Dr. Hertz peered into her eyes, commanding her to comply as he inspected the inside of her mouth. When she hesitated, he took matters into his own hands, forcing her mouth open, examining her throat with clinical detachment. Satisfied, he turned her around, scrutinizing her hands, ensuring the count of ten fingers. "Well, we know you can hear, that's for certain," he remarked, his tone brusque yet oddly intrigued. Leaning in, he whispered, "I believe that was Mendelssohn's violin concerto. Where did you learn that?" Gem Marie remained silent while maintaining a blank look on her face, her only response was slipping the paper flute discreetly up her sleeve. She stood motionless, meeting Dr. Hertz's gaze as he peered at Otis for a moment. In his cheeks, she glimpsed a faint resemblance to Monsieur Heritage, igniting a pang of longing and sorrow to her heart, she continue to stare and study his face while longing for home. Dr Hertz, who had just taken notice of her large walnut brown eyes saw something within them, he quickly walked away and sat at his desk and began writing something. Otis, who was now able to make eye contact with Gem Marie without the doctor noticing, gave her a glare as if her humming and instrument playing was worse than speaking. Gem Marie, feeling frightened, considered making up a lie to explain how she knew the concerto, but she couldn't think of anything that would make sense especially since she was supposed to be mute. So she continued to stand silently, glancing out of the window now and then. When Dr. Hertz finally rose, he handed Otis a few coins and a letter to deliver to his brother at the Canterberry Conservatory.

Otis, noticing he'd been given two extra coins, grinned and thanked Dr. Hertz repeatedly. He quickly took hold of Gem Marie's hand, along with the wheelbarrow, and the two headed out the door. As they walked down the long hallway, both of their hearts raced with the anticipation of reaching the outdoors. Otis wanted to ask Gem Marie about the mysterious song and how she was able to make those sounds, while Gem Marie was eager to see the letter without revealing her ability to read. They held hands, trying to stay calm as they made their way through the building. Once they were outside, Otis told Gem Marie to get into the wheelbarrow and cover herself. She nodded and asked him to give her Dr. Hertz's new note for safekeeping, mentioning it might slip through the large holes in his pockets. Though hesitant, Otis handed it over, feeling that she had earned his trust after her song had won him extra coins. Gem Marie lay flat in the wheelbarrow, curling onto her side. She took out the small cloth bag she had carried since her journey began and used it as a cushion for her head from the occasional bumps in the road. Hidden under the sheet, she listened to the sounds around her, people talking, voices shouting, horses clattering by, plus the shuffling of feet. Finally when everything grew quiet, she whispered from under the cover, "Otis where are we it's so quiet? It's so quiet now." Otis quickly hushed her. "Hush! We're by the trees. Don't speak again you never know who might be nearby, and I don't know these folks around here." Gem Marie agreed, and as she lay still, she carefully opened the letter from Dr. Hertz. It read...

Dearest Martin,

I trust this letter finds you in good health and spirits. I have come across something most unusual and captivating, and I felt compelled to share it with you. This young girl, no older than eleven or twelve years, is a true enigma. She appears to be mute, as she has not uttered a single word that anyone can recall. However, her silence has not confined her artistic expression, for she possesses a musical gift that I can scarcely believe. She was brought along by the boy Otis that collects animals for me, while waiting she began to play the 64th concerto by Felix Mendelssohn. Remarkably, she did not use a violin; instead, she produced the most exquisite melodies with her mouth and a piece of paper. As madden as it sound it is true. This inexplicable talent has left me both awed and bewildered. I cannot fathom how a girl who has never spoken a word could master such a complex piece. It is for this reason that I implore you to consider her for a thorough examination. I believe her case is one that deserves your professional attention. Should you decide to take her under your wing, please conduct any necessary tests to uncover the source and extent of her extraordinary gift. I am genuinely curious to learn more about this prodigious child and the enigma she embodies. Kindly keep me informed of your findings and the results of any examinations you may conduct.

With warm regards and brotherly affection,

Dr. Robert Hertz

Gem Marie read the letter once more, wondering if this man, Professor Martin Hertz, could truly help her find her way back home, and how her knowledge of music might aid in the process. Otis continued to walk through the quiet streets until he came upon a large, solitary building surrounded by rose bushes and an array of other flowers. From beneath the covers, Gem Marie peeked out, watching as flashes of color crossed her path brilliant reds, yellows, and purples. The sight of the rich purples instantly reminded her of the English bluebells that once blanketed the grounds of the Scotney. She took a deep breath, hoping to catch even the faintest whiff of their fragrance. But all she could smell was the metallic tang of the wheelbarrow and the lingering scent of the animals Otis had transported. Otis, searching for a side entrance like the one at Dr. Hertz's building on Medicine Row, found only a front and a back entrance both marked by red doors, identical to Dr. Hertz's office door. Standing before one of them, Otis knocked and promptly ordered Gem Marie out of the wheelbarrow. When no one answered, he banged on the metal door again until it swung open, revealing a man who appeared both annoyed and anxious. "What do you want?" the man demanded in a brusque tone. Otis, speaking quickly and with a trace of nervousness, replied, "I'm here to see the Doctor of Music, Martin Hertz. His brother, Dr. Robert Hertz, sent me with this letter." He reached into his pocket but suddenly realized that Gem Marie had the letter. She was already holding it out in her hand, when anxious man snatched the letter and scanned it briefly, then scrutinized both Gem Marie and Otis before opening the door wider. Gesturing for them to enter quickly, without slowing, he began to walk ahead them speaking to them and passing students he complained, "I don't know how Professor Hertz will have time to see anyone," he muttered. "There's an important event coming up," Two students ran out of a classroom and straight into the anxious man. " You two get out of my way and master your pieces at once." The man continued down a long hallway, "And here I am, answering doors and scolding unruly children. After this performance concert, I'll be leaving to start my own school with my own set of rules." The man continued to grumble about the school's busyness as they navigated the hallway until they reached a staircase. He climbed it, leading them to a single door positioned at the end of the floor's corridor. Pausing, he turned to them and warned curtly, "This is Professor Hertz's room. Keep quiet and speak only when spoken to." He knocked twice, turned the knob to check if it was unlocked, and carefully pushed the door open. Once they all stepped into the room, they saw a man seated at the center of the large space, playing a piano. Gem Marie, in awe, noticed that he was playing with his left hand while conducting with his right. He was speaking to some empty chairs that were arranged in orchestra seating positions. "Louder! Forte!" he shouted, as he played Mozart's *Violin Sonata No. 21 in C Major*. Delighted by the peculiar scene, Gem Marie smiled as she watched him command his phantom orchestra with precise movements. "Ritardando!" When he leaned in and scolded an imaginary violinist for playing out of key, "Bow one! More legato!" Gem Marie couldn't help but giggle. This drew a sharp scowl from Otis. The anxious man then called out, "Martin! Excuse me Professor," then waited a moment before approaching the professor and gently tapping him on the shoulder. Startled, Martin spun around and spoke in a sarcastic tone. "Ah, you've brought strange guests, Frederick? Why? Why, when I am preparing for the event of the year? An event people will talk about for years to come!" He resumed playing, this time more softly, and continued speaking. "Frederick, are you not answering me? Are you in need of a doctor?" Frederick replied, "Speaking of doctors, Maestro," and handed him a letter from Dr. Hertz. Professor Martin glanced at the letter and then at Gem Marie. He walked over to her with a skeptical expression and asked for her name. Before she could respond, Otis interjected, "She's a mute, sir. She can't speak, but she can hear and understand some. She mostly communicates through me, as I'm the only one who understands her half the time." The professor walked over to Otis and Frederick, placing a hand on each of their shoulders then swiftly ushered them toward the soundproof doors. "Wait outside," he instructed. Both men were taken aback but followed his command and stepped out of the room. Professor Hertz closed the door slowly in their faces, turning the key before slipping it into his pocket then patted it for safekeeping. He walked back to Gem Marie and playfully spoke, "Now that our interruptions have been dealt with, we can proceed with the testing. First, let me say I know you are not mute. I know that not only can you speak, but you might also be able to read music. I just need to know how much you know." He took Gem Marie by the hand and led her to a section of the room where several instruments were laid out on a table. "Which one is your favorite?" he asked. Gem Marie, startled by the question, said nothing. She hesitated, knowing not to respond too quickly. Besides, there was no harp among the instruments. Instead, she shook her head from side to side, testing the professor to see if he truly believed she could speak. The professor smiled. "Stop wasting time," he said. "The sooner you speak, the sooner I can help you." Gem Marie, who was enjoying the Professor's odd behavior, remembered that her goal was to return to the Scotney and now was being tempted by his bait. Overwhelmed by the thought of returning home She hastily said, "None of these are my favorite but I can play this one a little." She grabbed the violin and search for its Bow which she found lying on the ground . She then began tuning it, once she tuned the violin to the tone of her liking, she carefully placed the instrument under her chin. Professor Hertz, who was now smiling because his assumption of Gem Marie being able to speak was amazingly correct, he was taken back by her awareness of fine tuning and posture with the instrument. As Gem Marie looked around the room for a focal point, she finally found a blank white wall where she could comfortably rest her eyes on as she played. She arranged the shadows and the markings on the wall to form faces and began to return mentally back to the Scotney. Her careful manipulation of her illusions began working, she began to see Monsieur Heritage in the parlor, he was sitting with Auntie Elenor patiently waiting for her to return. Once he noticed her in the room, he order her to play the violin and not her Harp, he reminded her that he would be able to detect if she had been practicing. Gem Marie watched as Monsieur Heritage tapped his finger on the forearm of his chair and he gave a slight nod of approval as she had entered the second movement of the concerto. Auntie Elenor raised her kerchief and then laid it back on her lap as a gesture of uncontrollable enjoyment. Gem Marie, who was now smiling, began moving about the room in a way she had observed her music teacher move around when he taught her lessons. While sauntering across the floor, she caught a glimpse of the servants peeking into the parlor. Greta, who would sometimes peek through the crack of the parlor door stood with the servants and watched her carefully. Then with perfect timing she blew a kiss at Gem Marie when their eyes met. Gem Marie, who was just about to let out a small chuckle, was abruptly grabbed on her shoulder and spun around by Professor Martin who spoke very loudly. "Antonio Vivaldi Violin Concerto, this is impossible how can you play such a piece with complexity." He now held her by both shoulders and shook her slightly, "I mean it's impossible for your kind to know or comprehend such work! Tell me right now where did you learn this!" Gem Marie, who was now startled and frighten said nothing. Her mind racing, trying to come up with a believable excuse on how she could have learned such an intricate piece. She looked to the pale white wall for help from Monsieur or anyone from the Scotney but there was nothing there. Suddenly she thought of why she was in this predicament to begin with, she saw herself searching through newspapers for a man she had never known. She replayed the events leading up to her plan to run away in search of her true love. Now, with the clarity of hindsight, a wave of sadness and embarrassment washed over her as she realized how foolish it was to believe she could find a man who existed only in her imagination. Once she managed to push aside the persistent image of Christian Pierre's face from the newspaper, she felt control return to her voice. She stepped closer to Professor Hertz, no longer afraid. Quickly, she assessed his stature and attire. He bore no resemblance to Monsieur Heritage; he lacked the commanding presence of the Master, the most feared and respected figure at the Scotney. Monsieur ruled over a grand castle, vast lands, and the banks upon which the people depended. Professor Hertz had never earned a name or the respect she once attributed to the man she called her father. Now, seeing him for who he truly was, she could no longer be intimidated by him. As she moved closer, she looked into his eyes, and with each step, her courage grew. When she stood directly before him, she turned her gaze to the blank, white wall and spoke clearly, though softly. "My former master, Christian Pierre, commanded that I learn many compositions.

I practiced daily, for there would be consequences if I did not. To read the music and perform, he had to teach me to read and speak. I worked hard every day learning the music, finally before I was taken away and sold, I mastered Vivaldi which is not my favorite for that reason." Professor Hertz stood frozen, a surge of disbelief coursing through him as he recalled Christian Pierre a man whose presence had graced a few of their performances. Pierre was undeniably eccentric, known for his indulgent patronage of the arts and audacious flair. Yet, the notion of teaching a slave to master a concerto was beyond the bounds of propriety and openly defied the laws of the land. Professor Hertz years ago had heard of the whispers that circulated about Christian Pierre assembling an orchestra comprised of slaves and destitute widows. Their faces filling the concert hall as if mere placeholders in a spectacle driven by sheer desperation. "What could possibly be happening down in New Orleans?" Professor Hertz mused, the enigma gnawing at his thoughts. Why would Pierre lavish such attention on her, risking not only scandal but retribution? The professor's brow furrowed, and he made a silent promise to himself: he would journey to New Orleans before the year's end to uncover the truth behind this audacious gamble. Gem Marie felt her nerves tighten as the silence stretched between them. Professor Hertz seemed lost in an intense, private dialogue, his eyes fixed on her with an unreadable expression. Minutes slipped by, punctuated only by the faint ticking of the clock, but he remained wordless, his gaze unyielding. Carefully, Gem Marie set the violin down on a nearby chair, breaking the weight of his silence with a voice both soft and resolute. "Master Pierre told me never to play for anyone but him, and never to speak. If questioned, I was to give no answers." Professor Hertz's eyes softened, and for the first time, he spoke, his tone tinged with an unexpected gentleness. "So, to prove your loyalty, you silenced yourself. You refused to play, refused to speak. Even after being sold, you kept your vow. Such loyalty is unimaginable." Her words, combined with the haunting brilliance of her playing, unsettled him. It gnawed at his conscience how could he, in good faith, remain silent about such talent? His mind churned with thoughts, each more urgent than the last, until the storm of emotion made him falter. He stumbled forward, two shaky steps before his knees buckled. Reacting instantly, Gem Marie caught his arm and guided him to a large, cushioned chair. He sat there, breathing unevenly, eyes flicking from Gem Marie to the violin resting on the chair. His gaze lingered on the instrument before finally returning to her. Then, with newfound determination, he reached for her hand and pulled her closer. This is more tragic than Shakespeare," Professor Hertz finally uttered, his voice tight with emotion. "Although your secret is safe with me, you must continue to feign muteness. I cannot let you leave, not after discovering the knowledge you've been taught. You do understand your talents violates the law, and your life would be at grave risk outside these walls. You'll have to live in seclusion here at the school it's safer this way. You'll assist with errands and keep the place immaculate. Perhaps one day, your talents will be revealed, attributed to my teachings, as if acquired solely from your time here. But for now, you must never breathe a word about Pierre Christian, not even to my brother, Dr. Hertz. Do you understand?" Gem Marie nodded quickly, a secret smile playing at her lips. No more nights spent shivering on a cold floor or scavenging for scraps, she thought. Professor Hertz composed himself as if stepping onto a stage. With a deliberate grace, he moved to the soundproof door and opened it. He told Otis and the escort that he needed more time for testing and to leave Gem Marie with him. Otis, who was now alarmed when he heard the word test instantly thought about the animals that had been cut open by Dr. Hertz. Now, he was wondering if he had chosen the wrong words, when he asked him to see if his brother could run some test on Gem Marie like he did with the animals. Otis, who could think of nothing else to say to Professor Martin, told him that their Auntie would be upset if he did not bring her home to at least say goodbye, he web a tale about their auntie being worried due to Gem Marie's inability to speak. Professor Martin, who could sense that Otis was lying , quickly told Otis "Your aunt can come here and visit whenever she likes." Reaching into his pocket, Professor Martin drew out a coin and pressed it into Otis's hand, watching as his eyes widened. Otis cast a quick glance over at Gem Marie, a deep sadness settling in; he knew this might be the last time he would ever see her. After thanking the professor, he quietly asked if he could bid her farewell. Stepping over to Gem Marie, Otis positioned himself squarely in front of her, deliberately shielding her face from both the professor and the stern escort. In a low, urgent whisper, he murmured, "Now listen here. I reckon you'll be alright, but don't go breathing in no cloths if they offer them. And if he say he ever say he need to see what your heart or head looks like, you hear me, run as fast as you can, and don't look back. Cross the tracks, remember, and that's where you'll find me." He paused, his voice thick with worry. "Do what they say, keep your head low, and don't speak a word about England or no grand castles. I'll try to check on you when I can." Otis then pulled her into a fierce embrace, holding her tightly. In her ear, he whispered once more, "Remember, girl, your mind's your weapon." Gem Marie's heart twisted, realizing that since leaving the Scotney, Otis and Claudette was the closest thing to family she had left. Fighting back tears, she whispered back, "Tu es famille. You are my family, Otis." Professor Hertz, observing the intense farewell, nodded ever so slightly; their shared emotion was all the confirmation he needed to believe they were indeed kin. Professor Hertz interrupted their conversation with a firm yet subtle command, turning to Otis. "I have more tests to conduct, and this week is particularly busy for the school," he said, his voice curt but purposeful. Moving to his desk, he scribbled hastily onto a piece of paper, folded it, and placed it along with another coin into Otis's hand. "Deliver this to my brother at once," he instructed, casting a steady gaze upon him. Otis, astonished by the unexpected wealth now filling his pockets, felt an awe toward Gem Marie, sensing she held a power unlike any other slave around here. He stepped toward the heavy, soundproof door, pausing as the escort closed it firmly in his face. With a subtle nod, Professor Hertz redirected the escort. "Take Gem Marie to the costume area," he ordered. "Explain her arrangements in full. Make sure she knows the care required for the performance costumes I want precisely as I have ordered. Then, return for further instructions regarding the group. And at dawn tomorrow, bring her directly to me." The escort hesitated, his brow furrowed with concern. "Will rehearsals truly halt for this new project, Professor? The show is only a fortnight away. The backlash we faced last time was intense, remember? Many doubted that children could rival the performances of adults, regardless of the techniques taught." Professor Hertz dismissed the concern with a wave of his hand. "Today, individual rehearsals will suffice. Tomorrow morning, we resume group practice at six sharp." As Gem Marie disappeared down the corridor with the escort, Professor Hertz leaned back into his cushioned chair, his gaze falling to the violin she had played with such effortless skill. He was spellbound by the memory, awed by her talent a gift all the more remarkable given her sensory impairment. The thought stirred in him a deep and solemn question, "How might I safeguard this extraordinary talent from a world that would never see its worth? Right under my own roof. A darkie with such knowledge the " Once Gem Marie arrive at the room the boasted eclectic collection, ranging from animal ensembles to celestial bodies like the moon and sun nestled in one corner sent a surge through her. Gazing up at the high window, Gem Marie found solace in the moon and stars illuminating the space. Their reflection cast shimmering lights upon the costumes, adorning the walls and furniture with dancing specks of light. Tonight, however, was unlike any other. Gem Marie found herself overwhelmed with emotion, thoughts of Monsieur and The Scotney flooding her mind. Unlike previous nights filled with the comforting presence of Otis and Claudette tonight's solitude amplified her longing for home. It marked the first night since leaving The Scotney that she was left alone with just her thoughts. Unable to succumb to sleep, Gem Marie's tears stained a velvet gown that had been thrown at the head of a small settee that she laid upon. Before she resolved to explore the room, she had been forbidden to inspect earlier. With a decisive click, she locked the door from the inside and meticulously surveyed her surroundings. Making her way to the far end of the room, she discovered rows of garments piled haphazardly. Methodically, she began sorting through them, finding echoes of her own dresses left behind at The Scotney. Gem Marie found solace in sorting through the articles of clothing, each fold and arrangement offered healing to her lonely heart. As she reached the bottom of the pile, her fingers brushed against a large brass rack hidden beneath. Hastily, she sifted through it, setting aside a fresh ensemble of clothes before meticulously organizing them into their respective categories. Some garments were sorted by shade, others by the tales and authors they evoked. From the tragic romance of Romeo and Juliet to the dark intrigue of Macbeth, Gem Marie curated the pieces into orderly sections. A heavy robe caught her attention, adorned with stones and bearing the label "King William III" sewn into its lining. Struggling to remove it from the rack, she sensed it had been affixed to something before finally freeing it. Her heart skipped a beat as she uncovered a cherrywood harp nestled beneath the weighty fabric. Though its strings were badly tuned, some missing, and layers of dust accumulated, Gem Marie tenderly cleaned it with a torn shirt she found nearby. With care, she polished the brass and tightened the loose strings, restoring the instrument to a semblance of its former glory. Once finished, she reverently returned it to its corner, concealing it once more beneath the regal robe. Gem Marie felt a surge of joy at the sight of the harp. It reminded her of her cherished old companion, which had brought her solace and comfort on countless evenings. Exhausted from her cleaning and organizing efforts, she allowed herself to succumb to drowsiness. Nestling into a plush settee, she reflected on the fabricated story she had recounted to Professor Hertz about Christian Pierre. She replayed it in her mind, ensuring she wouldn't forget any detail in case of further questioning. With her eyes closed, she made a silent wish upon a star, hoping that somehow, Christian Pierre would find her and propose, returning her to Monsieur Heritage's care. She envisioned his gentle eyes, knowing that a man who loved music as she did must possess kindness. As fatigue overtook her, she imagined him patiently waiting nearby, perhaps seated in a chair, until she completed her rest. Drifting into slumber, she conjured an image of him tenderly placing a goodnight kiss upon her forehead.

Chapter: 10

Christian Pierre

Christian Pierre sat on his veranda, sipping wine, as he watched a family of foxes dart across the lawn of his expansive estate. The amber-furred creatures paused and stared at him, and in that moment of stillness, Christian pondered his life. Despite his wealthy and influential reputation as a businessman, his numerous handshakes, and escorting some of the loveliest women to high-profile events, he still longed for something more. His extensive wealth and influence, coupled with his philanthropic endeavors, had made him a beloved figure in society, yet he spent most nights alone. Christian's magnetic presence ensured his name frequently appeared in newspapers wherever he traveled, but this fame held no weight in finding a mate who was his equal. He recalled the last article that appeared in both Parisian and London papers, praising his handsome looks and intricate attire, yet neglecting to delve into the details of his self-written concerto. Despite putting together his own orchestra and composing his first musical piece, which many local elites attended, the event was only briefly mentioned, and he was merely labeled a lover of music. This prompted him to seek alternative recognition for his works. Years ago, when he announced his departure from Paris to America, his family was shocked and disappointed. They assumed a woman had stolen his heart and that his decision was guided solely by love. Feeling slighted that no one inquired about the concerto he had tirelessly spoken about and created the year before his departure, Christian used their reaction as fuel for his motivation. He interpreted his family's nonchalant behavior toward his love for the arts as a clear sign that no one in Paris cared or was listening to his music. Christian often traveled throughout Europe acquiring numerous lands and mansions but for some reason he was drawn to America and a small section of Luisiana called the French quarter. So, when he made the announcement as the eldest sibling that he was leaving for America and relocating in a section that had a reputation of being a replica of France, everyone was appalled that he would forsake his true heritage for a copy. Christian felt by planting roots there he would have the best of both worlds although after the battle of eighteen fifteen the area was becoming more Americanize, he was still drawn to the quarter's French characteristics. Christian insisted on staying true to his roots and on his twenty-acre estate, the entire feel of the property was almost a replica of the French quarters in Paris with paintings paying homage to Paris on every wall. Many of the elite who traveled to New Orleans would pay fees to stay on the estate in order to be in his presence and get an authentic feeling of Paris. Christian Pierre's estate in New Orleans began as a small, secretive community of elegant, stately homes nestled amid sprawling fields. Initially welcoming occasional visitors, Pierre later transformed the property into a full-time plantation, closing its gates to outsiders. When first established each grand house boasted six or more bedrooms and became home to a diverse group of women, most of whom were refugees from across Europe, having fled the chaos of the Napoleonic Wars and other revolutions. These women represented various walks of life, and each house was assigned distinct responsibilities to ensure the plantation thrived. They cultivated raw honey, cotton, and a remarkably pure well water that became legendary in the region. Pierre's plantation followed an unconventional social structure that was kept hushed where Black and white residents sometimes worked side-by-side, picking cotton and sowing seeds across the fertile land. The work assignments rotated frequently, adding flexibility to the tasks each house managed. Soon, rumors spread that Pierre's methods were radical; locals whispered that he treated his enslaved workers as if they were free. Some speculated that the estate's unusually large female population was Pierre's harem and that he bred slaves for his own purposes. Others believed he aimed to recreate the elegance and intellectual atmosphere of the Cabildo's grand salons, where nobility and free people of color once mingled. Yet, within the estate walls, masters, slaves, and servants labored in harmony, blurring the lines of conventional hierarchy. As the estate grew more self-sufficient, outside labor was rarely needed, and those within the plantation had little reason to leave. Pierre's methodical approach included assigning unique names to each house, creating a structured society within the plantation. He gave select enslaved individuals leadership roles, ensuring that if any house failed in its duties, he could hold those responsible accountable to the estate's own rituals and laws. Remarkably, Pierre was known to leave his estate without fear of his slaves escaping, as they were encouraged to resolve their disputes amongst themselves. Locals who had never been permitted on the plantation frequently criticized his lenient approach, warning that it would lead to rebellion. Unmoved, Pierre designed a meticulous security layout that allowed him to monitor any attempts to enter the plantation grounds. Overnight guests, who were rare, were housed in a separate guest home directly behind the main estate house, watched closely around the clock. No guest, regardless of their status, was permitted to roam freely. Here's a refined, organized version of your text, with enhanced clarity, intrigue, and historical atmosphere. Amid the sprawling gardens filled with apple, peach, and pear trees, mingling with the delicate scents of jasmine and magnolia, guests of Christian Pierre's estate found a sense of rare tranquility. His reputation as a successful plantation owner spread widely, not just for his crops but for his exceptional honey and fruit business. This prosperity blossomed further when he took in a Spaniard, rumored to be a descendant of one of the original Honey Hunters. The Spaniard's mastery over the bees and understanding of their hives allowed Christian to cultivate honey of unparalleled quality, strengthening his influence in New Orleans. But as Christian's honey business flourished, it caught the eye of Woolfolk, a notorious slave trader with ties to the infamous Slaytter brothers. Woolfolk, suspicious of Christian's rising success, demanded full records and origins of every slave on his estate, hoping to uncover any leverage against him. Christian refused, promptly enlisting the support of a trusted friend a colonel with influence in the Senate. With pressure from the colonel, Woolfolk was forced to withdraw his demands. As a gesture of apparent goodwill, Woolfolk attempted to smooth things over, gifting Christian a slave named Simone. Simone, though aging and without children, had long been obedient in Woolfolk's service, once even his favorite. Shortly after her arrival on Christian's plantation, however, Simone gave birth to twin boys fathered by a mulatto slave. Upon hearing this, Woolfolk was deeply affronted. He had convinced himself that Christian must have arranged the union, a blow to his pride that this woman, who had served him without bearing children, would bear "two strong bucks" soon after leaving his control. In an attempt to reclaim Simone, Woolfolk slyly offered Christian a trade, suggesting he would exchange two others for her return. Christian responded coolly, his voice calm but firm, "Once I own a slave, I never sell or give them away." Christian was not married, but rumors swirled that he could have a different woman every night. These whispers grew so extravagant that some women even gave mock interviews claiming to be his hidden wife. This was never taken as official information, but it was sometimes brought up a the lady societal luncheons that fueled for more gossip. Christian often spent his days and evenings immersed in the classical orchestra he had personally assembled. When not seeking new art pieces during his travels, he would visit music conservatories or other institutions in search of fresh talent. Christian devoted some of his time to a woman named Lelina Devereux, the daughter and heir of a wealthy oil and land-owning family. Unlike many others, Lelina was not swept away by Christian's good looks and charm. She seemed to genuinely love him, but her mother's constant reminders of the rumors about his many illegitimate children on the Pierre Estate often drew her away. Whenever Lelina questioned him about these rumors, Christian never admitted or denied them. He remained unapologetic about any of the children growing up on the estate. Lelina admired his ability to stay calm and collected amid gossip and chaos, which intrigued her. Lelina, the daughter of a war hero and a blue-blooded Southern belle, was cautious about being seen in public with Christian. Held in high regard, she could not risk ruining her chances with a proper suitor, as her mother put it. Although Christian lived a quiet life, rumors of his numerous affairs and the many women on the estate persisted. His silence and refusal to defend himself only fueled these stories. It was said that four of the children on the estate were his, born to two widows and two servants. Women who had never courted or had known him in that a way often embellished tales of supposed evenings spent with him, but none ever described him as anything less than a gentleman. One night, while attending an elite dinner party, Lelina gathered the courage to bring up a particularly bold woman. This woman had claimed to lose all composure at a ball where Christian was present, her animated account of events were so detailed that Lelina couldn't help but confront Christian afterwards. Pleading for the truth she politely requested the facts, Christian all too familiar with the fabricated story reminded her that every woman who read about him in the papers felt they knew him, and many had no problem concocting stories about secret rendezvous that never occurred. Lelina knew in her heart that not all the stories were true, but she could not risk her reputation by considering a serious relationship with Christian Pierre without marriage. She loved him, but the fear of her parents' disapproval plus any tarnish to her reputation kept her from showing her true feelings. In an effort to get him to propose, she would occasionally let her jealousy surface, which Christian oddly enjoyed. Those were the only moments he was given a glimpse of Lelina's authentic emotions. However, as she spent more time with Christian, she realized his true passion lay with music, surpassing any love he could have for her or any other woman. Lady Lelina who had grown an appetite for social status, was more concern with the opinions of the women at her societal luncheon believed. After three female slaves of Creole decent all became pregnant at the same time and were never paired with a stud, refused to give the names of the potential bucks that impregnated them, the suspicion grew greater. Great suspicion arose concerning the methods of reproducing the population on the plantation. Especially when Christian Pierre refused to inflict physical punishment in order to obtain the names of the possible men that impregnated the woman. Even after stating that he would not bring harm to his unborn property the woman and men remained silent concerning the children. Instead, the children were classified by color and mother. Rumors surfaced that he himself had mated with the women, although each child was born with different colored eyes whispers of jealousy and envy plague every social club. Lady Lelina began distancing herself by immersing herself with more charitable duties. By evening, a messenger delivered the news to Lady Lelina that Christian would be traveling to Maryland to finalize an investment. Lelina was unsurprised by the absence of an invitation; even if extended, it would have been a mere formality, and she would have declined. Christian often cloaked his pursuits of music and art in the guise of business, returning from his travels with a newly discovered composition or an instrument. Before departing, Christian requested that Lelina check in on the women at Honey Water and provide them with charm lessons—an area in which she excelled. Reluctant at first, Lelina found herself unexpectedly moved by the experience, particularly after her interactions with a woman named Margret, whose sincere gratitude resonated with her. Christian's dedication to the high standards of the plantation masked a deeper, restless void within him. Mastering his estate had lost its luster, and his nights were plagued by fitful sleep and unsettling dreams. One recurring vision haunted him: he was conducting an orchestra, transfixed by a woman playing an instrument with her back to him. The closer he approached, the more she receded into the shadows. When he finally reached her and touched her shoulder, she turned, revealing a face that was featureless no eyes, no nose, no mouth. The sight stole his breath and jolted him awake. He sat upright, drenched in sweat, trying to decipher the dream's meaning. The image of the faceless woman with cascading hair lingered in his mind. "Please, explain," he whispered into the emptiness. To his astonishment, a voice replied, "Play something." Heart racing, Christian sprang from his bed, hurried down the hallway to his music room, seized his violin, and began to play. Though he hadn't mastered the instrument, he always played it before creating a new concerto. Scrambling for pieces of paper to jot down the melodic wave that had overtaken his mind and body, Christian played and wrote notes repeatedly until he heard the roosters crow. Only then did he stop to prepare himself for the day. Summoning his servants, he announced that he would be leaving for his trip in two days instead of two months. The news of the spontaneous departure surprised everyone, especially Margret, a servant who had risen in rank after taking the initiative to learn the harpsichord. Scowling at the instructions, Margret asked, "Shall I notify Lady Lelina and arrange for our lessons to continue after your return, sir?" Christian, caught off guard by the remark, paused before quickly instructing one of the butlers to notify Lady Lelina at a reasonable hour after his departure, explaining that he left urgently for business. Satisfied with the turn of events, Margret returned to her quarters, devising a plan to speak with Lady Lelina without Christian ever knowing. Margret was uneasy about the relationship that had quickly developed between Lady Lelina and Christian devised a plan to become closer with her. Once Lady Lelina questioned Margret one the number of female servants and slaves that resided on the Honey Waters estate. She secretly confided in Margret that if she ever married Christian, her first act would be to sell off half of the female slaves and servants. Assuring Margret that she would never sell her off lady Lelina encourage Margret to provide her with updates on Honey Waters. Christian who took pride in stating that he had never increased his slave population himself had only fell victim once. It was a late summer's evening, and Margret, in a desperate bid to secure her place at Honey Waters, set a trap for Christian. She concocted a potent mix of wine and ale, timing her scheme perfectly after the enslaved residents of the manor had been sent to work in the fields. Margret devised a plan after noticing Christian had already downed two bottles of wine while absorbed in his work. After midnight, when all was sleep she appeared in the parlor doorway, clad only in a thin petticoat, her lips stained dark from raspberries. Breathless and wild-eyed, she claimed a spirit had visited her in a dream, whispering a secret melody that haunted her even now. Her words ignored Christian's protests as she hurried to the harpsichord and began playing a tune softly unfamiliar to him, her fingers moving feverishly. Drawn by the haunting melody, Christian eventually joined her at the bench, caught in the trance of her music. As the evening wore on, Margret persuaded him to drink from her goblet. Weakened by wine and the pull of loneliness, Christian succumbed to the one night's temptation, unaware of the later consequences. Margret kept her pregnancy hidden, but the weight of grief fell upon her when she was unable to carry the child to terms. Obsessed and unwilling to let go, she devised yet another plan to bear Christian's child. Margret's schemes did not go unnoticed. After a failed attempt at seduction, Christian ordered her to the farthest fields with two others, stripping her of any semblance of privilege she once held. Her demotion cost her respect among the other servants, and she seemed banished from Honey Waters entirely. But Margret was nothing if not determined. She convinced Lady Lelina to teach her the art of charms, and her efforts soon earned her a place back within the estate walls. However, life had shifted. Margret entered a union with another man among the enslaved, her obsession with Christian gradually fading. She then earned her position as the keeper of the garden. As she let go of her schemes and desires for Christian's heart, she resigned herself to a new life, finally surrendering the ghost of her ambitions.

Chapter: 11

A Vow Within The Scotney

It was a cloudy cold morning when a messenger riding in on an oversized black and white colt delivered a letter to Monsieur Heritage. As the messenger approached the moat he was stopped by some of the castle's guards and footmen. The young messenger insisted that the long-scrolled letter sealed with the crown and leaf birch be handed to Monsieur Heritage by him only. Once escorted inside then and only then he released the letter to Monsieur Heritage. Monsieur was careful to examine the scroll to confirm if the seal had been tampered with. He knew it contained pertinent information concerning Gem Marie, so he interrogated the young carrier by quickly hurling a series of questions, while giving him no chance to fabricate a story. He snapped at the messenger, " Can you read lad?" "No Sir," he was quick to respond, "But I can write my name." he lastly said before committing to silence. Monsieur now felt more comfortable in allowing the young man to sit and wait, for he knew depending on what the letter stated he would have to respond to the sender immediately. He summoned for Greta and Madam Henry to watch over the young messenger he instructed them to continue questioning his wits. Greta and her mother knew exactly what to do for this was not the first time they used hospitality and cleverness in order to get workers and messengers to expose their souls. Meanwhile Monsieur sat in his library behind his large Victorian French desk and began reading the letter slowly, it read.

My Honorable Monsieur Heritage,

I trust this letter finds you in good health. I pen this missive with a heart heavy with both sorrow and hope, seeking your assistance in a matter of great importance. It is with immense relief and a modicum of joy that I write to inform you of a discovery that has consumed the better part of my existence. Your beloved daughter, Gem Marie, who was abducted and carried away on a cargo slave ship bound for

America, has been traced to the shores of the New World. The vessel in question seems to have played host to a most extraordinary event, the details of which have come to light through the whispers of seamen and overseers. It appears that two remarkable women of darker descent, whom the overseers referred to as Darkies," managed to stage a daring escape somewhere between the shores of Virginia and Delaware. Rumors speak of their cleverness, and it is said that one of these women possessed the ability to converse in fluently in French, a skill that proved instrumental in creating a diversion, affording them the opportunity to flee. The destination they purportedly sought was the abode of wealthy slave owners and traders, among whom a man of considerable influence is named The Slayter brothers and Christian Pierre. Regrettably, the tales cease there, and the fate of these courageous women remains shrouded in uncertainty. The last reliable sightings place them alive and well, but the trials they may have endured during the arduous transatlantic journey are beyond my ken. I must now humbly request your continued assistance in this matter, as the funds I initially provided for the procurement of this information have been fully depleted. It pains me to impose further, but the exact location of their departure remains elusive, and I fear that more resources may be necessary to unravel this mystery. Your reputation for diligence and discretion precedes you, Monsieur Heritage, and I beseech you to lend your expertise to this pressing matter. I await your guidance with bated breath. My next letter will be sent to the old man at the mill.

Yours sincerely,

Baron Braydon Fitzgerald.

Monsieur Heritage reclined in his chair, allowing the weight of the information to settle upon him like a heavy fog. Christian Pierre those two words echoed incessantly, a relentless refrain haunting his thoughts. They were the same words he had stumbled upon in Gem Marie's treasured keepsake, now etched into his consciousness like an ominous warning. With each beat of his racing heart, Monsieur felt the swell of anger, a tempest rising within him. Who was this Christian Pierre, and by what twisted authority did he wield the power to snatch innocence away, both in body and spirit, Monsieur's mind pondered. The crackling of the fireplace interrupted his reverie, drawing his attention to the dancing flames and the poker resting beside them. His gaze fixated on the iron object along with a silent promise of retribution that formed in his mind's eye. He envisioned confronting Christian Pierre, pinning him against the wall with the menacing tool pressed against his throat, demanding answers about Gem Marie's whereabouts. The mere thought of seeing fear reflected in Pierre's eyes brought a grim satisfaction to Monsieur Heritage knowing that his quarry would have no escape, no sanctuary to flee from justice. In a low, deliberate voice, he uttered the words, the syllables heavy with resolve: "Tu connaîtras le goût de la mort." (You will taste and feel death's bitter embrace.) As he pondered the contents of the letter, a surge of realization swept through him. The mention of the woman's fluency in French and her cleverness was the only thing that sparked a calm reassurance within him. Pride swelled in his chest as he reflected on all he had imparted to Gem Marie. Each lesson, every piece of wisdom, had been absorbed by her with a remarkable competence. She had not only embraced her precocious nature but wielded it to her advantage, enabling her daring escape. The anger that had consumed him began to ebb away, replaced by a sense of triumph over Christian Pierre's reprehensible abilities. Gem Marie, though not his biological daughter, bore the unmistakable traits of his lineage. The image of the once tiny girl he had nurtured, teaching her to speak and write, to entertain with imaginary performances, now outsmarting a ship full of men filled him with a fierce sense of vindication. Yet, amid the desire for vengeance against Christian Pierre, a sobering realization dawned. His priority was not just to punish but to locate Gem Marie. If she couldn't be found, then Christian Pierre would face the consequences for his role in her disappearance. Seating himself at his desk, he penned a letter to Baron Fitzgerald, detailing his urgent inquiries. Every word emphasized the value of any information leading to Gem Marie's whereabouts, promising substantial rewards to those who assisted. He stressed the urgency of the matter, demanding swift action and preparing for a voyage to America. Armed with the letter, sealed by the Heritage's family crest and clutched tightly in his hand, Monsieur Heritage strode purposefully into the parlor where the young messenger awaited. Every step he took seemed to echo the weight of his determination, casting a palpable tension into the air. As Monsieur entered, Greta and her mother were inquiring about his family and heirs, their curiosity evident. Yet, the young messenger's demeanor betrayed a hint of nervousness and discomfort, his face betraying his unease. It was in that moment that Monsieur Heritage recognized a familiar look, one he had seen before on the face of an onlooker the evening he had administered a brutal beating to the helpless cripple. Armed with the memory of that violent encounter, he approached the messenger swiftly, handing him the letter along with a small pouch of coins. With a stern gaze, he emphasized the importance of delivering the letter and its attachments to the Baron Fitzgerald before sundown, warning of dire consequences should he fail. "And if you have any doubts," Monsieur added, his voice laced with a chilling undertone, "Just recall the night at the dressmaker's shop." The young carrier, now consumed by fear, nodded wordlessly before hastening away on his assigned task. Meanwhile, amidst the confusion of the conversation, Greta seized a fleeting moment to speak with Monsieur alone. Casting a glance at her mother, who understood her silent plea for privacy, she departed the room without a word. Alone at last with Monsieur, Greta approached the window where sunlight filtered through the drawn drapes, casting her silhouette in a soft glow. It was a moment she had longed for, a chance to be in his presence without interruption, her heart racing with anticipation. She reminisced about the day Monsieur Heritage had bestowed upon her the sweetest of compliments, marveling at how the sunlight played upon her hair and eyes, lending them an ethereal radiance. Her decision to move to this secluded corner of the room had proven fruitful; Monsieur, drawn by the enchanting spectacle of her illuminated form, had approached her with an eagerness she could scarcely ignore. Standing before Greta, Monsieur was a portrait of conflicting emotions, his heart dancing with unspoken desires yet restrained by the weight of untold truths. "Where is our child?" he murmured, his words a delicate thread in the tapestry of their shared intimacy history. Greta, momentarily lost in the flood of memories his presence evoked, was always caught off guard when Monsieur acknowledged their son. "He is resting peacefully," she replied, her voice soft with a mixture of longing and apprehension. "Would you like to see him?" "Yes," Monsieur answered, his voice barely more than a whisper, laden with layers of complexity that echoed through the corridor. Together they made their way to Greta's chambers, as each step, of their footsteps drew closer, the sound a testament to the bond that still tethered them together. Entering her sanctuary, Greta's gaze fell upon baby Philip, nestled in slumber, cocooned in the warmth of his bassinet. Two brass pins secured him in place, a symbol of protection in a world fraught with uncertainty. The room was suffused with the gentle glow of a crackling fire, its warmth embracing them like an old friend. Greta was just about to pick baby Philip up when Monsieur Heritage entered and told her to let him sleep. He stood by the doorway for a moment watching Greta as she stood by the baby awaiting her next instructions. As he stood silently while tracing her silhouette, he reveled in his thoughts, of how he was at an advantage by living at the Scotney. On any day he could show his true feelings whenever he felt without eyes or ears of judgement upon him. Only his own conscience could toil with him at times but for the most part he was living in a world that he alone had created. To him that was living in his true power and strength. Not by the dominance against men and women's will or the brut intimidation that was commonly depicted as normal in society. No, he carefully created his own society where he had sowed his own seeds of true love, that he had cultivated and watched bloom while its pedals of chance grew with reciprocation without nudge. He now knew he loved Greta, Philip, and Gem Marie, all of which were created by his own desires and not by traditions or laws. By his faith and will a sphere bonded by love came int existence, now a part of his circle was missing, his faith consumed by the fear that Greta and the baby could slip away right under his nose also. This union with Greta was missing one key factor, perhaps the vital part that could have kept Gem Marie content the figure of a mother and wife. With the thoughts and feelings welling up inside as he continued to watch Greta standing over his male heir, he could no longer contain himself with the persistent thought of possibly losing her plaguing his mind. He walked up and stood in front of her and while grabbing her hands he began questioning her. "Are you the mother of my child, yes?" Greta said nothing, she just stood there in shock, for although he never denied he fathered a child with her to hear the words in his own voice sent chills through her. Monsieur noticed her distant gaze, a knot of worry forming in his chest. He reached out, shaking her almost violently, desperation seeping into his voice as he asked again. Her silence felt like a cold wall of rejection. "You are the mother of my son, yes! he shouted, his tone raw with emotion. Greta, feeling a rush of fear, stammered, "Yes, I am." Taking a step back, Monsieur studied Greta's face intently, searching for any flicker of recognition. "Then you must understand," he continued with a mix of determination and urgency, Then, with a solemnity that sent shivers down Greta's spine, he declared, "Without the consent of the king's laws, or the merry witness of others, I declare today, on this land of my own, that you are my wife, and I am your husband, your protector, ruler, and keeper." Greta stood frozen, unable to form words. She tried to convince herself that she was simply lost in a dream, that none of this was real. Closing her hands into tight fists, she dug her nails into her palms, hoping the pain would jolt her awake. But the reality remained stubbornly present, leaving her adrift in confusion, waiting for the dream to guide her next move. With an escalating irritation coursing through him like a tempest, Monsieur seized her shoulders, his grip tight and forceful. The delicate silk shawl, a token of his affection on a distant evening, cascaded to the floor, forgotten in the turmoil. His voice rose to a crescendo, nearly a roar, as he confronted her with raw emotion. "Do you not hear me, woman?! I implore you, do not consign me to this torturous limbo! The vultures of my conscience relentlessly tear at me, and you are my sole sanctuary from this torment. Speak to me, my gentle hands that have absolved shame and blood from my soul without condemnation." Greta, engulfed by a deluge of memories shared with Monsieur, found herself overwhelmed. Each recollection crashed upon her mind like waves against the shore, leaving her breathless and disoriented. Her mouth, as dry as desert sand, refused to obey her commands to swallow. Beads of sweat traced paths down her neck and temples, while her heartbeat thundered in her ears. The sensation of impending faintness whispered to her like a tantalizing escape from this nightmare that had been thrusted upon her against her will. She welcomed the thought, for she imagine if she fainted, the impact of her body hitting the floor would somehow shatter the dream world she had been drafted into against her will. Suddenly Monsieur, who could not make reason of why Greta was not speaking, let out a deep groan before speaking again. This time. It was as if someone had struck a hard blow to his mid-section and rendered him almost unable to speak. Monsieur's words resonated with unwavering conviction as he declared, "My world shall not be merge with the silenced toll of the crushed Blue bells, which lay helpless and tattered beneath the relentless march of my stallion's hooves. Everything I have nurtured and cherished will soon cease to exist." Greta, overcome with a newfound conviction of Monsieur's impassioned speech, trembled uncontrollably as his words pierced through her with stark clarity, instilling a fear deeper than the darkest abyss. Never before had she encountered or even heard a man speak in such a manner. How could a servant be summoned to be the master's wife, the notion both bewildered and petrified Greta to the core. Even the stories that were spoken in whispers of the servants who had given birth to many offsprings for only the master of the house, were never referred to as his wife. Greta thought about baby Philip and all that had transpired between her and Monsieur she now believed that by their actions they had gone against nature and the laws of the land and now as her punishment would be to live in mind's cruel fictious place that it had created. She would damned to listen lies and illusions of Monsieur Heritage professing his love and demanding to be her husband. Nothing could halt the vicious loop of Monsieur's voice repeating itself. As if a refreshing mist enveloping her senses, a new voice shattered Greta's catatonic state, jolting her awake. "Wake up," it demanded, resonating with urgency and determination. Emerging from the shadows of the doorway, a figure approached, their presence commanding attention. The shadowed figure slowly walked in the room and continued speaking, "You foolish child do not mimic my life for you owe no loyalty to the sadness and loneliness I have burden you with. Do not allow the fear I have cast on you for years to imprison and lame you. Walk my daughter walk to a life I was never offered. Go forth and live to tell the tales of happiness all women have dreamed of." Madame now fearing that Greta may have already lost her chance spoke aloud again, "Unmute your tongue daughter and speak what is in your heart!" Monsieur, who now at a loss of words, was in disbelief at the eloquent words spoken by Madame Henry who stood in the doorway. Greta, who had followed monsieur's stares locked deep within his eyes once he finally turned away from her mother. With Greta's trance finally broken, she cultivated the courage to speak with confidence, "I Greta Martha Henry, living daughter to my mother Madam Daphne Henry and Father and former Master Francios Bordeaux. I Declare on this day I am the wife to Monsieur Philip Adam Heritage. He shall be my husband, master, and ruler over the Scotney. On this day I vow never to leave his side, for I am the mother of his only heir and son Philip Adam Heritage, and I shall be the mother to all his children to come. I now know that this shall be my place in life for now and eternity." Monsieur stood frozen eye to eye with Greta, the weight that held a tight grip on his mind and heart was now loosened, suddenly baby Philip let out a whimper almost as a call for his grandmother. Madam Henry quickly ran to his aid and removed his pinned swaddle. She spoke softly and held him closely; she insisted that he needed to be attended to. She continued to hold the baby close in her arms as she walked out of the room, not before giving Greta a brief smile of approval. Once the door closed Monsieur asked Greta, "Do you speak from the truth of your heart or does your tongue speak from the silent fear that once gripped you" Greta replied, "Both, my love and heart have been reborn, and you are the father of its joy. I only fear that one day you will see beyond the Scotney walls and a woman of virtue that is seen as your true equal shall render you smitten for her. For I am just the daughter of a slave and a servant, with no rights, and only a promise to comfort me. Should today, Monsieur, should this day become just a memory that must wither away, and I am made to vow never to speak of it again. Then you must know I too will die along with the love I am forced to forget. For after you there will be no other man my husband." At that moment Monsieur held Greta in his arms, he pulled her close so that his lips rested beside her ears as he spoke, Greta could feel the warmth of his breath and the vibrations from the baritone of his voice as he spoke. "There shall never be another woman of virtue, for the only one I love, she stands here now and forever before me. She is draped in all that I have adorned her with. Her scent is that of a Moon flower and I would know it in darkness as if it was my own. For I have laid in it many nights in servitude and gratitude. For it is my sanctuary, my haven of healing and it is all that I have ever known and want to know. You must never doubt this love, daughter of a slave whose head is fit for a crown. "I swear upon my life, you will never be made to forget the man whom you have blessed with an heir," Monsieur declared passionately, his words sending shivers down Greta's spine. Each syllable seemed to caress her skin, igniting a tingling sensation that left her breathless. His lips moved like dancers, leaving a trail of anticipation in their wake. With every utterance, she felt herself weakening, succumbing to the weight of his words and the gentle brush of his touch. In that moment, she needed no further confirmation that their destinies had intertwined, merging into one undeniable truth.

Chapter: 12

Felines Trapped In Rose Bushes

Gem Marie sat alone in the dimly lit room, her only companions a meager offering of bread and cheese pilfered from the abandoned remnants of a lavish spread. This was her clandestine refuge, a sanctuary snatched from the clutches of the bustling school corridors teeming with students. Forbidden from mingling with the students that populated the school during daylight hours, Gem Marie's existence was confined to the solitary confines of whichever classroom she was tasked with polishing to a gleaming perfection. Her very presence was a stealthy shadow, her movements shrouded in secrecy to avoid arousing the curiosity of the students and staff. She had been sternly cautioned by Professor Hertz against attracting undue attention upon herself. She was made to wear a maid costume borrowed from a long-forgotten theatrical production penned by the professor. Gem Marie was rarely seen by anyone, to the unsuspecting eyes of the student body, she was merely a humble servant. Invisible to most she was the backdrop of their academic life, her true talents obscured from view. Yet, hidden beneath her docile facade, a passion burned fiercely within her. On one serendipitous occasion, as the strains of a rehearsal and an upcoming show drifted through the air, Gem Marie seized a fleeting moment of respite to immerse herself in the ethereal melodies of Bach. She picked up a forgotten violin that had been left abandoned on a chair within one of the nearby rooms. Unbeknownst to her, the delicate threads of fate wove a curious tapestry that day, as two students, named William, and Mary, chanced upon the room just as Gem Marie's impromptu performance reached its crescendo. As they stepped into the room, Gem Marie swiftly resumed her menial task, her fingers brushing against the polished surface of the chairs and tables with practiced precision. Yet, in that fleeting moment of connection, a silent understanding passed between them, a shared recognition of the hidden depths concealed beneath the guise of a humble servant. Mary a very wealthy arrogant student, inquired about the source of the violin's melody that had drifted into their conversation. Startled by the question, Gem Marie shift in posture now portrayed an expression of fear. William who now took notice applied swift intuition, intervening he reminded Mary, " You know she is both mute and lacking in intellect. She is clearly incapable of identifying the music. Notice the sloping forehead a clear indication of some form of deformity. Why I doubt she even knows what a violin is." As the conversation veered into disparaging remarks about Gem Marie's intelligence, she recognized the duo from her clandestine visits to the balcony, where she would observe them in rehearsal from her concealed vantage point amidst stored props. A particular memory surfaced, Mary's struggle with a segment of Johann Sebastian Bach's harpsichord concerto in A major during one rehearsal. Gem Marie couldn't help but smile, reassured by the knowledge that she could flawlessly perform the piece since she was eight despite the violin not being her preferred instrument. She had learned it out of deference to Monsieur Heritage, who favored it the piece. Mary, catching a glimpse of Gem Marie's facial expression reverting to satisfaction, grew irritated and suggested to William that they speak to Professor Hertz and suggest Gem Marie undergo evaluation for possible madness, citing the act of smiling to oneself without apparent cause as a symptom. William, now feeling a pang of sympathy for Gem Marie, who continued her dusting duties, interjected, reminding Mary that she was attending the school to study music not the servants. With a bellowing laugh, the two hurried away, leaving Gem Marie behind as they slammed the door upon exiting the empty classroom. Alone, Gem Marie listened as the echoes of footsteps faded down the corridor, leaving a hush that settled around her. She paused by a nearby window, her gaze drifting to the scene below a couple alighting from a carriage, the man offering his hand gallantly to help the woman step down, her arms wrapped protectively around a tightly swaddled baby. Watching them, Gem Marie's thoughts turned to baby Philip and Greta; she wondered how much he must have grown by now. But the sorrow that usually accompanied these memories softened she reminded herself that she needed a plan to return to the Scotney. Thoughts of concertos and students couldn't be allowed to distract her now. Gem Marie knew it was only by her careful planning that she and Claudette had managed to escape unnoticed, her clever distractions kept the overseer unaware. Now, she resolved to stay hidden, listening through the walls until the students began practicing for the upcoming performance. Despite her determination, when she heard the familiar notes, Gem Marie couldn't resist the urge to join in. She picked up her phantom harp, strumming along softly whenever she felt the harp's voice was needed, weaving her melody into the distant echoes. Professor Hertz's voice boomed as he urged the violinist to go faster, and Gem Marie couldn't help but smile. In her mind, she was part of the performance. She imagined herself drifting among the students, moving from instrument to instrument. Her imagination took flight as she moved from violin to harp, her spirit untethered, dancing through the music, unable to contain her passion within the limits of just one role. She began to wonder on how she would make it back to the Scotney. Then, a voice within urged her to abandon foolish thoughts of performing and to focus solely on planning her escape. Yet, each time she attempted to devise a way out of the school, her mind wandered back to her harp and the faint music she could hear drifting through the walls. To distract herself, she began polishing every brass and silver item she could find, wiping each piece until it gleamed. She stood back, admiring how the candlelight and sunlight reflected off the polished surfaces, illuminating the room with a newfound brightness. She gathered her belongings and moved on to the next empty classroom, repeating this ritual of cleaning until fatigue overcame her. Her back and arms ached; she was unaccustomed to such strenuous labor. The only cleaning she'd ever done was when her beloved dolls, seldom out of place that may have required her attention. These porcelain dolls, gifted by Monsieur Heritage, were always treated with special care. Each one arrived in a custom carrier, announced by Monsieur their origins China, Spain, India each clothed in fabrics from their homelands. If a trace of dust ever appeared on their delicate porcelain faces or velvet gowns, Gem Marie would clean them meticulously with soft silk cloths, stitched especially for this purpose by Greta. She watched as her hands brushed dust from porcelain plates and odd figurines, the pieces she felt were undeserved by the rude students who struggled with their concertos. After completing the rooms she returned to her only sanctuary the costume room, she laid back on the settee, listening to the faint sounds of lingering practice sessions. When Mary's part was about to begin, she sprang up and hurried to the old harp concealed beneath the king's robe, and began strumming. She played until a string snapped with a harsh, discordant twang that jolted her back to the dim quiet of the costume room. Pulling her hands away from the harp, she began to weep, realizing how foolish she'd been to fall in love with a man she had never truly known. Tears streamed down her face, exhaustion overtaking her again now made her unable to stay awake, she returned to the settee, finally surrendering to sleep. Gem Marie slept soundly until Professor Hertz burst through the door, his voice commanding her to awaken. Jolted out of her sleep it took Gem Marie a moment to realize she was not in the Scotney but in the costume room. She rose to her feet quickly and tried to appear awake. The Professor scolded her advising that she should be cleaning his room and not sleeping. He grabbed her by the arm and ushered her out of the room and into the hallway, chastising her all the way to his room, he warned her of the consequences of not completing her work. Once they arrived in the room, she quickly removed a cloth from her apron pocket and began polishing some chairs. After witnessing her intense scrubbing for a minute professor Hertz walked over to the piano in the middle of the room and played a few notes, he banged some keys that made notes linger in the air with frustration. Professor Hertz now becoming aware that his playing sounded so angry that he abruptly stopped and walked over to a violin and began playing it intensely. Gem Marie listened as she continued to clean. She could hear the pain and frustration in his playing. Unable to bear the harsh sounds she walked over to a small throw the professor kept on a large armchair and picked it up and walked over to the door. She stepped slightly into the hall at the door's thresholds. Slightly closing the door behind her she stood halfway in the hallway and shook the dust off the throw. Listening to the imperfections that Professor Hertz played she wondered why he attempted to alter the piece. Every now and then he would stop and write something down as if he were adding to the piece that was already well put together. All of a sudden, she heard voices from the distance in the hallway, it was William and Mary. Gem Marie quickly stepped back into the doorway out of their sight while the professor began playing again. Once he stopped playing, she stuck her head out and peeked around as if she was making sure no one was around. Then as soon as Professor Hertz began playing again, she pulled herself back into the doorway's threshold out of sight. She heard Mary's voice over the violin telling William that she knew she was correct and that the darkie can play. Just as the professor ceased playing again, Gem Marie peeked out from the doorway once more, this time ensuring her eyes locked directly with Mary's. The moment their gazes met, she quickly pulled back pretending to enter the room. As she heard footsteps approaching, she carefully nudged the door open, positioning herself so that the professor couldn't be seen from the other side but would still be able to hear any voices. When the professor noticed the door swing open without anyone entering, he set his violin down and began walking toward the crack. Just as he reached for the handle, William and Mary came upon Gem Marie standing in the doorway. Mary, her voice dripping with arrogance, spoke sharply. "Well, darkie, what do you have to say for yourself? That was the most horrid performance I've ever heard in my life. I've heard wildcats caught in rose bushes hit better notes than whatever that was." Gem Marie remained silent, her deliberate lack of response fanning the flames of Mary's anger. "How dare you act mute and simple, sneaking around and trying to steal my piece! I'll see to it that you're flogged and punished for touching such a fine instrument. You're nothing but a talentless thief!" Mary spat, her voice growing louder. "I can't decide if I should have you thrown out for that awful playing or for pretending you didn't understand me the other day." William, unable to hide his amusement, chuckled and interrupted. "Now, Mary, give the girl a chance to explain herself." He turned to Gem Marie, grinning. "Come now, speak up. Who taught you to play, darkie? You must be able to talk if you can almost play as well as we can." Mary's eyes flared with indignation. "Almost play as well as us? William, you can't be serious! You're insulting us by comparing our skill to *that* if you can even call it music! It was simply dreadful." William raised his hands to calm Mary down. "Now, now, Mary, let's not get carried away. I'm just trying to make sense of things. Of course, she can't play like us." William now with a cross look on his face directed his irritation towards Gem Marie, "Speak up, girl! Who taught you!" Suddenly, the door behind Gem Marie swung wide open. Professor Hertz stormed into the doorway, his voice booming with authority. "No one! No one taught her anything because it was I who was playing!" Professor Hertz, now seething with anger, stormed fully into the hallway, and demanded silence. His voice echoed with authority as he barked, "Everyone, back to the auditorium! Now! Rehearsal isn't over!" He glared at the group with disdain. "Here I am, wasting my time simplifying this piece and why, because your uninspired playing couldn't handle it in its true form. The audience beyond the third row can barely hear you, and when they do, it's an assault on the ears. Instead of dedicating yourselves to practice, you wander the halls, mistreating the staff and distracting them from their work." His voice rose with the weight of his frustration. "This isn't just about playing the right notes. It's about discipline and responsibility! Our performance is less than two weeks away, and you choose *now* to indulge in childish antics?" Professor Hertz stepped closer, his anger evident, he roughly ushered Gem Marie back toward the classroom. "And you!" his eyes now fixed on Mary. "You waste time causing trouble, when your renditions of Vivaldi wouldn't even impress a pig in the filthiest corner of pig town!" Now shifting his attention onto William he spoke with contempt. " And to think you William would dare treat her that way when your own playing is far from adequate. Your index finger has placed so many assaults on that Stradivarius it should be severed at the joint." Mary gasped in horror, her eyes brimming with tears, while William fumbled to apologize, his words a tangled mess as he tried to soothe her. Professor Hertz's words lingered like a dark cloud over them. Each syllable a reminder of the crushing weight of their shortcomings. Now aware of the other students gathering around Professor Hertz's temper began to taper off. With all eyes focused on him, he made and loud final announcement, his voice louder than usual as he singled out briefly another set of children who also frequently roamed the halls, "No one is to wander on this hall ever again, the silence in the hallways must never be broken. Do you understand?" Everyone nodded and quickly scurried off down the steps. The only sounds left were feet shuffling and instruments being bumped against one another. Gem Marie, who had eased back into the room smiled and began folding some items and placing them on a chair. She quickly picked up some instruments and started polishing them in order not to vex the professor any further. Once professor Hertz heard complete silence from the halls, he slowly closed the door and locked it with a key. He sat back around the piano and with frustration slammed his fist onto the keys. His posture slumped in a position that reflected some emotional breakdown. Gem Marie picked up a nearby violin, then slowly walked over to him and sat down beside him on the bench with her back to him. With one leg elongated she softly began playing a piece that she had learned from her French music teacher, he had warned her that the musical piece was considered to be romantic. With the right precision and tone it was guaranteed to calm any savage beast. Gem Marie now recalling that whenever she would practice it, Greta, and all the servants would gather in the parlor and listen some of them would have a look as if they were going to drift off to sleep. Without fail the servants would search for something to clean or tidy while she played so that they could remain in the room. Monsieur, who would sometimes question why did all the servants have to clean one room all at the same time. Even he himself would also stop what he was doing and listen her play attentively as he relaxed in an armchair.. Greta would blush and secretly blow a kiss to Gem Marie as she left the room. Gem Marie never understood then why this particular piece had such an effect on everyone. She just knew that the castle was often calm and peaceful after she played it. It even seemed like the birds sang louder and clearer in the garden after. Once again it was now having the same effect on Professor Hertz. For once he heard Gem Marie playing, he stopped ringing his handkerchief and listened in awe. Once Gem Marie cease playing, he turned to her and said "Chopin nocturne in E flat that piece is relatively new how on earth did you learn that. Did Christian Pierre teach you that also? Don't answer that, So, you can play the violin well what about the piano? Tell me blessed talented one, what else can those gifted little petite fingers play and do? Then professor Hertz looked into Gem Marie's eyes, as if he had just noticed her almond shaped chestnut brown eyes and was now becoming hypnotized by them. He gently removed some dust from her face then slid closer to her and whispered, " Where are you from?" Gem Marie, who was taken back by the change of the mood in the room, quickly rose from the bench and stood at the end of the piano. Now frighten by the professor's tone of voice she redirected the attention on his upcoming performance. She asked him, "What is the most troublesome part of the performance." He told Gem Marie that he was not really sure because on certain days they play with perfection and other days there are obvious weak points. He stated that he was trying to accommodate the piece so that the student's imperfections would go unnoticed. Gem Marie ask him if he could show her what he meant. As soon as Professor Hertz began playing the piece again, Gem Marie picked up the violin and began playing along. She looked for a focal point on the wall, once she found an area the was clear and white, she began seeing figures moving on the wall. She continued to stare until the figures took shape, like a moving picture she saw herself back in the parlor at the Scotney. She let out a sigh of relief and continued playing once she saw the imaginative figures of Monsieur Heritage, Greta, Aunt Elenor and all the servants. They were standing around watching her in amazement. Right in the middle of the piece Greta spoke out and said, " She must never leave us again." Monsieur Heritage nodded in agreement then he turned to his left where seated next to him was a younger version of Gem Marie. The smaller version of herself was about five years old she was playing with his hand and humming a song. Gem Marie felt like she was now caught between being a spectator and a participant of her own performance. As she continued to play, she searched Monsieur Heritage's face for his usual approval of her musical rendition. She played more passionately, stepping closer to him with each note, but each time she moved forward, he turned his gaze away. Now, standing directly before him, she poured even more intensity into her playing, her fingers pressing into the strings as the bow glided fervently across them, trying to capture his attention. But the more passion she infused into her performance, the more Monsieur seemed to ignore her. Finally, Gem Marie closed her eyes, unable to bear the sting of being overlooked. She let herself listen as the piano swelled in the background, harmonizing with her violin, until, at last, the only sound she heard was the shriek of her bow dragging across the strings. Opening her eyes, she saw Professor Hertz standing before her, watching intently. Without a word, he reached out, pulling her into a tight embrace, his hands trembling. Gem Marie, frightened, felt herself begin to shake as well. Their trembling bodies pressed together, blurring the lines of whose tremors were whose, as they held onto each other in unison. His voice filled with firmness and desire. "Where did you come from? I know you say Christian Pierre taught you everything you know. Professor Hertz continued probing, "But I must understand the origin of your bloodline. No one with your... hue could possibly possess the mental faculties to grasp such a complex piece. Surely, you must come from a place where freaks of nature are more common." Gem Marie was stunned, trying to process Professor Hertz's words. *Her hue?* What could he possibly mean by that? She couldn't fathom what her skin color had to do with anything related to her intellect or capabilities. She had received an exceptional education since the age of four and, according to Monsieur, often excelled independently in her studies. *What did the color of her skin have to do with her mind, her hands, or her ears?* This world beyond the castle consumes themselves with less irrelevant things. Now taking a mental survey of the schools daily operation she thought, " No one has attended to the land or the animals, the garden was neglected with only two rose bushes and some wildflowers. This is a school of music with a Headmaster only concerned with the student's geography." Gem Marie pondered to herself again, "Why does a brilliant man of music speak so foolish and obtuse." Professor Hertz now slightly irritated at Gem Marie' lengthy silence demanded to know the reasoning to her behavior. "Why do you stand there with star gazed eyes? Answer me now, you are terrorizing to my soul.

Don't you understand you have just played Mozart's Alla Turca without a flaw better than my own students that I have trained for years. I'm even afraid to admit maybe better than I. Some of these students have traveled to Italy and stayed for years in order to gain a moment to study under the great students of Mozart himself. Now you stand before me, as the child or woman of no name, no father, no explanation and play without effort like you had been born with the instrument." The professor, now sensing the reality of his words, moved in closer to Gem Marie. "I demand to know now What is your name girl!? Do you not hear me?" Dr. Hertz, now feeling overwhelmed and engulfed by Gem Marie's whole presence, grabbed her hands, and held them tightly in a plea for truth and honesty from her. "Woman! with the hue of a beehive honey speak now, and unveil your origin. My brother has sent you here to me to find logic and reason for your rarity, but I believe you were sent here to torture me, a curse perhaps. Some rare debt I owe to the powers unseen. Perhaps you are as rare and odd as the five-legged calf." Professor Hertz, now becoming calm the concept that he may have just stumbled onto his very own musical protégé, he moved back towards Gem Marie and without thought he pull her into an embrace and began confessing his soul. "As I hold you in my arms now my tremors have subsided but yours have risen like the waves in the Atlantic. You must speak child now because you have come too far to go back to your fabricated tales of being a mute. Professor Hertz's tone now soaked in desperation threaten, "I demand you answer me now girl or I will flog you to an inch of your life do you hear me!" Filled with mixed emotions without thought he kissed Gem Marie then quickly turned her loose then glided across the room in delight. Gem Marie in shock said nothing as the professor spoke. Her mind was racing, trying to process the first kiss ever given to her. Now trying to determine if she should just tell the complete truth about being raised in the Scotney. Should she reveal all the teachings she had received since age four or should she remain silent. She pondered again and asked herself, "Why did he kiss me is he in love with me like I was with Christian Pierre." With not enough time to gather the proper game plan within her head she continued her nonresponsive status while savoring the last couple of seconds of her silence. Professor Hertz, still examining her, had now grown impatient. In an attempt to get her to speak he raised his hand in the air, the sole intention of the gesture was to place fear within her. Now with his hand in a position to strike her face, his eyes danced with confirmation that his action was no façade. Right before he was about to release his hand back down to solidify the action with her cheek, Gem Marie out of pure fear quickly spoke loudly, "My name is Gem Marie, and I do not know where I am from because I was found at age four. Christian Pierre took me away with him after I was abandon by a woman who was said to have stolen me from my true mother. From the age of four I was locked in a room similar to this one and given various instruments. I was told they would lay them down in front of me and whichever one I selected or touched I was then made to learn it and master it. With no contact with the outside world, every day I was only given music and a few books. I was not allowed to move on to another until I had completely mastered the one before. I did not clean rooms, nor did I work fields, I did not play nor was I ever struck. I stayed alone in a room with instruments, it was them and the birds in the trees that were my only companions. I knew nothing about the world cursing my hue because music was my master and the only world I knew were the notes to be played. So, if you must strike me Professor Hertz, for a skill I was threaten and tortured in solitude to master, step forward my new gatekeeper. I only played to try and bring comfort to you like I had often done with Christian Pierre. But you are not the same. You are different, you do not sit in a high back chair and revel in the beauty of the piece or cradle yourself in the comfort of the notes. No, you my gatekeeper are the master of the origins with hue indifference your allegiance is not to the music itself. You prefer to strike me. Not for my follies within the piece but for mastering it too well. According to you my hue in your world could never master such a sound. I ask you now Professor Hertz self-proclaim ruler of the Canterbury Conservatory are you and Christian Pierre not comrades. Are you not a lover of the music itself regardless of the hands that have produced it." Gem Marie knew that by comparing professor hertz to Christian Pierre social elite levels would make him resort back to his more civilized ways. From what she had read in the newspapers about Christian Pierre's many accomplishments, she knew that Professor Hertz was nowhere near his level. Monsieur heritage' and Christian Pierre were both men of power that ruled over many lands here and abroad they were men that did concern themselves with the laws of the land because they had created their own worlds with their own laws. She knew by making him believe that she viewed him on the same level as Christian Pierre was enough for his ego to make sure that his temper remained calm as a gentleman should. After absorbing every word Gem Marie had shared, he

144

added one sentence of observation, "You were given an educated also. Christian Pierre has given you the knowledge that could cost you and I our lives. He's simply gone mad." Professor Hertz quietly withdrew, retrieving an old violin ensconced in a weathered brown cloth bag from a nearby mantel. With delicate care, he unveiled the instrument, cradling it tenderly upon his lap, his fingers caressing its weathered frame as if coaxing secrets from its very soul. For a lingering moment, he sat in silent contemplation, his gaze fixed upon Gem Marie, each syllable of her narrative still echoing in his mind. Eventually, he beckoned her forth, and she approached him tentatively. With a graceful gesture, he extended the aged violin towards her, entrusting it into her care. He imparted a solemn instruction, to cleanse and safeguard this instrument, for it bore the weight of sentimental significance. It was the inaugural gift bestowed upon him by his father. Despite its imperfections, it was the catalyst for his profound lifelong love affair with music. Gem Marie, now handling it with care diligently polished the violin, then tenderly placed it amidst a tableau of cherished treasures upon the mantel. flanked by two brass goblets adorned with glistening rubies. As she meticulously tended to the room's artifacts, she began to discern the meticulous curation of Professor Hertz's collection, each item a testament to a cherished memory or passion. Meanwhile, Professor Hertz, now seated at the piano, softly tinkered with the keys, his gaze drifting towards Gem Marie with a sense of quiet admiration. He outlined a role for her, a way to incorporate her great talent without anyone becoming aware. She would be concealed behind the stage curtain, she would act as a guardian of musical integrity. At critical junctures, when William and Mary faltered, Gem Marie would intercede, her violin resounding boldly to cloak their errors in a symphony of harmony. Eager anticipation kindled within Gem Marie's heart at the prospect of this performance, a departure from her accustomed routine within the conservatory. Professor Hertz's unwavering belief in her abilities stirred her with newfound confidence. Unable to contain her enthusiasm, she implored him for an opportunity to rehearse immediately. With a nod of acceptance, Professor Hertz granted her wish, setting the stage for a hidden collaboration that would weave together their talents in a tapestry of musical mastery. Now with the door locked tightly and the freedom to manipulate the instrument without qualm. Gem Marie held the violin in her hand, she looked around the room until she locked eyes with a velvet piece of cloth. She draped the violin across her left shoulder and gently strummed the first note of Mendelssohn's violin concerto. Monsieur had insisted that she learn the piece, despite her music teacher's reservations, who believed it was too challenging for her. Gem Marie had expressed her unease to her teacher about the rapid finger movements required by the piece. However, it wasn't until one afternoon when Monsieur Heritage informed her, "The violin will come to your aid one day. You will thanked me for putting a short halt to your love affair with your Harp." He then requested to hear how much of the concerto she had mastered. When her teacher informed Monsieur Heritage that he had changed her assignment to a Bach piece she already knew well, Monsieur Heritage swiftly reprimanded him along with questioning whether the teacher was concern with her abilities or was he afraid that she may surpass his skills. Gem Marie felt a swell of pride at Monsieur's confidence in her abilities and became determined to master the concerto quickly and flawlessly to please him. Now, standing in the room with Professor Hertz, she felt the weight of expectation pressing upon her, knowing she had to perform the piece with absolute perfection. As Gem Marie reached the midway point of her performance, Professor Hertz reached for a handkerchief and gently dabbed his eyes. When she finished, he sat in silence, his gaze fixed upon her. Feeling a hint of discomfort, Gem Marie finally broke the silence and asked, "My playing brought forth a tear from your eye. Does my performance not please you? I must confess, I detected only one mistake throughout my playing; please forgive my error." Rising from his seat, Professor Hertz responded, "Your rendition has indeed brought me great joy. However, my tears were not from disappointment of your skills but rather of sorrow of your absence. It pains me to realize that despite your magnificent talent, you may never have the opportunity to be appreciated by an audience. There will be no bravos nor roses tossed at your feet. Because society fails to recognize the power of your music, you are relegated to remain behind the curtains, while those less gifted are praised for their mediocrity." Listening intently, Gem Marie came to a stark realization: the world was not as magical as she had imagined. It was rife with prejudice and individuals unable to express their true selves. Professor Hertz acknowledged that Gem Marie's playing was far from subpar, yet he remained fearful of society's judgment, thereby denying her the chance to perform openly. Behind a black heavy curtain, she would have to remain for the entire performance. Now recalling the incident with the newspaper had disillusioned her. It had led her to believe in the existence of interesting people and places to explore. Now, she was certain that the articles Monsieur had removed from the paper might have contained the truth. In that moment, she resolved to play like never before, producing a sound so profound and distinct that anyone with an ear for music would be captivated. As the performance approached, only twelve days remained. Gem Marie, who had been stealthily tucked away in the balcony during rehearsals, had diligently absorbed every note, with her already familiarized with the works of the great composers. The only remaining challenge was the professor's original composition, particularly a concerto that had posed difficulties for William and Mary. One morning, after a night of intense practice of the original piece, Gem Marie dozed off in the professor's music room, while he reclined on a nearby lounge, still fatigued from his own efforts. As dawn approached, they both rose and stood by the window overlooking the morning rituals of the town. While observing the bustling activity below, Professor Hertz noticed Gem Marie's fascination with the morning scene, he seized the relaxing moment to inquire about her experiences back when she served Christian Pierre. "Did you witness scenes like this back home?" he probed. Gem Marie, sustained by the liveliness outside, replied, "No, Monsieur ensured that everything was in order by the time I joined him for the morning meals. I was not allowed to question the outside world nor was I ever permitted to go into town." Her slip of referring to Christian as Monsieur startled her, she anxiously awaited the professor's reaction. Sensing her discomfort, Professor Hertz delved deeper into her past, questioning her about Christian Pierre's management of his plantation. "You address Christian Pierre as Monsieur instead of master. Why does he insist on such French formalities?" he inquired. Gem Marie, feeling a twinge of relief at having avoided revealing too much, responded calmly, "I was instructed to call him so in private, especially during musical endeavors. But if you prefer, I will not use that name again." Gem Marie, now feeling her self-consciousness intensifying, began to pondered whether she should be more meticulous in her choice of words. She tried to recall the speech patterns of Otis and Claudette, now considering their dialect to be the more appropriate one. After all, this was America, not France or England, and customs differed. Professor Hertz, now intrigued by Christian Pierre's unconventional approach to raising slaves and his evident fondness for Gem Marie's musical talents, listened intently, realizing there was more to this enslaved musical protégé. As Professor Hertz gazed out the window, a determination stirred within him to delve deeper into the enigmatic mind of Christian Pierre. The notion of peering into the inner sanctum of such a brilliant individual both intrigued and compelled him. Just as he poised to pose another probing question, his attention was diverted by the sight of a young courier hastening towards the school. Swiftly composing himself, he gestured to Gem Marie, urging her to maintain absolute silence and refrain from unlocking the door under any circumstances. With a deliberate pause, he withdrew a key from his jacket pocket and meticulously secured the door behind him, leaving Gem Marie alone in the music room. Meanwhile, Gem Marie edged closer to the window, her curiosity piqued by the scene unfolding below. She observed a slender, tall figure adorned with a saddle bag approaching, unmistakably, the usual young courier. Professor Hertz emerged, unlocking the heavy metal door to greet him. In a swift exchange, the young man proffered a letter, accompanied by some undisclosed words. With equal swiftness, the professor produced coins from his pocket, exchanging them with the messenger who promptly darted off towards the bustling marketplace. Gem Marie hastily settled into a nearby chair, her mind racing with curiosity about what had prompted the young man's sudden departure after speaking with the professor. When Professor Hertz reentered the room, she watched intently as he carefully re-read the letter for the third time, folding it with precision and tucking it into his jacket pocket. With an air of mystery surrounding him, he then approached Gem Marie, leading her to a music stand displaying the piece he had composed. In a tone tinged with impatience, the professor queried Gem Marie about her musical literacy. Sensing an air of unpredictability in his demeanor, Gem Marie felt a pang of unease, reluctant to reveal the extent of her musical knowledge. Choosing her words carefully, she hesitantly confessed, "I'm familiar with the basics, mostly playing by ear." Growing visibly frustrated, the professor handed her a sheet of paper and instructed her to study the sheet music and play what she could. Gem Marie studied the musical composition before her, marveling at its intricate complexities. It bore a striking resemblance to the piece she had heard the professor play, yet it held an additional allure, a fleeting nod to Bach's motif nestled within its notes. She wondered why then, hadn't the professor performed the piece as it was written? Was he so preoccupied with adjusting certain passages to suit William and Mary's preferences that he forgot the piece true composition. But even that didn't elucidate why he hadn't presented it to her in its original, unaltered form. Gem delved into the sheet music, scrutinizing each note, recalling the teachings of her music mentor, Monsieur Francois Pasquier. In the margins, inconspicuous annotations beckoned her attention with a subtle guide, perhaps mistaken for mere scribblings. Gem Marie, however, discerned their significance a roadmap to a hidden motif. Only once she had meticulously internalized every note did she dare to attempt the phantom playing in her head. Observing from a distance, Gem watched as the professor, seated at the piano, grappled with frustration, sporadically hitting keys amidst muttered expletives. Some phrases like "ninny" and "goose cap" rekindled memories of overheard conversations, snippets of which had echoed from the horse stalls on the Scotney. Though the meanings of all the unfamiliar terms eluded her, she couldn't ignore the crease of worry etched across the professor's face. She turned away and allowed her mind to drift away, with a blink of her eyes she found herself swiftly immersed in the parlor of the Scotney. Draped in a pale blue gown adorned with intricate gold trimming. Atop her head rested a delicate circle of baby's breath, the perfect crown fit for a musical sovereign. With grace, she lifted the violin from a nearby chair and raised the instrument to her chin, positioning the sheet music upon her lap, while extending her right leg forward for stability. As her fingers danced across the strings, she meticulously adjusted the tempo, slowing in areas marked for emphasis and accelerating through passages where notes had been struck out. With closed eyes, she traced the melodies, humming softly to synchronize her inner symphony with the harmonies emerging from her fingertips. In her mind's eye, she soared, carried away by the music, transported to the familiar embrace of her homeland at the Scotney. There, amidst the ethereal strains, she envisioned faces emerging from doorways, welcoming her with warmth and familiarity. "Welcome home," a voice whispered, echoing through the chamber of her consciousness. Following that a sharp crack of thunder, jolted Gem Marie back to reality as the Professor abruptly snatched the violin from her hands. Her eyes fluttered open, meeting his furious gaze; his face was flushed with anger. Accusations flew from his lips like lightning, accusing her of espionage and questioning how she wielded the complexities of music so effortlessly, as if she were a master. Stunned, Gem Marie struggled to comprehend the sudden hostility. Where was the reverence for music, the appreciation for its power? Confusion creased her brow as she pondered his accusations, trying to uncover the true motive behind his outburst. She turned and walked slowly to the window, gathering her thoughts. With nowhere else to turn, Gem Marie decided to cast off the pretense of ignorance she'd held for so long. She turned to the Professor with newfound confidence and revealed her mastery of music, recounting how she'd learned to read compositions after being sold and entrusted with forbidden pieces of music scores she was never allowed to replicate, as they bore illicit origins. The Professor's face showed disbelief. "Stolen? From Johann himself? Good heavens, are you certain?" Gem Marie, emboldened by his reaction, overjoyed by his ignorance of the Bach method, she directed him to examine the corner of the sheet music. She pointed out a specific corner and urged him to read the notes carefully. Confusion crossed his face as he recited, hesitantly, "B, a, c, h." His eyes widened in horror as he uttered the final letter. Gem Marie swiftly reclaimed the sheet, now fully aware of her command over these musical resources. Speaking with calm authority, she laid out her terms: to reach the pinnacle of performance, she must play the piece solo, hidden behind a curtain, while the others provide a soft, repetitive accompaniment. She walked up to Professor Hertz and instructed the layout of the upcoming performance. Each musician would be strategically positioned to muffle the others ears, so that would only be able to hear themselves playing Ensuring that only Gem Marie's melody reached the audience's ears. Gem Marie requested a list of supplies, to which Professor Hertz promised to furnish a list of requirements for the construction of a device to amplify her sound, Gem Marie stipulated that no questions be asked while she worked on the apparatus. As the professor's piercing inquiry cut through the air, Gem Marie found herself under the spotlight. "From whom else did you learn to play? I know of your tales with Christian Pierre, but surely, you've been exposed to someone else. I'm in shock that he would invest so much time in training you, only to swiftly release you into the squallers. Surely, your hue may have influenced your current whereabouts, but are you certain about the reason for your departure from Christian Pierre?" Gem Marie's initial confidence wavered slightly as she began to regret divulging the extent of her training to the professor. Yet, bolstered by a newfound resolve, she pressed on. No longer shackled by the fear of repercussions, she embraced her musical prowess. In that fleeting moment, she tasted freedom once more, unencumbered by societal expectations. It was then that she realized her yearning for the outside world had led to her imprisonment. The bars she once perceived as confining her within the castle were, in truth, erected to keep the chaos of the outside world at bay. With a disdainful glare out the window, she pondered the professor's probing question. The bustling figures below resembled ants in an intricate ant farm, each with their own purpose and destination. Why should they concern themselves with a young girl blessed with musical talent? Beyond the castle walls, there existed no true freedom, only the illusion of it. Now, her longing to return to the Scotney outweighed her apprehensions. Turning to the professor, Gem Marie's voice resonated with passion and certainty, a beacon of defiance against the constraints of her reality. "My journey has been far and wide compared to the my years. If I spoke of castles and gowns, you would call me a liar and flog me for being insubordinate, Yet my exposure to diverse cultures and esteemed dignitaries was orchestrated by Christian Pierre. He confined me, shielding his prized gem from the outside world, as he often dubbed me. Only he, and now you, professor, are privy to my talents." Her words hung in the air, overflowing with significance. "You may question how I acquired such refinement, or we can forge ahead with plans to craft one of the most remarkable performances this school has ever seen." The professor found himself deeply immersed in the enigmatic allure and unexpected twists of Gem Marie's narrative. The recent wire message he had received confirmed the attendance of several important guests appearance at the upcoming show. Faced with such compelling circumstances, he couldn't decline Gem Marie's proposition. With a tender gesture, he escorted her to a nearby chair, where he delicately placed the violin in her lap after gently wiping a bead of sweat from her brow with a clean kerchief retrieved from his pocket. Taking his seat at the piano, he explained, "As you prepare to play, I will transition from the role of maestro conductor to positioning myself at the piano in front of the stage. I'll commence the piece with you, discreetly, so none of the students are aware. My actions will serve as a deliberate distraction, drawing the audience's attention towards me. It's during this diversion that your performance must captivate. Remember, you mustn't falter." Gem Marie, pleased that her persuasive discourse had convinced the professor, couldn't suppress a smile, mirroring his own expression, reminiscent of the gaze Monsieur once bestowed upon a freshly prepared rack of lamb. "Please, call me Gem Marie. It's a name I've chosen for myself," she insisted. Agreeing with a nod, the professor raised his right hand, signaling Gem Marie to begin the piece.

Chapter: 13

The Device

Three days before the show, a young messenger boy arrived, carrying a sack filled with various items, its weight evident as he constantly shifted it from one arm to the other. Gem watched eagerly from the window as Professor Hertz greeted the boy, taking the sack from him and kindly slipping him a few coins in thanks. Bursting with excitement, Gem knew the sack held the essential components for building the mechanism that would amplify her playing. Without mentioning to Professor Hertz that she had already painstakingly built a smaller prototype back at the Scotney, she had requested these parts to be delivered within a day. This inspiration came from Monsieur Heritage, who had one day returned to the Scotney brimming with enthusiasm after seeing an apparatus displayed in town by a local inventor named Edward Hughes. The device had instantly captivated him, as it could amplify voices and music, making them sound fuller and clearer. Gem Marie had become utterly captivated by Monsieur Heritage's tales and detailed descriptions of a device known as the carbon microphone. Her fascination grew so intense that she begged him to uncover its secrets. Unable to refuse her, Monsieur devised a plan. During his next visit with the inventor, he would subtly inquire about the key components while discussing the banking industry, hoping to gather just enough information. Monsieur soon gathered the necessary parts, trusting in Gem Marie's abilities even more than his own capacity to teach her science. Under his guidance, she carefully assembled her own version of the device. As she completed it, a faint echo of sound emerged, signaling her success. Standing before the microphone, Gem Marie began to hum a tune, and Monsieur immediately recognized the significance of her creation. Gently, he took it from her hands for safekeeping. "This is not a toy like your dolls, mon amour," he said softly. "This is a great invention." Although she never saw the microphone again, Gem Marie remembered every detail Monsieur Heritage had shared with her in order to bring it to life. Professor Hertz entered the room carrying a sack, and Gem Marie, who had been pretending to dust, watched him closely, stealing glances from the corner of her eye as he began unloading its contents. Her breath hitched when she spotted a megaphone among the items a new addition she hadn't seen before. Unable to contain herself, she let out a squeal of delight. The professor, sensing her excitement, finally turned to her with an amused yet wary expression. "So, Gem Marie, what do you plan to do with all these things? Some of them I had to acquire through my brother, who was quite puzzled. He questioned what instrument could possibly need such... peculiar items. Naturally, he assumed I was trying to amplify sound for the upcoming performance, yet you gave no clue as to their purpose." Gem Marie, still keeping a respectable distance and waiting for his permission to touch the objects, responded with barely concealed joy. "They're not meant to be added to the instrument itself. They're to be arranged around it... to make its sound louder." The professor froze, processing her words, then strode over to her and seized her arm, steering her firmly toward the table where the items lay spread out. His voice was sharp, almost cutting. "Again, you reveal knowledge that is far beyond your kind knowledge forbidden for someone of your color. Christian Pierre is reckless, a madman, teaching you language, now science? Absurd! We could both be jailed and hung for such a matter." This time, the professor's harsh words barely grazed her, his words were becoming gibberish the more he spoke, Gem Marie knew, deep down, that when he had agreed to fetch the items on her list, his curiosity about her talents had begun to outweigh his fear of her forbidden knowledge. She could see he was growing intrigued by her, her hue no longer a factor his fondness for her was now far greater than any laws or rules. Though the very thought of her abilities seemed to unsettle him, to the point of almost frightening him with its intensity he knew he was witnessing greatness at first hand. If he hadn't seen the construction of it himself with his own eyes he would have declared it impossible. Gem Marie simply smiled at the professor and walked over to the corner of the room where he kept all his tools for the instruments. She quietly began creating a replica of the device she had made once before. After growing tired of watching her, the professor moved to his piano and began practicing. An hour later, at eight A.M., there was a knock on the door, the morning rehearsal had already begun. The student had been waiting for Professor Hertz to arrive, one of the students, Frederick, spoke through the locked door. He first inquired if Professor Hertz was feeling well and then asked if he would be attending the rehearsal. The professor, unaware that time had slipped away, quickly replied that he would be there shortly and instructed Frederick to begin without him. He reminded Gem Marie, as usual, not to open the door and to remain silent until he returned. Gem Marie, engrossed in her work on the device and eager for him to leave, nodded quickly, dismissing him with a wave of her hand. The professor, taken aback by her attitude, walked over to her, and grabbed her wrist so tightly that a piece of metal fell from her hands. Quickly regaining his composure, he smirked at her defiance, then raised her hand, and kissed the back of it. Quoting Shakespeare, he said, "Make the doors upon a woman's wit, and it will out at the casement. "Unable to maintain her submissive facade, Gem Marie retorted, "Shut that, and 'twill out at the keyhole; stop that, 'twill fly with smoke out at the chimney. "In complete astonishment and rage, the professor drew back his hand and slapped her across the face. Shocked by his own lack of control, he stood still, watching her reaction. Gem Marie felt a stinging sensation instantly, reminiscent of a summer incident when a young colt with an unusually long tail swatted her as she stood too close behind him, admiring the silky quality of his tail. But even that couldn't compare to the blow the professor had just inflicted. She had never been struck by Monsieur or anyone else, and she stood in silence, bewildered by why the professor, when angered, always resorted to threats or violence. She pondered in comparison while tracing the imprint of his hand. Fear was always his motivation when resorting to violence, afraid of anyone the barbaric behavior was becoming redundant. "Was this a rule in America that didn't exist in the Scotney? Is that why Monsieur never displayed such distasteful behavior? Perhaps he was aware of not only the physical pain it caused but the internal ache the blow left behind. Gem Marie facing the professor stared while trying to fathom why he had resorted to such behavior could say nothing else but "Forgive give me sir." Now, looking into her tearful eyes, Professor Hertz detected a genuine look of confusion and hurt. Observing this, he muttered, "I favored you more when you were a mute," he then proceeded to the door, he removed a long skeleton key from his pocket and locked it behind him. Gem Marie, now alone, rubbed her face one last time then diverted her attention back onto the device. The stinging on her face was quickly forgotten as she picked up the piece of metal that had fallen to the floor and resumed assembling the parts. She worked diligently, trying to recall everything she had learned while at the Scotney. Once the device was complete, she placed it on the table in front of her. Nervous about testing it, she hesitated, strumming a single note on the violin.

The sound was faint, making it difficult to determine if the device was working properly. Fearing the possible repercussions of being overheard, she decided to wait until Professor Hertz returned from rehearsal. In the meantime, she studied the sheet music again, silently practicing the violin in her head. Afterwards she moved over to a opposite end of the room where a room divider sat. There under a large dusty throw was a gown hidden beneath She dusted and wiped the gown clean. It was just her size, adorned in elegant purple lace, she rehearsed the words she would say to the professor in order to get him to allow her to wear the gown to the performance. Although she knew no one would see her, she still felt the desire to wear something elegant. Reflecting on the gowns Monsieur Heritage had given her, she realized how fortunate she was. She understood that appearances mattered; those who looked like Monsieur Heritage were often seen as natural leaders. Gem Marie's view of the outside world was bleak, it seemed poor and cruel, lacking the castles and gardens of bluebells she had once known. Most of all it lacked the love and kindness she was use to, as a trail of bitterness travel through her she wondered why Monsieur had never warned her about the world's fickle and harsh ways. Gem Marie walked to the window, watching as people loaded into carriages, the anticipation of the upcoming concert evident. Packages were being delivered to the school, and various people were buying tickets. Only now did it dawn on her: the performances she had once read about in the newspapers would soon include her own. Several coaches arrived, and one of the younger students, dressed as a jester, ran to one of the carriages with two pieces of paper. He played the role of a court fool, handing the papers through the coach's open door. Gem Marie couldn't see inside the carriage, she only caught sight of a man's hand reaching out to accept the papers. The hand had a large ring on one of its fingers that glittered in the morning light, and the edges of the man's sleeve were adorned with gold trim which in return handed the student a piece of paper. In all her days of peering out of the window, she had never seen anyone dressed in such clothing. As the coach pulled off, she could see the professor peering out of the front door, he quickly snatched the paper from the student's hand as he held the door open, still watching the carriage as it travel down the path. Then without warning he quickly slammed the door behind him. The sight of the mysterious man's hand made Gem Marie long for the Scotney. Determined, she decided to prepare herself and come up with a plan in case there were any visitors from England at the show. Later that evening, Professor Hertz returned to the room surprisingly in better spirits. He informed Gem Marie that very important guests would be arriving and that she must make herself scarce. He pulled out a piece of paper out his inner jacket pocket on which he had sketched the final layout of the orchestra seating. Pointing to an area on the paper, he spoke sternly to Gem Marie, " Quickly come closer, see there? That's where you will be sitting, behind the curtains on stage. You must not let anyone see you. If someone does see you, just nod and smile and start straightening and cleaning. You are a mute to everyone here except me, and you will continue to behave as such. Now, I've waited long enough, show me what that contraption does that you have spent so much time assembling." Gem Marie, now bursting with joy, eagerly complied. She quickly grabbed her violin and seated herself next to the device. Before playing, she envisioned the auditorium filled with people. In the front row sat Monsieur Heritage and Greta. Next to Greta was a tall, refined man who smiled and nodded as if to say, "Please begin." Gem Marie raised her bow and gently laid it on the first string. She began playing the section assigned to her by the professor. In the background, she could hear William and Mary attempting the same section, prompting her to strum the bow louder and faster. As the echo of her music resonated through the device she had constructed, she felt herself being transported. She was no longer in the auditorium; she was now in the brand-new gallant Music Hall in England. She sauntered down the grand stairs that Monsieur had described one evening after attending a concert there. The melody consumed her, prompting her to sway back and forth. Unaware she had risen from her seat, Gem Marie found herself standing in front of the newly assembled device, enveloped by the melodic vibrations. Her attention abruptly snapped back to the present when Professor Hertz shouted, "Bravo!" Gem Marie had reached the end of the concerto without realizing it. Professor Hertz with love and admiration in his eyes walked towards Gem Marie. With his arms held up open in front of him he approached her while speaking, "You still have plenty of life in you, my old friend." Gem Marie now confused watched Professor Hertz as he carefully removed the violin from her hands. "Father said you would last for years and bring me great joy. You've allowed yourself to be handled by another, but only with my blessing." Gem Marie continued to watch as Professor Hertz spoke to the now cradled inanimate object. "You give all of yourself, as you know no other way but greatness. Though slightly worn, your capabilities far exceed your years. You were the one who awakened my true love for music. Now, you must give yourself again on the day of the performance without hesitation." Gem Marie watched in amazement and silence as the professor then held the violin upright and kissed its neck softly. His lips brushed against a section of the Alpine spruce that had lost its shine and smoothness. He quickly reached for some Danish oil that he kept in a small sack on the mantle. Astonished she watched the professor as he wiped and smoothed out the instrument. He spoke again, this time acknowledging Gem Marie. "The sound was remarkable. I've never witnessed such a thing, once again you have managed to awaken the piece in so many ways. I had forgotten the power of its melody. Tell me, you say Christian Pierre had one similar constructed in secret correct. Oh, its Magnificent! This is a very unique device, almost a breakthrough. However, you won't be using it. Its greater purpose will be used for far greater use. My soloist will be singing, and I shall place it right beside her, in conspicuously of course, and I don't want it moved. I was fortunate to have her participate in this production as it is, and this will magnify the performance to levels unheard of. I won't have it any other way." Gem Marie, shocked, bit her tongue to suppress her scream. Professor Hertz had known all along that he would not allow her to be heard; he only wanted her to construct the instrument for his own use. Furious, she bit her tongue again, the pain sending a jolt through her body like cold water thrown on her. She watched as he examined the device, rubbing his finger against the metal she had meticulously hammered together, while tugging on a small string that was wrapped around it. Her realization was clear: the professor had never intended for her talent to shine, only to exploit her craftsmanship for his own acclaim. The bitterness of betrayal and the sting of unacknowledged brilliance surged within her finally after several minutes of her standing in silence. Taking matters into her own hands, Gem Marie positioned herself strategically near the violin, seizing a moment of opportunity she began speaking, "Your vision is truly remarkable, sir," she interjected calmly. "Surely, the anticipation for your showcase will be immense. Will the newspapers grace us with their presence?" Professor Hertz, still basking in the glow of his impending triumph, confirmed the widespread interest in the event. With the professor's attention focused upon his own ego, Gem Marie deftly steered the conversation back onto the device. She had taken the time to construct the apparatus, and she was not going to allow it to be used by anyone unworthy.

She paused for a moment then took some steps forward towards Professor Hertz. Running her finger across the device she spoke calmly, "It will be a wonderous thing if the Newspaper are in attendance, don't you agree. With all the practice you've done I just know William and Mary will give their greatest flawless performance which will complement your soloist. Of course, with the aid of the device their wonderful playing will definitely be magnified by the unique device," Gem Marie remarked, injecting reassurance into her tone as she took note of the professor's facial expression. A flicker of concern crossed Professor Hertz's face as he mentally summarized the extent of William and Mary's inadequacies. He had just chastised them in rehearsal this morning for their inexcusable faux par. Gem Marie's smile widened as she stood with her back turned, transmuting the weight of expectation that was settling on the professor's shoulders. With the impending scrutiny of critics, parents and newspapers looming, the success of the upcoming performance was paramount. Sensing an opportunity to solidify his fears, Gem Marie pledged her full commitment to ensuring the event's success sarcastically. "Rest assured, sir, I will play with vigor, enhancing your piece without compromising its integrity," she declared with conviction. The realization dawned on Professor Hertz that any misstep could jeopardize not only his reputation but also the patronage upon which he relied. Gem Marie's words resonated with the gravity of the situation, prompting him to redouble his efforts to ensure perfection. The trust of the students' parents, who had entrusted him with their children's musical future, hung in the balance. William and Mary's parents, were known for their generous contributions to school fees, wielded considerable influence over others in the community. The rumors of a new school on the horizon near Virginia provided a tempting alternative for some parents if dissatisfied with current performance levels. After composing himself, Professor Hertz strolled purposefully to the violin he kept delicately laid on the mantel. With a determined gaze, he turned to Gem Marie and spoke with conviction. "I shall prepare the new strings for this instrument, while you, my dear, will perform with the contraption behind the curtain. I only realized my soloist has a very strong healthy voice and will not require the device. Together, we shall unveil a rendition of the piece unlike any ever heard before." Gem Marie smiled internally, her mental semantics on the professor had worked. Now her playing would definitely be heard although behind curtains out of sight she did not care, the concert would mark her first performance on a stage in front of an audience. With one more day before the performance, Gem Marie stood at the window, watching the daily lines of people purchasing tickets for the next day's event. They were socialites from all over, Gem Marie amused herself by trying to guess their origins. Based on the fabrics of some of the women's gowns she concluded that great majority were from America and Europe. Some sent their own messenger boys, while others dispatched their coachmen to stand in line for the remaining tickets. Those with formal invitations were greeted by students in costume and given formal invitations. As visitors arrived at the entrance, their first glimpse of the school was immaculate and inviting. Statues were brought from storage and placed strategically. Everything was in its proper place, adorned with fresh roses and lilacs that transformed the classrooms into breathtaking spaces. Fresh pinecones and wild mint were placed in all the fireplaces, just as Gem Marie remembered Madam Henry and Greta artfully arranging them around the Scotney, creating a crackling, scented invitation for relaxation. She meticulously recreated these Scotney touches throughout the entire school, often feeling as if she were at home. When Professor Hertz caught the cozy aroma wafting through the halls, he was so pleased that he brought Gem Marie a piece of fresh fowl and a large slice of cake that evening. With the performance just a day away, the professor seemed both terrified and exhilarated. His demeanor shifted at times during the day, causing Gem Marie to speak only when spoken to and to carefully stay out of his way. Each time the professor left the room, she would meticulously organized his notes and instruments in the precise order he preferred, often dusting, and wiping until everything gleamed. The usual young messenger boy who delivered letters to Professor Hertz had appeared three times that day. Immediately after his third visit, Professor Hertz rushed into the room, quickly locking the door behind him and wedging a chair against it for added security. With a stern wag of his finger, he demanded that Gem Marie play the Bach section of her piece exactly as she intended to during the performance. Slightly unsettled by the professor's intense demeanor, Gem Marie lifted her violin to her chin. Just as she was about to begin, she paused and informed him that the strings he had attached hadn't dried completely. Before she could finish, he interrupted sharply, insisting she play immediately and forbidding any further delay. Reluctantly, Gem Marie began. Her sound was beautiful until she reached the demanding section with a crescendo, the rigorous strain on the bow caused one of the strings to snap. Professor Hertz quickly seized the instrument from her hands, demanding to know why the string had failed. Calmly, Gem Marie explained once again without interruption that the strings hadn't fully dried before he attached them but mentioned that there were more by the fireplace, which should be dry and ready for use. The professor, who had learned how to make violin strings from his father as a child, knew Gem Marie was right. In his eagerness, he had restrung the violin prematurely. Noticing his frustration, Gem Marie quickly poured a glass of wine into a King's goblet. The professor, amused by her choice, smiled, sat down at his piano, and drank from the cup that was given to him as a novelty item. He took a deep breath and ran his fingers across the remaining strings of the violin. Speaking softly, he said, "This performance will be one to remember. There are many important constituents in town, there is one in particular who has been very generous to me. He and his wife have postponed their trip to the south of France, in order to grace us with his presence. "I need you to play exquisitely while remaining completely out of sight. You must not be seen by any of the guests. I promise you will be rewarded for your outstanding performance." Professor Hertz, now heading towards a harpsichord that he seldom played since Gem Marie took residence at the school, sat lavishly at its bench, and began playing various excerpts from different pieces. Noticing Gem Marie's vacant look, he continued speaking directly to her, softening his playing. "I had a pillow constructed for you, made out of down feathers, large enough for you to rest your precious head on tonight. I'm certain with its assistance, you will sleep peacefully. I also have a fresh basin with rose petals soaking in it, especially for you to cleanse yourself. You might not be aware, but that is symbolic of royalty. Oh, did I mention I spoke with my brother? He says your cousin Otis has become quite the apprentice. He has risen up and is officially my brother's one and only assistant. I'm not surprised; his loyalty and diligence have placed him where he belongs. Who knows, there could be something similar in the future for you. Well, not working on animals, of course, but it all depends on how this performance goes." Gem Marie watched as he abruptly ended his playing after his last sentence. She could tell he expected her to be overjoyed by the pillow and rose-scented water. However, Gem Marie had slept and bathed with far greater luxuries. She had once worn pure olive oil from Italy and bathed in a potion composed of frankincense and lavender from Egypt. She knew that her fate hinged on her reactions and how well her playing was received. Hidden behind the curtains, she would have no way of seeing any nods of approval. She couldn't witness the tapping of elegant hand fans from the elite women that were scheduled to fill the auditorium. There would be no external clues to gauge her performance just her alone behind the curtains, with the music as her only companion. For the first time in her life, she had to play and genuinely believe she was magnificent without any outside confirmation. The professor's behavior conveyed a sense of urgency, as if more than just the school's reputation was at stake. Fearful of revealing any skepticism, Gem Marie smiled and repeated, "Down feathers, down feathers? You are too good to me, Professor." Professor Hertz stood up from the harpsichord, goblet in hand, and walked towards the window, peering at the people bustling about. The line for the performance had dwindled, with only a few stragglers still attempting to purchase tickets. It seemed that people were more inclined to shop and stroll in the park than attend the performance. On the day of the concert, many chose to linger on the front lawn, listening to the faint strains of music that drifted through the open windows. Professor Hertz had a habit of leaving a window or two ajar, allowing the music to spill out onto the streets. "The commoners are entitled to good music too," he often proclaimed to those who mentioned hearing his concerto. Gem Marie, feeling a surge of nerves, walked over to the fireplace to check on the string she had been drying. She glanced timidly at the professor, silently asking if he would like to inspect its condition. Professor Hertz walked over and examined the string, then sat down to carefully strung the violin. "You are a creation of Christian Pierre and much like this string I have created," he began. "You will use your talents from within. This both troubles me and excites me. Your knowledge and talent will shine behind a crimson and gold curtain, all the while playing with the skill of a porcelain debutante. I could be put to trial, but again I am not your creator. That cross and burden belongs to Christian Pierre. He alone without fear implanted seeds of gifts within you and allowed it to grow." Professor Hertz , watching Gem Marie in the distance with her back turned slowly walked over to her from behind, "Answer me truthfully," Professor Hertz grabbed a handful of Gem Marie's hair and yanked her head back, "Did he prick his finger and hold your head back like so," now with her neck exposed and her eyes focused on the ceiling he continued, "Just enough to allow the secret ingredient of his blood to wonder through your voided wilderness. If so was it sweet?" He moved closer and inhaled the aroma off her neck, "Yet, still fate has brought you to my doorstep to provide the melodic relief needed for my empty soul." He kissed Gem Marie's neck softly then released her and returned to his violin, "My rightful place in this town will be secured and unshaken because of you." The professor, having finished stringing the instrument, grabbed Gem Marie again and held her tightly. With tears brimming, he implored, "You must promise never to run away or let yourself be taken. Remember me always my child." Gem Marie taken aback by the intensity of his emotion, was rendered momentarily speechless, as she observed a solitary tear tracing its path down his cheek. It seemed as though the professor pinned his hopes on her musical performance as the key to unlocking some unseen shackles that had kept him from reaching his true potential. Restricted to practicing the piece, she was only permitted to leave the room to attend to her cleaning duties. Her interactions were confined to conversations with him only, predominantly spent in listening. Like a loyal pet, her efforts were rewarded with morsels of food for her achievements. However, now confronted with his vulnerability and frailty, Gem Marie found herself unable to do anything but return his embrace. As he sank from her arms unto his knees, his tears staining her dress, she enveloped him in the folds of her frock, comforting him as he wept, his anguish echoing the innocence of a child's sorrow. Leading her to the realization that she had traded her Scotney prison for another.

Chapter: 14

The Performance

In the early hours of the day of the performance, Gem Marie awoke with a start. She gazed out of the Victorian window, entranced by the dark blue and amber colors outlining the skyline. Professor Hertz laid asleep on an overstuffed cot he had assembled after two goblets of wine. At the foot of the cot, Gem Marie, curled into the fetal position, nestled her head into a down feather pillow made especially for her. She had slept well, waking only once during the night, when the professor's heavy snores filled the room. In the stillness of the school, she tiptoed to the back door, carefully propping open the door that led to the hen house. Armed with a single lit candle, she deftly retrieved two eggs without disturbing the hens, a skill she had mastered by the age of nine at the Scotney. Before returning to the room, she ventured to the stage and auditorium to study their layouts, the to the kitchen where she removed one large orange, and she returned to her room before the morning chef could wake and began preparations. While the professor slumbered, she mixed flour with wheat and milk in a small black Dutch pot and placed it on the low flame of the fireplace. By the time the professor awoke, fresh well water, eggs, sliced orange, and warm biscuits awaited him. Still slightly hungover, he smiled and took two small bites. Though the show was that evening, his appetite was minimal as his thoughts turned to the guests, making his entire body tense. The sun had yet to rise, and the low-wick candles cast dancing shadows on the walls. Gem Marie sat at the piano, her hands unconsciously sweeping across the keys, playing a warm-up melody favored by Monsieur Heritage. Searching the room for his approval she abruptly stopped, remembering she had never revealed to Professor Hertz that she was versed in piano. "Why did you stop? I was enjoying it," the professor asked, turning to her. Gem Marie, trying to recover from her mistake, replied, "That is all I could remember." The professor sat in amazement, letting out a sigh of relief. He told Gem Marie it was good she had knowledge of the piano, as it gave him something else to ponder other than the evening's performance. The night before, as he took his last sip of wine before falling asleep, he had mumbled to Gem Marie about her being taken away, regurgitating a slurred story of her separation from Christian Pierre. He spoke with contempt, predicting that the Gods would curse Christian Pierre for allowing her to be taught such knowledge and language skills and music. After a restful sleep, his demeanor possessed a newfound tranquility and stillness. It was as if he had come to terms with the fact that the show could be perceived in two ways: good or bad, depending on the ears and eyes of the beholder. The time for practice had passed; he would have to face fate, which would be sitting in the audience. Dressed in the finest garb with undivided attention an audience of elites would hold his fate. Professor Hertz paused as he heard footsteps echoing from the distant halls. Rising quickly, he bolted towards the door to confirm that it was locked. Just as he ensured its security, a knock and a voice came from the other side. It was William and Mary, inquiring if he would attend the brief morning rehearsal. "Yes," he responded quickly, providing them the confirmation they needed to rally the other students. He then instructed Gem Marie that after rehearsal, he would bring the device behind the curtain to her designated spot. Next to the covered device would be a chair with a violin on it. He warned her not to make a sound until the designated section of the piece. Gem Marie nodded as Professor Hertz took one last bite of his biscuit and hurriedly left the room for the auditorium. As the students began playing, Gem Marie could hear the music through the walls. It seemed as though performance date propelled the students to reach their peak of playing. Now she could understand why the professor praised them without season, so they were incredibly talented ages ranging from nine through seventeen. Gem Marie quickly grabbed the violin and began playing along, she could hear William and Mary struggling with the Bach interpretation. Without a care, she played loudly, drowning out the noise around her. She effortlessly covered the piece, enhancing William and Mary's playing with her own flair. Suddenly, there was a knock at the door. She knew it wasn't the professor; he would have simply used his key. Frightened, she remembered his stern warnings to remain quiet and out of sight. She held her breath, staying silent until the knocking ceased. She listened intently, holding her breath as the footsteps faded, dissolving into silence. Shaken and nervous, she reached for the goblet the professor had nursed the night before. What was it about these fermented grapes that held such a strange allure, she wondered the way adults sipped, savored, and sometimes avoided each other's gaze the next day?

Bringing the goblet to her nose, she inhaled the rich, slightly tangy aroma, then lifted it in a mock toast to an imaginary friend and took a hearty sip of the sweet yet metallic-tasting burgundy liquid. It burned as it went down, leaving her lightheaded and unsteady. She reached out, gripping the edge of the cot as the room seemed to sway around her. After a moment, she staggered to the table, where the morning meal she'd prepared for the professor sat untouched. She grabbed the glass of fresh well water and drank deeply, trying to clear her head. The room still felt close, thick with the lingering effects of the wine. Desperate for fresh air, she went to the window, pressing her fingers into the heavy, dusty frame. It hadn't been opened since her arrival, but with a determined push, she managed to lift it about two inches, allowing a cool breath of air to seep in. With one final effort, she raised it another inch, and a gentle breeze flowed into the room, refreshing her senses and grounding her once more. Deciding she wanted nothing more to do with wine, she walked over to a pile of old costumes the professor kept on one side of the room. There lay the maiden's gown, white with the purple lace embroidery, draped in dust and stripped of its petticoat. Gem Marie carefully cleaned it with a rag again, marveling at how it matched her size perfectly. She undressed and stood before a basin filled with rose petals, dipping a torn cloth into the sweet-smelling, murky water. She meticulously cleansed herself from head to toe, then she poured the remaining water over her hair, while sitting in front of the fireplace. She allowed the warmth air to dry her skin. Slipping back into her old dress, she decided there was no need to ask Professor Hertz for permission to wear the hidden maiden's gown she had found since she would remain behind the curtain, unseen. As the wine slowly continued to take effect, she lay down on the cot and closed her eyes, dreaming of cradling an infant who looked like baby Philip. In her dream, she sat on a hill, singing softly to the sleeping child. Lost in a sleeping slumber for what seemed like hours Gem Marie was awaken when Professor Hertz returned. Startled and shocked to find her mumbling in her restful state, he rudely shook her awake, demanding an explanation. " What are you doing? You are an omen! Why else would you be asleep on this of all days? You should be quietly practicing and studying the sheet music. How disgraceful to try and sabotage my production. Now stand before me and answer truthfully for your wicked insubordination." Professor Hertz, whose dramatic anger had frightened Gem Marie out of her sleep, leaned in closer intrigue by her wide frighten eyes, tilting his head to peer in closer. "Wine! I smell the grapes from the vineyard! You drink wine and wallow in drunkenness on the day of my most memorable performance. You, who secretly conspire to folly. Tell me, child, why do you hate me so?" Gem Marie, unable to comprehend Professor Hertz's behavior, stood in silence, fearing that any rebuttal she could give would be perceived as wicked and deceptive. Unable to endure the professor's verbal torment any longer, Gem Marie rushed to the violin she had placed on the chair. She raised the bow in the air before her like a sword in a stance she had seen monsieur do many times. Immediately silencing the professor, she placed the violin on her shoulder and began to play the piece from start to finish. Midway through, she walked over to a device she had constructed and leaned into it. During her interpretation of Bach, she wielded the bow in a way that sent the violin's sound vibrating through the room. As she played, Gem Marie's heart ached with longing for home, and tears streamed down her face. She whispered the names of the Scotney household, her voice barely audible. Feeling weak, she leaned back, almost losing her balance she completed a graceful three-hundred-and-sixty-degree turn. Her trance-like movement enchanted the professor, his anger dissipating and replaced by a look of complete bliss and lust. "Remarkable," he whispered, Gem Marie now standing at completed attention continued playing while looking into the professor's eyes. The professor now feeling her unspoken temptation locked eyes with her his mouth now salivating over her playing, he spoke to her as she continued playing, "I must say, this performance is thrilling. What a pity if you were placed in their vision their minds would not allow them to enjoy the beauty of the music. Their ignorance clouds their view with superficial prejudgment." Unable to maintain a distance between them he beckon for her, " Come here, my child, you are safe here." Gem Marie continued to play now softly and lower as she moved toward the professor, now standing in front of him the music gradually transformed the room's tension into a serene, almost magical atmosphere. Rejuvenated and sharpened by the melody's quiet power. The professor's breath quicken as he continued to listen overtaken by the allure of Gem Marie's new melody he question, "What is that you play now so softly with intentions that warms me. Within." Gem Marie remembering the words of her music teacher drew her bow slowly with an added vibrato to the sensual note. The professor overtaken let out a moan arouse but frighten by the power of Gem Marie's music he quickly rose to his feet. Fleeing to the door he spoke no words while fumbling for the key to unlock the door he left the room once more, now prepared to assist with the evening's performance preparations. Gem Marie now filled with satisfaction with her discovery of her new power smiled as she laid the instrument down and returned to the window, gazing down as the unfolding scene took shape in the school's garden. She pulled a large chair near and sat and watched After some hours, Professor Hertz reappeared briefly, his exhaustion evident, he poured himself a restorative sip of wine before joining her at the window. Standing before her with an air of anticipation, he presented himself for inspection. Gem Marie straightened his lapel and handed him an orange peel, recalling Monsieur Heritage's habit of rubbing it on his hands before important meetings at the bank. She wiped away the excess scent with a gentle touch, saying with a smile, "Now you'll have a pleasant aroma." The professor chuckled, then began to review his final instructions, reminding her to enter the stage from the back room and assuring her that both the device and violin were set behind the curtain. Unexpectedly, as he turned to leave, he asked what she planned to wear. Gem Marie dryly noted she'd found a gown suited for the occasion one, she added, that no one would ever see. Professor Hertz barely registered her sarcasm, giving her an awkward pat on the shoulder as he handed her an extra key, instructing her to use it to unlock the door when she returned after the performance. Immediately after Professor Hertz locked the door, Gem Marie removed her clothing and began dressing for the performance. She carefully put on the maiden's gown, fixed her hair, and picked up the sheet music Professor Hertz had given her. Although she had already memorized it, she brought it along with her for reassurance. She carefully removed a single candlestick from the mantel near the fireplace, its flickering light casting shadows on the walls. With cautious steps, she tiptoed along the back of the school, heading towards the seldom-used stairway that led to the auditorium. The narrow entry and poorly lit passageway deterred most, but Gem Marie navigated it with a determined grace, creating her path to the back of the stage. Every movement was calculated, her senses heightened to detect any sound. The only noise was the soft scurrying of a mouse, soon pursued by the school's white Angora cat. The hallways were eerily silent with the faint sound of the music coming from the auditorium, as all eyes and ears were captivated by the performance on stage. It was the end of the second act, and the soloist was commanding the audience's attention for the third. Gem Marie slipped quietly towards the backstage area of the auditorium. It was shrouded in darkness, except for the faint glow of a small candle on a table near the device she had crafted. Beside it, a chair that held her violin and placed there by the professor. With a deep breath, she prepared for what was to come, every detail meticulously planned, every move part of a larger, enigmatic scheme. Behind the thick, black, and red curtains, no one could see or suspect her presence. She lit the candle she had brought with her from the diminishing flame left by Professor Hertz. Quickly removing its cover and positioning herself near the apparatus, she waited for the soloist to complete her last stanza. William and Mary's part would be starting soon, her heart pounding with anticipation as the cellist, a young girl named Ingrid Wolfgang Hertz, had just begun to play. Ingrid had been adopted by Professor Hertz and his brother, who changed her name to Ingrid Hertz after she was orphaned. Rumors whispered that she was a distant heir of a famous composer, but nothing was proven. Her parents, refugees who had fled to America, met a tragic end when they were killed for possessing books in German. In the small village they took resident in they had been wrongly suspected of having a book containing pagan spells. Later, it was revealed that the books were actually Lutheran Bibles. Ingrid often pondered this misfortune, echoing words from Professor Hertz whom she sometimes fondly called "father" as she searched for meaning. One evening, after the other students had left for supper, Gem Marie slipped in from backstage, as she often did, assuming she was alone. Unbeknownst to her, Ingrid who also thought she was alone knelt on the auditorium floor while picking up sheet music that had been left scattered by other students. Muttering curses in her native German language Ingrid paused, speaking aloud in a frustrated tone, "Gibt es niemanden, der mich verstehen kann?" ("Is there anyone who understands me?") A voice responded softly from the shadows: "Nur jemand, den du nicht sehen solltest." ("Only someone you're not supposed to see.") Startled, Ingrid followed the voice's trail to where Gem Marie stood hidden behind the curtain. As soon as Ingrid laid eyes on her, she wrapped her arms around Gem Marie without hesitation, not questioning her presence. "You speak German, but how? You're just a mute servant, a slave. So, you're not mute you *do* speak but German?" Ingrid replied happily. "Yes, but only a little, and I clean only in the shadows never to be seen or heard," Gem Marie replied in German. From that first encounter, the two kept their interactions brief and secret, never uttering a word to Professor Hertz, the two never revealed their communications. Seated beside the device, Gem Marie waited, her heart beating in time with the music as she listened to Ingrid play. She adored the way Ingrid brought her cello to life the way her emotions flowed through each note. No one played quite like Ingrid. The two shared an unspoken bond in their music, each understanding the other's rhythm and phrasing. Ingrid's part was always perfectly placed, right before William and Mary's solo. Her precision set the stage for Gem Marie to enhance the performance with her own interpretation. The moment was approaching. Ingrid's cello was poised to release the final low note of C, but Gem Marie's sharp ear detected a subtle shift. Ingrid had unexpectedly replaced the C with a lingering G, a subtle alteration that enriched the piece's conclusion. As Ingrid's final note loitered in the air, Gem Marie noticed that William and Mary had missed their cue. They hadn't picked up on Ingrid's improvisation, which had served as an unspoken signal for their entrance. With their instruments lying idle, Gem Marie's instincts took over. She played a bold, commanding note into the device, prompting William and Mary to join in. As they quickly regained their footing and continued, Gem Marie paused, listening intently. Something about their performance felt off fragile, perhaps, unsettled by her unexpected intervention. Unable to endure their faltering any longer, Gem Marie took the lead, hoping they would regain their confidence. Her gaze fixed on the flickering candle, which now seemed to dance to the music, she converted her vision from the moving flame to the sight of the Scotney. The servants, and Monsieur Heritage, now all dancing and smiling, rising from her chair, she approached the device. The Bach interpretation was nearing, and she could hear William and Mary struggling with its intro. She swiftly strummed her bow against the strings in front of the device, her hand commanding the bow up and down against the strings. A voice in her head yelled, "Speak music!" her playing surprising everyone and eliciting a thunderous applause that made her heart leap. The entire student ensemble, inspired by her boldness, began to play with newfound energy and improvisation, as if this were their only chance to unleash their true, hidden talents. Gem Marie continued playing, her neck and face drenched in sweat. She watched as beads of sweat flew from her face and forehead in slow motion onto the instrument. Now in a complete trance with the sweat from her brow stinging the corners of her eyes, she continued playing lost in her own perfection. Suddenly, she heard Ingrid, who was not included in this portion of the piece, strum a loud B, as if to break the trance like spell everyone was under. Gem Marie glanced over at Monsieur Heritage, who was beginning to fade away while his lips were shouting, "Bravo!" It was then she realized the piece had ended, now met with the thunderous applause and yells of the audience. Out of breath, Gem Marie placed her instrument on the chair and ran to the center of the stage and carefully peeked through a small crack in the curtain. Her eyes, which washed over the packed to capacity auditorium, was met with a breathtaking sight of over a hundred exquisitely dressed people who were applauding and throwing roses. Professor Hertz made his way to center stage, bowing gracefully and acknowledging various sections of the orchestra. He gestured to Ingrid and the other students, and finally, with a flourished wave and bow, towards William and Mary. The crowd erupted in applause at the gesture. Gem Marie knew it was her playing that had elicited such a reaction. Bursting with excitement, she vicariously listened as the Professor gave an eloquent speech then thanked everyone and announced they would be moving to the ballroom for refreshments. As the audience began to file out, Gem Marie peeked through the curtains, her gaze fixed on Professor Hertz, who was being swarmed by a throng of admirers. One woman, her laughter infectious, boldly linked arms with him and whisked him away. Meanwhile, ecstatic students were enveloped by their parents, their joy echoing throughout the auditorium, celebrating the success of the evening's performance. Gem Marie watched in silence as, one by one, the crowd thinned. The only person remaining was Ingrid, who stood alone. With her true parents no longer living Professor Hertz was her only source of support. Yet even he seemed too preoccupied with his admirers to notice. Gem Marie couldn't help but feel a pang of sympathy as Ingrid slowly moved across the auditorium clearly stalling the inevitable: standing alone in the vast, empty space. Ingrid, as if sensing something or someone nearby, paused. Her gaze shifted toward the stage, her eyes scanning the curtains with quiet intensity it was if she knew her secret friend was near. Gem Marie, fearful of being discovered, shrank further into the shadows, creating a tiny crack in the fabric from which to observe. She watched Ingrid's every move, wondering if she might make her way toward the stage. Ingrid carefully gathered her cello, but as she neared the exit, she hesitated, casting one last glance over her shoulder at the stage. Slowly, she set the cello down by a nearby chair and walked back toward the center of the room. Just as she was about to ascend the stairs to the stage the sharp click of polished shoes on the floor broke the silence. A well-dressed man entered the auditorium with, spotting her, he called out, "Hello there, Cellist. Might I have a brief word with you?" Ingrid, startled, turned away from the stage her attention now upon a the man walking towards her. Gem Marie's heart pounded as she held her breath, hoping the pounding of it in her ears wouldn't be heard. The man, refined and carrying a walking stick much like Monsieur Heritage's often did, quickly approached Ingrid with his hand extended to assist her. "Here, madam, let me help you." Gem Marie noticed the large ruby ring on his hand, it was the same hand that was extended out of the carriage that delivered the letter to the students for Professor Hertz. "My, you gave a wonderful performance this evening," he said. Ingrid, studying the gentleman's appearance, blushingly replied, "Thank you very much sir. It was a pleasure to perform for you and the other distinguished guests." The man, now fully visible in the bright candlelight, continued, "Your playing was truly inspirational. You added touches to the piece that were both refreshing and unexpected. It was a delight to hear such creativity." Ingrid smiling was now curious about how the strange man could have known about her subtle changes. Gem Marie, equally intrigued, wondered who this mysterious music connoisseur was that could so easily detect the embellishments. Ingrid, her mind racing with the thought that others might have noticed the subtle alterations in her performance, responded with a calm, polite smile, "The excitement of a live show often brings a fresh perspective, even to a piece we've rehearsed for weeks, perfecting it in its truest form." The man, clearly amused by Ingrid's subtle evasion, leaned forward and spoke with confidence, "Ah, but young lady, I know there were changes made to the piece because I *wrote* it." Behind the curtain, Gem Marie gasped, her heart skipping a beat. She had suspected that Professor Hertz may not have been the sole composer of the piece, but this revelation suggested that someone else had written it entirely. Ingrid's eyes widened in surprise, but she quickly regained her composure. "You wrote it? I was under the impression that Professor Hertz composed it. There were a few minor adjustments during the performance, but I did my best to accommodate them." The man, now thoroughly intrigued by her response, leaned in even closer. "So, you are Ingrid, the cellist... daughter of the Hertz brothers, are you?" You were trained by Professor Hertz, and he has done a magnificent job teaching you about the cello. But my question is about a violinist. I heard a Bach interpretation played flawlessly, and it did not come from the professor's prize pupils, William, and Mary. They were not taught that part of the piece correctly. No, the person I'm looking for has a vast knowledge of music and comes from the highest lineage." Gem Marie, behind the curtain, stood frightened. Surely the man was telling the truth. His ability to detect the alterations was clear proof he had written it. "Excuse me, my dear. I neglected to properly introduce myself. My name is Christian Pierre." Gem Marie, now in a petrified state, began to tremble. She did not recognize him from the newspaper article, and though he was from Paris, this man spoke with a slight southern drawl. She could hardly believe her eyes. Her escape from the Scotney had led her, inexplicably, to the very man now standing in the same room. *"How could this be?"* she thought, her heart pounding. She wrestled with the urge to run to him, to pour out everything she had endured, all in the name of love. Yet, before she could collect herself, she heard Ingrid's voice break the silence. "Nice to meet you, sir. If you're interested in a violinist, why not ask Professor Hertz himself? He would surely know more about what you seek. As for me, I'm simply his orphaned cellist, doing as I'm told, without question. But perhaps I could fetch the professor for you?" "No, that won't be necessary," he replied, a trace of a smile in his voice. "If the professor intended anyone to know of this remarkable violinist, they would already be center stage." His gaze shifted to the cello resting in Ingrid's hands. "That cello you hold it appears to be one of the finest. Was it a gift from Professor Hertz?" Ingrid glanced down at the instrument, a masterpiece of polished mahogany that gleamed even in the dim light. She remembered the evening it had been presented to her, just last spring. After playing a new piece with flawless precision, she had earned her mentor's approval. Within a month, this beautiful cello had been crafted just for her, given as a reward for her performance, handed to her during an unforgettable dinner. Ingrid now realized that one of the generous donors the professor often spoke about was standing right before her. Unable to speak for fear she might say something incorrect that could jeopardize the school's funding, Ingrid stood in silence. Gem Marie watched and listened, as Christian Pierre professed, he wanted to meet and speak with the person who had interpreted his music. She could not say a word for she had told Professor Hertz an embellished story that she was once taught music by him. Christian Pierre, sensing Ingrid's uncomfortable demeanor, spoke again in a calming manner. "You played beautifully, and I sensed there was a muse among you all, maybe in spirit. Perhaps I could coax your father to allow you to join me for a lovely boat ride at the harbor tomorrow. I'll come by early and speak with the professor, then later, we can discuss your future and the cello." Ingrid smiled and nodded, now feeling more at ease, she took Christian Pierre's arm as he extended it and escorted her to the ballroom. Gem Marie, heartbroken, watched as they walked off. The dashing gentleman who held all the answers to her problems had just charmed the only friend she may have had. She stood alone in the back of the dimly lit stage area, hot and hungry. The sweltering heat was beginning to take a toll on her, the gown she wore was now soaked with perspiration. She removed it now only clad in her under garments, it would be hours before all the guests had left and the professor was too preoccupied to check on her. She pulled another chair close, sat on one, and rested her feet on the other. Staring at the reflection of the candlelight dancing on the curtains and walls, she thought of various scenarios she could use to convince Christian Pierre to take her away and return her to the Scotney. A mischievous smile crept across her face as she replayed her earlier performance in her mind. She could still feel the exhilaration in her veins, the way the audience had applauded, captivated by the sounds that came from her. She let her eyes close, savoring the triumph, imagining the whispers of her name if they had known it was she who created the masterpiece that had won their hearts.

Chapter: 15

Cake

The next morning, Gem Marie finally returned to the room, having waited patiently for the entire school to fall silent. She lingered in the dim corridors, listening as the last echoes of laughter and conversation faded. Moving lightly on her feet, she slipped through the hallways, stealing glances at the odd sleeping arrangements of visitors scattered across the ballroom floor with bottles of rich, fermented wine by their sides. When she reached the room, Gem Marie knocked softly a few times before carefully sliding in the spare key that Professor Hertz had entrusted to her with. She pushed the door open slowly, only to find the room empty. Professor Hertz had left for the night, likely in the company of the mysterious woman who had taken his arm in the auditorium. It seems that during their tour of the school, the woman had become acquainted with a cozy, empty costume room. Intrigued by the organization of costumes and the quaint setup inspired all by Gem Marie. The woman insisted that they talk in the meticulously arranged room the was encapsulated with the smell of pine. After several glasses of wine, Professor Hertz and the mysterious woman had awoken together before dawn. Still buzzing with excitement from the evening's performance, Professor Hertz quickly arranged a carriage for her journey home and promised to pay her a social visit in a week. Tucking her in tightly with a costume robe from one of his older plays, he left her smitten by his thoughtful gesture. Now free from the unexpected romance of the night, Professor Hertz hurried to the room, key in hand. Once he arrived, he found Gem Marie sleeping peacefully on a cot. Proudly, he tapped her arm and whispered, "Bravo." Startled and overwhelmed, Gem Marie quickly sat up, rubbing the sleep from her eyes. Professor Hertz, without haste began recounting the entire performance, detailing the various reactions from the audience. He shared how his heart had nearly stopped when William and Mary faltered, leaving him at a loss for words and looking to the heavens for guidance. Then, as fate would have it, she began playing the crowd that was unaware of her assistance, were extremely impressed with her handling of the piece, with nods of acceptance

174

professor Hertz stated he was able to breathe once again. Suddenly in the middle of recounting the events the professor paused and rushed out of the room leaving the door half a jar as if he had forgotten something particularly important. Moments later, he returned with two large slices of cake and water for Gem Marie, he insisted she try it at once. He boosted it was chocolate and that the chef made it especially for the days performance. He told her in detail of a couple from Boston who had strong ties in the music department at the University that wanted to invest in the school. Gem Marie, who had not eaten anything, devoured the cake with the large cup of well water. Professor Hertz watch in delight as she sat silently while engulfing the rich cake. As Gem Marie finished the last morsal of the first slice she thought about Christian Pierre and his possible unannounced visit that he could pay to the professor. According to what she had overheard he was going to stop by to inquire about Ingrid and maybe discuss the violin solo. Gem Marie waited patiently until the professor completed his animated tales of the performance. Once he had settled back down to himself again, she spoke carefully, " I have something to inform you sir last evening when everyone had retreated to the ballroom. Someone returned back to the auditorium, It was a man I couldn't see who he was, but I did hear him speaking from behind the curtain. A man approached Ingrid while she was gathering her things he began questioning her. Of course, they had no idea that I was behind the curtains so two answered freely under the assumption they were alone." Professor Hertz, now surrendering his full attention, stood with a look of puzzlement, and gestured for Gem Marie to continued informing him of the events. "The man complemented Ingrid on her playing and stated that he had never heard anything like it before until the piece reached to the violin section, he swore he heard similar playing years ago. Ingrid who sounded slightly confused quickly gave all praises to William and Mary but the gentleman that I could not see at all would not hear of it, he spoke out and said, no it was something else not William and Mary. Ingrid, now utterly confused, told the strange man she didn't understand what he meant. Professor Hertz, pacing the floor with a look of concern, quickly turned to Gem Marie. "Come now, you must have seen his face or recognized his voice. Was he someone you've seen around the school?" Gem Marie, feeling a subtle satisfaction at the professor's anxious demeanor, insisted, "'No, I've never heard of him. The curtains were a barrier, and they weren't speaking loudly. It was only because I was determined that I caught part of his statement. But that's not what concerns me, sir. He told Ingrid he wanted what was rightfully his returned. Poor Ingrid was confused as I was, she offered him her cello, thinking he might have mistaken it for his own. I think he was a vagabond looking for expensive violins to steal." As Gem Marie continued speaking, Professor Hertz listened intently, taken aback. He wondered if Christian Pierre had indeed recognized his protégé's playing. He questioned Gem Marie about the man's appearance once more, 'You're certain you didn't catch a glimpse of him?' Gem Marie adamantly repeated that she stood behind the curtain and listened attentively. Reluctant to attempt seeing him for fear of being discovered, she remained hidden, waiting as instructed." Professor Hertz was now convinced that Gem Marie was unaware the man she had heard was Christian Pierre. He estimated the time she had been away from him and concluded that it was enough time had passed between the two, combined with his voice being distorted from behind the curtains, to obscure his identity. According to the professor, Gem Marie had brought a newfound respect to the school with the accolades from last night's performance. Several people had already requested to enroll their family members, eager to join the prestigious institution. The school had finally attained the esteemed image he had longed for, with the wealthy couple from Boston expressing their desire to move to town and enroll their daughter, Professor Hertz knew the performance had sparked a lucrative curiosity in the school, Christian Pierre's presence, however, threatened to unravel everything. He could potentially reveal that he had written the piece performed so brilliantly by Gem Marie and had allowed the professor to use it. Seeing the success, he now wanted to reclaim his work. Although Christian Pierre's name lacked influence in the concerto world, last night's performance could change that. Professor Hertz realized that Christian Pierre, due to the response of the audience finally has recognized the alluring complexities of the piece. Unaware of its unique style he had foolishly handed it over two years ago. Noticing the distant look on Professor Hertz's face, Gem Marie knew she needed him to return to a relaxed state. If Christian Pierre arrived, she wanted the professor to be comfortable when caught off guard. Professor Hertz, feeling confident that he had truly won Gem Marie's allegiance, interpreted her eagerness to report about a stranger as a sign of her loyalty. It was still fairly early in the day, and he wondered if Ingrid too, would mention her conversation with the inquisitive stranger. Drawing his attention back to Gem Marie he watched her thin frame as she randomly wiped and polished things around the room. As a gesture of his gratitude, he inquired if she wanted more cake. Although not in the mood for cake, she said yes, knowing she would need sustenance for later also wanting the professor out of the room to slip on the handmaiden's white gown again. She replied again, trying to coax the professor out of the room, "Please forgive my hunger. I didn't eat anything while waiting behind the curtain, nor did I have anything after I returned. I was just so pleased that my playing was satisfactory." Professor Hertz smiled and nodded, then removed a key from his pocket and headed toward the door. Once he exited, Gem Marie quickly donned the gown, adjusted her hair into a bun, and let some curls fall elegantly to frame her face. She checked her reflection in a small silver tray and made a few final adjustments. When the professor returned with two slices of cake and a small glass of wine, he was shocked into silence. He noted how beautifully she wore the gown, as if it were made for her, and admired her transformation. Placing the tray on a small table by the window, he slid a wooden chair in front of it. "Is that the gown you wore behind the curtain last night?" he inquired, right before he was startled by a knock on the door he had neglected to lock. Voices called out, "Professor! Martin!" a voice called urgently. Then a quieter, more tentative, "Father?" as the door began to creak open. Professor Hertz turned, his eyes widening while the door continued to open. It was Ingrid, accompanied by Christian Pierre. "Ah, Martin," Pierre said with a genial smile, peering in through the barely open door. "I hope we're not intruding." Reacting instinctively, Professor Hertz gave a quick, discreet wave toward the long, heavy drapes by the east window. Without hesitation, Gem Marie slipped behind them, concealing herself just as Pierre and Ingrid stepped fully into the room. "Ingrid, my dear, you're up early. And with such esteemed company!" he greeted them warmly, his eyes betraying only the faintest flicker of apprehension. "Mr. Pierre, welcome. What an unexpected pleasure. And Ingrid, thank you for escorting him. You may return to your lessons now." Ingrid, clearly disappointed, cast a lingering look at Christian Pierre, who gave her a courteous nod. "I shall see you again soon, Miss Hertz," he assured her, his voice gentle yet firm. Reluctantly, she obeyed, though her gaze swept the room one last time before she withdrew. Left alone with the Professor, Christian Pierre let his gaze roam the room, eventually settling on the professor's prized harpsichord. As he stepped closer, his hand brushed a familiar sheet of music, one he had recently composed and recognized instantly, though it had been transposed by another hand Gem Marie's, though he couldn't have known. With a casual movement, Pierre shifted the sheet music beneath other papers, his face betraying nothing. "I must offer you my sincerest congratulations, Martin," he began, his tone almost admiring. "Your performance last night was nothing short of remarkable. I could scarcely believe the progress you've made since last we met. That you managed to decode that elusive section…" He trailed off, his words lingering with just a hint of suspicion. Professor Hertz stiffened slightly, struggling to recall every detail Gem Marie had provided about her interpretation of the piece. He forced a calm smile. "I merely placed my students in their proper places and let fate reveal their talents. Decoding such a challenge was simply a pleasure for me." "Indeed," Pierre replied, his gaze sharp yet affable. "The accomplishment was talked about all morning. People marveled at the skill displayed, claiming they had never heard anything so stirring. But tell me, Martin" Christian paused, his eyes narrowing, "There was a particular violinist who… stood out. It was as if their bow wept, the sound was so hauntingly beautiful. Who was it?" Professor Hertz's heart quickened. He hesitated, torn between attributing the playing to William and Mary, the students who had claimed the spotlight, or acknowledging Gem Marie. In his eyes, Gem Marie now belonged to him, and she had developed a loyalty towards him. As far as he was concerned, Christian Pierre had discarded her without a second thought. Only now, after witnessing the effort the professor had put into her development, did Christian want to reclaim her. Slightly irritated, Professor Hertz contemplated contacting the authorities. No slave trading was conducted within the harbor's realm without the Slaytter brothers' involvement. Christian Pierre's influence was stronger in the Deep South and Europe, but Professor Hertz mentally prepared himself for the challenge. "Christian, what you heard was the collective effort of the children's determination to bring the production to its highest standards. You must know I run a strict school with rigorous lessons and rehearsals. What you heard was an example of perseverance, the transposing of the piece, and recreating it to a level that would leave a lasting impression on anyone fortunate enough to witness the first performance of Hertz's concerto." Gem Marie, who stood still as an oak tree behind the thick velvet curtains, listened closely. She detected the contempt in Professor Hertz's voice as he took credit for Christian Pierre's work. The embellishments and new arrangements were done by her, not the professor. It was now clear that for the professor to maintain his newfound fame, he needed Gem Marie to stay permanently. Her mind flashed to his prior conversation about Otis being loyal to his brother and remaining with the doctor. Gem Marie listened to Christian Pierre's response. It was not a strong plea; he had given his piece to the professor for improvement, hoping it might be heard. But now, the professor had let the fame and attention consume him, even changing the name of the piece to his own. Christian Pierre, now regretting his actions for losing faith in himself, wanted credit and acknowledgment for his own work. He told Professor Hertz that due to a hasty decision he relinquished something that he truly had no intention to. His response was ineffective on Professor Hertz who replied arrogantly by mentioning something about confirming missing cargo with the Slaytter brothers. Gem Marie's heart raced at the thought of being referred to as cargo and questioning slave traders. Without Christian Pierre making a proper plea for her now and the possible confirmation with the Slaytter brothers, she would never return to the Scotney. The professor would surely try to keep her hidden, forcing her to remain behind the scenes and under him in order to gain more musical power. Frighten by though of being reported and unable to hold her tongue, Gem Marie stepped from behind the curtains and addressed Christian Pierre directly. "You were changing your voice when speaking to Ingrid. You Mr. Pierre, who stand there now like you have seen a ghost. You must have been aware of the sorrow I have felt after being taken away from you. You knew I was behind the curtain all along, didn't you? Once you heard my playing, you knew it came from the one you taught everything and had abandoned. How could you? You taught me how to play, you who dared to go against the laws of man and gave me the knowledge of various instruments. Sold me off as if teaching me all those things was just a hobby, and you were ashamed of what you created. " Christian Pierre stood in shock as he watched and listened to Gem Marie, who walked and talked as if she knew him intimately. The story was so unreal, yet he craved to know more about his musical maestro's life that was being narrated by this enigmatic young girl. He studied her closely to reassure himself that he had never met or seen her before. Yet still there was something familiar and captivating about this young girl who wore an elegant ball gown and speaking as if she had received the best schooling. Gem Marie's dramatic and eloquent tales of their encounters were almost theatrical. Every so often, she would lock eyes with Christian Pierre, gesturing for him to pay attention and take note of a particular

179

part of the story. "I always wondered if you valued me. I received my answer when you traded me away. At first, I thought it was a cruel joke for not learning the piece quickly enough. Then, when I was taken away, I began to think that I truly had no value that my darkness and being a woman in this world marked me as one of the cursed ones. Just a product of fate, placed among the misfortunate." Her voice trembled slightly, but she continued with unwavering resolve. "Then, when I arrived here, I could hear the music again. The professor gave me an opportunity to display my talents. When I heard the piece, I read it and thought to myself, "I know this piece. Then I saw the notes written on the sheet music, and I knew it was you. Then I thought, the writing, the Bach interpretation. It had all of your touches. Yet, I still doubted it." The professor, who worked so hard in bringing life to the piece, stood in silence with patience as he listen to Gem Marie's disclose her and Christian relationship. Christian Pierre's heart raced as he listened to the fictitious accounts. The mystery of her identity and the haunting familiarity of her words drew him deeper into her story. Now fully immersed in the flamboyant tale he grew a deep desire for the mystery woman who spoke without error. "I knew this day would come when you would find me and return me home. Your creation Mr. Christian Pierre is here before you and your music is here as well. Will you live up to your duties as a noble man and start again. With the love and courage that you have within you will you continue where you left off. I only ask that you allow me to return to the school once a year to join Professor Hertz and play behind the curtains." Christian Pierre stood speechless, staring into Gem Marie's eyes. Her gaze was radiated compassion that perfectly matched her words. As he pondered the decisions he made about music all his life, he identified the moment as an omen. His conscience told him that walking away from this mystery girl might cost him far more than any concerto ever could. He turned his piercing glare on Professor Hertz and spoke calmly as he directed his words towards Gem Marie. "Your tongue is sharp and wise, I see things have not changed. I have no more time to waste proving my ownership to a man who uses my gifts and talents as his own. I don't know how you ended up here at the school. What I do know is your playing ability is rare just like the pure ivory on a wild elephant in west Africa and it should because I created you that way. Go and gather your things gifted one. I have been searching far and wide for you." Gem Marie ran to a pile of costumes across the room and retrieved her cloth bag she had once worn beneath the belly of a wagon. After collecting her things, she quickly returned to Christian Pierre's side. The two of them now staring at Professor Hertz, whose face betrayed no emotions. He couldn't believe what had just transpired the gem that had been given to him by his brother was leaving. The thought of losing Gem Marie filled him with dread, he had grown accustomed to her presence and was relying on her talents to propel the school to new heights. She had stir a feeling within him that required just her music. The young musical protégée was leaving forever. He feared the possible repercussions if word ever got out that Gem Marie had played the piece, and the philanthropist Christien Pierre was the true composer of the music. If Christian Pierre ever decided to share the chains of event with any of his local constituents, the school's reputation would suffer. Professor Hertz, who had positioned himself in front of the door, blocking their paths after a moment stepped aside, and allowed them to pass . Just as they were about to step past him, the professor moved and block their way once more. With his feet firmly planted in a stance of defiance, Professor Hertz spat, "Tell me, Pierre, you have come back to claim what is yours. Your sweet protégé, immersed in all your teachings of great music. Tell me, what do you call her?" The professor now staring into Gem Marie's eyes , "What is her name? this talented girl that wheels her bow like a sword and renders any listener helpless. I myself, I just call her 'girl, 'gal, darkie or whatever comes to mind. But you, Pierre , who have spent so many days and nights together, surely you have given it a proper name." The professor now flooded with jealousy tried to contain himself took a deep breath and stepped away from Gem Marie. Christian Pierre, taken aback, realized he had no idea what the beautiful young woman with the walnut-colored eyes was called. No name seemed befitting for the woman who had convinced him to join her grand scheme of escaping from Professor Hertz's grips. Before Christian could ponder any longer, Gem Marie looked sternly into his eyes then she slowly traced them along his shoulders down his left arm to his hand, where she fixed her gaze on the bright red gem on his ring finger. The professor to self-indulged in the allure of Gem Marie and the quest to prevail over Christian Pierre was unaware of their unspoken communications. Following his instincts of doubt the professor asked, "Pierre, surely you don't need assistance in confirming her title? I only ask because hearing it from your mouth will give me comfort that she was returned to her rightful owner. Also it would confirm that she will return to the conservatory once a year, as agreed." Gem Marie, not fully aware of the professor's plan, spoke quickly. "You need me here only once a year? Good, so you will have more than enough time to prepare a decent meal for me other than cake. Or as you say, let them or excuse me, let me eat cake." With her last sentence, she walked away from the professor and quickly glanced at Christian Pierre with a smile and headed to the old slice of cake that sat on a table by the window. She took a bite then walked back to the professor as she licked her fingers. Christian Pierre, now intrigued by the young woman who knew Bach and quoted Marie Antoinette, spoke with newfound annoyed confidence. "Martin, I have known you for quite some time and have never broken a promise. I will have her back here once a year to perform for you. Oh, Excuse me I mean I will have Gem Marie back here, although she won't be able to stay long, she is one of my own prized pupils." Gem Marie smiled and curtsied, confirming his statement. Once given her approval, Christian Pierre took her hand, and raised it to his lips, he then laid a deliberate kiss that flowed in Professor Hertz's ears. "I made the terrible mistake of giving away one of my true gems Martin. Starting today, my days shall be spent rectifying my poor judgment. There is a lot of work to be done and I'm afraid we must leave now; everyone at home will be delighted to see her again. Come Gem Marie the carriage awaits." Professor Hertz, truly flabbergasted, asked, "There is more than one? Surely you can't be serious you said one of your prize pupils. Christian have you taught more than one to master music? This is unlawful, how many more are there? My guess three maybe." Christian Pierre, enjoying the professor's growing appetite for the confirmation of the number of possible women, smiled and replied, "Calm yourself Hertz there are only two." The professor, unable to contain himself, grabbed Christian Pierre's arm, leaned in closely, and whispered, "Share one with me old friend, I promise to handle with care." Christian Pierre's ego beginning to swell retorted, "Now, professor, we mustn't be greedy the deal is once a year you will see Gem Marie again, you have my word. I see you two have grown to trust one another. I wouldn't have it any other way." Christian turned away, smiling, and held out his arm for Gem Marie, who quickly wrapped hers around it as they began to walk towards the door. The steps towards the door seemed endless for Gem Marie she could feel Professor's Hertz's eyes peering on her back. She nervously squeezed Christian's arm once they made it to the hallways, following Gem Marie's grip growing tighter, he advised her, "If you are tempted to look back for confirmation that you are free from the hell you were once confided of, don't, for any reason. Your future lies ahead." As they walked through the school corridors, they were met by whispers and gasps that bounced off their aura then back into classrooms. Lesson plans and practice were abruptly halted and replaced by pointed index fingers. Gem Marie who was mimicking Christian Pierre held her head straight, she caught a slight glimpse of Ingrid in her peripheral vision. Ingrid, standing in a classroom doorway, waived her hand in an attempt to obtain Christian Pierre's attention. She quickly retracted it after she saw no acknowledgment from either of them. The two continued walking, ignoring all idle chatter once they were outside, where Christian quickly ushered Gem Marie into a carriage with the help of a coachman. The white and black carriage was adorned with red curtains which concealed the interior. Once they were settled inside, they spoke no words to one another. as the carriage set off. Gem Marie's heart was still racing as the carriage rode through the harbors of Baltimore and then Medicine Row. She peeked through the closed drapes, hoping to catch a glimpse of Otis one last time, but he was nowhere in sight. She stared long and hard at the good doctor's building, hoping Otis had felt her through a window or from behind a bush She whispered, "Goodbye, cousin," as she gazed at the town where she'd rarely spent any time outside in public. As the school gradually settled after the dramatic departure of Gem Marie and Christian Pierre, whispers circulated about Ingrid, who had prematurely boasted of her invitation to the lake by the wealthy Christian Pierre. With a sense of urgency, she dashed toward Professor Hertz's room. Out of breath she entered abruptly without invitation, "Father, I just saw Christian Pierre leaving," she informed, her voice strained from both the exertion and the weight of the cello. "He didn't say a word to me and he was walking hand in hand with that mute darkie," Ingrid quickly recounted the details she had just witnessed in the halls. Professor Hertz, maintaining his composure, side eyed Ingrid as he removed a key from his breast pocket and locked the door behind her. Ingrid, unsettled by his calm demeanor, embellished the details about her encounter with Christian Pierre the night before in order to gain a reaction from Professor Hertz. "Father he practically courted me right there in the auditorium he even held my hand, Knowing how protective you are I didn't want to vex you with his level of boldness. No, I couldn't it was your night to enjoy. He complemented me and said he was impressed with my playing and wanted to discuss my future with him." Professor Hertz now providing his undivided attention to Ingrid, "He was very interested in my inspiration, why he even went to the lengths of inviting me to go on the lake with him of course I didn't confirm anything without your permission." She paused, catching her breath, hoping her words would elicit a reaction from the nonchalantly acting professor. The professor, who had gone back to shuffling papers absentmindedly, suddenly paused and let out a thundering laugh. " Did you say take you on the lake? My dear, that was merely a ploy to extract information from you. Christian Pierre had no intention of taking you anywhere. He was here to claim his property, Gem Marie." Ingrid, surprised and annoyed, exclaimed, "Who? You can't be referring to the darkie! You mean, he traveled all the way here to retrieve a slave girl? A servant? But why? She practically mute." Professor Hertz, now faced with the reality of Gem Marie's absence, realized her talents far surpassed those of any student at the school. He could only hope that Christian Pierre would keep his word and allow her to return once a year to assist with the annual productions. Slightly annoyed by Ingrid's probing, he advised, "That darkie learned everything about music structure and composition from that man. She was so skilled that it was her you heard in the background, effortlessly fixing the mistakes when William and Mary faltered during the show." Ingrid, in shock and horror, covered her mouth to stifle her gasp, after a moment she asked, "Father, did you really have that girl play along with us during the concert? Did you truly give her the lead? That's an outrage! Father are you well." Professor Hertz now irate retorted, "Outrage! How dare you, Ingrid. You too are not free from fault, when it comes to the piece..." Ingrid, now trying to calm Professor Hertz down switched her tone, "I mean, father If you had only told me your concerns with the piece, I could have helped. Didn't you hear the crowd's thunderous applause after I played?" "Yes, I did," Professor Heartz retorted. "But I also heard how your selfish decisions in changing the keys caused William and Mary to falter. It was Gem Marie who quickly corrected the mistake and restored order back to the concerto." Ingrid, now more concerned than jealous replied, "Father, do you really believe that my small alteration is the cause for William and Mary to faulter. I assure you those two need no help with that trait. If those two spent more time practicing, then gossiping and stealing from the distillery they would play much better." Professor Hertz, taken back by Ingrid's contempt for her classmates, waited in silence for more brutal confessions. "Father please don't be cross. I played my best as I always have. You've never had a problem with my playing before. What is it about this strange slave girl that makes you doubt my own abilities now?" Professor Heartz, not wanting to add more insult to injury, kept quiet about Gem Marie's remarkable musical talents. Instead, he looked at Ingrid and saw a young girl in desperate need of his approval. He had never experienced her to be so vocal, so he walked over to a chair, removed the violin he had been given as a child, and handed it to her. "Take this," he said, "and learn to love it like your cello." Ingrid, surprised that he would entrusted her with his prized possession, smiled, feeling reassured she held it close. As she admired it for a brief moment, she wondered if Gem Marie had been allowed to play the instrument as well. She glanced around the room and noticed an older, battered violin with a bow next to it. It sat near a table with a tin cup and an old slice of cake. She walked over to it and picked it up, and examined the strings. She noticed that the common stringing method Professor Heartz usually used had not been applied to this violin. Instead, the neat knotting method looked as if it had been done by a professional. Ingrid placed the tattered violin down on the chair that sat before the small wooden table and stared at the setting. There she noticed a small, torn cloth, examining it with the careful eye of someone piecing together the remnants of a mystery. She couldn't help but notice the handkerchief was delicate, the fabric finer than anything worn by the average house slave. The initials, "G.M.," were amateurly stitched in fine thread at the corner, as if Gem Marie had claimed her place in the school through quiet acts of defiance. Ingrid's mind whirred as memories surfaced of her own brief lessons in Europe before her parents uprooted their lives for the promise of America, where their lives were tragically cut short. The hallmarks of European refinement in Gem Marie's life were unmistakable to Ingrid: the careful placement of the utensils, arranged with a practiced hand, as though honoring an invisible code of table etiquette; her hidden fluency in German, concealed even from her own father. Gem Marie had clearly been taught to read, write, and play music luxuries no American slave owner would bestow upon their so-called property. Ingrid's gaze shifted to the portion of cake left on the table, untouched but clearly offered with a sense of reverence. "This is where she played her music," she thought, envisioning Gem Marie seated gracefully, her fingers dancing over the keys or strings while her father stern yet softened in her presence watched in awe. "She has a life I cannot understand," Ingrid mused. "Christian Pierre, smitten by her brilliance, has whisked her away, like a hero from one of the stories hidden in her father's forbidden books. But who are you, Gem Marie? A slave girl that can speak many languages where do you come from, and why were you here?" Just then, Professor Hertz stirred from his reverie by the window, his gaze heavy with memories. Ingrid noticed his melancholic expression as he murmured, almost to himself, "She was meant for something greater than this place." Ingrid's curiosity tightened into resolve. She knew, now more than ever, that she had to uncover Gem Marie's past, to understand her connection to her father and the mysterious life she had left behind. With a final glance at the initials on the cloth, Ingrid threw it into the raging fireplace. It had been months since Gem Marie vanished, and Monsieur Heritage's patience was threadbare. The man he had paid handsomely to unearth her whereabouts had delivered no word, leaving Heritage in an uneasy silence. The gravity of her absence weighed heavily, but it was only after witnessing the death of a calf in the barn its small, fragile body lying lifeless that the bleakest thought took root in his mind: Was Gem Marie, too, lost to the world? He shuddered at the notion. How could such a bright soul, a child who cherished her dolls and played her harp with a grace beyond her years, be swept away by the world's cruelty? He knew well how indifferent society could be, a world where a child, especially a girl of her complexion, bold and intelligent was at risk for simply existing beyond the narrow expectations cast upon her. The world would care nothing for the heartache of a man who, orphaned and alone, had taken her in as his own blood. They would overlook the care he had poured into her upbringing, the gentle instruction, the unwavering love. No one would spare a glance at her gifts, her cleverness, her talents that shone like rare jewels. They would see only the child's skin, her gender, and deem her unworthy. As if haunted by his own despair, a voice echoed in his mind: *"Killed without hesitation for being intelligent and gifted."* He shook his head, trying to silence the unbidden thought, yet it lingered, as bitter as the taste of iron. On his lap sat a small handmade doll that Gem Marie had created one day from leftover mane from one of the stallions. she use wood, string, and scraps of cloth for the body and dress. Deep in thought Monsieur looked down at the wooden doll and thought of all the horror tales he had overheard from crude overseers, he crafted images of the horrid abuse Gem Marie may have endure. Without warning a single tear fell from his eyes and onto the doll his tear stained the face which caused the image of the doll's features to be smeared. With a deepen sorrow overwhelming him like grief he pondered on the reality that it was against the laws to teach her kind to speak many languages and to read and write. Now realizing he had been selfish and arrogant in believing that she would never leave the Scotney. His arrogance created a façade that he alone could protect her from the outside world. He was determined to find her dead or alive he wanted her body back on Scotney soil. Greta who sat back on a large chair with baby Philip in her arms, watched her beloved husband that she worshipped without hesitation sit wrenching his hands while staring at a doll. The absence of Gem Marie had also broken Greta's heart she knew of no way to ease her own pain much less Monsieur Heritage discomfort. The only thing that removed the sadness sometimes was baby Philip who had been growing very quickly. Greta watched monsieur as he pulled a book from one of the shelves in the parlor, he randomly turn the pages of a book and turned it upside down. When she saw what appeared to be at tear roll from his eye onto the book she. She quickly rose and walked towards and spoke calmly, "Darling, could you please hold baby Philip while I excuse myself, I have to check with the cook for the meals she has been very forgetful lately." Monsieur without a word held out his arms to receive Philip and placed him onto his lap. He peered into the eyes of the replica of himself that had grown so quickly. He examined his features and skin tone and determined if you knew his background and searched for it you could find traces of his mother in some of his features. The majority of his appearance came from Monsieur's lineage there would be no problems for baby Philip to live his life as a French man. No door would ever be closed to him unless he wanted them to be, and he would only leave the Scotney when fully prepared and ready. Once Monsieur had found the various newspaper articles in Gem Marie's things he deemed it the culprit for her running away and forbid anyone to bring a newspaper on Scotney soil. Whenever he rode into town, he would purchase a newspaper and sit in a coffee house on the hill ad catch up with current events when done he would drop it in the nearest fire pit. The last time he had visited the coffee house he heard whispers stating, "There goes Monsieur Heritage he walks in sorrow for his lost daughter." Enrage at the tone of pity in their voices he walked across the road to the printing press and demanded to see the editor he instructed him to run an article about a lost girl from the Scotney that is fluent in multiple languages and a master of the harp and violin. Monsieur provided a generous sum of money to the printer if he could see that word of it reached the papers in America. He also included a reward to anyone with any information of her whereabouts. Once the printer received the money for the task, he prepared his apprentice to leave on the next ship for Boston there he would connect to a distant relative of a printer that lectured at the University of Amherst once there, the two would have the article ran in the school paper and the local print. The apprentice was armed with enough money to get an article done mapped out his journey for Boston then Connecticut and New York. Once the article was completed a rough draft was sent to Monsieur Heritage that stated, "Young girl taken, she possess the ability to play several instruments. Her rare capabilities to speak several languages can be distinctly detected if heard. The girl is petite and clever and will respond to the name Heritage if spoken. All inquiries must be able to confirm girl's name and birthplace to be considered for a very handsome reward granted if successful." Once Monsieur received the draft, he approved the printing and set off to meet the old man he had paid for information on Gem Marie's whereabouts. This man had hired a young lad named Baron Fitzgerald, who had written a letter reporting that two clever women had managed to escape capture in Baltimore. However, the old man, who ran the mill and lived next door with his family, hadn't supplied Monsieur Heritage with any new information. As Monsieur approached the house, two little girls in long aprons ran up to him. Their hair and clothes were dusted with mill residue, their cheeks flushed, and their noses runny. Laughing, they called out, "Father a gentleman approaches with important papers!" Surprised by the girls' quick observation of the newspaper article in his hand, Monsieur felt a pang of nostalgia. The girls were small and bright-eyed, their worn clothing reminding him of the day he had been given Gem Marie. He stopped, knelt down and wiped both girls' noses, then handed the eldest his handkerchief, instructing her to walk with it and keep it clean. The girls ran off, shouting for their father as they took turns placing the embroidered handkerchief on their heads like a crown. Monsieur Heritage was soon greeted by the old man who walked with a slight limp in the distance. He quickly transformed his stride with vigor once he realized it was Monsieur heritage calling upon him. The old man made a detour to a nearby water barrel where he rinsed his hands and face. With his clothing covered in saw dust he began informing Monsieur that Baron Fitzgerald had just become a high seaman and would be returning to England very soon. He spoke with enthusiasm which gave Monsieur comfort, "The Lad Baron is a bright boy with two years of schooling, he has decided his kinship with the waters is better home for him. He set out for sail after the first time we spoke, and he immediately had that letter sent once he been given some information. That would be the letter I rushed to you that spoke about the two women's daring escape. "Apologies for my delay, sir. I didn't inform you sooner because I didn't want to raise any false hope. However, I've just received word from a fellow who claims to have crossed paths with Baron Fitzgerald at the docks of Castle Garden in New York. Although he didn't receive a letter from the Baron, he did speak with him briefly. He reports that Fitzgerald is heading south and that your daughter may have been taken as part of cargo moving past New York. The Baron plans to return immediately once he has her location, though there's no telling how far she may have been taken. If I know the Baron, sir, he'll return with your daughter in his arms if he finds her. He mentioned there are rumored places where runaways are kept; he may be able to track her down from there." The old man, beaming with pride at bringing this news, grinned broadly, revealing gaps where three teeth were missing. "Pardon me again, sir, but may I ask why you didn't want her description noted? I only mention it because it could improve our chances of finding her. For example " he continued, hitching up his trousers as he spoke, "if we knew whether her hair was red or her eyes were blue, we might locate her more quickly." Monsieur, slightly annoyed at the man's suggestion to draw attention to Gem Marie's features, stepped closer. The faint scent of ale drifted from the man, prompting Monsieur to retrieve a handkerchief and hold it discreetly over his nose and mouth. With a steady, gleaming gaze, he spoke calmly. "Old man, do you remember the evening when I had a disagreement with that young fellow now known as the crippled boy?" The question seemed to sober the old man instantly. His grin vanished as memories of that cold night behind the seamstress shop resurfaced. Fearful of saying anything further, he focused intently on Monsieur Heritage as he lowered the handkerchief from his face. "Remember, her hair is long and black, and her eyes are light brown. Don't trouble yourself with the other details. I have faith her remarkable talents will make her stand out in any crowd even among the crippled." Shaking uncontrollably, the old man nodded, confirming he'd relay any information as soon as the young Baron returned. Monsieur Heritage then mounted his stallion and rode toward the Scotney, swift as the wind. Thoughts of everything he had taught Gem

Marie raced through his mind. The countless days of music lessons might have outweigh the numerous math and science lessons he was now wondering if she had retained the more important things that he felt could help her escape from slavery at the moment the word pierced through his mind, slavery was something that was not permitted on his land or so he thought. He had enslaved Gem Marie without knowing it, that's why she sought freedom he rationalized. In his mind she was not going to explore the world, she was running away from him. At that very moment, a hanging tree branch struck him in the face and caused him to be thrown onto the cold dirt. His body sprawled on the cold soil as he laid there motionless, his horse still trotting and finally stopped in the far distance. There was not a home in sight or anyone else, a black crow squawked above his still body that sent a piercing ring to his ears. He opened his eyes now focused on the clouds in the sky moving west. Taking deep breaths in he could feel the soreness to his rib grow stronger. Monsieur watch the marvel of the sky as the clouds formed shapes of objects and people. He turned is head left and right and stared down the road he had just left and down the one that led to home. Once he confirmed that there was truly not a soul in sight, he let out a loud painful yell that ended with him calling out Gem Marie's name, which sealed the sound. He stared back up into the sky and saw one of the clouds had formed the shape of a harp it was clear as day the forty-string instrument almost resembled a painting. Monsieur Heritage reach his hand in front of him as if he were pulling down the instrument closing his hands to an empty fist he wept again as his hand grew heavy and fell to the ground. He whispered into the wind, "Happy birthday my darling I hope you've had your cake."

Chapter: 16

Your Home Now

Gem Marie and Christian Pierre rode to the docks in tense silence, their only form of communication being the occasional glance through the curtain that concealed the carriage. The journey ahead weighed heavily on them both. When they finally boarded the large vessel bound for Louisiana, Gem Marie's nerves tightened with each step. She was leaving behind the only place she had come to know outside of the Scotney, with no way to inform Otis that she had fled Baltimore. Once aboard, Christian Pierre swiftly escorted her to a cabin, instructing her to get comfortable and rest before dinner. The room was modest yet welcoming, filled with fresh fruits, bread, ale, and a basin of clear water. As soon as he closed the door behind her, Gem Marie found herself momentarily captivated by her surroundings, the unfamiliar stillness of the ship amplifying her thoughts. She rinsed her face and hands quickly before shedding her travel-worn clothes. Pausing in front of the looking glass, she was struck by the reflection before her. It had been so long since she'd truly seen herself, not since her departure from the Scotney. The figure staring back at her seemed foreign, her body had developed in ways that surprised her. She studied her curves with an almost detached curiosity, feeling as though she were seeing them for the first time. Reaching for a piece of fruit, she crushed a small piece of orange between her fingers, letting the juice run before dipping her hand into the basin of water. With slow, deliberate movements, she rubbed the scented liquid over her skin, the simple act grounding her in the present. But despite the luxury of the moment, an unsettling emptiness settled in her chest. Here she was, finally in the presence of the man she had run away to find and yet, victory felt hollow. Trying to recollect how long she had been in Maryland, she concluded it had been close to a year. The tumultuous events had thrown off her sense of time so much that she couldn't remember if her birthday had passed. Monsieur had always reminded her when it was coming. He would encouraged her to prepare her wishes, for on that day they would surely come to pass. The last wish she remembered making was to meet Christian Pierre. Now, here she was standing naked in a cabin he had placed her in, and she was not happy. All the imaginative escapades she had concocted alone in her room at night now disturbed her. There were no more wishes to be held in his arms as they exchange stories of how wonderful life was. The rigorous training she inflicted on her body to endure the wagon trip seemed like a waste of her life. The betrayal of hiding this secret from Monsieur plagued her. Christian Peirre was no friend, she dared not tell him about the newspaper clippings and the romantic letters she had written and hidden in walls of the Scotney. What should now be a dream come true was now a living nightmare. Even if she could trick her mind for a moment that she was somewhere else, he was her reminder that she had ran away from home and might never see her family again. Monsieur Heritage's enigmatic assurances had always filled her with anticipation. Each time he spoke of wishes, his voice carried a promise of magic and fulfillment. Her reflection in the brass-looking glass was the proof of Monsieur's truth. Her fantasies, once a source of secret pleasure, now seemed like cruel jokes played on her. "I'm I really here she asked herself," she had made a wish and now it had come true a voice now shouting in her head, "Make it go away now!" The grueling preparation for the journey, the endless hours spent strengthening her body, felt like they had been in vain. She had dared to hope, dared to dream of a romantic encounter with Christian Pierre, only to find herself standing in the dream she wished for. The only price was to be ripped away from home and thrown into filth. The fear of being forever separated from her family weighed heavily on her heart, turning what should be now a joyous occasion into a haunting reminder of her isolation . "Why did he not tell me that I was different," she whispered. Gem Marie now drenched in despair believed Christian Pierre would never return her back to England. He was utterly fascinated by her ability to play and comprehend, and that seemed to be his only concern with her. Otis and Claudette had taught her she was a nigger, outside of the Scotney, she was seen as worthless and troublesome. A darkie with no home only a corner to sleep in with rodents as companions. All meals provided by the master, a slave was not taught to read or play concertos. Their clothing was torn and riddled filthy, there were no moments of laughter to engage with family. Those that didn't live on a plantation fended for themselves and worked for various people every day like Otis, only to have at least one person declare permanent ownership. None of the newspaper articles could have prepared her for this outside life. Christian Pierre was a man so passionately devoted to creating great music that he would help a stranger he'd never met escape all for the mere promise that she might one day perform one of his masterpieces. Gem Marie believed that if he knew that she came from wealth and wanted to go home he would send her to the Slaytter brothers. Out in the world she was consider a runaway. She knew her musical talents was her only saving grace with Christian Pierre and she was not going to reveal her true origins. The world was very confusing with no logic and decisions were made irrationally and all based on hue. Gem Marie could see that anyone so consumed by his music would never love anything or anyone as much as his musical creations. That was the one thing she knew for certain about Christina Pierre, music would always come first. She stared into the glass and looked into her own eyes, and told herself, "You are clever. You must find a way to help you. Your home is forever the Scotney, not here in the world." With only one bag left from her journey, she took inventory of it. In her possession was the sheet music for Christian Pierre's piece that she had taken from Professor Hertz. She still had the newspaper articles, she glimpsed over it then folded it into a smaller size, and placed it back into the sack. Which she then tied under her gown as she told herself sternly, "He must never know about the feelings you once had for him. Fighting back her tear she scolded herself, "You must put away those imaginative girlish ways in this cruel world your heart's history and sincerity are of no value here." The naïve girl that once ached to look into his eyes now feared his intentions. Gem Marie took a deep breath and finally sat on the plump small bed that was filled with cotton as she kept her eyes on the beams. She felt a sudden jerk, as the boat began rocking, the motions of the tides now beating against the ship was an indicator that the boat had now departed. The constant crashing of the water was a clear indicator that they were headed for Louisiana. Another place where she knew no one and would be a stranger to it. The boat rocked again the movement was different from the ship she had traveled in, she felt lightheaded, her stomach ached from hunger but at the same time she felt nausea. She placed her head down on the bed and looked up at the wooden ceiling above her pieces of shredded wood hung from it. Soms even dangling from thick cobwebs a large lizard scuttle across the rafters above her head, causing her to scream. She quickly rose to her feet and moved away from the bed where the lizard had affixed himself over. Moments later, Christian Pierre came rushing into her cabin, flinging the door open. "Are you hurt?" he asked, breathless, his eyes scanning the cabin. Gem Marie, shocked and surprised, quickly grabbed her dress and informed Christian of the lizard hanging from the beams. To her astonishment, he seemed amused by the long-tailed creature that had taken refuge in her cabin. Gem Marie, held her dress up against herself as Christian began to speak, "Did you know that lizards help keep snakes away and can even detach their own tails if needed?" Gem Marie, entertained by his odd submission of lizard facts, inquired, "And why would a lizard ever need to dismantle its own tail?" Christian Pierre, now taking the time to get a full, uninterrupted look at her, became intrigued by Gem Marie's brown eyes, which seemed to dance as she stood on edge awaiting his response. Sensing his captivation, Gem Marie adjusted the pattern of her gown in front of her in an attempt to lure his fixated eyes elsewhere. "Well," he explained, "when faced with danger or a very uncomfortable situation," he stated as he moved closer to her. "The lizard will wiggle its tail in order to create a distraction, by confusing its predator and granting it more time to escape." At that very moment, the lizard, which had been clinging to the rafters, fell and landed on a nearby chair before scurrying into a crevice. A frighten Gem Marie who lunged forward, was thrown off balance by the boat's rocking, she stumbled into Christian's arms. Christian, now positioned to get a better look into Gem Marie's eyes, noticed the small specks of amber that lingered around her chestnut-brown pupils. "You smell of oranges how alluring," he remarked. Gem Marie uncomfortable with his observation pulled away still holding her dress asked, "Do you have any instruments on this vessel? I would like to play; it calms me." Christian Pierre, who had been still examining her, sensed her discomfort but disregarded it as overreacting. "There will be time enough for playing. Dinner will be served shortly, and I want you to join me. Please get dressed immediately, the chef is preparing Irish stew, and I have a full staff on board to cater to our needs for this voyage. Elizabeth is a kind ship; she has never failed me. Let us show our respect to her and share your welcoming dinner together. Oh, and you need not worry about the lizards. The two cats on board Dorthy and Paulina will maintain order amongst them." Surprised by Christian Pierre's choice of words and playful demeanor, Gem Marie found him both amusing and mysterious. She agreed to his orders with a nod, her curiosity about the voyage and her enigmatic host growing with each passing moment. They sat at a large dining table bolted to the floor, eyeing one another as the ship's unpredictable sway sent plates gliding across the polished wood.

The servants stationed at either end moved swiftly, catching the wayward China and restoring order. As the vessel eased into calmer waters, the pair settled, savoring the rich aroma of rabbit stew wafting from their bowls. Seeing Gem Marie begin to relax, Christian seized the opportunity, his gaze sharp and probing. "There's an accent, faint but I can hear it distinct. You're well educated. Now, tell me, where are you truly from? And don't insult my intelligence with an American city. I know a European tongue when I hear it." Gem Marie's mind raced, every instinct finely attuned to the delicate balance of truth and deception. She had exhausted the tale that cast Christian Pierre was the benefactor of her education and multilingual skills. Now, she sensed that the truth or at least some sliver of it might be her only weapon. She measured her response with a faint smile. "I am from England," she answered, voice steady. "As for where, I couldn't say. My schooling was hardly geographic. It was languages they trained me in. *Parlez-vous français?*" Christian's eyes narrowed, the faintest hint of a smile playing at his lips. "Yes, but let's keep to English for now. Tell me, who was your master, and what is his lineage?" Suspicion lingered in the air between them. Gem Marie knew she was walking a narrow line and decided to challenge him, hoping to draw out his intentions. "Are these questions," she asked coolly, "designed to send me back? Or perhaps you intend to return me to him yourself?" Christian's expression flickered just enough to show she'd struck a nerve. Christian sat back in his chair and eyed Gem Marie, fully aware of her tactics to avoid his questioning. He had no intention of returning her anywhere. She had been groomed and molded into a well-rounded aristocrat, and it was obvious she had not been sold the details on how she arrived in Maryland were not clear, but he was determined to find out. "Why would you say that my dear? I'm just getting to know you. From what I've seen thus far, I rather enjoy your company. What gives you the impression that I want to return you? Who might you belong to?" Gem Marie, shocked at Christian Pierre's ability to see through her tactic to silence him, sat and pondered for a minute. Finally, after what felt like hours, she spoke, "There is no one to return to. I have been orphaned since the age of four and was sent to live with nuns. There, I was allowed to play what they considered holy instruments every day. Forgive me, but that is the story the whole truth I told Professor Hertz only instead of the nuns, I used your name in place. I did this because the newspapers were covered with stories about you, and when I heard you arrived at the school, I wanted to go with you. I knew only a great man could have composed such a piece as yours. From the very first time I heard it, I knew Professor Hertz was not its true composer. His ignorance of the Bach interpretation revealed his true level of music comprehension." Christian Pierre was now totally immersed in Gem Marie's dialogue. He had been sipping some wine the entire time she had been speaking. Once Christian heard that it was Gem Marie who had uncovered the hidden Bach method noted on the sides of the paper, he quickly handed his glass to the nearby servant. "So, it was you who helped incorporate it into the performance? But how? Surely the nuns could not have taught you how to distinguish that. "Gem Marie, now stunned, realized Christian was correct. Nuns, no matter how musically inclined, would never have been skilled in hidden interpretations unless they had studied under a great composer. After what felt like hours, she finally admitted to Christian that a wealthy bank owner named Monsieur Heritage often visited the convent due to an unpaid debt on the convent's land. Gem Marie skillfully conveyed the tale based on a book she had read about a poor family who owed money to a merciless bank owner who harassed them until the father fell ill. Christian Pierre, now further immersed, proclaimed that church and state had already been separated, and Gem Marie was much too young to have experienced that. Convinced that Christian Pierre was no hoax and knew his history well, Gem Marie told herself she would have to be more careful when fabricating stories with him. She decided she had no choice but to villainize Monsieur Heritage. How else could she explain why he would be trying to collect money from nuns? She continued with her elaborate tale about Monsieur and the nuns, "I now know the proper laws, but Monsieur was a ruthless man who took advantage of the nuns' naivety. He knew they had no way of knowing that he was not allowed to continue collecting on their land, to which had been paid off years before. The nuns, without argument, paid and deemed it God's work. One of the head older nuns, afraid and troubled by the thought of not having enough to pay, worried herself into sickness and then death. Christian Pierre eyes widen in disbelief To ensure the convent was still functioning with integrity and virtue, Monsieur Heritage made frequent visits and would teach me various subjects. From music to geography, he became intrigued with my ability to learn. I became well-versed, his demands of my comprehension were high, yet he never imagined that I would one day be released from the confines of the nunnery. So, he taught me almost everything he knew." Christian listened and smiled. He held out his hand to the servant on his right, who quickly placed his wine glass back into his hand. "You intrigue me, Gem Marie. You must tell me more about Monsieur Heritage and your moments together. I would love to hear about the many things he has taught you, but now it is late, and I have grown tired. The stew and wine are taking their effects on me." Gem Marie, now taking note of his facial expression, watched as the smirk faded on and off his face. His speech lacked any indication of whether he believed the story she had just told. Growing nervous due to her inability to read his demeanor, she held her hand out in an attempt to mimic his wine request. A servant quickly placed a glass of wine in her hand. She smiled and took a large swallow in an attempt to portray herself as a connoisseur. The rapid ingestion of the wine sent a rush to her head, coloring her cheeks a rosy red. This time, the fermented grapes were much sweeter. It did not burn but quickly quenched her thirst and sent a warm sensation through her body. She handed the now half-empty glass back to the servant, then picked up a piece of bread and bit it aggressively. Christian Pierre in an attempt to stifle his laughter let out a small chuckle at her mannerisms, clearly reflecting the effects of the wine. Gem Marie, now growing more relaxed took her liberty and ignored Christian Pierre's request to retire. "You know, sir, you appear to be a noble man, and I admire you for your greatness. You must know how much you are revered; the papers frequently echo the public's admiration for you. Today, I declare, is my day of gratitude for you and your generous nature. Your benevolence with your stew, wine, and boat solidifies your unique royal qualities that the newspapers often reference." Gem Marie inadvertently raised her glass of wine in a gesture, found it filled once again with a new glass of wine. Without hesitation, in a defensive reflex, she took another swallow, which tasted sweeter than the first. She motioned to the servant to remove the half-empty glass, then demanded that her harp be brought to her. The room seemed softer now, as if she were looking through water-filled eyes. It was the wetness of a single tear rolling down her cheek that awakened her from her brief illusions. Embarrassed and now taken with sorrow, she spoke to the room as if her lineage had been questioned. "Excuse me, my head has grown weary, and I too believe the wine and the stew have taken their effects on me. You look at me as if you see into my world. On this day, I sit on a rocking ship and believe I am with all that was once mine. I am considered strange in your world, a rare find. You sit opposite me and watch with grins because you believe I am a mere child. I speak no lies, for the wine will not allow my tongue to recite Aesop's fables. "Your great land of Louisiana will not bestow heaven under my feet. I am a virtuous girl from another time and place that is not permitted here. Maryland has crowned me a darkie even branded me a nigger, and I say, I will stand on the highest precipice and throw that common headdress of thorns they unwelcomed chose to bestow upon me into the Dead Sea. Look upon my face sir, and see it covered in glee as I watch it sink into the murkiest waters, for I know who I am. I will not allow strangers or circumstances to tell false tales of me. I am the daughter of the highest lineage bestowed upon Europe. I am Gem Marie." Her words lingered in the air, captivating and mesmerizing Christian Pierre. Intrigued by the poetic, educated slave girl, he demanded to know her exact origins. "She speaks as if she were Shakespeare himself, yet not well enough to reveal where she is truly from. Disclose your origins now and relieve your shoulders from the weight of mystery. You say you were raised by nuns and who else? Speak, please. I doubt that you lack the words. You seem to have the perfect ones for our first evening together. Miss Gem Marie, I assure you, what you see sitting across from you is your biggest admirer. I only long to know the source of your knowledge. I did not free you from that school to label you with the vulgarity of the ignorant. You must remember my purpose was thrusted upon me without choice. It was you that took my hand. I beg you to see clearly the wine has made you emotional, and you judge me like a suspected foe. The day has been long, and you are now weary. It is time you lay down and allow today to become yesterday." Christian Pierre rose to his feet and walked over to Gem Marie, who was now completely still and silent with her head down. The boat was calm and growing darker as the sun departed from one high portal window. He stood over her, then turned her chair to face him, then quickly picked her up without effort and carried her to the cabin he had placed her in earlier. He gently placed her on the plump overstuffed bed then stood in the doorway watching before walking away, "Sleep mysterious one for you need not prove your beauty to me." It had been almost a month since Gem Marie and Christian Pierre first boarded the ship together. Gem Marie, who had become quite familiar with the ship's workings, suspected that Christian's insistence on her learning about the ship was a ploy to distract her from wanting to play an instrument. She had grown so comfortable with the ship that when it finally coasted into the harbors of Louisiana, she stood in the captain's cabin, watching as the ocean and land slowly intertwined. Once the ship was docked and anchored, the two were quickly led to a grand carriage that would take them to Christian Pierre's estate. Gem Marie admired the view as the sun hung low in the sky, casting a warm golden hue over the landscape. The carriage, drawn by a pair of majestic bay horses, began its leisurely journey along a dirt road flanked by sprawling plantations and verdant fields. The air was thick with the sweet aroma of magnolias and jasmine, their blossoms releasing a heady perfume that mingled with the earthy scent of freshly tilled soil. The crickets and Cicadas provided a constant, rhythmic background hum, their chorus rising and falling like the waves of a distant ocean. The occasional call of a mating bird or the rustle of leaves as a gentle breeze passed through the towering oaks added to the natural symphony. As the carriage rolled along, the wheels creaked softly, and the horses' hooves made a steady, comforting clip-clop against the packed earth. The road was bordered by rows of towering sugarcane, their stalks swaying gently in the breeze, creating a soothing rustle that harmonized with the sounds of the journey. Beyond the fields, dense groves of cypress trees, draped in Spanish moss like ghostly curtains, stood sentinel, their roots submerged in the still waters of hidden bayous. Passing by grand plantation homes, their white columns gleaming in the fading light, Gem Marie caught glimpses of life in the antebellum South. Elegant verandas were adorned with wicker furniture and colorful potted plants, while the sounds of laughter and the strains of a piano wafted through open windows, hinting at the evening's revelries yet to come. "Welcome to Louisiana, Gem Marie. I can tell you this is just a small taste of her goodness. My estate, 'Eaux de Miel,' will be your home away from home, wherever that may be," Christian Pierre said warmly. "Honey waters? Why is your estate called 'Eaux de Miel'?" Gem Marie asked, her face now filled with curiosity and captivated by the sweet smell of jasmine, as a butterfly perched on the carriage window like second nature. "My estate is as busy and productive as a beehive's intricacy. The greater part of my plantation's population is women, just like the best and sweetest beehive it is too also ran by a queen and her best workers, which happen to be females. The people on my plantation flow as smoothly as water, why sometimes they appear to be floating. I seldom have any qualms, I have no runaways and no issues with the law. I consider myself a fair peaceful man with integrity, and you, my darling, have just joined the hive." Gem Marie sat back in the carriage, watching as the butterfly lifted off into flight, their journey continuing onward. The landscape shifted subtly; the road dipped and rose, revealing hidden lakes and ponds, their surfaces like mirrors reflecting the brilliant hues of the sunset. She had never heard a man speak in such a manner. He spoke as though Honey Waters was truly her home now, a place she had chosen willingly. Her hands grew cold, and her heart fluttered at the thought of spending years there. Monsieur Heritage was the only man she knew who spoke with such grace, a poignant grace that held her captive to his charm. Christian Pierre's eyes, speckled with emerald, commanded attention with every gesture he made. His words needed no convincing; they were calming and persuasive all at once, leaving her entranced by the possibility of a life she had never imagined. The carriage turned onto the Honey Waters estate, they were greeted by a long line of women and a few men standing on both side of the path. The path led to a grand mansion in the distance, a large white home with two imposing columns. The front of the mansion featured six expansive windows with black shutters, both top and bottom, and a spacious balcony in the center, high above. The grounds were adorned with an assortment of various flowers. The line of women, dressed in coordinated brown and yellow, waved, and smiled as the carriage passed. Some bowed, others curtsied. Christian Pierre smiled and adjusted the brim of his hat as he passed a few servants he greeted by name. The women were of all ethnicities and colors, young and old, with hair ranging from silver to jet black, styled in ways Gem Marie had never seen before. One woman, with striking silver and black hair that flowed below her waist, waved, and the ivory bracelets on her wrists clinked melodically as she moved her hands. The men stood at attention, reminiscent of Confederate soldiers, with varying shades of skin and even some with fiery red hair. Gem Marie blushed when one male servant locked eyes with her, tipping his hat. His piercing grey eyes and freckled skin glistened in the last rays of sunlight, casting an almost otherworldly glow on his face. As the carriage continued its way towards the big house the lines of servants joined hands together as they walked behind the carriage trailing the way. When the carriage stopped at the house a servant by the name of McCoy greeted them and took Gem Marie's hand as he assisted her off the carriage. "Master Pierre I am so delighted to see you back safe, there has been quite a few visitors that have stopped by since your departure. Also, some small changes to house were done, nothing too large. I hope you don't mind I came up with the changes based on some paintings you left in the parlor. Sir I am delighted that your back home again. Honey Waters is never quite the same when you are away." Christian Pierre smiled feeling at ease at the warm welcome McCoy always exuded whenever he returned from a long trip. As McCoy continued to brief Christian Pierre on the current affairs he escorted Gem Marie up the stairs into the entrance of the house. Once they entered into the foyer. Christian Peirre walked back to the front porch he beckoned for Gem Marie who stood by his side, now looking into the crowd of servants that resembled a sea of multicolored faces. Gem Marie had never seen that many people of so many different shades their hair and clothing different she heard whispers and then a hush went over them as Christien Pierre spoke. "My beautiful Honey Waters family I am happy that I am back amongst you all as I look around, I see that you all have done your part in maintaining our beautiful estate. Today I have with me a new addition her name is Gem Marie let us give a great Honey Waters welcome." Together in unison the crowd repeated, "We are happy to have you here welcome Gem Marie 'ou lakay ou kounye a' (You are home now.)" Christian Pierre nodded his head as an indicator for the crowd to disperse and return to their quarters. Gem Maries was lead back into the house and into the parlor where she was given a glass of lemonade and made to sit on a chair. Christian Pierre instructed McCoy on where Gem Marie should be placed. He advised that she be confined to her room for the rest of the evening, provided supper, and then put to bed and not to be awakened until dawn. As soon as Christian walked away to the veranda, McCoy removed the half-drunk glass of lemonade from Gem Marie's hand and led her down into the cellar. "You are a house servant, can you remember that?" McCoy said sternly. Gem Marie nodded and continued walking down the long, narrow hallway to a room at the far end of the cellar. It was the only room that stood alone and had a small, high window with a view of the path leading to the big house. "Master Pierre has placed you alone in this room. I wonder what special gifts do you possess." McCoy eyed Gem Marie one last time before exiting the room. she studied the room then she took a step back from the window, where she could see some grass, a few flowers, and squirrels that scurried by. The first few days at Honey Water she followed the same routine, Gem Marie woke at dawn to assist with breakfast and then was sent back to her room. She remained there until supper, which was served to her after everyone else had eaten. Once during supper, Gem Marie questioned the dish she had been given. It was a spicy but delicious soup containing a variety of ingredients that she could not help but question. She was quickly reprimanded by one of the other servants, who spoke quickly. "It's gumbo. Now, hush!" was all that was said. Since her arrival, she had been isolated and barely allowed to speak more than two words. In the evenings, she could often hear Christian Pierre entertaining guests, near the veranda. A woman named Lelina would frequently visit with her driver. She would court Christian Pierre on the veranda, exchanging pleasantries before the conversation inevitably drifted to Christian Pierre's unconventional methods of running his plantation and the extensive freedoms, he granted his house servants. Lelina wasn't typically one to offer advice on plantation operations, but Christian Pierre's methods were starkly different from those of her own father. She felt compelled to start sharing her concerns after a conversation with Margret, who had warned her that some of the house servants were taking large liberties. When Lelina informed Christian Pierre of the events that had taken place while he was away, she grew upset and annoyed when he brushed off her concerns with laughter "I'm afraid your adventures across the waters have left your house open to insubordination Mr. Pierre," she insisted. "You may not deem this serious now, but take note, some of your darkies have gone rogue right under your very own roof. It just frightening to imagine having such unruly spirits in the same house while you sleep. Are you aware that they are eating strawberry jam with cornbread, frog legs and turtle eggs? I mean, really Christian, frog legs and turtle eggs." Christian who was more amused than concerned let out a chuckle. Lady Lelina now embarrassed and annoyed continued, " You may laugh now Christian, but your attitude may change once you know that they have been conspiring in a secret language." Christian Pierre, who was amused by Lady Lelina remarks now was becoming slightly annoyed, "Now Lelina, Creole is no secret language, it's French mix with a little some other things and I have you know my slaves do not conspire. I leave the matters of conspiring slaves to those that are beaten regularly and seldom fed." Lady Lelina in shock at his response was determine to make Christian see the severity of the matter, "French or not, they are still conspiring. I have reason to believe it's all true. A trustworthy source, who wanted no part in such unruly behavior, informed me immediately in hopes that I might be the voice of reason to talk sense in you." Christian now fully aware Margret was the only one who spoke with Lady Lelina frequently while taking etiquette classes from her. "Lelina may I ask who this trustworthy birdie, which has been informing you of my servant's breakfast habits?" Christian inquired. Lelina, now flustered by Christian's nonchalant demeanor, replied quickly, "I can't say for fear they might be isolated and punished from speaking the truth in the days to come." Christian Pierre unfazed by the exaggerated tales of extravagant breakfasts stolen by slaves, felt a distance growing between himself and Lelina. At that moment, he realized he had grown weary of her and her superficial ways. She showed no interest in his love for music, preferring instead to dispel the latest rumors about him and the servants along with idle talk that held no significance for Christian's true worth. His trip to Maryland had introduced him to a talent beyond his imagination. Gem Marie, a rare presence in Honey Waters, was in the cellar below his feet possessing some of the greatest talent. He had no idea where she came from, but he wondered if her kind was common in her homeland. For years, Christian Pierre had scoured the globe for hands that possessed the rare skill to bring his creation to life. Doubts plagued him, whispering that he was merely a businessman, not a maestro. Yet, now, the key to his long-awaited masterpiece lay hidden in his very own cellar. As he listened to the idle chatter about stolen meals, a thrill of anticipation coursed through him his moment had finally arrived and was waiting for him to seize it. Christian turned to Lelina who was still prattling along about meals and late-night journeys to slave quarters and addressed her without allowing interruption. "Lelina, my dear, you look peaked. Perhaps you would like something more to drink or eat. Excuse me while I confer with the cook. I'll be right back," Christian said, hurrying into the house. He glanced over his shoulder one last time to see Lelina spreading open an embroidered hand fan. Once inside, he instructed his butler, McCoy, to prepare a tray of lemonade for Lady Lelina. Christian then descended into the cellar, giving the cook orders to prepare a lavish full-course meal for her. As he ventured deeper into the cellar towards Gem Marie's room, he called out but received no reply. Panic set in with the oppressive silence. Rushing to the door, he found Gem Marie sprawled across the small bed in nothing but a petticoat, drenched in perspiration and mumbling incoherently. Unable to determine the nature of her ailment, he sprinted back to the kitchen. Without a word to the cook, who was already busy with Lelina's meal, Christian grabbed a bucket of water and returned to Gem Marie's room. He scooped water into a nearby tin cup and held it to her lips, forcing her to drink. She choked, spewing water onto herself before quickly closing her eyes in exhaustion. Christian laid Gem Marie gently on the bed, tearing away her remaining garment, exposing her neck and chest. With urgency, he splashed the last of the water from the tin cup onto her face and body. The cold shock made her cry out and mutter incoherent words. She weakly raised her hands, waving them feebly as beads of sweat rolled down her face. "The heat... is unbearable, Monsieur. May I play my harp today? My head... struck by rocks and pebbles. My harp, please, Monsieur," she pleaded before slipping back into unconsciousness. In a desperate panic, Christian tore the bottom of her chemise, leaving her chest bare and her lower half scantily clad. He retrieved a handkerchief from his pocket and fanned her face until she stirred slightly. He scooped more water from the bucket and pour it down her throat until she coughed and sputtered. Alternating between drenching her and fanning her with his handkerchief, he fought to keep her awake. Finally, Gem Marie's eyes fluttered open, and she reached for the tin cup. Christian eagerly assisted her. "More, please," she whispered, finishing the cup in one gulp. Christian obliged, dipping the cup into the cool water once more before handing it to her. Gem Marie, now regaining her strength, drank deeply without pause. She sat up on the bed and asked, "Where am I?" Christian Pierre, relieved to see Gem Marie regaining her faculties, smiled gently. "My dear. You are much closer to heaven. You are at Honey Waters plantation." "Heaven!" a voice shouted, "Mr. Pierre, what are you doing with that half-naked darkie? Oh, my Lord, I'm going to faint." Lelina leaned on the wall for support, "I can't believe the rumors are true. Here I am, worried that you may have taken ill from being gone for so long. So I alone travel down into this dark dreadful cellar to find you perfectly well, discussing heaven with your half-naked slave." Lady Lelina stood in the doorway with her hand perch on the doorway her posture now reflecting as if she were about to faint. Christian Pierre, in shock, glanced at Gem Marie, who was visibly frightened by Ms. Lelina's tone. She quickly reached for an old throw on the bed and covered herself, her eyes darting between the two. "Lelina, there is a perfectly good explanation for this situation. If you calm down for a moment, I'll explain. I came down here to make sure Cook had prepared a special meal for you. Well, while I was here, I found my new house servant, Gem Marie, half clothes and half dead from the heat. I paid a pretty penny for this European gal. Unfortunately, she hasn't grown accustomed to our heat yet. Rightfully so, as she just arrived less than a month ago. I keep her down here, away from the others, because I haven't learned her habits. Frankly, Lelina, I'm surprised that you would perceive me as a man who would congregate with his cargo while the beautiful lady in waiting is right above my head. Why, just to ponder on such an event has me wondering where the motivation for your thoughts lies." Lelina's eyes narrowed, suspicion etched across her face. "My thoughts? You speak of a slave as if she is your equal. What do you care if your new darkie is overwhelmed by the heat? Cook and the others can look after her. Why I myself was left unattended on that porch in the heat, I might add. Thank goodness for my specially made hand fan my daddy bought back from North Carolina, or I don't know how I would manage. The sun has been unusually high today. I think I feel something coming on right now." Christian stepped closer, his voice dropping to a conspiratorial whisper. "There, there never you mind. I had Cook make you some fresh Lemonade. I distinctly told him to put fresh mint leaves and some sugar cane just as you like it." Lelina hesitated, the promise of her favorite drink momentarily distracting her. But a flicker of doubt remained in her eyes as she looked at Christian Pierre and then back at Gem Marie, the tension in the room evident. Christian Pierre took Lelina's hand and gently raised it to his lips for a tender kiss before speaking again. "You ought not come down to the cellar again. This is no place for a lady. Cook! Come here boy, and assist Lady Lelina. Have you prepared her drink with a freshly picked mint leaf, as I instructed?" Cook, met Lady Lelina and Christian Pierre at the top of the steps, escorting her the rest of the way to the parlor. He seated her in a large, cushioned chair where two servants stood on either side, each holding a large hand fan ready to assist. They fanned her and applied a cool rag to her wrist. Cook, who had overheard the entire commotion from Gem Marie's room, had arranged for another cool glass of lemonade for Lady Lelina. Grateful for the cook's quick thinking, Christian Pierre called out for a status update on the meal. "How long until Ms. Lelina's meal is ready?" "Any minute now, sir. The servants are setting the table as we speak," the cook replied. Lelina reclined in the chair and stared at Christian Pierre, noting his newfound attentiveness. She felt a sense of power in the way her accusations had made him uncomfortable. His eagerness to please her only made him more alluring. Her curiosity about the new servant gnawed at her. The young woman's face and eyes hinted at origins from distant lands. Lelina replayed the incident in her mind, focusing now on the gown that lay draped over a chair. Despite being covered in dirt, the garment's fine fabric still reflected its high quality, almost resembling a princess's gown. Christian Pierre sipped on a glass of lemonade watching Lelina sit in silence. She stole glances at him, while her mind was clearly elsewhere. Christian grew increasingly uncomfortable, his thoughts drifting to Gem Marie and her near-death experience. Lelina's idle chatter only added to his unease. Gem Marie's reaction to the heat was telling, she had never endured hard manual labor or been exposed to extreme weather. This young, exotic beauty, fluent in multiple languages and skilled with instruments, could not have been born a slave. He yearned to speak with her, to uncover the truth about her origins and her presence at the school. To quell his impatience for Lelina's departure, he summoned Cook for an update on the meal. Cook replied with a smile, "Dinner is prepared and waiting Sir." Christian Pierre led Ms. Lelina to the dining area, where they enjoyed a lavish meal and planned their upcoming outings. Cook, pleased with the reception of his meal, returned to the cellar to check on Gem Marie. When he arrived, he found Gem Marie being chastised by McCoy. "Now gal, I don't know where Master Pierre got you from, cause I'm trying to figure out, what kind of nigger can't take the heat in the cellar on a day like this one?" McCoy's voice was laced with disdain. Gem Marie, trembling and fearful, had not fully recovered from the heat. She winced at McCoy's use of the word that Monsieur Heritage hated, it was the same word Otis had called her. Too afraid to say anything else, she replied in a quivering voice, "I had no water or food today, and the room was very hot." "Did you hear that, Cook?" McCoy sneered. Cook now amused shook his head and nodded. McCoy smiled, in an attempt to control his irritation. "Are you crazy, gal? Do you think I'm supposed to serve you? Here you are, with Cook just three steps away from you, and you too damn lazy to get up and get your own water. You listen here and listen good, Honey Waters is one of the best plantations. We got no hangings here, and I haven't seen a man whipped in over three years. Ain't that right, Cook?" "Yessir, and ain't nobody ever run away from Honey Waters either," Cook affirmed. McCoy now moved in closer to Gem Marie as he lowered his voice, "You see, gal, we do as we're told here and it's like we free here. We got strawberries in the morning with biscuits and gravy. And Gumbo and cornbread in the evenings. We got the cleanest well water in all of Louisiana, ain't dat right Cook." Cook nodded his head with a large grin a drop of perspiration hung off the tip of his nose. " Master Pierre even got me my very own colt. Now, you name one nigger that got his very own purebred colt from a white man for nothing." "There ain't none!" Cook quickly replied, eager to show his support for McCoy. "Where you from, gal? With dem cat eyes? You ain't Creole dats for sure, your skin brown and green." McCoy continued to study her face, his gaze sharp and unyielding. Gem Marie, now shaking uncontrollably, found herself unable to speak. She squeezed her eyes shut, hoping to awaken from what felt like a horrific nightmare. But there was no escape from the harsh barrage unleashed by McCoy and Cook. As she heard the slur "nigger" repeated, she covered her ears, recoiling inwardly. In her mind, she imagined herself back at The Scotney, running to the parlor in search of her harp. The castle was dark and hollow, each room she entered barren and cloaked in dust. She climbed the stairs to Monsieur's room, but it, too, lay abandoned. Frantic, she rushed downstairs to Greta's quarters, only to find the room empty, save for a bassinet emitting the cries of a baby. Desperation gripped her as she hurried over to cradle baby Philip, the one familiar presence she could sense in the desolate castle. The wailing grew louder as she neared the bassinet, where a white blanket lay draped over the infant. But when she lifted the blanket, she found nothing—an empty bassinet, yet the haunting cries continued without a source. The eerie sight struck her like a blow, forcing a high-pitched scream from her lips as she cried out, "Monsieur, help me!" "Her cry was so unexpected that it startled both Cook and McCoy, who froze in place. Ms. Lelina dropped her napkin, staring at Christian Pierre in horror. Christian hesitated, torn between investigating the noise or remaining seated. Ultimately, he stayed in his chair. "Christian, are you really just going to sit there while that deranged darkie screams in your home?" Lelina's crude remark enraged him. "Clearly, I was mistaken," he responded. "She hasn't been overtaken by the heat; she has what I first suspected a fever. Possibly Dengue, I believe." "Dengue? Well, Christian, which calls for immediate care her own kind should be attending to her. But it's late, and I'll be heading home now. Thank you for your kindness and hospitality, as always. It's been a pleasure. No need to trouble McCoy; my driver is waiting on the veranda," Lelina replied, with a coldness that Christian couldn't ignore. Taking note of Lady Lelina's discomfort, Christian nodded. "Of course, Lelina. Thank you for coming. I'll be in touch for our next outing," he said, relieved as she prepared to leave. Standing on the veranda, he waved as her carriage disappeared into the night. As soon as it was out of sight, he rushed to the cellar. When Christian arrived in the cellar, he stood in the hallway, watching McCoy and Cook surround Gem Marie, who was still shaking. "Gal, have you lost your mind? Master Pierre's up in the dining room with Lady Lelina, enjoying dinner, and you're down here howling at the moon like an old hound dog," Cook exclaimed, still startled. "Who dat she calling? Ain't nobody by dat name here at Honey Waters," McCoy interjected, his voice trembling. "This gal gon' cause problems I feel it." At that moment, Christian Pierre entered the room, his eyes scanning everyone before he fully stepped in. "Now, what is going on in my home? Unnatural screams coming from the cellar during my supper? It was so loud, Ms. Lelina and I had to cut our dinner short. Well, somebody say something." McCoy nervously spoke up, giving Gem Marie a quick evil eye. "We ain't done nothing, sir, 'cept come to check if she need more water. Then she got to moving around strange-like, ain't that right, Cook?" "Sure is, Master Pierre," Cook added. "Then her eyes got to rolling and closing, and den she just screamed out, 'Monny sore!' Just like that, Master Pierre. I swear we ain't harmed a hair on her." McCoy nodded in agreement, timidly adding, "Master Pierre, I beg your pardon, sir, but dat gal don't seem right. It's like she got something trapped in her." Christian Pierre, now certain that Gem Marie's tales of Monsieur Heritage was a half-truth. He was convinced that Monsieur Heritage must have been her master and she, his mistress. "Thank you, men, for your help, but I'll handle this. You gentlemen can go upstairs and share that delicious meal Cook prepared with the others. I've got this under control." The two men, now grateful for Gem Marie's behavior, smiled and nodded at Christian and then at Gem Marie. Their jovial voices faded away as they headed upstairs confirming two blueberry pies. Christian Pierre walked out of the room and descended into the cellar's kitchen. He grabbed a bowl, filled it with potatoes and gravy that the cook had set aside, and picked up a biscuit. Returning to the room, he handed the bowl to Gem Marie and ordered her to eat. He watched as she took small nibbles of the biscuit, then, growing impatient, he snatched the bowl from her hand. "I'm not going to wait for you to decide if you want to eat or starve," he said sternly. He told her to open her mouth wide and shoved a large spoonful of gravy and potatoes into her mouth. To Gem Marie's surprise, the food was tasty, as she realized just how hungry she was. She quickly chewed the remaining food, opening and closing her mouth to Christian's orders like an infant. When she was done, she reached for the tin cup of water placed on a small table. Christian Pierre chastised her again, "If you think I'm going to feed you and fetch water for you, Gem Marie, you are sadly mistaken. You have legs get up and grab that tin cup now." Gem Marie stood up, holding the fabric she had been using as a cover. She turned her back to Christian Pierre, tied a knot in the fabric around herself, then quickly grabbed the cup of water and drank it down, then hurried back to bed. Christian stood up then advised her, "Tomorrow, you will rise with the sun and help with the meals alongside the cook and the others. After you are done, you will report to me and explain everything concerning Monsieur Heritage and this time I want the truth."

Chapter: 17

Soon

As night fell and the air grew cold, Monsieur Heritage regained consciousness. The only light came from the last quarter moon, casting a dim glow across the landscape. Around him, he could make out only the faint shimmer of leaves and the scattered sparkle of stones on the ground. No living thing seemed to stir only a few fireflies danced in the distance. His head throbbed slightly from the blow of a tree branch that had thrown him from his horse. Desperately, he scanned the darkness, searching for his horse, Kennedy, but there was no sign of him. Suddenly, two round, glowing reflections appeared, weaving in and out of the distant brush. They were slowly approaching. Monsieur Heritage strained to make sense of the blurred, shimmering image. Placing both palms flat on the ground, he braced himself to rise. Just then, the clouds in the sky shifted, as if parted by unseen hands, revealing the bright full moon. Its glow bathed the area, casting a light brighter than any candle. Monsieur Heritage's heart pounded as his gaze returned to the two glowing orbs. He now realized they weren't fireflies, but the gleaming eyes of a large wolf. Gripped by fear, he locked eyes with the lone wolf, its gaze unyielding and its fangs bared. Moving slowly, he reached down into his boot and drew a large dagger. Without breaking eye contact, he adjusted his grip, bracing for an inevitable attack. The wolf continued to advance, then abruptly paused, its attention diverted by a sound behind it. In the chilling night air, Monsieur Heritage could only see the wolf's misty breath hovering around its head. Scanning the surroundings, he confirmed that the wolf was indeed alone, with no pack in sight. A low rumble suddenly rose from the distance, accompanied by a familiar warning snarl, Kennedy, his horse came to a halt right behind the wolf, who immediately tensed, now aware of Kennedy's presence. Fangs glistening in the moonlight, the wolf crouched, ready to strike. Monsieur Heritage, holding the brass-handled dagger tightly, called out, "Kennedy! Danje!" With marksman-like precision, he threw the dagger, striking the wolf squarely in the throat. The wolf let out a piercing howl, cut short as Kennedy reared up, his powerful hooves crashing down onto the creature's head. The impact sent the dagger skittering across the ground, landing by Monsieur Heritage's feet. The wolf scrambled back into the darkness, a streak of blood marking its retreat. Monsieur Heritage retrieved the dagger, admiring the blade's craftsmanship and Kennedy's unwavering loyalty. He wiped the blood from the steel on his sleeve, then carefully slid it back into his boot. Swiftly, he mounted the formidable stallion, giving a single command: "Rentrer à la maison!" Upon reaching Scotney, he headed directly to his room, craving the solitude of the night. But as he opened the door, he froze, startled. Greta was there, seated calmly in the dim glow, her presence both unexpected and unnerving. Eyes narrowed, he demanded, "You sit here, alone, in my room. Who else knows you're here?" Greta's expression betrayed a hint of emotion, though she held her composure. "No one," she replied softly. "I entered when I saw you approaching in the moonlight." His voice dropped to a warning whisper. "Then see that it remains so. We must not invite suspicion." "Our arrangement is not for others' eyes. This union requires no other acknowledgement." Taken aback by the urgency in his voice, Greta responded, "Everyone is asleep. The cock will crow soon, and you will once again don your stained garments. My dear husband, it was you who entrusted me with our love. It was you who gave me title as wife. I only ask that you keep nothing from me that burdens your heart. I want to help you. I grieve for Gem Marie too; she is the daughter that I did not carry. She prepared me for our son, her inquisitive nature and warmth banished all my fears of motherhood. I beg you, Monsieur, do not continue to seek revenge in the dark. She will return home." "Seek revenge?" he echoed, a dangerous edge to his voice. "The man who has stolen my daughter has no need to worry about revenge. It is death's certainty that should concern him." "I will not stop until she is returned," he vowed, his voice steely. "And you speak in riddles, woman, why waiting in darkness for my return. I ask you why? What troubles you now? Does the bed of fine linen not ease your doubts? Who dares contest what we have vowed to hold? Not a soul! Then why must you torment me? Speak now, what truly lies in your heart. Is it a new dress? More scented water? Does not our son give you peace and joy. Or do you hide behind mystery because you desire to be known in my bedroom also?" Greta's eyes widened in astonishment, welling up with tears and anger, she walked over to Monsieur and slapped his face. "Torment you? To be known? My dear husband, you have blood on your clothes again, yet you explain nothing. You want my heart's truth? Answer me this: when you have blood on your clothes and I look upon you without judging eyes, am I to be your servant or your wife?" Monsieur, now growing weary, felt the lingering sting of the tree branch's earlier blow trickle down his forehead. He sighed, the sound heavy with exhaustion, and slowly reached down into his boot to retrieve a dagger. Holding it up to catch the dim candlelight, he admired its blade before setting it on the table. "That dagger," he began, voice thick with an unyielding calm, "carries the blood of a great wolf a beast that lunged at me after I was thrown from my horse by that cursed branch. And you wonder what you are to me now, as I stand before you bruised and weary, roused from a sleep fit for the dead?" He paused, his gaze unwavering. "You are both, my lovely Greta. Now, make haste and remove my clothing." With his final command, Monsieur turned his back to her, giving Greta no choice but to comply. Resentful yet steeled by her own lingering anger, she reached for the dusty jacket draped over his shoulders and peeled it off. Her steps deliberately, she circled him slowly, calculating her next move. She paused to face him, her fingers finding his collar as she undid the first two buttons, her eyes fixed intently on his. Then, with a swift and sudden motion, she gripped his shirt and tore it open, the buttons scattering onto the floor. Monsieur watched silently, his expression unreadable as Greta's gaze lingered on his bare chest, her eyes tracking the steady rise and fall of his breath. The longer she watched, the faster his breathing became. "Philip Adam Heritage, you once pillaged the nourishment for our child from me, then asked if I had known its taste. I spoke no lie when I insisted it was foreign to me. Yet from that day, you have made me grow accustomed to the taste of my own. Tell me, husband, ruler, and master, what have you grown accustomed to?" Monsieur Heritage, standing bare-chested before Greta, picked her off her feet and carried her to his large king bed, placing her gently on the plush sheets. Suddenly, a loud banging echoed from the castle door. A bell sounded just as the cock began to crow. Shouts reverberated throughout the castle, calling for Monsieur Heritage. It was the footman with some of the field servants. Greta sprang from the bed and peered out of the large window. She saw a strange horse tied to the garden entrance. As daylight began to break, she spotted two other male servants running towards the castle. It appeared as if Scotney was under some form of attack. Heart pounding, Greta darted away from the window and toward Monsieur, who quickly reached for a formal shirt, slipping it on with practiced haste. A sharp knock suddenly pierced the tense silence.

"Monsieur Heritage, it's Madam Henry, sir! Please, open up there's trouble at the moat. A man has stormed through without warning!" Terrified by her mother's sudden appearance and dreading who else might be with her Greta shrank behind the wardrobe, holding her breath as Monsieur opened the door. "My apologies, sir, forgive the intrusion " Madam Henry began, her voice laced with urgency. "But a young man on horseback has forced his way past the gates and over the moat I am certain I've never seen his face before. I worry what mischief he may intend." Monsieur's jaw tightened, his eyes darkening as he seized the dagger from the table. With a curt nod, he brushed past Madam Henry and strode toward the stairs, his steps quickening as he made his way to confront the intruder waiting at the front door. Madam Henry jostled as she stood in the center of Monsieur's room, peering around in silence. She picked up a blood-stained shirt with missing buttons, looked around the room again, and spoke aloud, "You can come out, daughter. Your jasmine scent lingers, and your son will wake soon." Greta slowly emerged from behind the wardrobe, mustering enough courage to hold her head up and face her mother. "I waited in the dark for him. He rides late and returns with blood on him." Madam Henry quickly retorted, "You must know your place. He has taken you as his wife with no regard for what the outside world can do. But remember, Gem Marie holds his heart as well. You cannot allow yourself to be seen by others. If it were revealed that he has willingly fathered a child with you out of love, I shudder at the thought of what could be done. Listen, daughter, you must contain your urges and remain a woman of virtue." Greta, now irritated by the continued assumptions of her presence in Monsieur's bedroom, walked over to the bedroom door and closed it. "My urges? My urges! Mother, I am no mare in heat. I came here out of concern. Yes, I have laid with a man, and he has fathered a child with me, but I am no whore. He loves me mother, and has taken me as his wife. But I am no fool. I know my place here at the Scotney and out there in the world. I am just as confused as you are when I am reminded by our son. Look at me, your daughter, chosen by the master of the house. He lays with no one else. I am the creator of his only heir." Madam Henry, shocked by Greta's outspokenness, exclaimed, "Your tongue is brazen! You speak as though you were born free and were the lady of the house. Remember, though we are on Scotney soil, beyond these gates lie ropes and lashes that silence such talk. If you ever feel free enough to run away like Gem Marie, think clearly you are no child. The comforts you enjoy here are clear, from the embroidered linens on your bed, which I wash and hang for all to see. He hides nothing anymore, requesting hats and gowns from the seamstress, carrying them openly. I'm left making excuses for his bold displays of affection towards you. "Greta, startled by her mother's words, suddenly realized she hadn't noticed all the new gifts Monsieur had bestowed on her. "Mother don't be foolish; no one notices these things but you. Madam Henry now frustrated at Greta's blatant denial, " I'm forced to tell the others that he misses Gem Marie dearly, that your closeness with her brings him comfort, and that he has no one else to lavish with gifts in her absence. There are things we cannot speak of here, things that should never leave these walls. But I must ask, daughter: are you certain there is no other woman outside of the Scotney? Are you certain that when he rides off alone, he only searches for Gem Marie? Why does he return, night after night, with blood on his clothes, right before dawn unconcerned about you waiting in the dark in his chambers?" Greta, embarrassed by her mother's words and unsure if she'd overheard intimate conversations, retorted, "Do you dare eavesdrop on us? Why do you linger in the corridors, hoping to hear my so-called follies? I know the laws, and I will never speak of the child he's fathered with me. Why must you torment me so, Mother?" Greta raised her hand as if to strike her mother, unable to bear the shame of her knowing the depths of her affair with Monsieur. But Madam Henry swiftly caught Greta's wrist in a tight grip. "Foolish girl," she warned, "be careful your obsession may drive you mad. Look there, on the table: his shirt is stained with blood, clear as day. You dare strike me, the one who has protected you all these years, who shielded your life so you may stand before me without fear and speak of a man who is not your equal. You lie with your master for comfort and risk all our lives, should anyone outside discover that we live as though we are free." She released Greta's wrist and turned to leave. "I will not burden you further, daughter. I will leave you to your own choices. But now, you too should leave the master's chambers and go tend to your son." Greta, now feeling regret welling up within her, looked away from the bloody shirt, realizing how deeply her paranoia and the love for Monsieur had consumed her. Madam Henry, who was headed downstairs, paused for a moment, she could hear voices coming from the parlor. She slowly took two more steps right before she reached for the parlor door, she stood outside of it and listened attentively. She could hear Monsieur speaking to the young rider called Baron Fitzgerald who had charged the moat. Every word seemed to hang in the air, filled with ominous tension. Madam Henry pondered, "What secrets did the blood on the shirt conceal? And what truth lay hidden in the conversation beyond the parlor door?" As Madam Henry strained to listen, her heart pounded with the suspense of what she might uncover. "So, you're certain Gem Marie was taken from New York to Maryland? But how can you be sure it was my Gem Marie?" Baron Fitzgerald, visibly uneasy, lowered his gaze, his eyes tracing the intricate patterns on the floor. "Well, sir, word has it that a remarkably talented girl was bought and taken to serve as a maid at a prestigious music school for some of the wealthiest children in the area. Forgive my bluntness, but they describe her not as brown or mulatto, but as exceptionally beautiful and foreign but no one has actually really seen her. As soon as I confirmed she was alive, I returned to England without delay. Her last known location was indeed Maryland. "I must warn you, sir, that particularly ruthless slave traders operate in America, and I fear they may soon target her for a profitable trade. It seems that slaves with European training are in high demand among affluent slave owners further south." Monsieur Heritage, now both relieved and deeply unsettled by news of Gem Marie's survival, felt a surge of anxiety and fury at the thought of her being captured by a slave trader. He understood that to reclaim her, he could not approach her as a father but rather as a master or a merchant. Monsieur Heritage, now resolute in his pursuit of Gem Marie's exact location, gave orders to Baron, "I need the names of the wealthiest men. And this music school, who runs it? If there's any culture within the school, surely someone has traveled to Europe at least once. Investigate the school thoroughly from top to bottom. I want the headmaster's name and the names of their family members. Gather all this information you can within two days. There are men returning from the sea daily; one of them must know something. Prepare yourself for travel as well." With grim determination, Monsieur Heritage crossed the room to a shelf near the window, seizing a large brass bell. He rang it vigorously, the clamor echoing through the castle. "Attention! Attention! Tout le monde se présente au parloir maintenant! Everyone to the parlor, now! "The entire castle was alerted. The emergency bell, unused for years, tolled with a deep resonance that stirred memories of the great storm, when windows had shattered, and animals needed urgent tending. This, however, was no storm, every servant and worker was summoned scurried about. Those laboring in the fields were beckoned urgently to the castle. Madam Henry waited, her heart pounding, listening for the first servant to approach before stepping from behind the door and entering the parlor. Greta soon followed, trailed by the other servants from the cellar. Within moments, the parlor and its doorways were filled to capacity. The young rider, now observing the assembled staff, noted the diverse appearances of the castle's residents. Some seemed as regal as royalty, while others bore the humble look of the working class he had seen in town. His gaze finally settled on Monsieur Heritage, and he began to understand the whispers about the reclusive, wealthy banker who rarely ventured into the town. "Everyone, listen to me," Monsieur Heritage's voice commanded attention. "I have good news. Our Gem Marie is alive." The room erupted with joyous exclamations. "This young man has found her, and he and I shall soon depart for America to return her safely. I cannot say how long we will be away, as this is one of my greatest tasks the return of Gem Marie. I'm sure you all remember her, the one whose feet echoed through these halls as a child, then stolen from the Scotney." A female servant let out a terrifying gasp, and soft whispers spread through the crowd, many having believed Gem Marie had run away. Monsieur Heritage continued, his voice strong and commanding. "Our soldiers will be heightened around the castle and the moat. No strangers are to be permitted on this soil. The Scotney will be managed as usual during my absence, with only a few small changes. I want all younger servants and children under careful watch. Greta and Madam Henry are to take inventory of everyone daily. The castle will be run just as if I were standing among you. Gem Marie was taken in the dead of night because she is a member of the Scotney, you are all unbelievably valuable. You must remember that if things are done as you are told under my rules and leadership, all will be safe as long as you remain here. I will not tolerate any of my people being harmed or taken. What is here at The Scotney must remain at The Scotney. I will leave soon and return with Gem Marie. "Salut au Scotney pour toujours et à jamais!" The weight of his words hung in the air as the castle's inhabitants chanted together in French and English, "Hail to the Scotney forever and ever," bracing themselves for the journey ahead. Greta and Madam Henry nodded in agreement, confirming their commitment to maintaining the house's status. "So, my incredibly beautiful daughter, the master of the house recognizes you as the lady of Scotney. Whatever love you have shown him, it is working. Remember to provide him with a proper goodbye; he will need your love to be his strength during his journey." Greta, taking note of her mother's proud and straight posture, replied, "You speak of my love as if it were a plan to lure him, my sweet mother. There is nothing to work on; it is he who craves me. We have created a union that not even the king's law could destroy." Madam Henry, with a confident smile reminiscent of her daughter's, retorted, "Careful, my daughter. You speak of the King's law as if you are not bound by it, and with only one heir." Greta, now observing Monsieur Heritage as he continued to rally the servants, noted how he controlled them as if soothing commoners, reassuring them that no one could infiltrate the Scotney. He reminded them once again that Gem Marie's talents made her a highly sought-after possession. " This vessel, crafted by the inventor of steamboats himself, Robert Fulton, was one of the safest and fastest, and the only one of its kind in England. It was thanks to the assistance of his father, Jean Paul who kept the word of Monsieur Gracieux, that the seaman had been able to purchase the boat. Monsieur Heritage who had been given a box with items from his father and grandfather pulled out an item and handed it to Baron with strict instructions. Monsieur Heritage's plan was set in motion, a journey shrouded in mystery and anticipation. Greta continued to watch Monsieur Heritage from a distance as he meticulously reviewed the details and orders for the upcoming trip. Her eyes sparkled with admiration as his display of authority seemed to overshadowed Baron Fitzgerald. She turned away and headed for the cellar to find her mother, who had gone down with the others. Remembering baby Philip, she quickened her pace, eager to fetch a piece of the morning's biscuits for herself. As she hurried, she was stopped and cornered by Livingston, one of the servants who had kept a watchful eye on Greta ever since baby Philip's birth. Unknown to Greta, Madam Henry had once threatened Livingston with scissors at his throat for calling Greta's unborn child a bastard. "You're in a hurry aren't you Greta." Livingston appear from out of the shadows impeding Greta's way, "So tell me you and your mother are in charge of what exactly? Oh yes, the children, and rightly so. However, it is not the children Monsieur Heritage should be concerned about," Livingston spoke, his tone laced with mockery. Greta, now agitated, realized Livingston had cornered her in a rarely traveled, dimly lit area. Aware of her isolation, she adjusted her demeanor and retorted, "Oh, and what should be his concern?" Livingston, relishing her attention, replied, "The sea, of course. Traveling to America is fraught with danger. There are tales of pirates who slit throats for gold and storms that can

217

capsize boats, sending them crashing. Then, once in the water, the sharks circle. There are even fish that can fly." Greta, initially captivated by his gruesome tales, lost her interest upon hearing about flying fish. Now slightly concerned that Monsieur Heritage might face unknown perils, she pushed Livingston aside. "Get out of my way, Livingston, with your foolish talk of flying fish. Monsieur Heritage wants everything in order before he leaves. He has left my mother and I in charge and he has made a list of all to be done, and whatever is not completed, I am to report." Realizing Greta's true authority in managing the castle, Livingston moved aside but not before grabbing her hand and kissing it. "I too, like Monsieur, was born in France. Greta, I am a gentleman always. Pardonne-moi," he said, a sly smile playing on his lips. "You know, Greta, I see how you look at him, always staring with such admiration in your eyes." Livingston moved in closer, almost pinning Greta against the wall. "What are you thinking about when you stare at him? Do you daydream of him? Ah yes you wish he was the father of that bastard child, don't you?" Enraged, Greta raised her hands, ready to strike Livingston for his disrespectful tone, his words cutting through the desolate cellar hallway like a knife. "Calm down, Greta. You wouldn't want to hurt that delicate hand of yours. Those hands were made for picking flowers and stirring porridge." Livingston continued as he held Greta's wrist tight. "All I want you to know is that I can help you with your baby, I can tell Monsieur I am the father, and I want to be truthful now since we will be married soon." Greta's eyes widen as she listened to Livingston bare his true feelings for her. Livingston still holding one of Greta's hand moved in closer, "He almost looks like me," Playing with a strand of Greta's hair while the breath of each of his syllables brushed up against her cheeks. "If we had known one another at least once. I would have given my life and sworn he was from my loins." Greta, now amused by Livingston's delusions of baby Philip's features, gave forth a sense of pride that was permeating all over her body. The truth in knowing she had only given herself to Monsieur Heritage and him alone cultivated a rush of courage. "Help me with my son? Greta now aware of how close Livingston had positioned himself near her, turned her head so her lips met his. Now with only an inch between them she retorted, "Surely you don't believe my bastard child resembles you?" Greta let out a light chuckle that almost resembled a witches tone it caused her body to shake and brush up against Livingston. "You will never know who fathered my child and you cannot help anyone because you Livingston weep at night in your sleep." "Lies! Greta, you lie!" Livingston shouted in anger, "I speak the truth as always. Tell me, who is the woman you call out to that causes tears to run down your face while you dream? I witness it and took pity on you, could it be the mother you have never known." "Silence! Greta you are a Liar. A Liar and a whore is what you are. You dare to speak such things. You who wears the smell of Jasmin to lure men into deception. Why won't you reveal who fathered your child. Perhaps because there are so many, you cannot choose." Livingston now regaining his pride smiled with contempt as he gazed at her. Greta, now even more amused at Livingston's jealousy, began taking her power back. She strategically repositioned herself and leaned in closely to Livingston and whispered, "Of course I know who fathered my child. Surely when I laid down with him, I kept my eyes open and watched as he forced himself upon me with merriness" Livingston, shocked by Greta's retort, stepped further away from her and stammered, "Your mother should hear of your talk. Greta, you are not the virtuous woman I once knew. Look there" Livingston now pointing to Greta's chest continued, "Your shoulders are revealed and even your breast plate lays open beckoning for touch. Your lips tainted with raspberries, speak in the ways of a woman that has seen many days in the world." Greta now unbothered an annoyed with Livingston retorted, "And I have grown tired of you Livingston, you long to smell the jasmine behind my ears. Leave me alone you've held me captive long enough. I need to tend to my son, I will not play foolish games of taunt with you." With a loss of appetite and sprinting on toes, Greta quickly retreated up the back stairs that led to the parlor. The intrigue and tension of Livingston's true confessions impeded her journey, but her thoughts remained on the immediate care of her son. Almost to the verge of tears she ran past the parlor that was now empty, all the servants had dispersed. Through a large bay window she could see Baron Fitzgerald mounting his horse for departure. Still in search of her mother she saw no one, while heading for her room she thought of baby Philip, hungry and pinned to his bassinet and maybe in distress. Certain that he must be weeping from hunger she rushed towards her room while loosening her blouse simultaneously as she neared the door. She heard no cries coming from inside as she quickly unlatched the last button of her blouse and pushed the door open. There she saw Monsieur Heritage standing in the middle of the room holding baby Philip with his back turned, he was rocking and comforting him and whispering. "You are hungry my son, and your mother is off picking flowers for her scented water but do not cry my son she will be here soon to feed us both." Baron Fitzgerald took off on his horse with the speed of lightning. Despite his haste, he managed to reach the town intact and well while there was still ample daylight. His next task was to meet with the old seaman, a rendezvous that required some preparation. He stopped by the local tavern and purchased a bottle of high-end rum that had just arrived from Barbados. The proprietor, shock by his purchase, stared at the shiny coins as he retrieved them from the bar counter. With the funds and the advance Monsieur Heritage had provided, Baron was well-equipped to secure everything on his list. The most challenging task, however, would be convincing the old seaman. Known throughout the town, the seaman's reputation was legendary; the tales of an enormous great white shark mounted above the entrance of his gate was testament enough to his prowess at sea. Baron made a stop at a tailor shop, picking up a few essential items, then proceeded to the smoke shop, where he purchased a fine clay pipe and some premium tobacco. After carefully strapping his acquisitions onto his horse, he set off for the old seaman's home. As he rode through England's picturesque countryside, he caught sight of the seaman's house from the top of a hill. The rumors were true: a massive piece of a ship rested near the entrance, a feat of relocation that no one could quite explain. Baron approached the imposing gate adorned with the thirteen-foot great white shark. The gutted creature, its skin stretched over a metal frame and stuffed with hay and feathers, greeted visitors with its menacing teeth protruding in a frightening display. It was an effective deterrent for unwelcome guests, but Baron, with his carefully chosen gifts of rum and tobacco, was determined to gain an audience with the elusive seaman. By the time Baron arrived and tied his horse, he noticed a figure standing in the window, watching him. He untied the two bags from his horse, which contained the items he had purchased, and walked toward the large front doors made of metal. He banged on the door with his fist and yelled, "Hello in there! I'm looking for Captain Sheldon McGee. I have important news." The door remained closed without any response. Baron knocked again, then took a couple of steps back to get a clear view of the windows facing the front entrance. Once in view, he removed a large bottle of rum from his bag and held it as if he were about to take a drink. He quickly walked back to the door and banged on it again, speaking with urgency this time. "Please, I need to see Captain Sheldon McGee. I was sent on important business related to the king's laws, and I cannot leave until I see the greatest captain who ever sailed the high seas." After a moment of silence, the heavy, rusted front door slowly opened with a squeaky sound and the scraping of the bottom. A woman appeared. She wore a thin dress, her brunette hair cascading down her back, and her blouse hanging off one shoulder. Smiling at the sight of Baron. She asked, "Who are you, sir, and what message do you have for Sheldon McGee?" "My name is Baron Fitzgerald. May I please come in, madam? I've been up all morning, and I'm a wee bit tired and thirsty," Baron stated as he held up the bottle of rum. The woman opened the door wider, propping it open with her bare feet, and guided Baron into the house. She quickly retraced her steps then shut the door behind him, sealing them in a world of their own. Leading him through a dimly lit corridor, she brought him to a spacious sitting area dominated by a solitary chair that sat in the center of the room. The chair faced a large window, its view obscured by heavy, dusty drapes. The woman approached the window and drew the drapes open, as if to let the sunlight pierce the shadows and illuminate Baron's face. Baron slowly circled around to the side of the single high-backed chair, where an older man with a mix of black and silver hair sat. The man toyed with a small, white triangular object, its point tapping rhythmically against his fingertips that went from bright red to a pale white with each pierce. As the last folds of the drapes were pulled aside, and Baron stood facing his side profile the man finally spoke. "I'm Sheldon McGee, though at sea they call me Captain. On land, my mates call me Shelly, and my wife, well, she has her own name for me, isn't that right, love?" He glanced with a hint of amusement at the woman, "Here darling put this shark's tooth with the rest of them and mark number four on this one. It's been a long time since I've seen it" Now turning his attention back to Baron, "What can I do for you, lad? "Baron, clutching a bottle of rum in one hand and a bag in the other, set the bag down and cradled the rum bottle in his arms. He spoke with a mixture of apprehension and urgency. "I beg your pardon, Captain I mean Shelly, Mr. McGee. Your expertise is urgently needed once again on the seas. There's a critical task involving the acquisition of some property, and your exceptional skills are required, sir." Captain McGee, his sharp eyes tracing every detail of Baron's attire, lingered on the scuffed riding boots before speaking. "I no longer sail," he declared, his voice heavy with the weight of years spent at sea. "At sixty-three, these sea legs have found comfort on solid ground. You'll need to find another seaman for your venture these legs are anchored here." Baron, unfazed by the Captain's apparent reluctance, picked up the bottle of rum with a steady hand and scanned the room for a chair. Despite the Captain's commanding presence, his nerves remained unshaken. Spotting a small chair, Baron drew it closer with a disarming smile. "May I sit, sir? I find myself both weary and parched. Might I trouble you for a goblet? I'm eager to taste this rum, fresh from Barbados. Surely, a man of your experience would only return to the seas for a matter of great consequence. And indeed, that's why I'm here to bring news of just such a matter. The man who needs your help sir is…" Baron was abruptly interrupted by Captain McGee, who was slightly vexed that his earlier declaration had been disregarded. He cut into the conversation with a pointed head gesture and subtle nod, he invited Baron to sit, as Baron eased into the chair, McGee's wife appeared with two large goblets, her eyes unreadable. Baron, with a steady hand, offered the jug to Captain McGee. The captain uncorked it with a practiced flick, inhaling the potent aroma deeply before pouring a generous measure. "You know," Captain McGee began, his gaze drifting to some far-off memory, "I was but a lad of seven when the sea first claimed me. A family friend came to our house with grim news of my father's death. My mother, young and beautiful, despaired at the thought of raising me alone. In the dead of night, she kissed my brow and vanished. I later learned she had taken up with a wealthy older man, leaving me to fend for myself." McGee's voice grew quieter, almost as if he was speaking to himself. "For days, I was alone and hungry with just the woods and the animals to keep me company. Finally one day after rubbing wild berries on my fingers, I caught a rabbit. I waited patiently and coaxed him out of his hole then I quickly snapped it's neck. I put it in a pot of hot water with one old potato, and cooked it until the eyes bulged. I peeled the skin and fur off and I lived on that stew for a week. On the third week after my food was gone the man who brought the news of my father returned. He found me on the brink of death from hunger, I had only been eating a few berries I was lucky to find. The man took me away aboard his ship, declaring he would make a man of me by way of the sea." Baron listened as the captain's voice turned cold. "Thus began my life on the high seas, when he died, I was about ten years of age, left alone with his corpse adrift in the vast ocean. I sailed as long as I could, turning to his rotted remains for guidance along the rough sails. It was me alone until a band of pirates, a wretched lot they were, captured me. I sailed with them until I

222

could stomach their cruelty no longer. I remember the day they forced a man to walk the plank, with a rope tied to his ankle, dragging him through the waters like bait." McGee paused, his eyes dark with the memory. "Every creature in those depths of murky waters had a piece of him. When they finally hauled him back aboard, hours later, what remained was... a horror I can never forget." All three simultaneously, now sobering up from the last details of the gruesome tale, took a long hard swallow that sent jolts through their system as the captain continued. "By the time I was sixteen, they abandoned me on the shores of Paris and never looked back. With no ship to call home, I wandered the streets, taking on whatever odd jobs I could find, always with a restless spirit and no place to rest my head. Until one fateful day, as I sat in the corner of a tavern trying to remain unnoticed, I overheard a man lamenting his struggle to find a sailor for an ambitious voyage. Despite my grubby clothes and the stench of the streets clinging to me, I approached him, my pride far outweighing my disheveled appearance. The gentleman, clearly repulsed by my odor, lifted a kerchief to his nose as he listened to my tale. Yet, something in my story must have struck a chord, for he soon ordered me a bath and clean clothes. "I have a grand ship that is in need of a captain. What do you need to sail her?" he asked me once I was cleaned up and presentable. Now feeling like a new man I met his gaze, my voice steady as I replied, 'Tell me her size, sir, and I'll know exactly how to crew her, how to chart her course, and what supplies we'll need. The sea speaks to me, and with the right ship beneath my feet, there's no place we can't reach.'" To my astonishment, he granted me a ship of my own, a vessel meticulously crafted by the best shipwrights in the land. He asked nothing in return, save for my loyalty to sail whenever he called upon me. I was still young then, but for years I sailed under his command, retrieving treasures, and delivering cargo. 'Shelly,' he would say, 'you're a trustworthy man who's worked long and hard for me. When the time comes that you wish to settle, you'll never go hungry.' And that's how I returned to land, still in one piece, with both legs intact." Baron, who had been listening intently to Captain McGee's tale, reached into his bag and began searching for the item he purchased for Captain McGhee. "A small token of appreciation for the man who had sailed the seas and lived to tell the tale, Baron's expression thoughtful as now retrieving a clay pipe filled with fresh tobacco. The captain's eyes sparked with interest as he admired the pristine pipe, its wooden tip glinting in the dim light. Without a word, Baron extended his hand, offering the pipe to the captain. Baron began, his voice steady, " This is a gift from a man who desperately seeks your help. He wishes to sail to America to retrieve his daughter, who was stolen by a ruthless band of traders. They plan to profit handsomely from the very refined young lady, abducted from her bed in the dead of night, or so they believe." Captain McGee, who had been reclining casually, suddenly sat up straight, his demeanor shifting. "In the dead of night, you say?" he echoed, setting his goblet down on a wooden table with deliberate care. "Yes," Baron confirmed, leaning in slightly, "And her father is unwavering in his determination to see her returned. I've confirmed her location, they've hidden her away in a prestigious music school, capitalizing on her ability to play four instruments and speak as many languages as possible. Her father sent me to find the greatest man of the seas, and every inquiry led me to you, Captain McGee." The captain's eyes narrowed as he listened, but before he could respond, Baron, now feeling the warm effects of the Barbados rum, set his goblet beside him, and reached into his bag once more. This time, he pulled out a cloth-wrapped object, carefully placing it in both hands as if presenting a sacred offering. "This," Baron said, his voice now barely above a whisper, "Is another gift from the gentleman. It is the only gift worthy and befitting for a man with your unparalleled knowledge and mastery of the sea." Captain McGee's gaze fixed on the large, shrouded item. With a slow, deliberate motion, he began to unwrap it, his curiosity piqued as Baron Fitzgerald held it out before him. When the object was revealed, Captain McGee sat motionless, momentarily lost for words. He marveled at the item before him, his eyes shimmering with unspoken emotion, a smile playing on his lips, nearly bringing him to tears. His wife, equally entranced by its splendor, stepped closer for a better look. " Darling, why don't you…" "Hush, Love." Captain McGee gently interrupted her, now rising to his feet , he walked over to a well-polished brass plate, where he carefully placed a large tricorn hat, trimmed with gold and silver lace, and adorned with a merit pin at its center. The captain's gaze lingered on the pin, while admiration deepen in his eyes, before he reverently placed the well-crafted captain's hat upon his head. The craftmanship of the hat had brought him back to a time and place where he had ruled the waters. "What is the name of the man who has showered me with such lavish gifts?" Captain McGee inquired, his eyes still fixed on his reflection in the polished brass plate. "Philip Adam Heritage," came the reply from Baron who had now risen to his feet. "He says you'll know who he is by reading the engravement on the pin." Captain McGee's expression shifted as he carefully removed the hat, his fingers tracing the delicate design on the edges of the pin. Turning it over, he read aloud, "Monsieur Gracieux." The captain's hand tightened around the pin as he slowly approached Baron. "What is the meaning of this!" he demanded, his voice low and tense. "Monsieur Gracieux is the man I've been speaking of this entire time. He is the man who gave me my first ship and his son in law and daughter were my keepers for many years. But I know for certain that he died many years ago and his daughter and son in law peacefully laid to rest. So, tell your Monsieur Heritage he is no Gracieux and to keep his gifts; I do nothing for a man who pretends to be a noble dead man." Baron, now visibly shaken, quickly responded, "Captain, you must understand, Monsieur Heritage is the grandson of Monsieur Gracieux. He is the son of Madam Fleur Dior and Jean Paul Heritage." Captain McGee, now realizing the correlation, stood in silence, his gaze locked on the pin and the hat, the weight of the revelation settling over him. He carefully replaced the pin back onto the hat in its original place, then canvas the room taking a quick glance at his wife then at Baron, he spoke his voice commanding. "When would he like to leave?" "Soon, very soon" replied Baron.

Chapter: 18

Meet The Foxes

"Honey waters, that's what you live for. I live to go home and be free again." "Don't be foolish, you are home. Once again I tell you this is your home now. You're as free as a bird. Now sit down and start from the beginning." Gem Marie rose to her feet, standing in the middle of the parlor with a violin in hand. She lifted it to her chin and began to play the piece Christian Pierre had just written. As she played, her eyes locked onto his, unwavering. She strummed the instrument, letting the sound grow louder, drowning out the voices that were rising in her head. She could hear Greta calling for marmalade, and she squeezed her eyes shut, trying to block out the image of her face. But with her eyes closed, she could see Monsieur Heritage, smiling with approval as he watched her play a piece he had never heard before. "No, no, no! Please look at the sheet music if you can't remember," Christian urged. "I don't expect you to have it memorized; I just wrote it. Here, take it and study it some more." Gem Marie opened her eyes and took the paper from Christian Pierre, who was now distracted by something beyond the parlor window. She held the paper up to her face, pretending not to notice his anxious expression. Gem Marie sensed someone approaching—a presence Christian clearly didn't want knowing about her, let alone seeing her play. When he realized she was ignoring his gestures, he rushed over and whispered urgently, "Quickly, take the paper and go to the cellar. There are guests arriving, and you must be silent." Irritated, Gem Marie slowly lowered the paper and snapped, "I think I've got it now. Listen." She made an attempt to play, but Christian swiftly placed his hand over her bow, his tone now firm with authority. "There is no time for these games. You will behave like a proper young lady and do as you're told. *Il n'y a pas de temps pour ces jeux, vous vous comporterez comme une gentille jeune femme et ferez ce qu'on vous dit.*" Gem Marie, now seething, retorted, "A nice young lady? I am always a lady. But tell me—where is your walking stick, adorned with gold and crowned with a lion's head?" Christian, bewildered, replied, "What are you talking about? I have no walking stick." "Precisely!" Gem Marie shot back, her eyes blazing. "That's why you should never question my behavior as a lady. You neglect to carry a gentleman's proper necessity." "But I have no ailment that requires me to own a walking stick." Christian retorted confused and agitated. "You misunderstand," she countered, her tone sharp. "A gentleman needs no ailment to possess a proper walking stick. Now, send me home at once!" The sound of horses' hooves grew louder, each thud intensifying the tension as they neared. Gem Marie's heart raced with fear of the approaching guest. "Why must you always play these games? Come here!" Christian's voice was sharp as he seized her hand, dragging her toward the parlor doorway before steering her toward the cellar steps. Gem Marie resisted, her heels digging into the floor as though he were leading her to a dungeon. "I don't want to go down there," she protested, pulling against his grip. "I want to stay in the parlor and play. Your guest will understand me once they hear me. People always understand once they've heard me play. Listen to me please. The music it has powers master!" Christian Pierre stood frozen in silence, his gaze locked on Gem Marie, who was fully aware that calling him "master" was a calculated move, a subtle form of manipulation. His patience, already frayed, snapped. In one swift motion, he hoisted her over his shoulder and marched down the cellar steps. Once at the bottom, he set her down with a stern warning. "Now, go to your room and study the piece. Read it over and over until it's memorized. And be silent." "I'm not a child; I'm a woman now!" she retorted, her voice laced with defiance. "Then go to your room, woman who is not a child and stay silent," Christian snapped back, his words slicing through the dim hallway. As the sound of hooves echoed from above, their presence growing nearer, Christian's demeanor shifted. He bolted up the stairs, shutting the cellar door firmly behind him. He hurried to the main level kitchen, instructing a servant to prepare refreshments, then settled in the parlor. Lighting a cigar, he puffed slowly, trying to banish the image of Gem Marie's defiant face along with her haunting words from his mind. Despite his best efforts, a smile tugged at the corner of his mouth, her independence and defiance was... intoxicating. It was becoming increasingly difficult to keep his distance from her. From the first day she openly challenged him, Christian had resolved to send her back to Baltimore, to remove the source of his growing distraction. But her fierce independence, her unexpected intelligence, and her sharp tongue it was as if he were dealing with an equal, someone who matched him in every way. It unsettled him, yet intrigued him all the same. A wave of guilt washed over him, a heavy burden that settled deep in his chest. Locking her beneath the house felt like a betrayal a cruel irony that the one person who brought life into his music now languished beneath the floorboards. He was haunted by the thought of her confinement. Suddenly, the parlor door creaked open. "Master Pierre, Lady Lelina's carriage has arrived. She appears to have company with her," announced Cook, his tone respectful yet tinged with curiosity. Christian's heart skipped a beat. Lelina had brought someone with her? The prospect of dodging marital inquiries from one of her probing friends made him tense. It had been a moment since the two had seen each other and after their last encounter, her constant referencing towards more commitment and marriage was the last thing on his mind. "Of course, Cook. Show them into the parlor," he instructed, rising to his feet, bracing himself to greet Lelina. As his eyes moved to the center of the room, he was met by an unexpected figure, a gentleman with a tall, slender frame and a face drawn with sharp lines. The man stood confidently in the foyer, his presence commanding immediate attention. "Good day, Christian Pierre. It is a great pleasure to finally make your acquaintance," the stranger said, his voice smooth and deliberate, each word carefully chosen. Christian blinked, as he was momentarily thrown off. The man before him was unfamiliar. "Good day, sir. Might I ask with whom I have the pleasure of speaking?" Christian's tone was polite, but there was a slight edge to his words. The stranger's smile was polite, yet it carried a hint of something darker. "Bonneville Mercer, the fiancé of Lady Lelina." He paused, watching Christian's reaction closely. "She sends her deepest regrets, as she's been struck by a rather dreadful case of the vapors. Nevertheless, she sends her warmest regards. Our plans to spend the day with you , as agreed took a sudden change as she became ill, still she insisted I come alone. " Christian now in shock, Fiancé? The word echoed in his mind, sharp and unsettling. His face betrayed none of the confusion swirling inside him, but beneath the surface, his thoughts raced. Engaged? This was news to him, and worse, Lelina hadn't mentioned it once. Suppressing a surge of irritation, Christian forced a measured tone. "I apologize, Sir Bonneville, but it seems this plan must have slipped my mind. I wasn't aware things had grown so... serious between you and Lady Lelina. How long has it been? "Bonneville's expression brightened with a mix of triumph and satisfaction. "Three months since we became officially engaged, though I've been courting her for over a year. My frequent trips abroad made it difficult, but in my absence, she kept herself occupied... with your brotherly hospitality." Bonneville gave a knowing smile. "Assigning her as your etiquette instructor for your household servants, I believe? Quite a resourceful woman. Leave it to Lelina to place a fork and napkin in a darkie's hand." Christian's face remained impassive, though his mind churned. Lelina was clearly playing a dangerous game, weaving her life between the two of them. With a cool, practiced smile, Christian replied, "My servants have been using utensils since they were knee-high. I find it more efficient for them to learn proper etiquette early on." He allowed his eyes to linger on Bonneville, gauging his reaction. "And as for you, Sir Bonneville, it appears she's chosen a fine husband indeed." He gestured towards a plush armchair. "Please, have a seat. Join me for a drink." Christian's voice remained courteous, though beneath the surface, tension crackled. They walked to the parlor, where a rich haze of cigar smoke filled the room. The atmosphere was thick with unspoken words, both men acutely aware of the stakes beneath this polite exchange. As they settled in, Cook entered the room, carrying a tray with two glasses of fine whiskey. He had overheard enough of the conversation to know that this guest was truly uninvited. Cook's eyes flicked to Christian, his silent offer of support understood with a simple nod. Christian took a glass and, after a long sip, glanced at Cook. "Prepare your best lamb for lunch. I find myself in the mood for a slaughtered lamb, as they say." His words hung in the air with deliberate weight. Cook, catching the underlying meaning, smiled ever so slightly as he left the room to carry out the order. When he reached the kitchen cellar, he found McCoy, the head servant, and quickly relayed the news. "Bonneville Mercer," Cook said under his breath, "claims to be engaged to Lady Lelina." McCoy raised an eyebrow, pausing from his duties. "Engaged? But how she been coming around here to see Master Pierre" "That's not the half of it," Cook replied, glancing over his shoulder. "Something tells me that this engagement is just the beginning of trouble." Back in the parlor, Christian reclined in his chair, his mind racing as he regarded Bonneville across from him. Lelina's web was growing more intricate, and Christian couldn't help but wonder: Was this visit simply an introduction, or the first move in a far more sinister game? In the dim cellar, McCoy let out a low howl, "Ooooow wee! "curiosity stirring deep within him. The sound echoed off the stone walls, unsettling the silence. In the back of the cellar, Gem Marie carefully folded the sheet music she had been reading, and slipped it beneath her bed. She moved to her door and

229

strained to listen to the hushed voices murmuring in the hallway. "You mean to tell me that woman sent her new fella to Honey Waters all by himself, and Master Christian hasn't even laid eyes on the man before?" Cook's voice was heavy with contempt. "First time they meet, and he drops news like *that*?" McCoy, only mildly surprised, retorted, "And how do you figure *she* the one who sent him? Could be he caught wind of the rumors and decided to come see if they were true, all on his own. Heck anyone within a mile of New Orleans knows Lady Lelina and master Pierre been sweet on each other for years." McCoy's tone hardened, revealing his admiration for Lady Lelina. Cook, who clearly saw through her web of games, fired back with growing irritation. "You think that woman don't know that mam took a trip over here? Well, I *heard* that man say 'Lelina sends her warmest regards' on account of she got some illness that kept her from coming herself. Some strange sickness." Gem Marie listened intently, a wave of relief washing over her. This was the confirmation she needed that Lady Lelina's would no longer be making her sudden appearances anymore. Her constant visits is what had driven Gem Marie to hide away like a shadow in these cold dank walls. As she stood in the cellar listening to the men's chatter, she reflected on how the months had slipped by, yet she had made no progress in returning to the Scotney. It was as if Christian Pierre had tethered her to Honey Waters like a prized pet, unwilling to let her leave. His initial tone when they met in Baltimore came across as a fair man but there had been a change since Lady Lelina's presence. Lady Lelina, viewed as radiant and from a family of immense wealth, had now taken another man without warning or care. The news had struck Christian Pierre like a sharp blade, sudden, and devastating. Yet Gem Marie felt neither joy nor sorrow over it. In the months she had spent with Christian, his demeanor had proven himself far from the perfect of the man that the newspapers had glorified and portrayed him to be. Kneeling beside her bed, she searched for the loose floorboard and retrieved a travel bag that contained the articles she had often read before falling asleep at the Scotney. The words in that articles had crafted him into the man she thought she desired. But now, as she sensed the weight of his footsteps on the floorboards above, she could feel the truth of his persona seeping through the wood. "You are my illusion," she whispered, her voice trembling with resolve. "Go away with your lies. I will never be fooled by your charm again." Her longing to return home now eclipsed her love for him. She shut her room door with finality and placed the article on her bed. Then, she pulled a small chair into the center of the room, standing on her toes, ear tilted toward the ceiling. The chair wobbled slightly as she strained to catch the faint voices filtering through the floorboards. The men above had been deep in conversation for hours, but Gem Marie thought she heard a note of distress in Christian Pierre's voice. As their voices grew louder, her anxiety swelled. "Why should I still care?" she wondered, troubled by the thought that the visiting man might have uncovered Lelina's love for Christian. Desperate to distract herself, she hopped down from the precarious chair and began to strum her violin loudly. The music reverberated through the room, and suddenly, a loud thump resounded from the ceiling. She froze, her fingers silencing the strings. She sat on the edge of her bed, listening intently, but the only answer was silence. Christian Pierre and Bonneville had been in the parlor drinking for two hours. Both voices had grown louder as the cycle of slurred conversation continued, only broken by bursts of laughter and blurred words. "Mr. Pierre, I do believe you have howling coming from beneath you sir," Bonneville stated as he held his glass up and toasted to an imaginary glass. Christian slightly intoxicated knew the sound had come from Gem Marie, so he sat quietly and waited. Then he replied to Bonneville while quickly stomping his foot. "No, my good friend what you hear is a family of foxes that often use the cellar as a pathway to the garden, would you like to meet them I have named them after I had the pleasure of dining with them one evening." Bonneville who had become completely intoxicated from the last glass of Russian vodka. Christian decided to open it after a half bottle of peach Brandy had been devoured. "Why Mr. Pierre you're going to make a formal introduction to the foxes just for me? Well then of course I would be honored to meet them sir." The two men walked out of the parlor, Christian Pierre guiding Bonneville outside to the far end of the porch. The two stood on the veranda with drink in hand waiting patiently for the family of foxes to reveal themselves. Christian glanced over at Bonneville, who was leaning over the veranda, searching for the family of mammals. For a brief moment, Christian's thoughts drifted to Lady Lelina and her possible motives for sending her new beau over. Perhaps it was her last attempt to make him jealous, hoping for a proposal under pressure. He let out a sigh of relief any woman who would place her intended husband in such a predicament was hardly someone to be desired, let alone tempt him to reveal his jealous nature. "So, Bonneville, when's the wedding?" he asked.

Bonneville, still peering over the porch, replied, "It's in a month," his gaze fixed on the grass, looking for signs of the creatures' hideout. "Good," Christian said with a straight face. "You can have it here I wouldn't have it any other way." Bonneville smiled and, with sudden boyish enthusiasm, pointed to the fox family scurrying across the lawn. Just as Christian had described the family of six with bushy tails ran frantically. "Bonneville, I'd like to introduce you to the fox family," Christian said with a hint of satisfaction. Just then Cook appeared in the doorway and gestured for Christian Pierre, he announced dinner would be ready in fifteen minutes, in returned Christian instructed Cook to make certain that Gem Marie remained quiet for the rest of the evening. Cook eagerly complied and headed for the cellar steps Moving directly towards Gem Marie's room. he opened the door, and discovered Gem Marie standing in the center of her room holding the violin that Christian had given her. She was practicing his music without applying the bow to the instrument. She moved the bow back and forth without letting it hit the strings on the violin. Her eyes focused solely on her fingers movements. Back and forth as quickly as she could she pretended to play. Cook, who viewed her behavior as trouble, walked up to her without warning and ripped the violin from her hands. He then gave her a forceful backhand that sent her flying upon her bed. Gem Marie, with her hands trembling, held her face as she tried to make sense of Cook's sudden aggression. With tears welling in her eyes, her thoughts raced, searching for a reason behind his cruel behavior. Cook, noticing her frightened expression, grinned menacingly. His voice was low, dripping with malice as he spoke, "You'd better never, ever make a sound while Master Christian is upstairs entertaining guests. Now, you lay on that bed and think really hard about why I did what I did. And don't you dare make a sound while you're at it." In disbelief, Gem Marie stifled her cries, her heart pounding in her chest. She watched as Cook's face, twisted with satisfaction, gleamed with a dark pleasure at the pain he had caused. His eyes, filled with a sinister delight, bore into her soul, sending a shiver down her spine. Desperate to keep her sobs from escaping, she pressed her hands tightly against her trembling lips, struggling to contain the terror rising within her. Cook, now emboldened by her fear, let out a low, cruel chuckle. "Make sure you don't make another sound," he warned, his voice a chilling whisper. "Master Christian wants you quiet, or else I'll be back for you." With a fiendish grin, he slowly backed out of the room, his eyes never leaving her as he closed her door. Left alone, Jen Marie collapsed back onto her bed, her body shaking with silent sobs. She called out in her mind to her harp, the only source of love and compassion she had left. The blow from Cook made her ponder if the truth of the world had not been hidden by Monsieur Heritage she would have never ran away. She forced herself to remember every detail of her harp, the strings of the elegant instrument always brought her comfort. Serving now as a refuge from the harshness of her reality. But now, that solace seemed distant, almost unreachable. She had made a grave mistake in once falling for Christian Pierre, and now her life was a twisted web of physical and emotional pain. The man she had once loved had become a ghost, haunting every corner of her existence. He was never tangible for he was a article in a paper that she had developed an obsession for. Gem Marie laid there, her tears soaking the pillow, as she grappled with the crushing weight of her choices and the cruel fate that had befallen her. This was a torment beyond anything she had ever endured. Cook and McCoy were vile men, destined to meet their grim fate once her father found her. She squeezed her eyes shut, lying on her back as she wiped away the hot tears that stung her cheeks. Slowly, she raised her trembling hands before her, carefully positioning them as if she were seated at her beloved harp. Her fingers began to dance in the empty air, playing an imagined melody, soft and haunting. In the darkness behind her closed eyelids, she concentrated until tiny specks of grey and white began to swirl and form faint images. She remained perfectly still, her fingers moving with graceful precision, following the rhythm of the song that played in her mind. The outside world faded; even the voices of Cook and McCoy, still gossiping in the kitchen as Cook prepared the meal, became distant echoes. She found solace in the music in her head, each note she conjured carrying her farther away from the horror of her reality. She imagined the day her father would storm through the doors, his righteous fury sealing the fate of those who had wronged her. On the ceiling above her head, Christian Pierre sat at the head of the table, with Bonneville seated to his right. The two men were still caught in a laughing frenzy, their minds pleasantly hazy from the imported liquor as they headed back into the parlor for dinner. "I do believe that red fox has taken quite a liking to you, Sir Bonneville," Christian teased, his voice laced with a playful edge. "I can't recall ever seeing them so friendly and cozy on my veranda." "It's a simple joy to have you here at Honey Waters." Bonneville, having just taken his last sip of wine, nodded in agreement. "This has been one of my most memorable experiences, Mr. Pierre, your hospitality is unmatched. You truly are the gentleman Miss Lelina has spoken highly of. With your charm and her beauty, I can't imagine why the two of you haven't gone beyond the casual." Christian's gaze sharpened, his eyes glassy from another full glass of wine. His ego flared, pushing him to the edge. "Who says we haven't?" At that moment, the sharp crash of crockery hitting the floor from within the house shattered the night's calm. "Excuse me, sir," Bonneville stammered, hastily swallowing a large piece of potato. The combination of Cook's culinary prowess and Christian's bold admission had sobered him up quickly. Christian, suddenly aware of the potential consequences of his careless words, scrambled to redirect the conversation. "If I allowed my late-night reminiscing about Lady Lelina to escape my lips," he thought, this situation could turn dangerous." Christian quickly steered the discussion into safer waters. "I must clarify, Bonneville, when I offered my hand to Lady Lelina, she corrected me at once. She advised that we were better off as brother and sister. And she was right she's the only woman who could ever fill the place of the sister I never had. I commend you, Bonneville. The best man has certainly won, and now, I shall toast to your marriage." Feeling a surge of pride, Bonneville raised his nearly empty glass and drained the last of the wine. The men sat quietly, continuing to devour their meal, their drunken grins and sighs of relief echoing through the room. Between bites, they reached an agreement: the wedding ceremony would take place at Honey Waters, a lavish estate known for its breathtaking views of lush greenery and vibrant gardens, the perfect backdrop for a grand wedding. Christian Pierre leaned back in his chair, trying to envision Lady Lelina's face when Bonneville announced their wedding venue. This was more than just a generous wedding gift; it was a carefully crafted lesson for Lady Lelina. She had thought marrying another man would make Christian jealous, but she was playing a daring game with hearts. Christian had no intention of falling into Lady Lelina's carefully laid trap. His ability to maintain composure in the face of her blatant and manipulative displays of affection was a testament to the shallow depths of his feelings for her. He saw through her theatrics, recognizing them for what were desperate attempts to ensnare him in a web of emotional deceit. "Bonneville is the perfect pawn," Christian mused quietly, watching from a distance as he slept. Lelina had played her game, and Christian had no intention of being her next move. With calculated precision, he planned to walk away without so much as a backward glance, leaving her to the loneliness she had sown with her own hands. It was painfully clear that Bonneville's feelings for Lelina were genuine. Somehow, she had managed to convince him that her love was real even while keeping him suspended in uncertainty. Lelina's trips to Honey Water had grown frequent, her arrivals unannounced, as she carefully weighed her options with Christian. Now becoming aware that while she was visiting Christian she dangled the promise of marriage before Bonneville like a cruel taunt, savoring the power it gave her. But with Christian, she was more direct, presenting him with an ultimatum cloaked in the veneer of choice. "Marriage or nothing," she had told him one night beneath an ancient Alabaster tree, her voice cold and unyielding, each word cutting through the night like a blade. Yet, something about her sudden jealousy toward Gem Marie unsettled Christian. For a fleeting moment, he almost believed Lelina's reaction was genuine that beneath her relentless pursuit for social standing, there might be a glimmer of true emotion. But the moment passed quickly, and he reminded himself that appearances could be deceiving. "Don't let her fool you," Christian murmured to himself, lying beneath the tree, counting the leaves as they fell. His resolve hardened, his eyes narrowing as the realization set in. "She's playing a game, and I'm not the prize she thinks I am." For she had proven that his choices concerning he were the best, Bonneville was sitting across from him stretched out asleep. With that, he turned his back on the scene, his decision final. Lady Lelina could keep her games, but he would no longer be a part of them. As dawn broke, the men awoke on the veranda, having fallen asleep in two large comfortable chairs after chatting late into the night. Christian stirred first, leaving Bonneville snoring softly in the crisp morning air. He made his way into the parlor, where the staff awaited him with a wash basin and fresh clothing. As he disrobed and washed in the parlor one of the servant girls blushed, her eyes lingering a moment too long on his form. Unfazed, Christian dressed quickly, his mind already on the day ahead. McCoy entered the room, his footsteps soft on the polished floor. "Breakfast will be ready in moments, sir," he informed Christian. "Cook is in the cellar, putting the final touches on the meal sir." Christian nodded, his thoughts still on the impending announcement. "Good McCoy," he replied, his voice steady. "Let Bonneville sleep a little longer. He'll need his strength for what's to come. See that he is given a shave once he awakens." Christian then headed down to the cellar to Gem Marie's room, he could smell bacon frying and buttermilk biscuit baking along the corridors. Once at the threshold of her door, he found her still asleep she had some cloths scattered around her that she had been using for handkerchiefs. All around the bed also were papers one in particular seemed to be some sort of a love note that professed an undying love for a man far away. Along with another note there was some instruction on escaping from some land. There was also some newspaper articles that were dated two years prior. As Christian quickly read, he came to the realization that the articles were about him. In disbelief he pondered to himself, "How could she have kept articles about me for so long had she really crafted a plan to find me? Who is this young woman who professed her love in writing for two years that now sleeps in my house." Christian's heart raced as he scanned the papers. Between the article that boasted of his upbring and travels and the note that spoke of a relentless pursuit, a plan meticulously crafted to find him. His hands trembled as he folded the paper back into its original creases and placed it gently next to Gem Marie. He took a deep breath, in an attempt to gain composure from the emotions that now flooded within him. his mind swirling with confusion and curiosity. As he quietly exited the room, he stood in the dim hallway, grappling with his thoughts. "How could she have held onto an article about me for two years? And now, she is here, asleep in my home?" He pondered again in utter disbelief Who is this woman who has been plotting to find me, and what is her story?" Christian's thoughts raced as he contemplated the mystery of Gem Marie. What had driven her to such lengths? Love maybe, what did her presence in his home mean for both of their futures? Christian now feeling slightly unstable leaned on the cellar's walls for support. Cook, who stepped out into the corridor holding the breakfast tray caught sight of Christian Pierre and quickly returned to the cellar's Kitchen to place the tray down, he rushed over to him, "Master Pierre, are you alright sir? You look like you were about to fall sir." Christian still in shock from his revelation said nothing as he held unto the walls. "Master Pierre, you need to sit down and eat sir you don't look so good sir." Christian feeling slightly dizzy muttered something as he glanced at Gem Marie's room door. Cook now little annoyed that Christian Pierre would allow himself to be affected by Gem Marie replied, "Don't you worry yourself none about that gal. I quieted her down last night for playing that violin out of turn. Just like you said sir, from what I give her she won't be playing that thing again without your permission sir." Christian Pierre now becoming coherent to Cook's voice replied, "Quieted her down what are you talking about Cook?" Cook now a little surprise retorted, "Well master Pierre, I didn't hurt her none too bad just enough to get her in line with the way things should be done here at Honey waters. Sure, she cried a bit but then she settled down nice quiet like and stayed stilled just like you wanted her sir." Christian Pierre now trying to recall Gem Marie's appearance as he watched her sleep. "Jaimison Cook Blacksmith did you strike Gem Marie?" Cook now unsure of himself nodded his head and uttered, "Yes but she," before he could say another word Christian Pierre slapped him in rage. Cook who had stumbled slightly from the blow now swapped roles with Christian and held onto the wall. "In all your years here at Honey Waters have I ever struck you before Cook?" Cook, now afraid to speak, just shook his head like a child. Christian Pierre now in disgust with Cook's tactics continued. "So why would you lay a hand on that innocent child. Her rambunctiousness is not an invitation for you to abuse her. A stern talking would have been enough for her fragile feelings. You are never ever to lay a hand on her or anybody again is that understood." Cook who finally managed to speak in his defense, " But master Pierre she was playing that violin loud on purpose sir." Christian now becoming annoyed again removed his kerchief from his pocket and held it in a tight fist and let out a deep cough then held it up as he pointed in Cook's face. "I don't care if she was singing to the robins in her nighty. You are never to touch her again do you understand?" Cook nodded and apologized and swore that he would never partake in such behavior again. Christian Pierre walked away but not before ordering Cook to bring the breakfast upstairs immediately. Before reaching the top of the stairs Christian Pierre collected himself in hopes of displaying a neutral demeanor. When he arrived on the veranda Bonneville was tidy and had just had his morning shave completed by McCoy. With a healthy grin, Christian spoke, "You look splendid Bonneville. Simply dashing. McCoy, I believe it's my turn. Now be careful not to nick me; I know you're a bit heavy-handed. I need you to be mindful we have a wedding coming soon. "McCoy now looking alert replied. "Ah yes sir master Pierre my hand will be as light as a feather." Bonneville, now stroking his freshly shaven face, spoke with admiration for McCoy. "Christian, I do believe this is the finest shave I've ever had. Your servant is quite skilled. I must borrow him for the wedding." Christian Pierre, his thoughts flashing to Gem Marie, nodded in agreement. "Of course, it would be my pleasure to lend McCoy for your wedding. And as a special treat, I'll provide the music as well if you don't mind." Bonneville, clearly elated, replied, "It would be an honor! I've heard so much about your compositions. Tell me, is it true they're playing your music abroad?" Christian, now reclining in an armchair, closed his eyes and exposed his throat as McCoy carefully slid the straight razor along his neck. "I believe so, although my main concern is the smooth operations of Honey Waters." Bonneville smiled in agreement, "Yes indeed, This is a mighty fine estate you have, Christian. Thank you for your hospitality and graciousness. You're the true definition of a gentleman." I am so glad that you are understanding with Lady Lelina and our union she was worried that you may have been skeptical of me in a brotherly way of course." Christian with his eyes still close listen carefully. Unbeknown to Bonneville he had just given him the confirmation of Lady Lelina's true intention of her orchestrated meeting. Christian believed with certainty that she hoped for some discord between the two men, why else would she have any qualms about them meeting. McCoy, perceptive to Christian's quiet unease, quickly concluded his shave by placing a damp towel across his face. Christian relaxed and grateful beneath the cool damp towel welcomed the brief respite. Just then, a servant appeared, carrying a large basket overflowing with flowers. She was a striking woman of mixed heritage, her presence bold, her beauty arresting. Dressed in a gown she had sewn herself, its design tailored to her fit with the neckline dipped just low enough to raise eyebrows, if one paid attention. The woman moved with an assured grace. Her loose bun unraveled slightly as she walked, dark curls cascading to her shoulders. Bonneville, seated nearby, was captivated by her beauty and confidence, his gaze lingering on her as she climbed the veranda steps. He stared, intrigued until his curiosity soured as her ethnicity became unmistakable. Embarrassed by his attraction, he addressed her with a scoff, his tone dripping with haughty disdain. "You there, girl awfully bold of you to walk so freely upon this veranda in the presence of gentlemen. Christian, I must say, your darkies are both skilled and... unrestrained." Christian, still beneath the towel, removed it in time to see the woman standing at his side, her basket of flowers in hand. This was Margret, newly granted permission to approach the main house after a long absence. "Ah, I see you've met Margret," he replied smoothly, introducing her as he rose from his chair. "One of my most loyal servants and Lady Lelina's prized student in matters of the garden and etiquettes. She brings the morning flowers for our table and lapels." Margret stepped forward with calm grace, selecting a freshly cut carnation and placing it on Bonneville's lapel. The air filled with the faint, exotic scent of jasmine as her delicate fingers adjusted the flower. But in a flash, Bonneville's hand shot out, gripping her wrist and casting her hand aside with a violent, disdainful gesture. Margret's eyes darkened, but she held her composure, merely straightening herself as she turned to Christian and carefully pinned a flower to his lapel. Christian, still wiping away the remnants of soap, was oblivious to the undercurrent that had passed between the two. Margret withdrew quietly, disappearing into the parlor to finish arranging the morning's flowers. Bonneville's gaze followed her every step, his expression a mixture of scorn and fascination. "Christian, that woman carries herself with an unwelcome pride," he remarked, his tone icy. "I don't presume to tell you how to run your estate, but I'd caution you about a servants who holds themselves so high." Christian, sensing the bitterness in Bonneville's words but uninterested in indulging, steered the conversation to the waiting breakfast, hinting at the delicious delicacies being prepared in the dining room. Christian Pierre's greatest irritation stemmed from others' audacity to tell him how to run his plantation. He took deep pride in the fact that, unlike neighboring estates beset by unrest, his slaves never dared to flee or contemplated it. He knew other plantation owners resented his ironclad control, now an unspoken jealousy simmering beneath their strained smiles. As he and Bonneville entered the dining room, they found Margret standing at the far side with a tray of cool spring water. Bonneville, spotting her immediately, snapped, "Gal, bring me that water. My throat's parched from being shaved out on the veranda." Margret moved quickly, setting the glass before him without meeting his gaze, then retreated to her post at the opposite wall. Christian, noting her unease, gestured dismissively and excused her, instructing her to tend to the gardens. With a tone both instructive and expectant, he reminded her of the upcoming wedding and directed her to prepare the most splendid floral arrangements. The two men then turned to their lavish breakfast, exchanging laughter and half-veiled remarks as they discussed the wedding's plans. Christian reaffirmed that the ceremony would unfold at Honey Waters, his prized spot overlooking the lake, before he saw Bonneville on his way. But as he watched his newfound friend depart, Christian's expression darkened, shadows flickering behind his calm exterior. Lady Lelina had sent Bonneville over alone, hoping to provoke his jealousy over their upcoming wedding. Yet as Christian stared out over the plantation, he found himself unexpectedly disturbed not by thoughts of orchestrated deception, but by the quiet realization that his heart and mind had drifted elsewhere, "Gem Marie," he whispered.

Chapter: 19

They Set Sail

"I need her scrubbed clean and made ready again, from top to bottom. There'll be barnacles larger than the size of a man's fist clinging beneath her hull, and who knows what creatures have made their home under her belly during her long slumber. She's been asleep for many years, and I won't take her out unprepared. I want her shellac applied thick, and the hull layered thrice and pitched, the waters grow treacherous this time of year. Now, what's the target's name again?" "Baltimore," replied Baron, trailing behind the captain like an eager cabin boy, struggling to keep up with the seasoned seaman's long strides. "Baltimore!" McGhee echoed, his voice carrying the weight of disdain, as though the very word tasted foul. "You mean that cesspool of harbors where men's lives are traded as easily as barrels of rum? Are you speaking of the cursed harbors where men's lives are tossed aside like rotting timber? While vile congregation of scoundrels gather to decide which cargo lives to see the light of day and which is left to rot below deck? Aye, I know the place well enough. That's where the top hats, drunk on their blood-stained coins, make deals, trading flesh as casually as they indulge in their vices. Yes, the top hats, bloated on their blood money, make dirty deals while indulging in every depravity known to man. Tell me, Baron, that we are not sailing into the filthy ocean of the slave trade and dipping our toes into those foul waters, are we? This girl what has she to do with the dealings of the slave trade." Baron, taken aback by the captain's sudden vehemence, quickly stammered, "No, Captain, not at all! I share your distaste for such wretched business. When I last sailed from the Chesapeake and made a brief stop in Baltimore, well... the harbor alone was dreadful. The air thick with unsavory dealings. I too was in a haste to leave the place." Captain McGhee's eyes narrowed to slits, his glare fierce as if Baron had insulted his very honor. For the inclination that he may have been in a hurry to leave Baltimore meant that he may have harbored some fear for it. He snapped, his voice cutting like the lash of a whip. "Afraid of Baltimore, are ye? Me hah! Let me shed some light on you like the morning sun. Should I ever come face to face with a slave trader looking for a fight, I'll

241

doff my hat before reaching for my sword. Know With the truth of the virgin Mary Know that the edge of my sword has tasted the blood of many a fools who thought he could lay claim to my findings. Slave trade or no, I have no fear of what may lie in wait." McGhee moved to the ship's railing, inhaling deeply, as if he were swallowing the very winds coming off the ocean. Turning to Baron, his gaze sharpened, his voice low and deadly serious. "No man, no beast not even the largest great white leaping before me from the depths chasing a school of dolphins has ever been enough to turn me from my course. My blade has cleaved through the breastplates of many men who never saw it coming. So, you can mark my words lad. Captain McGhee always returns to land, and I doubt the search for a mere girl will be the one thing that tarnishes my record. While I've no qualms about the trade, I prefer to face whatever beast awaits me well-prepared. Be it man or animal, I'll be ready." Baron, once a man of quiet confidence, now stood visibly shaken, his earlier resolve crumbling like the weathered timbers of an old ship battered by relentless waves. The notion of remaining an unnoticed passenger, slipping silently through the shadows while gathering secrets to report back, had long since vanished. He was no longer an idle observer; he had been drawn deep into the crew's ranks. From the moment he informed Monsieur Heritage that Captain McGhee had accepted the offer to locate Gem Marie, the tide of Baron's fate had turned. He was now under strict orders to obey every command the Captain issued without question. McGhee, a captain as hardened as the sea itself, had made his expectations clear: Baron was to know every inch of the ship, from bow to stern, with no detail too insignificant. He wasn't merely expected to blend into the crew but to contribute, he was even responsible for recruiting men to their cause. However, there was a grim test awaiting every potential sailor. If any recruit so much as flinched or hesitated during their initial test, they were not dismissed with mere words. No, they were escorted off the ship by way of the water. "Best get used to walking the plank now," McGhee would say with a cruel glint in his eye, "for that's where you'll end up if fear controls your soul." The Captain made it clear: this was not a voyage for the faint-hearted. Baron, now well-schooled in the ship's operations, found himself standing at the helm, his hands gripping the wheel as tightly as he clung to his sense of purpose. His gaze drifted over the horizon, where the sea glimmered under the midday sun, the waves rising and falling like silver coins tumbling in an endless cascade. "What harm could we truly bring?" he wondered, his thoughts drifting like the ship itself. "We're only in pursuit of a lost girl. A girl who happens to be the daughter of one of the wealthiest men in all of England. And her whereabouts unknown, adrift like a phantom in the mist." For weeks, Monsieur Heritage had been preparing for his travel by rising before the first light of dawn, his routine more akin to a warrior preparing for battle than a father awaiting news. He would don his dueling attire and march to the barn, where he practiced with his sword, thrusting the blade deep into a sack of hay, over and over, each plunge driven by the same thought: Gem Marie. She had been gone for over a year now, and her absence weighed upon him like an anchor pulling him into the depths. Only young Philip, his son, could stir any joy within him. The boy had just begun to toddle on his own two legs, taking an interest in the dusty old piano that Monsieur had once crafted for Gem Marie when she was a child. Gem Marie, with her love for the harp and violin, had scarcely touched the piano in those days, leaving it to sit, abandoned in the corner. But now, baby Philip's curious fingers danced over the keys, striking notes that filled the air with a bittersweet melody. The sound both warmed and saddened Monsieur Heritage's heart, reminding him of the sister who should be there, to offer her gentle sisterly guidance. She had vanished like a breath on the wind, and now only memories remained. Armed with his sword and the meager information he had gathered, Monsieur Heritage carried the vengeance of twenty men within him. Whoever held his daughter would soon feel the weight of that fury. In three days he would embark on a journey to a distant land where the laws held no sway, a place where accountability was as rare as a calm sea in the midst of a storm. He had raised Gem Marie to live without restrictions, to believe that her freedom was not a privilege, but her right on the Scotney estate. And now, he feared that this very mindset, her unyielding thirst for freedom would be her undoing. With the resolve of a man who had nothing left to lose, Monsieur Heritage prepared for a journey that would test not only his strength but his soul. He knew, deep in his bones, that the pursuit of Gem Marie would either bring her home or doom them both to the dark depths of the unknown. "There you are! Monsieur, Philip darling you have not been to breakfast or seen your son today. You must not deprive yourself of sleep and food. I know you must do what is necessary to bring order back to the Scotney because Gem Marie's absence breaks my heart too. I too cannot rest knowing that she is away in a strange land. With your permission master your son walks and soon speaks,

243

and I only beg that you hold him before departure." Greta stood in the barn, her words sincere and her heartbeat quickened from the journey to the barn that she swiftly ran to. The two had been able to keep their relationship hidden from the staff and servants. Greta had convinced her mother that time was needed between the two due to the weight of Gem Marie being gone but in reality, the two had grown stronger together. Monsieur had convinced Greta that she must learn how to wheeled the sword during his absence. He warned her to not take the guarded entrance of the Scotney for granted. Instead he supplied her with a sword similar to his own and began training her in defense tactics. "My dearest Greta you worry and create burdens on your heart for me without warrant. My son knows me for I have seen him and held him in the dead night while you slumber after both he and I have feast on your essence without pause. We all share the same blood now and you and I have a bond like no other." Monsieur walked over to Greta and whispered in her ear, "There is no other man and woman who have shared what we have shared." He then stood in front of her and pointed to a pile of hay with his sword in hand then stated. "There, pick up your sword woman and prepare yourself for battle." Greta, moved by his kinship words, wiped a tear from her eye then picked up a brass handle sword that was lighter in weight than Monsieur and held it up to her face. With a swift motion she stepped back and held the sword out in front of her with her right arm stiffened and her left held in the air above her head she watched monsieur Heritage as he maneuvered around her. "Remember, be swift, Greta. If the enemy comes without warning, he will try to take you," Monsieur whispered, his voice low and commanding as he backed her against the barn's worn beam. Her back pressed into the rough wood, the scent of rotting timber filling the air. He was determined to harden her resolve, to make her unafraid while he was away, ready for any battle that may come. Greta's gaze locked on his lips as he spoke, their faces mere inches apart, his blade brushing lightly against hers, a metallic whisper in the air. "Your position is fatal, Greta. The enemy has you pinned. You may never see our precious son again, all that will be left of you is the smell of your jasmine. What will you do?" he continued, his voice dark and deliberate. "Will you cry and beg for mercy, or You will hope for pity just before he rips your blouse from your skin." Greta's breath becoming shallow, his words conjuring an image so vivid and raw that fury ignited in her chest. The thought of a stranger invading her land, with his hands upon her, possibly hungry for the essence she saved only for the man she loved and the child they shared was unbearable. Anger surged through her veins, mixing with fear, until the need to defend herself overpowered everything else. Her breathing quickening while her own blade laid diagonally across her chest. The sensation of the chill blade grazing her breast prompted a swift movement, with all her strength she shoved Monsieur back. Her sword gracefully following him with the tip of it pointed at his throat by her trembling hand. His eyes gleamed with approval as he stumbled slightly, then stood tall with pride etched across his face. He gave her a slight nod , his voice warm with admiration. "Bravo, well done. You have proven that when faced with the threat of being torn from our son, you will not cry but you will fight." Greta's chest heaved with fatigue and exhilaration, a smile tugging at her lips, along with the urge to correct him, but she did not. For it was not only the thought of being taken away from baby Philip that fueled her; it was the haunting possibility of never seeing Monsieur again. "There will be no invasion here, my love," she finally murmured, her voice soft but firm as she lowered the blade. "Everything will be just as you left it when you return. I will be here, waiting for you." Their eyes lingered, the unspoken longing thick between them, each moment heavy with the weight of their impending separation. Yet beneath the tension was a promise of love, loyalty and of reunion that needed no more confirmation. The morning air was crisp as the crew assembled, all eyes upon the grand ship gleaming in the early light. She was a magnificently crafted, ship dressed for the gods. her hull polished to a mirror's shine. At the top of the bow a figure head carved and carefully plated in brass. A depiction of a blind folded mermaid holding a scale in the air with one side of the scale holding a boat weighting it down. The other side a giant wave curled to perfection as if it could wash her away. The beautiful carvings, fierce and fair tell the story of the love and hate along with the power of the sea. Underneath it all a name etched beneath in large letters: *Annabelle*. Every man was made to kiss her long flowing hair that covered the main head rail before standing at attention. Monsieur Heritage stood by Captain McGhee's side, who's voice cut through the wind like the snap of a sail. "Men, we set sail for America on a voyage that will test your mettle and your very souls. *Annabelle* is no ordinary ship. She's been my faithful companion through storms that'd sink lesser men. She had taken me on voyages that have been kissed by the wing of angels, and then cradled in the very arms of hell. Annabelle can bear you to your destination without so much as rousing a kitten from its slumber. But beware she can also drop you to your knees and make you beg the heavens for mercy. While aboard her treat her as though she were the only love you've ever known, for I swear upon the salt of the sea if you give your love to another, you will feel her wrath. I do not play with the waters ever because only men that have gone into the depths of storms know that the sea can be the devil's own playground." Captain McGhee's eyes narrowed as they swept over the faces before him. "We are on a mission, lads, to find a young maiden. And we'll be charting through waters some of you have never sailed. We will plow through territories where men disappear, and ships vanish like smoke on the horizon. My command will not be challenged, nor broken. Any man who dares will pay with his life, and the cold, unforgiving waters shall be his eternal bed." Captain McGhee's gestured to his side, "This here is Monsieur Philip Heritage. He is the reason we shall drink ale, wine, and feast on lamb mutton instead of stale biscuit and salt pork. This man brings with him fifty-two barrels of fresh spring water such luxury I've never had in all my years at sea. Address him with anything less than the respect he deserves, and I'll gut your insides like a mackerel and crack you open like a clam." The captain's gaze shifted to a younger man standing nearby. "This here is young Baron, my assistant. Don't let his age fool you into thoughts of mutiny, for I've equipped him with the cat-o'-nine-tails, and he's quick to use it. And that old quiet sea man with the pipe is Smitty Lagoon he is the best ears and nose these seas have ever known. When he says a storm is brewing, you'll be wise to take heed and be on your marks, no questions asked." The captain paused, letting the weight of his words sink into every heart aboard. "Now am I understood?" Monsieur Heritage studied the faces of the men before him, their ages spanning decades. Some now looked more apprehensive after Captain McGhee's commanding speech, yet no one dared complain or retreat. Rightfully so word had spread about the provisions aboard: barrels of fresh water, meals that surpassed the typical fare, and beds lined with cotton and hay. There was the promise of five pence upon their return to England that had silenced any second thoughts. Even a few women requested to join as cooks, but were quickly turned away. His heart raced as the heavy anchor was hoisted from the depths, the ship creaking to life beneath their feet. He stepped forward, his voice carrying with authority, and the men listened, "Listen well, men," he began, his voice steady but charged with purpose. "Each of you is important to me, for you have all agreed to embark

246

on this brave journey. Together, we will face whatever may come. There will be no quarrels among us fighting will not be tolerated for we are now bound by a brotherhood that will not be broken." He paused, his gaze sweeping across the crew, locking eyes with several of them. "You are being paid well to complete a noble quest, and like your Captain, I expect nothing less than excellence. There is no room for error, no space for weakness." Then, with a fierce glint in his eye, he revealed the heart of the matter. "My daughter is lost in America, and I will stop at nothing to find her. This voyage, this mission is in her honor. We sail for her! Now, let me hear your voices shout 'Aye!' if you stand with me!" The ship sailed smoothly through the English Channel, with over three thousand nautical miles ahead before reaching Baltimore. Monsieur Heritage stood on the deck, watching the newly refurbished vessel cut through the waves with ease. Captain McGhee steered the ship with precision, while the crew tended to their duties, some gazing in awe at the vast expanse of the sea. Ocean spray misted their faces as the warm sun rested on their shoulders. The occasional flicker of marine life breaking the surface added to the enchantment of the voyage. For Monsieur Heritage, however, the tranquility of the scene was deceiving. A calmness settled over him, but it was laced with a deep, bittersweet nostalgia. His thoughts drifted back to his first encounter with Gem Marie, another voyage, not so different from this one. Rubbing his thumb against his forefinger absentmindedly, he reached out for the memory of Gem Marie's small, delicate fingers, as he had once held them as they walked the ship's deck. This time, there was only air, the absence of her touch ignited a wave of rage, reminding him cruelly of why he was aboard this ship. His mind, once lulled by the sea's harmony, now betrayed him. Dark thoughts whispered like a relentless wind: *"She's run away from you. Gone to find a man better than you. Her innocence likely stolen by the lowest of humanity fueled by their internal hatred for her kind."* Suddenly a burst of laughter broke through his spiraling torment. A group of men on deck were roaring at one sailor's fright at the sight of a large shark. Monsieur Heritage stiffened, startled by the sound. His eyes narrowed as his imagination twisted the scene, picturing a similar group of men surrounding Gem Marie, taunting her, stealing what was his precious child. He glared at the men, despising their carefree joy. From a distance, Baron, who kept a watchful eye on Monsieur, observed the swift change in his demeanor. He could see the storm brewing behind Monsieur's eyes who was being consumed by a growing fury. He began to move towards the laughing men, his steps heavy with intent as he held the rail for stability. Sensing danger, Baron quickly maneuvered through the deck, intercepting Monsieur before he could reach the unsuspecting sailors. "Monsieur Héritage," Baron said urgently, placing a firm hand on his arm. "Pardon me, but I need to confirm our arrangements once we dock in Baltimore." Baron locked eyes with him, determined to shatter the anger-filled trance that had overtaken him. "Sir, I suggest we survey the area first. Once we've assessed it, we can send one of the common men to gather intelligence find out who among them is friend or foe." Monsieur Heritage stood like a statue, his cold gaze unwavering as it flickered between the men before him. But Baron pressed on, undeterred by the silence. "Monsieur, forgive my boldness, but you must not let the torment of your thoughts consume you. Your daughter is safe. The way the overseers from both the north and south marveled at how such a clever girl escaped without a trace I'm convinced not a hair on her head was harmed. This voyage, sir, was declared peaceful by none other than yourself. Your brilliance is needed now, not the wrath that clouds your mind." Monsieur Heritage jolted, taken aback by Baron's words, his anger slowly dissolving. The storm inside him, once howling, began to ebb into a strange calm. His clenched fists loosened, his breath deepened. "Baron," he began, his voice carrying a newfound respect, "You are a good man. You were the voice of reason when I could not find my own, and for that, I am indebted to you. Now, tell me have you selected the two men I asked for? Did you choose them for both skill and character? Show me the three." Baron smiled, satisfied to see the fire in Monsieur's eyes diminish. "As you wish, sir. By the sail, there's Dillard. He's an expert with any axe, regardless of its size. I've witness him throw one four feet and strike his target without hesitation. Once, I witnessed him kill a wild boar with a small axe he had hidden beneath his cloak. The beast was three feet away he struck it squarely between the eyes. A perfect kill. The boar stood frozen for a breath, then collapsed as though life had been plucked from it by an unseen hand. It was almost eerie, watching it unfold. His ability to dismantle its body parts without effort was unbelievable." Monsieur Heritage studied Henry's face, clearly impressed by the man's hidden skills. He turned his attention back to Baron. "And the tall one there by the mast. Who is he?" Baron's grin broadened, pleased by Monsieur's sharp eye. "Ah, the tall one is Rupert, though he goes by the name 'Rascals.' He's a master with rope, as skilled as any sailor you'll ever meet. A peculiar man, to be sure. He can tie any knot you imagine, then free himself from it faster than a blink. He's designed traps so intricate that no blade can cut through them. His ability to bind any man or beast is unnatural. I've seen him snare wild animals without so much as a struggle." Baron's tone dropped to a bemused whisper. "They say Rascals spent much of his childhood tied up for mischief, learning to free himself out of necessity. Once, he was left tied in a barn for an entire day. By nightfall, he had not only freed himself but lassoed half the livestock in the pen. He can kill with a rope as easily as a man can draw breath." Monsieur Heritage's eyebrows arched, intrigued by the strange man's skill. "And yet," Baron added with a chuckle, "Despite all his mastery with a rope, he can't seem to keep his own trousers tied up. Quite the paradox, wouldn't you say?" Monsieur Heritage studied the two men intently, feeling the tension in his chest slowly ease. Baron was right Gem Marie is clever, raised with intelligence and a fierce independence. Although she was young, she was unmistakably his daughter resilient, resourceful, and completely beyond the grasp of the brutal, uneducated men who trafficked in slaves. They would need more than brute strength to capture someone as brilliant as Gem Marie. For the rest of the journey, Monsieur spent most of his time in his cabin, crafting his dialogue for when he'd confront the slave traders. He also sketched the notorious slave jail he'd heard about, the one owned by the Slaytter brothers. It was said that for a mere quarter, any ship's captain could store their slaves there while docking in Baltimore. The grim details came from various sources, including Captain McGhee, whose stories gave Monsieur much to consider. By the third week, the ship was sailing smoothly down the East Coast of North America, having passed Nova Scotia, and now docking briefly in New York for fresh water and supplies. Captain McGhee, who hadn't been in the city for over fifteen years, felt a wave of nostalgia as the ship pulled into the harbor. "Listen up, men!" he called, his voice commanding the deck. "This here ship's one of the finest to dock in New York waters, but mind ye this city ain't what it seems. Ye'll see men dressed sharp in their top hats and fine coats, but don't be fooled. Underneath all that linen, ye'll find scoundrels and thieves of every sort. They know these waters, and they'll take advantage of any fool who lets his guard down." He paused, casting a stern look at the crew. "Keep a sharp eye out, especially for ships that linger in the distance but don't dock. There's piracy in these parts, and they ain't the kind ye'll see comin'. I was once feared in these waters, but

now… well, now it's overrun with young fools who think they know the sea."
The crew, anxious to step on solid ground, stood in rapt attention as McGhee
continued. "Take yer rest while ye can, but don't forget at daybreak, we sail
again. If any of ye are thinkin' about lookin' for a woman's company, keep yer
coins close. And don't be drinkin' the ale they offer ye at the taverns it's known
to knock men out cold, and we won't wait for no one who's too deep in
slumber from a bar wench's brew." His warning hung in the air like a cloud,
thick with the reality of the dangers waiting onshore." The Captain now
satisfied that his warnings would be heeded and prepared to retreat to his
cabin. Monsieur Heritage stood at the prow of the ship, his sharp eyes fixed
on the horizon. He barked an order and gestured to one of the young seamen
and the ship's cook, "Fetch six large live fowls, a sack of flour, and sugar. Be
quick about it." With the cook dismissed, he turned his attention to Henry and
Rupert Rascals, gesturing for them to remain by his side. In hushed tones,
Monsieur briefed them on the notorious Slaytter brothers, infamous for their
dealings in the vile slave trade. He laid out their plan for an arrival in
Baltimore, methodically detailing every step. Henry and Rupert listened
intently, the creak of the ship the only sound breaking the stillness as they
plotted their next move. In the distance, a colossal ship loomed, its dark
silhouette wading near the shore. From this distance, they could make out a
figure standing at the bow, beneath a striking carving of a great white shark,
impaled by a sword that glimmered gold even from afar. The vibrant, almost
unnatural color of the shark's body was like a beacon, drawing the eye and
igniting unease. Monsieur Heritage, fixated on the bold carving, was snapped
back to the present by the booming voice of Captain McGhee. "Why, if I didn't
know better, I'd swear there were two of them cursed ships." His voice was
grim, his eyes narrowing. "After more than twenty years of dodging that
vessel, my karmic tragedy has caught up with me. To think, after all this time,
that beast has found me in a moment of weakness. My ship is the only one
with a cannon mounted at the stern I built it myself, for the likes of that cursed
ship you see before and it's captain. " At once, all the men left on the ship
gathered on deck, their bodies stiffened, eyes alert as they prepared for what
could only mean trouble. The massive, black, and red ship edged closer,
menacing on the waves. One of the younger seamen, his hands trembling,
pulled out a telescope. He raised it to his eye, scanning the approaching vessel.
A minute passed in tense silence before he spoke, his voice barely a whisper.

"Captain McGhee... they're pirates I see!. And the largest one among them... he's got shark teeth hanging' from his beard." McGhee's eyes flashed with recognition. "Shark teeth, you say. You'd best be certain, look again, and be sure to remove the morning from your eyes. " The young sailor, now visibly shaken, spit on the glass of his scope then wiped it clean with a trembling hand while using the tail of his shirt. He lifted the telescope once more, inching toward the stern to get a better view. The silence on deck was defining, every man awaiting confirmation. Finally, the boy spoke again. "Aye, Captain, many shark teeth in his beard. And... the crew's a scurvy lot, no doubt. But there's something strange on one of their sails, there's a mermaid, nearly identical to the one carved on your hull, sir." McGhee's face darkened. His voice, low and dangerous, carried across the deck. "I feared waking the seaman in me and taking on this task might bring out old debts to collect, but this... this is more than fate demanding restitution. This is the devil himself, still clutching his grudge. Men, ready your swords. This may be an old acquaintance come to settle a grievance, and Captain McGhee pays no man what he hasn't earned. Load the aft cannon and await my command!" At once, four men scrambled below deck toward the rear of the ship. Monsieur Heritage discreetly checked a small sword hidden in his jacket, slowly he raised his leg to ensure the dagger he always kept in his boot was secure. He then mentally calculated the distance to his cabin, where his sword awaited. Satisfied with his preparations, he turned to Captain McGhee. "And what, pray tell, is the nature of your dealings with this rekindled rival of yours, Captain? We've yet to set foot in America, and already blood is on the wind. Speak, what do you have to say for yourself?" Captain McGhee strode to the rear of the ship, his eyes narrowing as the rival vessel loomed closer. The clamor of voices and activity aboard the other ship carried over the water, growing clearer with each gust of wind. Monsieur Heritage glanced down at the once-bustling harbor that turned into deserted docks, now resembling a ghost town. Just then, a young seaman stumbled back aboard, breathless, and anxious, accompanied by two others carrying sacks of flour and sugar, as well as six live fowls in cages. "Sir, I retrieved everything you asked for," the seaman panted, wiping sweat from his brow. "I came as fast as I could, but the townsfolk below they're all heading inside, taking cover. Is there a storm coming, sir?" Captain McGhee, his face darkening with annoyance, responded gruffly, "Aye, lad, there's a storm coming, but not the kind you'd expect. Now get those supplies to the galley

251

and be quick about it. Then return to the deck." As the seaman hurried off, McGhee raised his telescope to his eye, scanning the approaching ship. After a moment, he lowered it with a satisfied grunt, then shouted across the water, his voice booming. "Still following me, are you! I see you've dressed up your ship with a mermaid on the sail! I could've sworn you were partial to sharks!" The other vessel, now stationary and anchored, a man with a wild grin, his beard adorned with shark teeth of various sizes, lifted a jug to his head and took a long swig before bellowing back. "By Neptune's trident, I'd know that voice and that ship anywhere! But tell me, am I seeing a ghost? For the man who owned that vessel swore once he caught a mermaid that he'd never sail again, and word has it, he died some years back trying to fulfill his wish!" Captain McGhee's face flushed with fury, his knuckles whitening as he gripped the ship's railing. He leaned forward, his voice a thunderous roar that carried over the crashing waves. "Died? Not on your best Christmas, I haven't! Look at me alive and breathing! Now tell me, what brings you here? Have you come to finally thank me for teaching you how to master the sea, have you?" The other captain, a hulking figure with a beard that bristled like a shark's teeth and intertwined with the individual tooth themselves, let out a deep, rumbling laugh, his words slurred with drink but dripping with arrogance. "Teach me? It was I who taught you the finer things, McGhee. I've hauled seven great whites from the depths and held a mermaid bride in my net. What I've done would fetch a fortune at any port stories you could only dream of old man." Captain McGhee's eyes gleamed with amusement, a sharp smile tugging at the corners of his lips. "Ah, you must sail in a waking slumber, Shark. It was I who secured that net of yours many storms ago, or you'd have drowned alongside your precious catch. Even Smitty can vouch for that! And don't you dare spin another yarn about Annabelle. Everyone knows I'm the only man to ever hold her hand. Her love for me runs deeper than any sea why else would she make the bow of my ship her home? Still tracing my footsteps are ya, from the mermaid at the helm to the very way you've set your sail, even down to that red-feathered cap you wear, like one of my own from days long gone." Captain Shark, unfazed, grinned and replied, "This old hat, McGhee, isn't just any cap. It's your hat, the very one you darned years ago. I came across it the day they told me you'd fallen overboard when Captain rancid Haggerty made you walk the plank." "Lies!" Captain McGhee roared, his voice booming above the creaking of the ship. "It was the north wind that blew my hat adrift! Haggerty must've fished it from the sea. I'd sooner fall on my blade than walk Haggerty's cursed plank." Captain Shark interjected with a calm but pointed tone. "We all believed it to be true, McGhee. We never saw you again. Haggerty had your hat perched atop a parrot cage, and with you gone, well, we had no reason to doubt it." McGhee, now eyeing Shark with suspicion, leaned in. "If that's so, Shark, how did you come by it? Surely any man who stumbled upon a great seaman's hat such as mine wouldn't part with it so easily. He'd mount it above a mantel for all to admire. Yet you claim to wear it without a second thought. Tell me, Shark, not only do you mimic me, but it seems you fancy me as well. Well let me remind you, my heart belongs to my wife... and Annabelle." At that, McGhee's crew erupted into laughter, their voices ringing out across the deck as Shark's face darkened in response. Captain Shark, with a sly grin creeping across his weathered face, held his tongue for a moment before finally retorting, "Fancy you? No, McGhee. I mourned you like any brother would. Our mother, Rosalee, always said you were a hard birth, stubborn as your father, Ransford that raised you." A hush fell over both ships as Captain Shark continued, his voice echoing across the calm waters. "My father, Archibald, was a handsome gentleman Rosalee's heart belonged to him, as you can plainly see. The apple doesn't fall far from the tree." Shark's booming laugh followed, rolling across the sea like a thunderclap, his thick beard shaking with every chuckle. Captain McGhee, face flushed with both shock and fury, shot back, "Lies! My mother was a blessed angel, young and innocent she never bore another child but me. You dare twist her memory! For that, I'll have your filthy, drunken tongue for supper!" Amused, Captain Shark watched as McGhee paced the deck, fuming like an untamed beast. With easy grace, Shark extended his hand, and a fresh jug of rum was quickly placed in his palm. He took a long swig before speaking again, his tone dripping with mockery. "Now, now, brother, no need for such venom. Do you remember when your mother left you? You were only five, if I recall correctly." McGhee froze. His mind flashed back to that time when his mother had vanished, supposedly to care for a dying aunt who had left her a fortune. When she returned a year later, she had persuaded McGhee's father to move the family closer to that same aunt's remote estate. It was only a year and a half later that Captain McGhee's father, Ransford, died. And after that, his mother abandoned him. McGhee now remembering in that village there was a blacksmith by the name of Archibald a man whose wife had died

253

in childbirth, leaving him to raise their newborn alone. McGhee recalled his mother Rosalee, had often helped the poor widowed father with the newborn. As McGhee pondered on the memory, Captain Shark spread his arms wide, roaring with triumphant glee. "Brother!" Captain McGhee, still reeling from the revelation, snarled, "Do not call me brother!" Captain Shark tried to lighten the weight of the truth, softening the harshness of their mother's Rosalee's abandonment. With a smirk that barely masked his own lingering bitterness, he said, "When we moved away, she eventually left me too. She used to talk about you, McGhee how much you loved wild berries. I figured when she left, maybe she went back to you." But Shark's words, meant to cushion the truth, only fueled McGhee's growing anger. The realization hit him like a crashing wave: his mother had left him at seven years old, not for him but to chase her own desires. Finally snapping back to the present, he shouted at Captain Shark, "You'd best be moving that sorry excuse for a ship before I blast it to the depths! And tell me, Shark, your little tale still doesn't explain how you got your hands on my old cap. Haggerty is one of my sworn enemies, he swore to take my hat to his grave if he ever had the chance. How did you manage to wrestle it from him?" Captain Shark paused mid-guzzle, wiping the rum from his lips with the back of his hand. With a dark gleam in his eye, he leaned forward and said simply, "Twas easy. I killed him, and the bird for it. Revenge is a funny thing." A deafening roar of laughter erupted from Shark's men. Their cackles spread like wildfire across the decks, reaching McGhee's ship. The laughter continued as the men exchanged taunts across the water with a camaraderie born from years of brutal rivalry. Monsieur Heritage motioned for Captain McGhee to approach, his expression solemn, yet carrying a newfound glimmer of hope. "Discovering that Captain Shark is kin," Heritage began, "is a stroke of fortune I never could have foreseen. His services may soon be needed my daughter's recapture could depend on it." McGhee nodded, his eyes steady. "Aye, I'll make the necessary arrangements. Shark and I will meet in Baltimore. I'll go over all the details with him." Captain Shark confirmed his intentions, eager to partake in the mission. He advised, "I'll sail first to Cape Charles, but I'll be in Baltimore soon enough. Your daughter will be found, I swear on a great white's tooth." With that, the large red-and-black ship, looming like a predator of the sea, set off toward its unknown fate. As dawn's first light broke across the horizon, a fully rested Captain McGhee steered his vessel toward the western shores. The ship cut through the water like a knife, eventually arriving at Fort McHenry. There, the crew encountered a heavily fortified defense a place known for its watchful eyes on all vessels, particularly those rumored to be carrying slaves. A soldier, armed and stern, stepped forward, his gaze hard. "What's the purpose of such a large vessel in these harbors, if it's not transporting cargo? By orders of Slaytter Company and the authorities, you must be unloading or picking up." Baron, well-versed in the dealings of the port, sensed the rising tension. His eyes caught Monsieur Heritage's subtle movement as the latter's hand drifted toward the coat pocket where he concealed his trusty dagger. Acting quickly, Baron stepped closer to the guard, a disarming smile playing on his lips. "Ah, good sir," Baron said smoothly, eyeing the soldier's worn boots with holes. "Your shoes they've seen better days. Yet here you stand, dutifully watching over Slaytter's strict entry policy. A man standing at such a pristine post ought to wear the proper footwear. Before you is one of London's most esteemed men a man of benevolence, searching for a fair-skinned maiden with a gift for music. She may have returned home to Maryland. She plays instruments with a skill so divine that she's stolen the hearts of many. Perhaps this small gesture will ease your burden and help you in your search for her whereabouts." Baron slipped one hundred dollars from his jacket and pressed it discreetly into the man's hand. The soldier's eyes widened in shock, and without hesitation, he pocketed the money before anyone could take notice. Monsieur Heritage, with a cool demeanor, handed the man two more dollars. "A drink, for you and your men," he said, his voice low and commanding. The guard, now practically beaming, replied, "My wife and daughter thank you, sir. They'll be needing new frocks, no doubt." He paused, lowering his voice conspiratorially. "Now, about the girl you're looking for the one skilled with instruments you might find her at the conservatory teaching maybe. I can arrange for someone to take you." Monsieur Heritage, his eyes narrowing ever so slightly, felt a growing unease at the guard's greedy nature, yet he masked it with practiced ease. "No, thank you. We'll rest first before any such meeting. Where might we find the cleanest lodgings?" The guard, eager to please, pointed up the hill. "There's a fine, quiet place called Caroll's Place. Large, clean, and respectable. You can't miss it's the largest house that sits on the hill pass the buildings, a very welcoming place I might add." With a nod of agreement, Monsieur Heritage, Baron, Dillard, and Rupert made their way up the hill, their boots crunching against the gravel as the ship shrank into the distance. Behind them, Captain McGhee stood at the edge of the dock, the sea breeze tugging at his coat, watching the four disappear into the haze of the looming fort. "Keep your eyes sharp," McGhee muttered, glancing over his shoulder at the crew still lingering by the ship. "Shark won't be long now." He reached into his pocket, retrieving a small leather pouch heavy with coins. "This should be enough to keep the local tongues busy if they start flapping before Shark arrives." He tossed it to one of his men with a sly grin. "Just make sure you don't get too generous." The men nodded, knowing all too well the price of loose lips in a town like this. Their orders were clear: keep quiet, keep watch, and wait. As the group began to disperse, they drifted toward the taverns nestled in the shadow of the fort, their presence deliberate but subdued. Each man blended into the bustling crowd of sailors and soldiers, but none were there to drink. They were there to listen and wait. Every glance, every whispered conversation, was carefully noted. The taverns might have been full of laughter and music, but beneath it all, there was an undeniable tension. The kind that only comes before a storm.

Chapter: 20

Lilac

"The wedding is approaching quickly, you must play with certainty," Christian Pierre's voice held a sharp edge, frustration laced in every word. "You've been playing as if this is your first time holding the instrument. Tell me, Gem Marie, what troubles you? Is it the piece itself does it upset you, perhaps? It has been months since I informed you that you'd be playing at Lady Lelina's wedding, yet you still behave as though you are unwell." Gem Marie remained distant, her fingers trembling against the bow, her gaze avoiding his. The idea of performing at Lady Lelina's wedding felt anything but comforting. She had been dreading it since she had been ordered to play. "I cannot play this piece, Christian," she finally snapped, her voice rising with emotion. "You composed it with the intent to outsmart Lady Lelina, why do you want me to play, and she dislikes me. Is that the reason you have selected me to play. Well I refuse I will not play for her." Christian Pierre's patience frayed. "You will play," he said coldly, stepping closer, "or I'll summon Cook to sit with you while you practice." Gem Marie froze, her face paling at the mention of Cook. It had been over a month since Cook had struck her for playing the violin inappropriately while guests were present. A memory she tried to buried deep but now it clawed its way to the surface, threatening to unravel her completely. Her voice trembled with fury. "You think you can frighten me into playing? Where is my harp?" In a fit of frustration, she stormed to the back of the parlor, where a harp sat gleaming under a veil of dust. Christian had had it delivered two weeks prior, at her request to learn how to play. but she had deliberately ignored it, refusing to pluck even a single note. A small revenge of her own that no one else was aware of, Gem Marie had been torturing herself by not playing the instrument she absolutely loved. She positioned herself behind the harp, her chest heaving with anger. "You want me to play the violin for a woman who flaunts her disloyalty in your face? A woman who shares no love for your music or for you. What is your plan, Christian Pierre?" Her voice cracked as she spoke, her eyes brimming with unshed tears. Without waiting for his response, Gem Marie's fingers began to move over the strings of the

Harp. The sound of the Harp filled the room, raw and haunting. She poured her anger, her hurt, her soul into the music. As the melody swelled, her mind drifted back to the Scotney, to a moment that had burned itself into her memory. In her recollection, she was no longer in the Honey Waters parlor. She was back in the Scotney garden, surrounded by roses. Christian Pierre was there too, seated beside Monsieur Heritage, while the staff, the servants, and the guests all watched her play. She could feel their eyes on her, the weight of their expectations crushing her spirit. Her fingers moved faster, harder, and a tightness began to form in her stomach, a violent wrenching that threatened to tear her apart. She could hear Christian calling her name in the distance, but she was lost in the music, unable to open her eyes or stop herself. The pain in her soul erupted through the strings, and the harp seemed to scream with her. And then, suddenly, a loud shout shattered the moment. "Bravo!" The word jolted her back to reality. Her fingers stilled, as she opened her eyes, gasping for breath. Christian Pierre stood mesmerized, his gaze fixed on Gem Marie as her fingers danced across the harp. He had never heard such a hauntingly beautiful style of playing before, each note resonating with a depth that left him spellbound. His voice softened, almost a whisper. "Remarkable... what other instruments do you play, Gem Marie? You must tell me at once. You were in a trance, where did you go? What place do you see when the music pours from your soul like this? Who taught you to play so, my darling?" Tears welled up in Gem Marie's eyes, her chest tightening with the weight of a secret she had buried for so long. This was the moment she had to decide. Should she weave another elaborate story, or would she finally reveal the truth? The truth that she had once been the daughter of Monsieur Philip Heritage, a man who owned no slaves, only servants. A man who ruled not a plantation but a grand castle, a life she had lost by her own hands. Christian Pierre watched her intently, noticing every tremble of her fingers, every breath she took, waiting for her response. His eyes seemed to pierce her, as if sensing the turmoil in her heart. Aware of his gaze, Gem Marie stepped away from the harp, the delicate notes still echoing in the room, crossed to the center. There, she picked up a violin and held it beneath her chin. Her voice, though soft, trembled with firmness. "I will play this violin as I truly know it should be played." With that, Gem Marie began. She started with Bach's violin concerto no.2, her strokes measured and graceful, then transitioned seamlessly to concerto no.1, the music swelling with intensity. Her movements became fervent, the friction of the bow sending warmth through her fingertips. But this time, she didn't close her eyes to escape. This time, she kept them wide open focused entirely on Christian Pierre. Every note, every stroke of the bow, was a confession. Through the music, she revealed her deepest feelings for him the sleepless nights, the unspoken promises, the yearning buried beneath layers of silence. The melody was a purging, a surrender of the soul she had once guarded so fiercely. When the final note faded into the stillness, she placed the violin and bow gently on the chair, her chest rising and falling with the remnants of the emotion she had released. In the silence, Christian Pierre's voice broke through, soft yet commanding. "Come here. Give me your hands." His tone left no room for refusal. Gem Marie hesitated but slowly stepped forward. He took her hands, his fingers gently enclosing hers as if holding something fragile and precious. "Please allow me to hold all that is true before me," he murmured, his voice low and kind. "You hold your tongue why? Is it because your music has spoken in a thousand languages? Your talent... it is greater than any I have ever heard." Their eyes locked, the air thick with the words they dared not speak. The distance between them, once defined by the unspoken rules of master and slave, seemed to blur in that moment, leaving only the weight of everything they had yet to admit. Gem Marie watched as Christian's touch grew softer, his hands lingering over hers in a way that made her heart quicken. Although Gem Marie's ignorance of her hue had once shielded her from the harsh realities of this world, she now found herself in a place that loathed her kind. Yet, somehow, she had escaped the more treacherous fates she overheard whispered among the other slaves. Today, that fragile innocence was about to shatter. "That, Christian Pierre, is what I will *not* do for Lady Lelina on her wedding day," Gem Marie said, her voice steely. "I will not bestow upon her the creation of hours of love and dedication." The room fell silent, Christian Pierre momentarily speechless, his gaze shifting from the harp to Gem Marie, who now refused to meet his eyes. The tension between them was unavoidable. "You speak with such contempt," Christian said, breaking the silence, confusion furrowing his brow. "Why? Why do you let anger consume you? All over a woman who masks herself in foreign fabric, seeking approval from gossip mongers? Why do you believe if you play that your music, your gift, would only be meant for Lady Lelina?" He rose from his chair, his steps deliberate, and moved toward Gem Marie, who stood stiffly in the center of the parlor. Her hands absentmindedly fingered the edges of her dress a gown once adorned with delicate beads, now barren, the threads that once held the decorations that dangled loosely. Cook and the others had forced her to remove the beads, reminding her she was not the lady of the house. She longed for the gowns Monsieur Heritage had gifted her, wondering now if she was no different from Lady Lelina desiring beauty that came from lands far from this plantation. Christian stepped beside her, his eyes tracing her profile. Her hair, unbound, fell past her shoulders, and the dress, once loose, now clung tightly to her form Surely, you've heard that Margret is to be married, beyond the fields, out of sight, on that very same day. It is no coincidence. Your playing will be a gift to her as well. She has finally revealed the truth about the father of her child. Christian Pierre paused, a hint of satisfaction lacing his voice. "I consider myself a fair man, and no one here at Sweetwater needs to fear love. I've given permission for Margret and Thomas to jump the broom in marriage. I've arranged for a beautiful gown to be made for you, Gem Marie, a dress of your own for that special day. My darling, all of New Orleans will gather here not for Lady Lelina, but to hear you play. And play, you will, my precious one." Gem Marie stood silent, listening without interruption, feeling the weight of what was being asked of her. She was to perform once more, but this time not from behind the veil of anonymity. Christian's touch softened, his fingers lingering over hers, sending a tremor through her heart. Although Gem Marie's ignorance of her mixed heritage had once shielded her from the harsh truths of the world, she now stood in a place that loathed her kind. Yet somehow, she had managed to avoid the cruelty whispered and endured among the other slaves. But today, that fragile shield was about to shatter. "That, Christian Pierre, is what I will *not* do for Lady Lelina on her wedding day," Gem Marie said, her voice steady but laced with defiance. "I will not offer her my music, hours of love and dedication, for a woman who cannot see me as more than a tool." Awkward Silence filled the room. Christian's eyes widened in surprise, caught off guard by her boldness. His gaze shifted from the harp to Gem Marie, who now refused to meet his eyes. The tension between them was evident. "You speak with such contempt," Christian finally broke the silence, his brow furrowing. "Why? Why let anger consume you over a woman who drapes herself in foreign silks, only to seek validation from those who thrive on gossip? Why do you think your musical gift is meant solely for Lady Lelina? " He rose from his chair, his movements deliberate as he approached Gem Marie, who stood still in the center of the

260

parlor. Her hands nervously smoothed the worn edges of her dress the she had taken from the music school, once adorned with delicate beads that now lay bare, the threads hanging loosely where Cook had one evening in the cellar had ripped them away, reminding her she never would be the lady of the house. Gem Marie longed for the gowns Monsieur Heritage had gifted her, wondering now if her desire too for beauty was no different from Lady Lelina's, yearning for treasures from distant lands while trapped on the plantation. Christian stopped beside her, his eyes tracing her profile. Her hair, unbound, fell in waves past her shoulders, and the dress, now tight against her form, seemed to carry the weight of unspoken sorrow. Her innocence, so fragile and untouched by the cruelties of this world, stirred something deep within him. She had turned to him once, silently, seeking comfort after Cook had struck her. The memory of her pain, her vulnerability, was too potent to leave unaddressed. Without warning, Christian took another step closer, turning her to face him. Before Gem Marie could react, he kissed her again. The act was sudden, unexpected. Her eyes widened with fear as she tried to pull away, but his grip was strong, unrelenting. She opened her mouth to scream, but the sound was swallowed by another kiss, more insistent than the first. Initially Gem Marie resisted, her body tense with fear and confusion. But then, in the stillness of the moment, something within her began to give. Her hands, which had been pushing against him softened as the kiss deepened. The world outside the parlor faded as they stood there, lost in a stolen moment, both unaware of their surroundings. It was the faint chirping of a bird outside the parlor window that broke the spell. Reality came crashing back as Gem Marie pulled away, her breath quick and uneven. Christian Pierre blinked, as if waking from a dream. Just beyond the double parlor doors, a shadow shifted a silent observer, or perhaps only the breeze. His eyes flicked toward the movement, his expression unreadable, though a trace of suspicion lingered. Still holding her hands, he gently guided Gem Marie to a seat by a small mahogany table. With quiet precision, he pulled out a sheet of fine parchment and a fountain pen, setting them before her. "Since you refuse to speak," Christian said softly, his voice steady yet filled with a quiet intensity, "Write it here. Tell me everything you know." Gem Marie hesitated, her heart racing. The man she had dreamed of, fantasized about for years, stood before her at last. His gaze, though calm, seemed to probe deeper than her words could convey. With trembling hands, she picked up the pen and began to write, her thoughts pouring onto the paper in a desperate flow.

I am a girl. I believe I am sixteen years old. I speak many languages, English, French Italian and German. I can play the harp, violin, and piano. I am still learning the cello, but I know a little. I do not remember my mother. My father is Monsieur Heritage the man who took care of me since I was four... I cannot speak his name anymore. It hurts too much. I betrayed and traded a place that worshiped for a place that despises me. The Scotney castle the place that taught me everything I know. I ran away, searching for a man I once read about in a newspaper. A man I fell in love with, without ever knowing him. I left behind everything to find him. Now, I can never return to the life I once knew. I am in the world alone, utterly alone. I want to know when you see me, what do you see. When you close your eyes and listen, what do you see as you hear. I am lost. I am stolen, I was and use to be, but now I am no longer.... Gem Marie.

When she finished writing, Gem Marie handed the paper to Christian Pierre, her eyes pleading for understanding. He accepted it with careful hands, standing silently by the parlor's window as he read her confession. Twice he read the words, and each time they sank deeper into him. He knew he was the man she had been searching for, but he would not reveal it not now. A single tear threatened to betray him, but he held it back, turning to face her with a mixture of tenderness and resolve. Holding out the paper, he spoke softly, "You are quite remarkable, Gem Marie. You are fortunate I play the cello as well. After Lady Lelina and Bonneville's wedding, I will teach you. Though now, I almost wish I could break my promise and say no to this wedding ceremony." He paused, as if weighing his next words. "You write beautifully, and your command of languages is extraordinary. Where were you taken from?" "Italy," Gem Marie whispered, her voice barely audible. Christian nodded slowly, his suspicion finally aligning with the truth. Her Mediterranean glow, the elegance she tried to suppress all made sense now. "Listen to me carefully," he said, his tone soft but firm. "What you have written must never be spoken aloud. Not to anyone. Especially not to the slaves." He studied her closely, his eyes filled with an emotion Gem Marie couldn't quite decipher. "You are no slave, Gem Marie. No one with your knowledge, your grace, could have been raised in such a life. This is why you know nothing of chores, or fieldwork. Your mannerisms they betray your charm, your education." For a moment, Christian lingered, the air between them thick with unspoken truths. Then, with a final glance, he stepped back, the weight of their shared secret hanging heavy in the room. Christian paused, listening to the unnerving silence that now filled the house, a stillness that stirred a paranoia he couldn't quite explain. He moved back to the window, his gaze drifting to the fields where slaves and servants worked tirelessly under the sun. His eyes caught on a large peach tree, where Margret labored with her infant strapped to her back. Without hesitation, Christian headed for the veranda, his voice sharp as he called out, "Margret, come here quickly!" Sweating and out of breath, Margret made her way to the veranda. For a brief moment, she observed Christian Pierre, her mind wandering back to the days when jealousy gnawed at her insecurities of Lady Lelina and her closeness to Christian. The memory vanished as Christian's voice cut through the air, authoritative yet oddly concerned. "Margret, have you fed your child yet?" he asked, his tone unexpectedly gentle. Margret, taken aback by his question, smiled weakly. "No, sir, I was tending to the peaches for preserving... for the wedding and storage." Christian nodded, pleased. "Good. But I want you to feed the child now. From this point on, Gem Marie will handle the baby's care while you're working. Whenever you're in the garden or dealing with the fruit, leave the child with her. That baby is not to come to any harm. Do you understand?" Margret, shocked by his sudden decision, felt an unexpected sense of entitlement, knowing Gem Marie had been assigned to care for her child. She quickly made her way inside, sitting in the parlor as she explained to Gem Marie the delicacy of the infant's head and body, Christian Pierre stood on the veranda, leaving the two women to come to terms with the new arrangements. As Margret began to breastfeed, Gem Marie watched with quiet amazement. Seeing the whole act from start to finish her curiosity got the better of her, and she gently asked, "Why are you showing me this?" Margret, now agitated, snapped, "Master Pierre says you are to care for my child while I work in the garden and the fields. You will do it right, and you will bring no harm to my baby girl or there will be a heavy price to pay. Do you understand, gal?" Gem Marie, silent and obedient, nodded. She watched the baby, now sleeping peacefully in Margret's arms as she fed her. Margret's eyes wandered around the parlor, landing on the musical instruments and sheets of music scattered on the mahogany table remnants of Christian Pierre's passion for music. "You play all this with Master Pierre?" Margret asked, her voice curious. "Where do you come from? Why are you here at Honey Waters?" Gem Marie said nothing, her silence heavy as she reached out her arms. After a moment's hesitation, Margret reluctantly handed over the small infant just as Christian entered the room. He stepped closer to Gem Marie, his gaze softening as he watched her cradle the baby. "Return to the garden Margret," he ordered, his focus now fully on Gem Marie. Once Margret exited the parlor, Christian settled into a nearby chair, watching Gem Marie with interest. After a long pause, he spoke again, his voice quiet yet probing. "Do you want one of your own someday?" Gem Marie's response was barely a whisper, but her quick nod said enough. She continued to cradle the infant, her eyes downcast as Christian's gaze lingered on her. Gem Marie's thoughts drifted back to Greta and baby Philip, recalling the days she spent playing with him, just the three of them. Now, a wave of curiosity swept over her, the unanswered questions bubbling to the surface to which Greta and Monsieur Heritage had always avoided. Without a second thought, her innocence shone through in the most unexpected way as she asked, "If you were to hatch one for me, which bird would you choose? I would like to pick my own." Christian Pierre, caught off guard, stared at her in disbelief, struggling to make sense of her words. With a slight chuckle he thought to himself, "Does she really believe? Wait," he began, his voice tinged with shock while fighting to contain his bewilderment, finally he asked, "Do You think that child came from a fowl?" Gem Marie smiled with amusement. "Yes, I saw a calf being born and a young colt too there was no egg. But baby Philip, I saw him after he was hatched from Greta, just like the hens." Christian Pierre, astonished, leaned forward and asked, "Who is Greta?" Gem Marie immediately regretted the slip of her tongue, revealing a fragment of her past. She hesitated before replying, "She was a woman I once knew." Sensing an opportunity to probe further, Christian pressed on. "And when you saw baby Philip after he was 'hatched,' where was he?" Without thinking, Gem Marie answered, "In Greta's chambers, in his bassinet. He was such a joyful baby always smiling and moving about. Unlike this little one she doesn't smile like Philip. She only sleeps peacefully is it because she is a girl, girls behave different from boys." Christian, now thoroughly puzzled, kept his expression neutral. "Perhaps this baby is missing your touch," he suggested tenderly. "With your constant care, she might begin to smile like Philip." "Perhaps," Gem Marie murmured, sniffing the baby's delicate skin. "She smells of lilacs. Why is that?" "Her mother gardens often," Christian explained, choosing his words carefully. "Margaret ensures Honey Waters is always in bloom, every inch of this land has something that has grown or is growing. She is in charge of caring for the flowers ensuring their healthy growth. She often carries lilacs and all sorts of flowers, she keeps her baby tied to her as she works, the child must have picked up the floral scent." Gem Marie smiled at the thought of the sweet-smelling baby, "Her name should be lilac." Christian now realized just how sheltered Gem Marie's life had been. She wasn't only born free she had been protected, hidden away from the harsh realities of the world. Only a man of influence could have guarded her so carefully. The thought lingered in his mind about the newspaper articles as he decided to reveal a simple truth. "Gem Marie," Christian said after a pause, "babies aren't born from hens. They are born from the love shared between a man and a woman. They often talk like you, and I are doing." Gem Marie listened intently as Christian explained courtship, admiration, and love. The things were so foreign to her that each word felt like a revelation. When he finished, she blinked, still processing the information. "So..." she asked, her tone genuinely curious, "who lays the egg the man or the woman?" Christian, once again shocked by her innocence, stared at her in disbelief. But instead of correcting her, a smile tugged at his lips. He couldn't help but wonder what other mysteries lay hidden in her past, waiting to be unearthed. This woman, with her strange knowledge, a Master of Music and sheltered life, intrigued him in ways he couldn't yet understand. The room grew quiet around them, the only sound being the soft breath of the baby in Gem Marie's arms. Christian knew that one day, the full story of her past would surface, and when it did, it would change everything. After some passing hours, Margaret entered the grand foyer of the big house, her steps slow and deliberate. The scent of fresh-cut flowers filled the air, mingling with the tension that always seemed to linger slightly inside the walls. She paused at the parlor door, her fingers trembling slightly as she smoothed her apron and cleared her throat. After a moment's hesitation, she stepped inside. "Master Pierre," she began, her voice steady despite the tightness in her chest, "all the gardens have been tended to sir. I placed some orchids on the veranda, just as you like. I've come for my child now, sir. It's time for her to be fed and cleaned." Christian Pierre, seated by the large bay window, nodded absentmindedly, his gaze distant. His eyes followed Margaret as she made her way to the corner of the room where

Gem Marie sat, cradling the baby girl in her arms. Gently, Margaret reached for the infant, her hands tender but purposeful. As she swaddled the delicate child against her chest, she allowed herself the smallest of smiles. But before she could make her escape, Christian Pierre's voice stopped her. "Ah, Margaret," he said, his tone almost casual. "Have you named her yet?" Margaret turned, her heart racing, yet she forced a smile to mask her unease. "Yes, Master. Her name is Sarah, after my mother." Pierre's lips curled into a slow, calculating smile. His eyes, however, held a predatory gleam. "Sarah? How... quaint. But a girl as sweet-smelling as she is deserves a name worthy of her uniqueness. I held her earlier, and she smelled of lilacs. Don't you agree Lilac is a more fitting name?" Margaret's stomach churned, the weight of his words pressing down on her like a stone. Her throat tightened, but she kept her face neutral, glancing at Gem Marie, whose naive eyes darted nervously between Margaret and Pierre, clearly uncomfortable but too simple-minded to understand the cruelty of the moment. There would be no support from her, Margaret swallowed hard and forced herself to nod. "As you wish, Master Pierre," she murmured, her voice barely above a whisper. "Lilac it is." The name her mother carried, that she had chosen with love, now ripped away and replaced with something as fleeting and fragile as a flower. Hastily, she turned and left the parlor, her vision blurred with tears she refused to shed in front of them. Her feet quickened, desperate to leave behind the suffocating walls of the big house. Outside, the wind carried the scent of the very flowers Christian Pierre had named her daughter after. It felt like mockery, her mother's legacy now erased as easily as the dirt Margaret swept from the veranda steps each morning. Margaret clutched her baby tightly, her arms protective as if shielding her child from a fate she could no longer control. Inside, Gem Marie's mood shifted. Elation danced in her eyes as she looked at Christian Pierre as the thought of him changing Margret's baby's name to her suggestion excited her. "When will you give me my baby?" she asked eagerly, the hunger in her voice unmistakable. "I'd like two." Christian Pierre rose from his seat and walked over to her, the same calculating smile playing on his lips. He knelt beside her, taking her hand in his and pressing a kiss to the back of it. His eyes never left hers. "Soon, my precious Gem," he promised. Gem Marie smiled unaware to the actual terms that came along with a baby now more cooperative she picked of the violin that had been laying on a chair and began playing a soft melody. The piece was so soothing Christian Pierre still kneeling began closing his eyes as he listened. After Gem Marie was finished, she told him, "That is for the wedding."

Chapter: 21

The Heritage Way

Ms. Carrol, I must express my deepest gratitude for your warm hospitality. Never before have I partaken in such a breakfast. You say the gravy was made from the very pork you prepared? Simply delightful, my dear," Monsieur Heritage remarked. His tone laden with sincere admiration. He, along with Dillard and Rupert, sat around the small breakfast table, greedily devouring what Ms. Carrol had proudly named a proper Southern breakfast. The three gentlemen had taken up lodging at a rooming house recommended to them by the port's guard. The house, a modest yet well-kept abode, was governed by Ms. Carrol with a strict hand and a motherly touch. The establishment was spotless, the scent of bacon and eggs greeting them each morning, while the rich aroma of hearty stew filled the air by evening. Ms. Carrol herself, a middle-aged woman of sturdy frame and soft features, had clearly taken a particular fondness to Monsieur Heritage. She offered him extra helpings with an eager smile and ensured his linens were always freshly laundered and replaced before his return each day. Monsieur Heritage, ever the curious scholar, had grown quite intrigued by the local medicines and remedies found in the town. A long street, lined with doctors and scientists alike, displayed an assortment of curiosities in their windows. One doctor, who proclaimed himself an expert in bones and animals, brazenly highlighted a human femur as a testament to his trade. Indeed, the area was full of strange happenings and peculiarities, which only deepened their interest. By now, they had been guests in the house for nearly a week, and it was at night, under the cloak of darkness, that the most unsettling sounds crept from the nearby woods. It was as if tortured beasts were prowling just beyond the treelined. When questioned about the eerie noises, Ms. Carrol assured them it was nothing more than wild animals, creatures known to wreak havoc upon the livestock if not for the diligent efforts of the young colored boy who set traps for them. She added, in a hushed tone, that according to one of the esteemed doctors on Medicine Row, some of these very animals were said to carry dreadful diseases. "Best keep your distance from them, gentlemen," she warned with a knowing nod, "for not all creatures roam the woods without cause." It was the fifth day now, and Monsieur Heritage took his usual stroll along Medicine Row, casting a keen eye through windows as the sick, both human and beast, went about their daily tribulations. On this particular morning, his gaze fell upon a tall, thin youth, pushing a wheelbarrow. Monsieur watched with growing curiosity as the lad wheeled the barrel, a large one, draped in a white sheet. As the boy advanced down the lane, the townsfolk seemed to part before him as water yields to a ship's bow, moving with an almost unnatural deference, as though he commanded their very steps. A couple hurried aside, offering the boy a quick bow as he passed. Intrigued by this strange procession, Monsieur Heritage followed the youth at a discreet distance, his curiosity piqued. The boy led him to a building that stood apart from the rest, lonely and peculiar. There were no bones hung in the windows, no painted signs of children with cool rags upon their brows nothing but a bright red door at the rear. The youth approached the red door, lifting a hand to knock, when Monsieur called out, "You there, young man with the barrel!" The boy paused, glancing over his shoulder, revealing a gaunt figure clad in a brown lab coat, its sleeves worn and frayed, his gloves missing their fingertips. "Yes, sir?" he asked, a slight smile forming on his lips. He surveyed Monsieur Heritage's attire, instantly recognizing that the man was no native of Maryland. "May I be of service to you? Should you wish to see the doctor, I could fetch him." Monsieur stepped closer, closing the distance until he stood within arm's reach. "No, I require no doctor, lad. But I must ask, I have seen you daily with that wheelbarrow. What is it that you transport with such care?" The boy's smile faltered, a shadow of unease crossing his face. He hesitated for a moment, then handed Monsieur a weathered note, hastily written and sealed with the name of Dr. Hertz. As Monsieur glanced down to read, a fetid odor assailed his senses foul and rancid. He recoiled, pulling a handkerchief to his nose, eyes watering from the stench. "My God, boy!" Monsieur exclaimed. "What lies beneath that cloth? The stench is unbearable!" Otis Baltimore, stiffened, his earlier smile now replaced by frustration. He pondered whether to divulge the truth to this strange man who, for all he knew, could be the new constable. For beneath the sheet was a creature, half-dead, its body riddled with maggots, desperate in its struggle to gnaw free its trapped limb. The truth lingered on Otis's tongue, but he hesitated, unsure if he should reveal such a grim sight to the curious stranger before him. The situation at hand would likely disturb the impeccably dressed gentleman with the foreign accent, Otis mused. Yet, after a moment of thought, he smirked inwardly, *"The sight will surely send the stranger fleeing,"* he considered. Without further hesitation, Otis yanked the sheet off and took a step back, awaiting Monsieur's reaction. "See, sir? Medical business for the good doctor," Otis declared. Monsieur Heritage gasped in abject horror. The creature beneath the sheet a large raccoon was crawling with maggots, which seemed to pour out of one decayed paw. The stench of its rotting flesh now hung thick in the air, seeping into Monsieur's senses. What had once been a pleasant morning was now ruined by the vile odor, the remnants of his breakfast, prepared so kindly by Ms. Carrol, rising unbidden in his throat. Unable to speak, Monsieur Heritage, his face paling rapidly, turned sharply to the side, unable to keep down the meal any longer. With a sickening sound, he regurgitated into a nearby bush, his body wracked by retching. Otis, uneasy with the scene, began to shift uncomfortably, backing away from both the wheelbarrow and the distressed gentleman. He stood frozen, eyes fixed on Monsieur's pallor, unsure of what to do next. The stillness was abruptly broken by the clanging of the metal door as it swung open. Dr. Hertz, both perplexed and visibly irritated, strode out, a cup in hand. With a stern command, he addressed Otis. "Boy, cover that monstrosity and bring it to the lab at once!" He then turned his attention to Monsieur Heritage, offering the cup. "Here, sir, drink this it will settle your stomach and ease the nausea." Monsieur Heritage, still shaken, grasped the cup with trembling hands and downed its contents in one swift gulp. The fine breakfast Ms. Carrol had prepared for Monsieur now threatened rebellion, lodging itself in his throat in a thick, choking lump of saliva. Dr. Hertz led Monsieur to a nearby bench, shaded by the grand branches of a maple tree. "Sit here for a moment, sir," he said, gesturing to the seat. "The air is clearer here, by the tree and the plants, that large box you see seated across from you is not for aesthetic its filled with the most exquisite night-blooming flowers that come alive once twilight sets in. Guaranteed to provide the right medicine needed, I often come to this very spot myself to gather my thoughts in the late night just so I can open the box and watch the beautiful flowers bloom right before my eyes in the moonlight" Monsieur Heritage settled onto the bench, his eyes now keenly observing Dr. Hertz's attire his long coat, worn shoes. "You are a doctor?" Monsieur inquired, though still finishing the last of the curious drink, the taste of saltwater and ginger lingering on his tongue. The concoction seemed to work quickly, soothing the nausea that had overcome him earlier. "Indeed, I am a doctor," Dr. Hertz replied, a slight smile tugging at the corner of his mouth. "Though I much prefer to be recognized for my scientific discoveries more so medical. You might say I am more of a healer by nature. Your reaction to one of my subjects is only natural the rancid odor of the creature, combined with its deteriorating health, serves a purpose in my experiments. You see, these animals respond much like humans, though I have never had the privilege of practicing on a human cadaver. Such things are frowned upon here, even if the person has passed on. Hard to believe isn't it." Monsieur Heritage, now taken aback, stared at the empty cup in his hands. A sudden realization dawned upon him he could very well have been given something lethal. His gaze darkened, suspicion creeping into his expression. Sensing the shift, Dr. Hertz raised a hand in protest. "Please, sir, do not be alarmed. What you consumed was nothing more than salt water and ginger, ingredients easily found in any mercantile. In fact, I dare say your own wife likely keeps them in her pantry." Dr. Hertz, still seeking to reassure the now wary Monsieur Heritage, cast a glance toward his office building. "I happened to notice you from my window up there. Your paleness was unmistakable, sir. And when I saw Otis, well, I knew at once what had happened. I've told that boy countless times not to lift the sheet until the note is delivered first, the note alone is always suffice." Monsieur, now feeling a sense of relief wash over him, softened. "I must offer my apologies, Doctor. I'm to blame, I pried further than I should have after Otis handed me the note. My curiosity, I fear, got the better of me. I thank you for the cure, but I shall take my leave now. I have some business to attend." Dr. Hertz, now inspecting Monsieur Heritage's attire, responded with a cordial smile, "You are most welcome, sir. Are you a visitor to Baltimore? Might you be in need of a doctor?" "No," Monsieur replied, his voice steady yet filled with purpose. "I seek not a doctor, but a young woman beautiful and gifted in the arts of music, a scholar in France. It seems she has followed the whispers of love, and my search has brought me to this city. Though, I am uncertain where she may be found here. A wistful expression passed over Dr. Hertz's face, and with a slight nod, he remarked, "Ah, matters of the heart seldom yield to reason, yet their truth requires no logic. I see it in your eyes this woman means the world to you. As for her presence in Baltimore, if she is as musically inclined as you suggest and seeking work, she may have sought out the conservatory, an esteemed place for such talent.

Fortune is on your side, for it is not far from here. Although, it would not do for a gentleman of your standing to walk such a distance. I shall have my servant, Otis, prepare a carriage for you." At the mention of a lead on the whereabouts of his beloved Gem Marie Monsieur's heart quickened. "Thank you, Doctor. I will have to find a way to repay your kindness, I have companions awaiting me at the quaint lodging, Carroll's Place I believe it is called. Have your boy meet me there just before midday, and I shall be ready for the journey." When Otis Baltimore arrived at Carroll's Inn, he wore a driver's hat and a clean shirt a suggestion from Dr. Hertz. He pulled the carriage alongside the inn, his eyes scanning the three men seated on the veranda. Their piercing gazes made Otis uneasy, as if they were stripping him down to his very soul. Monsieur Heritage, seated at the center, observed Otis carefully. He remembered Otis had unveiled the decomposing animal for Dr. Hertz's study. That moment had revealed much about him. Otis's mannerisms weren't born of fear, but of caution. He had found a strange, comfortable place under Dr. Hertz's wing. This was no ordinary servant or slave. There was a quiet confidence in him, masked by the veneer of obedience. Monsieur Heritage decided to test the man. "I'll ride in the front," he declared, climbing onto the seat beside Otis, leaving Dillard and Rupert to enter the covered coach. Otis, trying not to let his discomfort show, glanced sideways. "Sir, you're welcome to join the other gentlemen in the carriage there is much more comfort back there," he offered. Monsieur Heritage waved off the suggestion. "No need. Just go slow. I'd like to take in the scenery." "Yes, sir. I'll go slow," Otis replied, keeping his tone respectful. Monsieur Heritage leaned back, his eyes studying Otis as if weighing every movement. "Tell me, what is your name young man?" Otis's heart skipped a beat. He had never been called "Young man," by anyone of Monsieur Heritage's stature. It felt strange, almost like a compliment. "My name's Otis, sir. Otis Cecil Baltimore. That's my real name, I was named after Cecil Baltimore the man who discovered Maryland. Baltimore is named after him." Otis glanced around, suddenly aware they were nearing the side of town where things moved quickly but eyes stayed alert on someone like him. He tightened his lips, trying to make himself smaller. Riding up front in broad daylight with a well-dressed white man in a high-priced carriage wasn't just unusual it was risky. "They say, sir, and I don't mean to be disobedient, but they say I'm somehow kin to him, I mean really kin to him." Monsieur Heritage nodded, smiling faintly, though his eyes stayed sharp. "Interesting, tell me Otis are you aware of most things that happen around here in town?" Otis hesitated. "Well, sir, depends on what sorts of things you mean. If it got to do with critters and things that move in the dark, I probably know a bit. I been catching critters for the good doctor for over ten years now. I started when I was about eight. Folks around here use to be afraid of him back then. By him setting his own traps with blood on his coat and shoes, most people stayed away from him. But once I started helping him, bringing him the animals and hauling things around, it seemed to ease their minds a little." Otis paused, his voice dropping low. "You see, sir, what's under them sheets sometimes ain't no white man supposed to be walking the streets with the sight of that." The coach rolled on, but now the tension in the air was thick, like the humid fog that often cloaked the southern days. Monsieur Heritage looked straight ahead, but his mind was working furiously. Otis Baltimore was no simple servant, and he needed to gain his trust quickly. At that, Monsieur Heritage's gaze shifted from the vibrant flower fields back to Otis, who sat a few inches away. The look in his eyes was the silent confirmation Otis had been waiting for an unspoken promise that the man trusted him. It was a rare thing, to be trusted by someone of Monsieur's stature, and Otis knew that meant more than casual conversation. In their world, a man had to be careful about who he spoke freely to, and Otis had long learned the delicate balance of silence and secrets, especially when it came to those in power. "Otis," Monsieur Heritage's voice softened, but there was weight in it. "Do you enjoy hauling dead animals in the dark?" The question hit Otis like a stone, halting the steady stream of thoughts that had been running through his mind. No one, no one in all his years had ever asked him how he felt, not even Claudette, who had once accompanied him on one of those dark nights. She had never thought to question what he was doing. Otis let the moment hang in the air, his brow furrowed as he considered his answer. "Sir," Otis began slowly, his voice steady though his eyes flicked to the ground, "it's not that I enjoy it. I do it because no one questions me. Except maybe a stranger like yourself, who don't know me. Other than that, I'm a free man with that wheel barrel." The rawness of Otis's words lingered, and for a brief moment, Monsieur Heritage found himself moved. This young man no more than a boy, really had convinced himself that the stench of rotting flesh was as sweet as roses just to survive. Monsieur glanced back at the covered carriage, where Rupert and Dillard had fallen into a deep slumber, their stomachs content with

Miss Carroll's generous meal. The fresh scent of flowers in the air lulling them into dreams acting as a floral sedative. "Otis," Monsieur said, his tone shifting to something more secretive, "I have something to share with you. It's important so important that it requires your trust." Reaching into his coat pocket, Monsieur withdrew a handful of fifty crisp American dollar bills. He extended them toward Otis. Whose eyes widened in disbelief, his heart quickening for he had never seen that amount of money in his life. He cast a nervous glance around, scanning the surrounding foliage and vibrant flowers for any sign of life. The two were alone, passing through a quiet stretch of countryside, with no one else was in sight, Otis snatched the money and shoved it deep into his pocket. With quick, frantic hands Otis wiped the perspiration from his brow as he nervously questioned Monsieur Heritage, "Sir where did you come from?" Monsieur, now overjoyed that Otis had accepted his monetary agreement offer, ignored his question, and began speaking with a sense of urgency. "Otis, listen to me I am searching for a young girl beautiful, clever. She was taken from my home in England under dreadful circumstances, and I believe she's here, in Baltimore." His voice tightened as he continued. "The people in America may not understand who or what she is, or where she came from. But she is my daughter, and I've come to carry her home, where she belongs." His eyes, once filled with warmth, now darkened with a father's despair. "I shudder to think of what might have befallen her, alone in this foreign land." He paused, his fists clenched as if trying to contain the storm inside him. "I will not rest until I find her. I've sailed across the Atlantic with one purpose: to bring her home. And mark my words, any man who has harmed her and any man involved in her capture will pay with his blood." Otis, who had initially seen Monsieur Heritage as a genteel and composed man, now observed the change. The kindness in the man's eyes had vanished, replaced by the ferocity of a father determined to protect his child, no matter the cost. Monsieur Heritage continued speaking, seemingly oblivious to Otis's growing unease. "They say she escaped from a slave ship, armed only with her wits and an extraordinary gift for music. No one has ever heard anything like it." At that moment, Otis abruptly pulled the carriage to a stop. His hands tightened on the reins, and he took a moment to gather himself before turning to face Monsieur Heritage. His voice was low and trembling, but each word held weight. "Is her name... Gem Marie?" As the name left Otis's lips, it was as if the world itself had frozen. The birds hung motionless in the air, carriages and horses halted mid-motion, and the soft breeze that had rustled the trees fell suddenly still. *Gem Marie.* Still ringing in Monsieur Heritage's ears, an echo from the past flashed a small girls hand now reaching in the carriage for his own brushed up against his. His breath caught in his throat as the moment he had long hoped and prayed for unfolded before him. Finally, he had found the one who knew her name. Tears welled up in his eyes, his voice breaking as he spoke. "Yes... where is she?" Otis hesitated, his gaze falling to the ground for a moment before he began. "I met Gem Marie, and her friend Claudette. I'll tell you the whole truth." Monsieur Heritage inhaled deeply, gathering his thoughts as they both sat in the now eerily quiet street while Otis unfolded Gem Marie's past days with him. "After I discovered she could play, I knew she didn't belong here. It was too hard, too risky to try to make her into one of us. That girl was too smart, too special, she just didn't blend in, with all her fancy ways and talent. So I took her to Dr. Hertz for help, In return, he had me take her to the music Conservatory to work for his brother. Now his name is Professor Martin Hertz, and he teaches music to all the rich children. Folks sometimes come from far to put their children in there." Monsieur Heritage's face paled, his grip tightening on the seat of the carriage as if bracing for more. "Go on Otis and since then?" Otis swallowed hard. "Since then...nothing ." Otis leaned forward, his voice low and troubled, as he began to explain. "I ain't seen Gem Marie since the day I dropped her off. There was talk around town about a grand performance at the school, a night folks still talk about. Dr. Hertz didn't go he stayed down in the lab cutting and opening a baby bear I caught, can you imagine that?" Otis paused and studied Monsieur face, when he saw no judgement he continued, "Well I wasn't invited to the concert, but I snuck behind the rose bushes for a bit and caught some of it. And when I heard that violin so clearly, so beautiful, I knew it was her. I felt it in my bones. I don't know how he did it, but Gem Marie was behind that performance, I just know it." He paused, casting a quick glance back into the carriage to ensure Rupert and Dillard were still asleep, their breaths slow and steady. Satisfied, he continued, his voice tense with the weight of his memories. "Every time I tried to visit her, Professor Hertz drove me away like a dog. At first, he said I could come anytime, but that was a damn lie. Because each time I showed up, he gave me an excuse. Then he started threatenin' said he'd tell Dr. Hertz about me lurkin' around and straying away from work. But I couldn't give up on her. I started watching from a distance, seein' her sometimes at the window that overlooks the courtyard. She'd just be standin there, starin' off like she was waitin' for somethin'. She never saw me though, I always hid just in case the Professor Hertz was watching. After a while, she just stopped showin' up at that window." Otis paused again, his fingers nervously tracing the edges of the reins as he steered the horses. "I ain't had the courage to knock on that door again. But somethin' in my gut tells me she's alive. I just don't know what's happening behind those walls." His voice dropped even lower as he recalled an eerie encounter. "One day, I caught Dr. Hertz in another one of his rare, good moods. He'd just finished some kind of new experiment, cut the brain clean out of a dog. Can you believe it. Said if he had a real person he could cure some things and do more for folks. He seemed happy, so I took a chance and asked him if he knew where Gem Marie was. All he said was, 'She's highly sought after, a rare property,' and then... he never mentioned her again." Otis fell silent, the weight of the mystery and sadness hanging heavy in the air. Monsieur Heritage listened intently as Otis recounted the entire story, his mind was swiftly formulating a calculated plan to gain entry into the conservatory. He instructed Otis to securely hide and bury the money he had been given in a safe location. "Here's what you must do," he said, leaning in with a sense of urgency "First, bury the remaining money given to you in a safe remote place, somewhere only you would know." Then, he ordered Otis to immediately return to Dr. Hertz today and provide him with ten dollars along with this note, " Thank you Dr. Hertz for your assistance in locating my newfound love please assist Otis with the purchasing of two of the finest barrels of rum to be brought to the music conservatory by this afternoon for the grand celebration tomorrow late evening. It will be a joyous occasion of the discovery of love." Monsieur advised Otis should the good doctor inquire about the lady's appearance or his brother's involvement in the matter. Happily advise Dr. Hertz that his brother is overjoyed about the union. He warned Otis to make sure to describe the woman as having fair skin and cornsilk hair. Include that the couple plan to make a grand entrance together tomorrow evening. Monsieur carefully instructed Otis to deliver the barrels to the conservatory later today and leave the carriage behind and quickly return back on foot to Dr. Hertz. He was to advise the good doctor that the carriage would be returned the afternoon of the celebration, for his use of travel convenience. Otis listened carefully to Monsieur Heritage's detailed plans for the celebration. In addition, Monsieur gave Otis sufficient funds to purchase a pig for the slaughter, duck, rabbit, and pies, ensuring the feast would be worthy of the lavish occasion. He reminded Otis once more before finally sending him on his way, "And remember don't delay you are to return here as soon as you have purchased all the items then quickly return back to Dr. Hertz on foot. The preparation for those things need to be started today." As the men walked up to the courtyard, they approached the grand building with Victorian Architecture, Monsieur Heritage's gaze immediately found the window above the courtyard, the very one Otis had mentioned. It was wide and imposing, but empty with no sign of movement within, the men continued until they stood before the towering iron doors. Monsieur Heritage pounded them hard and fast, the sound echoing. Turning quickly to his companions, he whispered with urgency, "Remember, you were chosen for your gifts so let your demeanor reflect of it. And for heaven sakes remain silent and follow my lead." The doors swung open abruptly, revealing a petite pale young woman with a kind face, her cheeks softly tinged with rose. Her dress, old-fashioned but elaborate, seemed at odds with her youthful appearance. "Good evening, gentlemen. How may I assist you?" she asked with a polite smile. Monsieur Heritage, his eyes lingering on the ground as if distracted, followed a line of ants as they marched toward the threshold. After a moment, he slowly lifted his head, tipped his hat, and smiled warmly. "Good evening, my fair lady," he said, his voice smooth and genteel. "We are dear friends of the renowned Dr. Hertz and have come to speak with his brother, Professor Martin Hertz, about the exquisite music being taught here." Blushing at the kiss Monsieur Heritage placed on her hand, the young woman giggled softly. "I'm afraid Professor Hertz is out at the moment, but he should return until later this evening after he's finished cherry-picking." Ingrid, excited and happy to greet the outside guest, smiled warmly as she offered, "I can give you a tour of our conservatory while you wait. My name is Ingrid Professor Hertz's daughter, I am lead cellist of the school. Perhaps you recall my performance at out last concert?" Monsieur Heritage examined the young girl again, his mind already at work, searching for a way to extract information about Gem Marie. "No, Iso sorry I haven't had the pleasure to see it," he replied smoothly, "But I've certainly heard about it. In fact, word of your performance reached me across the Atlantic, which is part of why I've come to visit the school that has Europe buzzing. Tell me, where are you from? You don't seem like a commoner." Ingrid, taken slightly aback by his keen perception, straightened herself with a touch of pride. "No, I'm originally from Germany," she responded. "You say you're a friend of Dr. Hertz my uncle, but you've never met my father, Professor Hertz? How curious." Monsieur Heritage, now having gauged Ingrid's intelligence, smiled subtly. "My dear, whenever I'm in town, it's strictly for scientific matters, not musical ones. I handle important business mainly in Europe. "But tell me," he leaned in just a little, lowering his voice as if sharing a secret, "Have you ever drifted down the canals of Venice, with the soft strains of a violin whispering in your ears?" Ingrid's curiosity was piqued, her imagination stirred. "No, but I dream of it often," she admitted, her eyes gleaming. "Especially Paris." She added. "Why not go, then?" Monsieur Heritage asked, his tone persuasive. "I'm sure your father would be more than happy to take you. You're a remarkable cellist; such talent deserves to be rewarded." Ingrid, now even more intrigued, moved a little closer to him. "Perhaps," she mused, before adding, "Shall I give you a proper tour of the school before my father arrives?" Monsieur Heritage extended his arm with a practiced grace, and Ingrid delicately looped her arm through his. "On this level," she began, "we have several classrooms and a large auditorium towards the back, where all performances are held. I'll take you there." As Monsieur Heritage stepped into the grand auditorium, the scent of dust lingered in the air. Tall, velvet drapes were being unhooked from their brass poles, ready to be flogged and beaten clean outside. A handful of servants bustled about, dusting ornate carvings, and polishing the chandeliers. His sharp eyes caught a glimpse of movement on stage a young boy, dark-skinned with a rag, darting behind the curtains, vanishing the moment he noticed their presence. Monsieur Heritage's brow furrowed with interest. He leaned closer to Ingrid and spoke with a calculated edge. "I see you allow *darkies* in your school now. I had no idea you permitted such a thing. How long has this policy been in place?" Ingrid chuckled lightly, her lips curling into a smirk. "Oh, heavens, no. He's no student, just a cleaning boy. Comes once a week, father allows him unsupervised, mind you. Rest assured, sir he is well mannered. We have never accepted *darkie* students here. Not ever." Her words hung in the air with a casual cruelty, as if the thought only amused her. Monsieur Heritage's jaw tightened as the memory of Otis's words stirred inside him. He knew the truth ran deeper than Ingrid's surface niceties. "Come now, Ingrid, everyone's heard about the rumors of an unusual darkie she was said to have lived here, hidden away for years. Surely, you must recall."

Ingrid's smile faltered, and her eyes narrowed in a mix of annoyance and dismissal. "Idle gossip, I assure you. That girl was no student. She was a servant, a mere *possession* and she didn't stay here for years. We had no use for her, so she was quickly returned to her rightful owner, the elitest Christian Pierre, a wealthy man who came back to reclaim her." Her voice hardened as she added, "Even when we did have her as a maid, she was of high pedigree only here to clean, not to be educated. Gossip, sir is a dangerous thing." Monsieur Heritage felt his temper rising, but he hid it behind a thin smile. The confirmation of Gem Marie's fate burned like hot coals in his chest. Pierre had taken her, as he had suspected. "So she was returned to him?" he asked, his voice laced with false pleasantries. "I suppose she was sent to Virginia, where such things are more... *tolerated*." Ingrid laughed, genuinely entertained by his ignorance. "No, no. You mean New Orleans. I know that for certain. I courted Christian Pierre once, long ago. My father put an end to it, of course couldn't abide his dealings with *darkies*. He had his share of wealth yes, but even his riches couldn't make such matters acceptable here." Her tone was light, almost dismissive, but Monsieur Heritage could barely contain his anger. To know his beloved Gem Marie, reduced to a mere servant in the very halls where she should have been free. And now, confirmation that the man he loathed had taken her, ripped her away from him, leaving nothing but bitter memories behind. He clenched his fists as he stood in the very place she had once slept, his heart heavy with the knowledge that the world, and the people in it, had treated her like a common slave. The relief of knowing she was still alive was the only thing that steadied his racing heart. Monsieur Héritage, glancing back at Dillard and Rupert with a subtle nod, tightened his grip on Ingrid's arm as they walked. His eyes, dark and calculating, gleamed with hidden intent. "Tell me, dear," he said softly, his voice smooth but commanding, "when will your father be returning?" Ingrid, blushing under the intensity of his gaze, turned nervously toward the back entrance of the stage. "I'm not sure... When he goes cherry picking, he often stays until the late evening. He says it relaxes him, gathering the ripe, sweet cherries." Her voice wavered slightly as she added, "Do you like cherries? Forgive me, but I seem to have forgotten your name." Monsieur Héritage responded swiftly, his smile sharpening like a knife. "Where are my manners? Rupert. Rupert Dillard," he said, bowing slightly. "It is a pleasure to make your acquaintance, Lady Ingrid." Behind him, Dillard and Rupert exchanged surprised glances, their eyebrows arched in silent disbelief. But any expression of doubt was quickly erased as Monsieur Héritage shot them a cutting look, reminding them to keep their composure. Monsieur turned his attention back to Ingrid, his tone now velvet smooth. "Is there somewhere we can wait, you and I, until your father returns?" He lifted her hand to his lips, placing a lingering kiss on her pale skin. The sensation of his lips sent an unexpected shiver down her spine, one she had never felt before. For a moment, she froze, fear flickering through her. But then she recalled the tale she had woven of courting Christian Pierre, a fabricated story meant to project her maturity. Realizing that her falsehood may have ignited a dangerous desire in a man she barely knew, Ingrid quickly composed herself, not wanting to appear childish or dishonest. "There's a large barn," she said, her voice steadier now. "We keep the hens there, and my father's horse as well. It's quite well-kept... and secluded." Monsieur Heritages' eyes gleamed with something darker as he studied her, noting that she was not as innocent as she appeared. "That sounds marvelous," he murmured, with the edge of his smile twisting. "A perfect place indeed... for slaughtering the pig I've purchased for the celebration." His tone was smooth, but Ingrid could sense the underlying intent. "Will you show me?" he asked, the words a challenge as much as a request. "A celebration oh yes of course," Ingrid replied, her voice wavering slightly. "It's just up the trail behind the school. It's a white and black barn that sits on the hill. We can go now if you would like." Monsieur Héritage gave a subtle nod then walked over to Dillard and Rupert, lowering his voice as he whispered something to them. The last command he spoke aloud was, "Send the boy with the pig and the goods to the barn immediately." With that, the two men swiftly disappeared, heading toward the front entrance of the conservatory turning back, Monsieur Héritage offered his arm to Ingrid. "Shall we, my dear?" he said, gesturing toward the back door of the auditorium. Ingrid, her eagerness now tinged with an unsettling sense of fear, stepped toward the door leading to the barn. Her mind raced, but she took his arm, the two-walking hand in hand through the dew-covered grass. As they approached the large structure, Monsieur paused only for a moment to pluck a daffodil, handing it to Ingrid with a smile. The spontaneous gesture made her heart flutter whether from admiration or anxiety, she could not say. Once the two entered the barn, Monsieur's eyes swept over the scene with an intense gaze. Inside, a coop housed six hens, wired in to protect them from lurking predators. Two stalls stood empty, save for the bales of hay meticulously arranged in a circle, awaiting their next feeding. Without warning, Monsieur Héritage turned abruptly, spinning Ingrid to face him. His hand slid gently over her cheek, the touch both intimate and unnerving. "Tell me," he began, his voice soft but laced with something darker, "about your courtship with Christian Pierre. You still think of him often, don't you? Or are you thinking of him right now?" Ingrid's heart thundered in her chest, her breath catching as she struggled to find words. "No," she stammered, her voice barely a whisper. "I never think of him." "Lies!" Monsieur Héritage hissed, his eyes narrowing as he leaned closer. "You're thinking of every way he touched you. Your face... your hands..." His fingers trailed down her arm, sending a shiver through her. Then, with a chilling slowness, his hand wrapped around her neck. "Did he touch you like this?" he whispered, his grip tightening slightly. "Or like this?" Before she could respond, his lips brushed against her neck, the kiss slow, deliberate, and filled with unspoken menace. Ingrid, who had initially held herself rigid, suddenly felt her strength leave her. She pulled away, trembling. "Yes, you do think of him," Monsieur replied with quiet certainty. "No!" Ingrid shouted, her voice sharp and defensive. "I do not think of him at all! He left here with that dark girl, hand in hand, just as you so gallantly walked with me." Her voice shook with a bitterness that filled the room. "They stepped out of the school and into one of the finest carriages, and she" Ingrid's face twisted with disdain "She was wearing a white gown stolen from the costume room! Imagine, father let her wear it, while she hid behind the curtains playing dreadfully." Ingrid's voice grew colder. "I don't know what enchantment she holds, but both Father and Christian Pierre were utterly deceived by that... that nigger." Monsieur's expression darkened as Ingrid's words confirmed what he had long suspected Gem Marie was still alive, and perhaps unharmed. But what had truly befallen her? Had she too been kiss softly, or did they continue with no regard for restraint? His mind raced, conjuring dark images of what might have occurred. Ingrid, now watching Monsieur's face closely, saw the flicker of turmoil. Lead by inexperience she perceived his grimace as jealousy. Her voice turned venomous again. "He humiliated me in front of the entire school, and Father he laughed when I told him everything about Christian's promises, how he said he'd take me sailing, how he swore it was me he wanted." At that moment, the distant sound of hooves echoed across the fields. Ingrid pressed her face to the narrow crack in the barn wall and squinted. Her heart raced as she recognized the silhouette of Professor Hertz approaching on horseback, a large sack slung over his side. Panic seized her. "Father will be furious if he finds me here with a strange man," she thought, her breath catching. "I must get back to the school before he sees me." Monsieur Heritage, sensing her distress, gestured toward the small back window of the barn. He wasted no time, swiftly hoisting Ingrid through the opening. "Go straight to your room, and do not show yourself again until tomorrow's celebration, I will try to distract your father from seeing you." he instructed in a low, urgent voice. Ingrid nodded, her pulse pounding as she disappeared out of the back of the barn. Monsieur Heritage then turned his attention back to himself, adjusting his disheveled appearance. He splashed cold water from a nearby trough onto his face, hoping to sharpen his senses and calm the tension building in his chest. With a deliberate calm, he approached the barn door and gently pulled it open, watching as Professor Hertz's horse drew near. A flicker of confusion passed over the professor's face as he dismounted, his eyes scanning the barn suspiciously. He moved with a cautious grace, tying his stallion to a post before removing the large bag from the saddle. Every movement was calculated, his gaze flicking warily between the barn's shadows and Monsieur Heritage. Professor Hertz paused, one hand still gripping a sack of cherries. His eyes narrowed as he stepped into the dim barn, casting an unreadable glance back toward Monsieur. Something unspoken lingered in the air between them something heavy, and not easily ignored. Before Professor Hertz could speak, Monsieur began quickly, "Good evening, Professor Hertz. My name is Rupert Dillard. I am a friend of your brother, and he has sent me here in the hope that you might assist me in locating someone very dear to me, my lost loved one. He assured me that you may be the key to finding her. She is a striking fair maiden, with corn-silk hair, porcelain skin and a gift for music. Suggestion has it that she moved to this region, perhaps to teach her extraordinary skills in music." Monsieur paused briefly, his eyes scanning the barn again before continuing. "When I first arrived, I was told you were out cherry picking. I confess, I felt a pang of disappointment. You see, I have crossed the mid-Atlantic in search of this remarkable girl. Fortunately, I met your daughter, Ingrid a delightful young woman who kindly gave me a tour of your school." Professor Hertz, now feeling a slight unease with the direction of the conversation, kept a measured eye on Monsieur as he moved toward his horse's blacksmith tools. With a practiced hand, he picked up a chisel and knelt by his stallion, and began carefully removing one of the horse's worn shoes. The steady clink of metal filled the silence, only broken when he turned to stoke the small coal fire with fresh hay and additional coal, the embers glowing brighter. "Mr. Dillard, is it?" Professor Hertz began slowly, his voice low and deliberate. "I must admit, I'm uncertain as to why my brother sent you here in search of this girl. I know nothing of her, nor am I expecting any new music teachers. I am afraid you've been misled." He glanced up briefly, studying Dillard's expression as he continued. "My days are consumed with teaching and composing. I rarely have time for matters outside these walls, and as for young women who wander about, I know even less. My only concern is my own daughter, as you've met. She, indeed, is the one with a musical gift." Monsieur Heritage brow furrowed ever so slightly, as though the professor's indifference only deepened his frustration. Professor Hertz now feeling something unsettling about Monsieur's persistence, the way his eyes lingered just a moment too long on the professor's work, conveyed he was searching for hidden truths beneath his words. Monsieur growing increasingly irate, from knowing that the man who had once enslaved his daughter and later sold her stood right before him. With a voice laced in mockery, he addressed Professor Hertz, "Professor, you are absolutely correct, she is very musically inclined, and I must commend you on your daughter's home training. Such a well-behaved creature. She was a delight to taste, and her porcelain skin... quite arousing especially with the shade of barn hay laying beneath her. Her melodic moans of arousal, remarkably intoxicating." At that moment, Professor Hertz shot to his feet, eyes blazing with outrage. "I beg your pardon, sir?" Monsieur Heritage, reveling in the professor's shock, smiled slyly, and leaned forward. "Your daughter, unlike mine, now lies in her bed, probably still thinking of the kiss I placed ever so gently upon her neck." The professor's face turned red with fury. He lunged toward Monsieur Heritage, still gripping the chisel in his hand, moving with the rage of a man whose honor had been publicly scorched. "How dare you speak of my daughter in such a vile manner!" he bellowed. Without hesitation, Monsieur Heritage withdrew a dagger from his breast pocket, swiftly pressing the blade against Professor Hertz's throat. His voice dripped with venom and bitter contempt as he spoke. "Your daughter is no musical genius, Hertz. Mine plays three instruments, speaks four languages, and has had the finest schooling from here to Europe. But your daughter? She was all too eager to give me her most precious possession. And you, fool, were too ignorant to recognize beauty when it stood before you." At these words, Professor Hertz barely whispered, "Gem Marie..." His voice broke as he spoke Monsieur's daughter's name. "Yes, Gem Marie," Monsieur Heritage sneered, enjoying the professor's helplessness. The tip of his dagger pressed harder against Hertz's throat, enough to leave an impression, though not yet enough to break the skin. Suddenly, the clatter of hooves broke the tension. A carriage pulled up to the open door of the barn, and a voice called out, "Hello, sir! The girl told me you were in here. I've brought your barrels and the pig." Otis stepped fully into the barn, his eyes widening in disbelief at the scene unfolding before him. He froze, struggling to swallow the lump in his throat, but the dry air and dust filled his airway, burning his lungs as he stood paralyzed. Seeing a glimmer of hope, Professor Hertz spoke to Otis, his voice gentle yet urgent. "Otis, my son, leave now. Go home, tell no one of what you've seen, and forget this ever happened." Monsieur Heritage, still holding the dagger firmly against the professor's throat, smirked. "Otis, young man, the choice is yours. Whether you run for help or stay, this man will die. The only question is... how." Otis, trembling with fear, cautiously stepped forward, his legs and hands shaking as he approached the two men. Professor Hertz, with a calm but stern voice, warned him again, "Don't be a fool, Otis. You're just a boy you can't handle this . Go home and remember tell no one." The professor's eyes were saying the opposite as he kept eye contact with Otis. Ignoring the professor's words and coded eye movements, Otis halted. His eyes fixed on Monsieur Heritage as he slowly bent down, lifting a large bucket from the barn floor. Holding the handle of the bucket in one hand, while the other made an imaginary outline, "Begging your pardon sir but you need to move that dagger to the left side, then go up a hair, now when you run across that bulge go deep but quickly, no mess." Without hesitation, Monsieur Heritage followed Otis's direction and slid the dagger with deadly precision, slicing across Professor Hertz's jugular. Blood sprayed across the barn as the professor collapsed, a cascade of crimson stained the hay filled floor. Otis rushed to the professor's side, and positioned his slit throat over the bucket. Now letting the blood flow freely into the bucket, he shouted, "Hand me the dagger," Monsieur Heritage, still in a fog of violence, ignored Otis and bent down while once more he drove the dagger deeper across the professor's neck. This time, he didn't stop until the head was severed from the body. Unfazed, Otis walked to the coal fire, and retrieve a large branding iron. He pressed the hot iron against the stump of the professor's neck in a crude attempt to seal the wound. The flesh sizzled, popped and burned, while filling the barn with the sharp scent of scorched meat. As Otis applied more pressure the iron scorched away the thin attachment of skin that once held the head. Finally in a grotesque final jest, the professor's severed head blinked, startling Monsieur Heritage. Without missing a beat, Otis grabbed the disembodied head and placed it upside down into the bucket, letting the last of the blood drain back in the skull. He then gathered the blood-soaked hay from all around the barn and tossed it into the coal fire. The blood-filled hay popped and sizzled as the fire grew larger. Now as the reality of the situation settled in Otis sat down on the barn floor next to the professor's headless, twitching body. He then pulled a small flask from his pocket and sipped without offering. Slowly he placed it back into his jacket and said, while swatting mosquitoes from his face, his tone almost compassionate. "Don't worry, sir, his body will stop moving soon that's just the last of life leaving. It was mighty smart of you, getting them barrels to pickle him in. I'm Just wonderin' where you plan on keeping him?" Monsieur Heritage, now eyeing Otis with a mixture of respect and pity, replied, "At sea where the rest of the shark bait belongs. As for his head, there are some lovely flowers that bloom at midnight, I think that will be a proper home for it." Otis gaze unwavering. "I see. Begging your pardon again, sir, but you'll need something stronger than that dagger to get the joints loose so he can fit in that barrel. And you'll need to tie him up good and strong. I don't see nothing around here that can do that." Otis now eyeing the fire as the blood-filled hay continued to burn and pop, "I never did like him none, even after I told him Me and Gem Marie were kin folk he still never let me see her. It was like he knew it hurt me, and he liked it." Monsieur Heritage gave a slight smile, his voice cold and certain. "No need to worry. I've got the tools for both." At that exact moment, the barn doors creaked open. Dillard and Rupert stood in the doorway, their eyes wide with horror as they took in the grisly scene. Wordlessly, they shut the door behind them, sealing off the world outside. Staring at Otis and Monsieur Heritage in disbelief, both men spoke in unison, "Is it time for us to use our... talents?"

285

Chapter: 22

I Wish You Forever Love

"Where did you get that?" Christian Pierre's voice cut through the air, halting Gem Marie mid-spin. "I made it. Don't you like it?" she asked, her voice hopeful as she twirled again, the shells and beads on her dress catching the dim light. She had painstakingly re-tailored the old garment, soaking the hem in rose petal water for two days, and adorned her hair with a headpiece she had fashioned into a crown. Christian stood back, his arms crossed, eyes narrowing. "Take it off. Now. I mean it, Gem Marie. Right now." The brightness in her expression faded, and her shoulders drooped. "Why?" she asked, her voice trembling slightly. "I made it with my own two hands. I just wanted to look presentable when I play." Christian's gaze softened, but his words remained firm. He couldn't afford to bend the rules, not even for her. "You can't outshine the bride, Gem Marie. This is her day all the attention must be on her and the groom." Tears brimmed in Gem Marie's eyes as she struggled to comprehend. "I don't understand," she said, her voice breaking. "This America, This New Orleans, a place of celebration and beauty, and I'm expected to wear rags? What does 'outdo' mean? Christian, why do you hate me so?" Christian sighed deeply, his patience wearing thin but his heart heavy at her words. "I don't hate you, Gem Marie. Don't be foolish." His tone was softer now, though the authority in his voice never wavered. "You're a beautiful woman too beautiful in that dress. It's not about you, it's about respect. You cannot make a bride feel small on her own wedding day. Half of New Orleans will be watching. Now I've brought you a dress, just as fine. So, for the last time, take off that one. The guests will be here in two hours." With her back to him, Gem Marie allowed a small, defiant smile to creep across her lips. It was the second time Christian had called her beautiful, and that acknowledgment lingered. She considered another tearful outburst, but instead, she turned to him calmly and said, "Where is the dress, you'd like me to wear? I'll change into it in the cellar, though I hope it doesn't get dirty from being down there." Christian's jaw clenched, his patience fraying. Ever since it had been decided that Gem Marie would perform at the wedding, her behavior had grown unpredictable, and the only solace he'd found was when she held Margaret's baby in rare moments of stillness. "Nonsense," he snapped. "You'll change right here in the parlor and quickly." As Christian disappeared to retrieve the dress, Cook and McCoy exchanged a glance from the doorway ceasing the opportunity to warn Gem Marie of her spoiled behavior. The men took their chance. Cook, a burly man with a grizzled beard, stepped into the room while McCoy lingered by the door, keeping an ear out for Christian's return. "Listen up, gal," Cook growled, his voice as thick as molasses. "Today's Miss Lelina's weddin' day, and you better know your place. Margaret's jumpin' the broom deep behind the walnut trees, and you ain't gonna be the one to spoil it." His imposing figure loomed over Gem Marie as she met his stern gaze. "I don't know why Master Pierre's so taken with you, but mark my words you're gonna take off that fancy rag you stitched together and put on the dress master picked out for you. I swear gal you mess this day up, and when Master Pierre heads off to Georgia, you'll pay for it. You hear me, gal?" McCoy, a wiry man with sharp eyes, nodded in agreement, his arms crossed over his chest. "We ain't going to have no problems today," he muttered. "Do as you're told." Gem Marie bit her lip, her defiance threatening to rise, but she held her tongue. Outside, the world was preparing for a celebration, but inside, floating upon Honey Waters the power dynamics and expectations pressed down on her like a weight. She knew that she was walking a fine line. As she waited for Christian's return, her mind raced. She had been called beautiful, and that small victory, however fleeting echoed in her thoughts. But for now, she would do as she was told, even as her heart burned with a mixture of hurt and rebellion. Her mind shifted to the past months, Gem Marie had practiced the same piece beneath the sprawling branches of a Sugar Maple Tree. The slaves working nearby would pause to listen, some even humming along to the melody, their voices weaving into the rhythm like whispers on the wind. At first, there had been only stares, muttered comments, and, in the second week, silence just a ripe plum hurled at her from the shadows. The plum had struck her squarely on the shoulder, staining her dress and drawing the attention of a swarm of insects. Shocked, she stopped playing and stared down at the bruised fruit now lying at her feet, dirt clinging to its flesh. As she brushed the remnants of it from her dress, Christian Pierre strode toward her, agitation clear in his every step. "Why did you stop playing?" he demanded, his voice thick with impatience. Still staring at the dirt-covered plum, Gem Marie finally looked up, her eyes meeting his. "Someone threw that at me," she said quietly. "What does it mean?" Christian, now scanning the nearby trees for any sign of the culprit, raised his voice. "It means you're a great violinist and you must keep playing! For I will have the head of the man or woman who had the audacity to waste and throw my property." Without hesitation, Gem Marie picked up her bow and began again, the music flowing as if uninterrupted. Christian, watching her closely, walked to a nearby apple tree. He plucked a bright red apple from one of the branches, polishing it against his jacket until it gleamed. With a quick motion, he removed a small knife and sliced it in two and handed Gem Marie one half, lifting the other in a mock toast. "To your brilliant playing," he said, his smile warm and encouraging. The crowd that had gathered, curious and watchful, now fixed their eyes on the two of them as they shared the moment. Christian could no longer ignore the deepening emotions stirring within him. His feelings for her had become almost impossible to conceal. With a tenderness that caught even him by surprise, he reached into his pocket, pulled out a handkerchief, and gently wiped a stray piece of apple from her cheek. Gem Marie, who had grown equally fond of Christian over the months, whispered, her voice barely audible, "I'm all alone here." She resumed playing, her fingers gliding effortlessly over the strings, though her words lingered in the air between them. The weight of her confession did not go unnoticed by Christian. He stood in silence, watching her, knowing there was much left unsaid between them. Gem Marie, now brought back to the present time stared through the parlor window at the area where the wedding would take place. She realized today there was no time for her challenging words. It was the big day and there would be no velvet curtain to hide behind, no cellar walls to shield her from prying eyes. People from all over had come to New Orleans for the wedding, and the anticipation hung heavy in the air, thick as the scent of summer. Once Lady Lelina's telegrams were sent all abroad, messengers began arriving daily at Honey Waters, delivering notes of joy from those who would soon attend the grand estate wedding. The parlor, filled with anticipation, seemed to hum with the weight of the coming event. Yet in the midst of it all, Gem Marie stood in a daze, unaware of Christian's quiet return. He approached silently, laying the dress carefully on a nearby chair before stepping in front of her. His voice was gentle, but firm. "You must be strong today. There will be those who refuse to see the beauty in your music. But remember, there will also be others who will revel in the wonder and love you will pour into each note. Let that thought carry you through, and know I'll be with you, no matter what happens." From the shadows, Cook and McCoy stood, their usual banter silenced by the scene that unfolded before them. They exchanged a glance, stunned by the unexpected intimacy between Christian and Gem Marie. Without a word, they backed out of the room doorway, unnoticed. Once on the far end of the veranda, McCoy finally broke the silence. "What do you make of that, Cook? I don't want to say it, but" "Then don't," Cook cut him off, his voice sharp. "If it's that bad, don't let it leave your mouth." McCoy, unable to contain himself, blurted out, "It seems like he's in love with that girl. I know what you're thinking he could have any woman, with all these ladies waiting on him. But I'm telling you, Cook, he might have known her." Cook grabbed McCoy's arm and dragged him to the side of the house. His voice dropped to a low, stern whisper. "Listen to me, McCoy, don't you ever talk about Master Pierre laying with no slave. He ain't never done such a thing. He tells everyone he doesn't breed his stock; he buys them. So keep your mouth shut about things you don't understand." McCoy, now rattled and fearing the consequences of what he'd witnessed, stammered, "But I saw him, Cook. I saw him kiss her." Cook's eyes widened. "Are you sure? "McCoy nodded, his voice barely above a whisper. "I don't like her. She's bad luck, coming to Honey Waters like that hollering in the night. She even speaks better than some white folks. Now she's playing Master Pierre's music. You tell me where'd she learn to play like that? Hell, she might even know how to read." "Don't lose your head, McCoy," Cook muttered, though a note of fear had crept into his own voice. The gravity of Gem Marie's presence at Honey Waters now weighed heavily on him. But Cook, ever pragmatic, shook off his unease and leaned in close. "Mark my words, McCoy. That girl's gonna bring trouble to Honey Waters, and it's gonna end with a rope around somebody's neck." Gem Marie stood in the parlor, her heart pounding as she waited for Christian Pierre to leave. She clutched the handmade gown she had cherished, knowing the moment she dreaded was approaching. "Nonsense!" Christian barked, his tone sharp. "I won't waste another minute. Put the dress on right here, in front of me. I want no trickery Gem Marie. Our guests will be arriving within the hour." Gem Marie's frown deepened, but she knew better than to argue. Reluctantly, she slipped out of her gown and into the new one striking yellow dress adorned with delicate embroidery in brown and blue. The crown-like tiara she had crafted from baby's breath and daffodils only enhanced the elegance of her light, golden skin. Now fully dressed she began to see the beauty of the dress. "My goodness, woman, you could make a sackcloth look magnificent," Christian muttered, his eyes dark with admiration. Blushing, Gem Marie hesitated before crossing the room to awkwardly kiss him. The brief touch of their lips sent a shock through both of them a moment of simultaneous surprise and connection. Overwhelmed by a mix of emotions she could barely control, Gem Marie pulled away just as the kiss reached its most tender point. "There's something I must tell you," she said softly, her voice trembling. "I have something important to say but you must promise me you'll listen to me completely." Christian's expression shifted, his eyes locking with hers in deep contemplation. He knew exactly what she was referring to, her newspaper articles and the love letter she had risked so much to write. His jaw tightened, but he nodded slowly. "We can talk," he replied, his voice steady. "When I return from Georgia." The two stood in stillness, eyes locked in a gaze that spoke louder than words. In that fleeting moment, both Christian Pierre and Gem Marie realized that an undeniable true love had blossomed between them, silently but unmistakably. Suddenly, the sharp clang of a bell shattered the quiet intimacy, echoing through the open window. Outside, a stream of servants hurriedly fell into line, taking their appointed places. A commanding voice rang out, cutting through the air like a whip: "The guests from Honey Waters have arrived! Everyone to your positions!" Christian Pierre cursed under his breath, his usual composure rattled. "Damn it, woman! With all your wicked temptations, I've no time to finish dressing!" He fumbled hastily for his tie and jacket, his frustration apparent as he rushed to pull himself together. Once fully dressed, he carefully adjusted the yellow-and-white handkerchief in his pocket, smoothing it with precision. As he turned to leave, his eyes lingered on Gem Marie one last time before stepping toward the veranda. Gem Marie stood rooted to the spot, her heart racing. From the doorway, she watched carriages winding their way up the drive to Honey Waters. Beyond her, the frenzy of preparation unfolded as slaves and servants rushed to tend to last-minute details. Margaret was draping each chair and table with matching flowers, ensuring that every corner of the estate exuded elegance. But while everyone else moved with purpose, Gem Marie stood frozen caught between the life she knew and the love she had just discovered. The two stood there, locked in each other's gaze, a silent realization passing between them true love had just blossomed, undeniable and sudden. The moment felt eternal until the distant chime of a bell tower shattered their reverie. Through the open window, the commotion outside came into focus as servants hurriedly lined up in their assigned positions. A sharp voice pierced the air. "Honey Waters arrivals are here! Everyone, to your stations!" Christian Pierre cursed under his breath, hastily grabbing his cravat and jacket. "Damn it, woman, with all your devilish ways, I'm late again!" he muttered, struggling with his tie. Once dressed, he meticulously placed a white and yellow handkerchief in his breast pocket, giving it a final, perfect adjustment. As he made his way toward the veranda, he cast a lingering glance back at Gem Marie, his expression unreadable. Gem Marie, frozen in place, could only watch as the scene unfolded before her. Through the doorway, she saw the carriages rolling in the distance, making their way to Honey Waters. Servants and slaves alike moved with purpose, rushing to complete last-minute preparations. Margaret busied herself adorning every chair and table with delicate arrangements of matching flowers, the finishing touches of perfection. Gem Marie's heart quickened as the reality of the day settled in. Something more than just the arrival of guests was stirring beneath the surface, something that could change everything. The ceremony was enchanting. Under the canopy of the orchard, Bonneville and Lady Lelina exchanged vows, blessed by gifts and prayers from all who attended. Christian Pierre had prepared a feast fit for royalty a calf, duck, and rabbit, all roasted with vegetables, and an astonishing array of twenty-two different pies. Barrels of rum, jugs of ale, and fine wine flowed freely as laughter filled the air. The wedding taking place at Honey Waters was symbolic for his well wishes and detachment from Lady Lelina, he wanted no more unspoken games or taunting gestures of romance. Lady Lelina belonged to Bonneville now, he was the keeper of her chaos and Christian as all the better for it. As the guests of Honey Waters grew merrier and drunker on the evening's revelry, the servants and slaves slipped quietly away into the pasture for another, more secretive wedding, Margret's. the joyous union, Christian Pierre decided to entertain the remaining guests with his own violin, filling the night with music. Meanwhile, Gem Marie, carrying her own violin, stealthily made her way to Margret's gathering deep in woods. Under the stars, Gem Marie played a delicate Chopin piece for the hidden couple, each note a whisper of warmth and quiet joy, her fingers gliding over the keys as if every sound carried a secret. In the dim candlelight of the night, Margret and her groom swayed together in soft, measured steps, wrapped in the fragile intimacy of stolen moments. Their movements were slow, tender, as if time itself had slowed to honor the sacredness of their union. As the music hung in the air, they recited their vows, heavy with bittersweet sincerity. They promised to love one another until the inevitable day came when they would be torn apart and sold. Though Christian Pierre had long voiced his disdain for the brutal practice of severing families, deeming it against the harmony that Honey Waters was built on, Margret and her husband knew too well the grim reality they faced. As slaves, they lived in a world stripped of mercy, where no bond no matter how sacred was safe from the whims of those who saw their lives as mere property. In this world, anyone could be sold, lost, or discarded, if the price were right. Yet, despite the weight of this cruel truth, the day felt crisp, almost radiant, as if love itself dared to bloom amidst such sorrow. There was a bittersweet joy that lingered in the air, as if this fleeting happiness were a quiet rebellion against their fate. When her performance ended, Gem Marie stood alone in the shade, cradling her instrument, her heart heavy with unspoken longing. She watched the couple with admiration and envy, wondering if she, too, might ever know such love the kind Margret and her groom shared. And if, in some distant dream, Christian Pierre could ever see her as more than she appeared, as someone worthy of love in a world that allowed so little tenderness between two people of different standing. As she made her way back to the big house, blending into the shadows with the other slaves, the guests began to depart, their idle conversations punctuated by polite laughter and whispered intrigues. Lady Lelina and Bonneville stood at the grand steps, offering thanks and farewells to all who had attended. Christian Pierre, standing apart on the veranda, surveyed the scene with a rare calm, a sense of satisfaction swelling in his chest. The union of Margret and her groom had been sealed on his land, and in some quiet corner of his heart, he felt a rare sense of peace. The layout of the event, from the designs to the music, had been nothing short of breathtaking. Lady Lelina, unable to suppress her emotions, let tears fall freely as she turned to Christian Pierre, her voice thick with sincerity. "Thank you, Christian. This wedding is fit for royalty." Her words, spoken with genuine reverence, did not go unnoticed. Several guests caught the exchange, and soon, the crowd was abuzz with chatter, murmurs swirling like the soft winds that marked the end of the day. Yet, in the midst of all this, Christian Pierre stood unmoved, his eyes lingering on the couple and Gem Marie a woman whose silent yearnings remained as unnoticed as the moon behind the clouds. Gem Marie stood silently among the other slaves, watching the scene unfold. Following their lead, she bent to the ground, gathering the remnants of the evening the crushed flowers and discarded trinkets left behind by the guests. Her eyes darted toward a few slaves who, with quick glances and steady hands, poured leftover rum and wine from half-empty glasses into hidden bottles. No one seemed to notice, and if they did, they pretended not to care. The night, once filled with the music of laughter and clinking glasses, now grew darker, heavy with a strange mixture of exhaustion and the remnants of passion that had filled the air. As the last of the visitors departed, Honey Water, the grand plantation, fell silent. Christian Pierre, the master of the estate, gave a casual order to Gem Marie, "Play "his voice a command wrapped in indifference. She complied, taking her violin in hand and began playing while the others hurried about, clearing tables, their hands eager to finish the task and claiming their share of the sweet leftovers. Christian Pierre, seemingly uninterested in the laborious movements around him, retreated to his parlor. There, he sank into a chair by the window, a cigar balanced between his fingers. The thick smoke curled lazily into the air as he listened to the distant melody Gem Marie coaxed from her bow, the music drifting through the open window, lulling him into a state of deep relaxation. The other servants worked swiftly, their thoughts already on home, where they would gather to gossip over the day's events, sharing tales and savoring stolen bites of rich food. But Gem Marie's attention remained fixed on Christian Pierre, her fingers gliding with her bow against the strings, her gaze occasionally flickering to his silhouette framed by the window. In that moment, the feeling she'd buried long ago returned the same feeling she had experienced when she first saw his face in the newspaper, the article casting him in a light both captivating and dangerous. Christian Pierre let the soft strains of the music wash over him as his thoughts drifted to Lady Lelina. She, who had once professed an unshakable love for him, had now taken another man. It was his fault, he knew. His silence, his refusal to confess his love in return had driven her away. But now he realized it had not been fear that held him back. No, it was the lack of authenticity, of something real and true, that he had longed for all along. The love he sought was not with Lady Lelina, but elsewhere. His eyes closed as the music grew louder, more vivid. There, amidst the haunting melody of the violin, he sensed something stirring within him. When he opened his eyes, Gem Marie stood in the parlor, her fingers dancing effortlessly across the strings. She was the one. She had always been the one, even if he hadn't known it until now. Across the hall, Cook and McCoy lingered, on the verge of retreating to their quarters. They paused, watching with curiosity as Gem Marie entered the grand room unbidden. "There she goes again, walking into that house like she owns the place," Cook muttered, his voice thick with contempt as he took a swig from a flask still filled with wine from the wedding feast. McCoy shrugged, his expression unreadable. "I don't know what makes her so special, but he's in love with her, sure as the moon hangs in the sky. And she's got feelings for him too, though she's from somewhere far off. Best leave her be, Cook." They stood there a moment longer, watching the faint silhouettes through the dimly lit windows. Their curiosity eventually faded, and they turned to leave, but not before they caught sight of Christian Pierre at the window, his gaze fixed on the woman in the parlor. Inside, the air was thick with tension and unspoken words. Christian took a step closer to Gem Marie, his voice soft. "Gem Marie, how did you like the wedding?" She stopped playing, her lips curving into a soft smile. "It was beautiful," she replied. "The first wedding I've ever attended. Much less played for." Her words hung in the air, and in that moment, the quiet between them was more telling than anything could say. Gem Marie settled into the chair, her gaze fixed on Christian's back as he stood silhouetted against the window, bathed in the fading light. "I want to tell you where I'm from where I'm truly from, and you can make your decision based on your heart." she said, her voice barely above a whisper. Christian turned sharply, his expression one of surprise. "Go on," he urged softly. "Tell me everything." Gem Marie hesitated, gathering her thoughts before beginning the tale, one she had rehearsed many times in her mind. She spoke of her mother, Monsieur Heritage, the man who had raised her, and how her life had unfolded since then. She poured out the story she had been told growing up, carefully omitting the part about the newspaper article, the one with his name in it that had set her on the path of running away to find him. Christian listened intently, his sharp mind picking up on what she chose not to say. He knew. He had known for some time. Her abrupt departure, the hidden letters, and scattered articles he'd discovered that fateful day everything pointed to her flight. Yet, he held his tongue. There would be a time to confront those truths, but now it was not that moment. "You must return home," he said at last, his voice low but firm. "You are not a slave, Gem Marie. You belong with your family. I must help you get back to them." She looked up at him, her eyes wide, uncertain. "How?" "We will travel to Georgia first. "I have business to attend to," he explained, pacing the floor, his mind clearly working through a plan. "From there, we will make our way to Europe. You've been stolen, separated from those who love you and you must return to where you belong." The two had spoken late into the night, their conversation hushed as the lantern's flame dwindled, casting flickering shadows across the room. When the light finally went out, only the pale moonlight illuminated their faces as they drifted into a peaceful sleep, wrapped in each other's arms. Morning came with the harsh crowing of the rooster, rousing them from their brief rest. They moved quickly, to slip out of their wedding clothes as the weight of the day settled on their shoulders. Gem Marie hurried down the narrow cellar hallway, her footsteps quiet on the worn stone floor. By the time Cook and McCoy had made their way into the cellar's kitchen, Gem Marie had already changed into a plain dress and freshened up, she moved toward the stairs leading to the parlor, Cook, who had been boasting to McCoy about being on the plantation longer than anyone could remember, noticed Gem Marie and stopped her in her tracks. "Hold up there, girl," Cook called, his voice rough with years of suspicion. "Sit yourself down a minute before you go runnin' off to tend to Margaret's baby. I got somethin' to say to you. There's things you need to know about this here plantation about Honey Waters and how it really came to be that Master Christian Pierre started all this." Gem Marie froze, her pulse quickening. She glanced toward the stairs, her thoughts still on Christian and the night they had shared. But Cook's eyes bore into her, hard and unreadable, making it clear he wasn't asking. With a sigh, she sat down on the rough wooden chair Cook motioned toward. Her body was tense she had never trusted Cook. His watchful eyes followed her everywhere, and though he rarely spoke to her directly, his presence always made her feel like an outsider, like someone who didn't belong. And now as he stood before her, arms crossed over his chest, his brow furrowed, she could feel his wariness. Whatever he was about to say, it was meant to unsettle her. "You think you know this place," Cook began slowly, his voice low and gravelly. "But you don't. Not the way I do. Honey Waters ain't what it seems, and neither is Master Pierre. You may have charmed him, but you best believe there's more to him and to this

295

plantation than meets the eye." Gem Marie forced herself to nod, though her heart sank. She had poured her heart out to Christian the night before, and now here was Cook, determined to taint whatever happiness she had found. She listened, barely absorbing the words, her mind racing with thoughts of escape. If only she could break free from this cellar, fly far away like a bird to the Scotney. But as Cook spoke, she realized there was no avoiding the hard realities of Honey Waters and no escaping the ever-watchful eyes of Cook. Once cook was done speaking and gave a nonverbal nod of dismissal, she raced upstairs to find Margret waiting for her in the parlor. "My goodness, you'd think it was you who got married and had to soothe a fussy baby all night," Margret teased, though her voice was wearied. "Well, here she is. Lilac's just been changed, fed, and hopefully she'll sleep a little longer. Mind her head she's getting beside herself, trying to sit up already, but she's not strong enough yet. Margret gave a small, tired laugh, gently shifting the baby's weight. "I believe that's everything. I'll be in the garden and the fields if you need me." She turned swiftly, heading toward the door. Just as Margret reached for the handle, Gem Marie found her voice. "Margret," she said softly, "You were a beautiful bride. I wish you a lifetime of love." Margret froze for a moment, her hand resting on the door. Slowly, she turned her head, just enough for Gem Marie to catch the glimmer of unshed tears in her eyes. "Thank you for playing," Margret whispered, her voice tight with emotion. "It was beautiful. And I wish you forever love as well." Without another word, she opened the door and stepped outside, the soft creak of the hinges breaking the silence. From behind, all Gem Marie could see was the outline of Margret's back as she vanished into the sunlight. "You're welcome," she called after her, her voice echoing through the parlor just as the front door clicked shut. Gem Marie sat in quiet reflection, her thoughts drifting back to the grand wedding ceremony of Lady Lelina and Bonneville. She vividly recalled the moment when the officiant asked, "Who gives this bride away?" Lady Lelina's father stood with pride, his voice unwavering as he spoke of blessings bestowed and promises fulfilled. A pang of longing tugged at Gem Marie's heart would she ever see Monsieur Heritage again? Would he, with the same proud stance, give her away as a bride? Hope flickered within her, delicate yet persistent, thoughts of returning home filled her with a sense of promise. Just as she allowed herself to imagine such a future, Christian Pierre entered the room, his smile warm and disarming. "Gem Marie," he said with a playful glint in his eye, "I'm sure Margaret has warned you more than once about securing the child's head and neck. Let me show you hand Lilac to me." As Gem Marie passed the child to Christian, the air shifted, carrying with it an electric charge that awakened her senses. Thoughts swirled within her, each one a whisper of fate's unpredictable hand, intertwining lives in ways she had never anticipated. In that moment, she understood that destiny had a unique way of binding their paths together. Just as Lady Lelina had discovered her own happiness against the odds, so too did Gem Marie yearning for her own love that had matured into something profound and undeniable. Yet, beneath the burgeoning passion for Christian, a steadfast loyalty to her father held her heart in a delicate balance. As the world around her shimmered with the uncertainty of what was yet to come, she stood on the precipice of a new beginning, ready to embrace both love and loyalty in a life that was uniquely hers.

Chapter: 23

Honey Waters

The tide was low when the men finally set sail, their course set for New Orleans. They knew that once they arrived, it wouldn't take long to find Christian Pierre, one of the wealthiest men in the region. Pierre's name had graced the papers in both America and Europe, not only for his fortune but also for his reputation as a benevolent philanthropist. Monsieur Heritage, Dillard, and Rupert left the conservatory just before dusk. The celebration had already begun in earnest, the pig had been prepared and slow roasted in the ground, its sweet aroma filling the school's evening air. By the time they were ready to depart, the entire school was in a drunken stupor, lost in barrels of rum and ale. Ingrid, who had been handed a large goblet of ale and sent back to her room with a slice of cake, was warned to stay there until the pig was fully roasted. She was told, in a hushed tone, not to leave her room again that night. When the students questioned the reason for the celebration, they were quickly encouraged to eat, drink, and remain joyous. Meanwhile, a careful rumor was spread that Professor Hertz was in the barn with a woman from high ranking, a convincing distraction for those curious enough to probe too deeply. The tale was enough to spark remembrance of the professor behavior the evening of the school great performance, when he had awoken with an unknown woman. In reality, Professor Hertz was no longer of this world his body had been meticulously dismembered, tied, and hidden in a barrel of rum while the revelry raged on. The irony was cruel: while the students toasted and sang, Hertz's final resting place was nothing more than a makeshift casket. Otis, who had gained the trust of Monsieur Heritage, had walked briskly back from the conservatory to inform Dr. Hertz that the festivities had begun, and the carriage would be arriving later to collect him. He also mentioned, with a sly smile, that much of the school had been drinking and that the rumor about Professor Hertz and a mysterious woman in the barn was spreading quickly. Dr. Hertz, now irritated, replied sharply, "I've heard of this behavior before during the school's last performance, no less. There was talk of him waking possibly in the morning with the esquire's wife, but I casted it off as idle gossip in his defense." Dr. Hertz's temper was flaring, but Otis, amused by the gossip, leaned in with an over exaggerated demeanor, "Oh no, Dr. Hertz, I don't want to know about that! The esquire's wife, of all people? That's the worst thing a man could do. A man like me is not safe hearing things like this. Concerning the law." Dr. Hertz's scowl deepened as he thought back to how the esquire had once questioned some of his more peculiar experiments after a passerby pulled the sheet off one his wheel barrels. Yet, it was the doctor weeks later who had saved the esquire's life during a bout with fever. It was the result of Dr . Hertz meticulous bed side manner which seemed to silence any further suspicions. As he mulled over these memories, his eyes drifted toward the garden, where he noticed the carriage waiting, as promised. Otis continued adding more severity to the situation, " Do you know I could be hanged repeating somethin like this although it may be true it wouldn't matter I would be swinging from a Sycamore tree if I were to mention the esquire's wife with your brother. No sir wile horses could get me to repeat it." Dr. Hertz growing an intensified anger grabbed his jacket and headed towards the carriage. Little did he know that the host of the party was already sealed in a barrel, destined for a far different journey than he had ever imagined. Once Dr. Hertz arrived at the conservatory he was immediately met by a student with a glass of wine, she quickly handed it to him then ran off into the building. The front of the building was filled with students laughing and drinking. Dr. hertz who was puzzled and confused pondered his brother where abouts as he stepped over a passed-out student. His heart began to quicken for there was all sorts of galivanting taking place inside, with half-dressed students running from room to room. Some were bare chested playing their instruments. The auditorium was filled with students performing on stage, some meeting their fatal demise with fake blood upon their naked bodies, others dressed in full costumes acting like spectators. The stench of Ale and rum filled the room as they caroused as if a Shakespeare himself had been directing. Dr. Hertz, visibly shaken, grabbed a nearby student dressed as lady MacBeth and demanded, "Is this what also occurred after your noted performance?" The child, swaying on unsteady feet, nodded sluggishly, her breath reeking of ale as she curtsied and stumbled off. Dr. Hertz's voice grew sharper as he grabbed another student in a nightgown who was about to sprint off " You there come here at once! Where is Professor Hertz?" The incoherent boy, struggling to focus, slurred his response while pressing one finger upon his perched lips. "We're not supposed to say…" The unleveled boy spoke in a whisper, "He's with a woman… in the barn of high regards." A cold dread crept over Dr. Hertz. His heart quickened again as he released the grip on the young man and turned to two other students who seemed less intoxicated. "Listen to me, bring everyone inside, immediately," he ordered, his voice tight with urgency. The thought of his brother being in the barn with the esquire's wife made him lightheaded. As the students hurried off, Dr. Hertz pressed further to two students laying across some chairs, "Where is this barn?" The children merely pointed toward a narrow door at the rear of the auditorium, the very door through which Ingrid had led Monsieur Héritage through earlier. Fury and apprehension surged through him as he realized the weight of his brother's recklessness. Without delay, Dr. Hertz marched up the path toward the barn, his thoughts racing with prepared chastisements for his brother's irresponsible behavior . Upon reaching it, he flung open the barn door and found no one but Professor Hertz's horse, tethered and calm. The barn was eerily tidy, save for the large, smoldering pit in the back of the barn where a pig had recently been roasted. The scent of sweetly charred meat still lingered in the air, thick and unsettling. "Martin! Martin!" he called, his voice echoing in the silence. No reply came. Dr. Hertz's chest tightened as he called out once more, but the barn loomed ominously silent, a dark silhouette against the twilight sky. A gnawing unease gripped him as he turned away, retreating toward the Conservatory. He scoured every shadowy corner of the large school, from the dank cellar to the dust-laden rafters of the uppermost rooms, but his search yielded no trace of his brother. Exhausted and plagued by an escalating sense of dread, he paused to catch his breath after inspecting the last room on the top floor. It was then that he stumbled upon Ingrid. Her cheeks were flushed with a feverish glow, the scent of alcohol thick in the air, and she was draped in the trappings of celebration. Wrapped in a sheet over a very thin sheer dress her eyes sparkled with a tipsy joy as she slurred, "Don't trouble yourself about Father, Uncle Robert! Come, drink and feast! Today is a day of merriment!" But her words only deepened his concern. Something was terribly amiss. Before he could ponder further, Ingrid seized his arm and led him downstairs she held his arm as Monsieur had held hers. "There's a delicious roast pig and cake! Please, have some rest. You're sweating profusely!" With one last wary glance around the school, feeling outnumbered he took a deep swallow of wine, its richness slid down his throat like velvet that initiated a warm feeling. Without warning

Ingrid placed a small piece of succulent pig in his mouth. The delicious flavor hit his taste buds followed by some frothy ale. The tension in his shoulders begin to ease as Ingrid continued coaxing the ale in his mouth. Yet, even as the revelry surrounded him and Ingrid suggestive mannerism continued, the unsettling feeling in the pit of his stomach lingered, a harbinger of darker truths yet to be unveiled. It was near the late hours when the festivities had begun to die down. Behind the school's locked doors, most of the students had succumbed to their drunken slumber, their laughter and chatter now replaced by the quiet hum of the night. None seemed troubled by his brother's absence, Dr. Hertz, however, couldn't shake the unease gnawed at him. Now with the night fallen completely, Dr. Hertz and a bottle of wine plus a hefty portion of roasted swine, carefully climbed into his carriage to return home. With the dark road offering a little more than time to reflect. He thought of his younger brother's disturbing absence, strangely missing without a trace, he manage to push aside worry for now. He rationalized it with Martin's accomplishments. After all he had built something remarkable an academy filled with gifted minds, which had a reputation of greatness. That should have been enough, yet his recent rendezvous with the esquire's wife continued to occupied his thoughts. "Perhaps he was falling in love with a married woman?" The idea unsettled him, as did the nagging realization that, despite the doctor's long nights and rigorous studies, his own career had not flourished as he had imagined. There were no great performances or outlandish parties to recognized his breakthrough in medicine. Arriving at his office, he dismounted, pausing to stare at the lonely building. The nights were always the same: an empty bed followed by early hours of dissecting half-decomposed animals, trying to unlock the mysteries of life and death. There were rumors of a new school opening one that encouraged radical thinking, a possible teaching hospital. Could he fit in there, or had he already fallen too far behind due to isolated methods? Pushing the thoughts aside, he turned toward his garden instead of the door for solace. The garden scented and peaceful always brought him serenity, a small sanctuary where the weight of his scientific failures seemed to melt away even if only briefly. He sat on the worn bench and uncorked the wine bottle that he had taken from the foyer of the school as he exited. A deep breath escaped him as he prepared to watch the nightly bloom of his prized flowers that he loved so much. Upon opening the wooden box beside him, Dr. Hertz's breath caught in his throat. His eyes fluttered, disbelieving. The wine bottle slipped from his grip, shattering as it struck the ground. He rubbed his eyes, certain it was some trick of the darkness. Surely, the bright moon casting its silvery light had unleashed some form of witchery. Yet there were two glares, eerily familiar, peering at him through the sweet-smelling Casablanca lilies. His heart pounded as he stumbled backward, his mind racing to make sense of what he saw. With trembling hands, he rushed to his carriage, fumbling for his lantern. He returned, the kerosene light flickering across the box's contents, inside, nestled amid the bed of flowers, was his brother, Martin. Reflecting off the lantern's light and glowing into the night. It was only his severed head, his neck grotesquely scorched and twisted like a knotted rope. Dr. Hertz's breath quickened, his chest tightening, as he clutched at his heart. Surely this was a hallucination, brought on by exhaustion and the wine. Just as he felt the edges of unconsciousness closing in, the eyes blinked. Shock overtook him. He leaned closer, peering into the box, before swiftly removing his jacket and wrapping it around the head. His gaze darted around his moonlit garden, every shadow now teeming with sinister intent. His hands trembled as he lifted the severed head and carried it inside, laying it carefully on the laboratory table. His mind whirled, struggling to stay grounded as he removed his jacket to reveal his brother's face. His voice, however, remained unnervingly calm, as if speaking to a patient. "Martin…" he whispered, his throat tight with grief. "I'm so sorry for your misfortune. Not in my worst nightmares could I have foreseen such… horror." His voice broke, tears streaming down his face. His heart ached as he choked out, "Who could have done this to you, my dear brother? For you had no enemies only your love of music consumed you." Then a small single flower petal drifted from Martin's ear, and Dr. Hertz suddenly understood. The careful placement of the head was a message one from someone who feared neither law nor consequence. Pulling up a stool, he sat to examine the grotesque craftsmanship more closely, his mind moving between sorrow and cold deduction. After allowing the reality to slightly seep in Dr. Hertz spoke again to the severed head, "But Martin," he began softly, "you must have known… frolicking with the esquire's wife would not end well. Mother always warned you, your reckless nature at times would bring harm if left unchecked." He paused, the weight of the moment pressing down on him like a stone. "This is a terrible fate, brother, but I promise, you will not be forgotten. For what you've left behind will serve a higher medical purpose.

I put my life on it." But then, in the dim light, something impossible happened. The faintest twitch crossed Martin's face. A flicker, A blink. It was as though the dead had given him a nod of approval. Dr. Hertz leaned in, his heart thundering in the oppressive silence. Had his brother just blinked again? The night, once peaceful, had turned ominous. It was only the beginning. Dr. Hertz's voice cracked with sorrow, his younger brother now gone forever. he whispered staring at his brother's severed head, "Rest in peace, Martin." "I've got a pet shark in the Atlantic he will be so please with this bountiful treat you have bestowed upon me brother McGhee." It was one of the last thing Captain Shark stated to his half-brother Captain McGhee. Before setting a sail, "I see you lads have got a taste for mischief," his voice rumbled before letting out a bellowing laughter. "I shall be coming through New Orleans to check on you, I mind you all to take heed down there they don't take kindly to placing aristocrats in rum barrels." Monsieur Heritage nodded with a tip of his hat as the ship and the entire crew departed from Baltimore's fort. It was the evening of the school's celebration before Dr. hertz's arrival that they set sail to New Orleans. Baron informed Captain McGhee that a new state named Florida had recently been established and they would have to go around it. Captain McGhee, who emphasized there was nothing new about the piece of land. It had just been recognized by the top hats and given a name. It had been close to fourteen hours the ship had been a sail, and the plan was laid out perfectly. Once he set off to Christian Pierre house Monsieur Heritage had two hours to locate and retrieve Gem Marie if not the crew would have to find him. The plan had been laid out Monsieur would enter town first where he would question some locals on where Christian Pierre was location. After he would advise Baron, who would be lingering nearby, would be tracking his every move if more time were needed he would return to Baron to give him the status of Gem Marie. Upon his return to her location they would leave quietly together or if needed she would be taken by force. When Monsieur Heritage arrived in the bustling port city of New Orleans, he wasted no time in acquiring a horse, although a fine stallion the creature was in desperate need of new shoes. He led the animal to a nearby blacksmith a who turned out to be a helpful resource for information. A seasoned man whose hands bore the marks of years spent shaping iron, the blacksmith deftly resized the horse's hooves, all the while boasting of how long he'd been in the trade. He claimed that nearly every man in the city had at least once relied on his craftsmanship.

"What good is horse with poor shoes," he stated to Monsieur Heritage who listened carefully, eyeing Baron across the road at a local tavern. Monsieur casually mentioned he had not seen an old friend, Christian Pierre, since his return from Europe. He watched the blacksmith's reaction closely, knowing full well the name carried weight in the area. The blacksmith's hands momentarily paused mid-task before he spoke again, lowering his voice to a conspiratorial whisper. "I've known Christian Pierre for years," The blacksmith murmured, casting a quick glance around to ensure no one else was listening. "His plantation Honey Waters is different from the others. Some say the he and the slaves live like they're in their own world." Monsieur Heritage's brow furrowed at the cryptic remark. "What do you mean?" he asked, curiosity piqued. The blacksmith gave a curt nod, as if reluctant to say more. "You'll see for yourself. Honey Waters ain't like the rest but I take it you must know a little about your friend's choices." With a slight tremor in his voice, the blacksmith provided directions to the elusive Honey Waters plantation, a place that, by all accounts, carried as many whispers of mystery as it did intrigue but respect. After relaying his findings from the blacksmith to Baron, Monsieur Heritage rode ahead, an unsettling thought gnawing at him what truly lay behind the gates of Honey Waters? The blacksmith had provided clear directions, but instead of the dense woods Heritage anticipated, the path ahead was unexpectedly lined with wildflowers. The air was thick with the heady perfume of lavender and Lilac, so intense it felt surreal, like a scene plucked from a dream or a painting. The idyllic surroundings painted Honey Waters as a tranquil, serene place, yet deep in his gut, Heritage knew it was merely a facade hiding something far more sinister. Any man that could take child from her home and then surround himself with such opulence must be demented. As he neared the entrance, four men stepped forward in front of a long gate, blocking his path. Their expressions were hard, suspicious. "Who are you sir?" one of them demanded. This was unusual black and white together guarding an entrance armed with swords. Monsieur Heritage smiled, trying to maintain his composure. "I'm a dear friend of Christian Pierre from London," he explained smoothly. "I've come for the celebration." The men exchanged glances, and one of them frowned. "Sir, you mean yesterday's wedding?" Heritage's heart skipped a beat, but he forced himself to remain calm. His mind raced, what had happened? Why didn't the blacksmith mention it. "Yes, of course," he replied, his tone steady despite the panic rising in his chest. "My ship was delayed unexpectedly, which threw off my schedule I forced to spend a night in Florida. But I'd still like to see Christian Pierre. It's been years since we last met." The men eyed him warily, but their gaze lingered on his fine attire, a mark of his social standing. After a moment of hesitation, the men stepped aside. Monsieur Heritage exhaled in relief, though his unease remained. He offered each man five dollars, flashing them a charming smile. "Thank you, gentlemen, I may have some friends arriving behind me. Should they appear, do allow them through, though I'm not certain when they'll arrive. Thank you again." The men nodded, still cautious but swayed by his confident demeanor and generous tip. As Monsieur Heritage passed through the gates, a chill ran down his spine. The beauty of Honey Waters had lulled him, but now the weight of mystery and the unknown settled over him once more. What had happened here, and what would he find when he finally came face to face with Christian Pierre? He rode with fierce determination, adrenaline coursing through his veins as he tore through the well-manicured grounds. Ahead of him a grand house rose from the heart of the plantation, standing like a monument to its owner's wealth and power. Without waiting for his horse to come to a full stop, he leapt from the saddle, sprinting up the porch steps two at a time and bursting through the massive double front doors. Inside, the house was empty and lavishly decorated, but he had no time for the opulence surrounding him. The large foyer blurred past him as he strode with purpose, his ears picking up faint voices, a woman's laughter echoing down the hallway. He slowed his stride as he continued to follow the sound, every step weighing heavier with rage, until he reached the doorway of a parlor on his right. His hand moved instinctively to his breast pocket as he slowed his pace to the sound of a male voice. Across the room, sat a beautiful young girl, her hair long to her shoulders with small streaks of sunburned hair. Her smile was bright as she cradle a baby her arms petite and gentle. Monsieur look again now deep in focus. It was Gem Marie her features now slightly mature her skin brown as honey due to the southern sun. Holding the infant in her arms, she held it up and inhaled deeply, her gaze tender as she looked into the child's innocent eyes. Monsieur Heritage watched while standing above her, emersed in the entire scene was what appeared to be a Christian Pierre. He stood over her with watchful eyes as he occasionally removed strands of hair from her face. He causally placed his hand on her shoulder to which she slowly ran her fingertips against the back of his hand.

Monsieur Heritage now remembering a small girl sitting on a yellow satin chair as her fingers stroked a custom-made harp. The thought of her precious beautiful instrument being replaced by baby infuriated him. The sight sent a wave of fury crashing over him rage and betrayal flooding every inch of his being. She had been taken not given and forced to convert to the life as a breeding slave. The tears that filled his eyes turned his focus to a blurred cloudy view. With one blink the tears rolled down his face and unto his lips. remnants of salt water linger in his mouth as he pierced his lips together in rage. Here he stood, finally face-to-face with the man who had shattered his world and everything related family he had created. From a distance, Christian Pierre had been a phantom, a figure cloaked in philanthropy and praise through glowing newspaper articles. But now, under the same roof, he could see the truth the man was nothing more than a deceiver, a manipulator of young girls. This was the monster who had stolen her from England and had taken her innocence, the man who had pierced his heart with the anguish of a thousand knives for so many sleepless nights. As he stood there, mere feet from the man he despised, memories surged through him. Christian Pierre was not just the villain of today he became every man who had ever harmed his daughter. He was the father who had no name who had abandoned her, He was the boy who had once hurled cruel, filthy name 'nigger' at her, while never knowing the purity of her heart. He was the man who had found her, captured her, treated her like an object, a piece of cargo to be tossed around and used as he pleased. And now, Christian Pierre had taken the ultimate from her, robbing her of her innocence before she even had the chance to fully become a woman. He had violated her not just to satisfy his lust, but as a display of his power a reminder to everyone that he controlled everything, even the purity of a young girl's life. The weight of the moment pressed down on him, his chest heavy with a grief so fierce it burned. The man who stood before him was not just Christian Pierre anymore he was the embodiment of every wound Gem Marie had ever suffered, and in that moment, nothing mattered except retribution. Monsieur Heritage, his heart now blackened with hatred and jealousy, suddenly cried out, "Thief!" His voice was coarse, loud, and raw, like the scraping of jagged stone. The shout reverberated through the room, startling the two occupants. Christian Pierre, wide-eyed and disoriented, stared at the stranger before him, his mind struggling to comprehend the scene. Gem Marie, though shaken, was not frozen. Her gaze locked onto the face she

306

hadn't seen in years, one she had once known as her protector, her teacher and her father now seemed almost like a ghost from her past. Her mind raced to make sense of it, was this apparition real, or had her memory conjured him from the depths of her imagination? In her arms there was no violin, no harp there was no wall with smiling figures cheering her on. Her voice, barely more than a trembling whisper, escaped her lips. "Monsieur? est-ce vraiment toi," Tears welled in her eyes, clouding her vision as she fought to hold herself together. She repeated again. "Is that really you?" Monsieur Heritage's hand, still gripping the dagger hidden in his breast pocket, trembled as the weight of the moment bore down on him. Slowly, he released his hold, now pressing his palm against his heart, feeling its thunderous beat. His eyes flickered with a mix of rage and sorrow as he beheld the young woman who had once been so small clung to his fingers aboard that ill-fated ship. "I have come for you Gem Marie." A single tear escaped, trailing down his weathered cheek. For a fleeting moment, he was lost in their past. Until Christian Pierre, broke the silence with a voice as cold as steel, demanded, "Who are you, sir and what are you doing in my home?" The sharpness of the question jolted Monsieur Heritage back to the present, his brief tenderness vanishing like mist in the wind. The baby in Gem Marie's arms began to stir, wiggling against her chest, its soft cries filling the tense air. Monsieur Heritage's tightened his grip on the dagger again. His eyes darkened, fury overtaking him as he quickly charged toward Christian Pierre, throwing him to the ground with brutal force. Christian's breath was knocked from his lungs as the weight of Monsieur's body pinned him to the floor. Monsieur raised the dagger, its blade gleaming ominously, in Christian's face. His heart raced as he desperately pushed against the enraged Monsieur, holding his daggered held hand at bay, Christian's free hand frantically searched the floor. Scrapping and fumbling the floor with his fingers the debris of the shattered vase and table rolled under his fingertips. The once opulent parlor now in utter chaos. The two men, locked in a desperate struggle, wrestled violently on the floor, each fighting for his life. Gem Marie, frozen with fear, clutched the baby tightly to her chest and hid behind the harp across the room Christian purchased. Her voice trembling as she called out, "Monsieur!" Her cry caused the slightest flicker of distraction in Monsieur Heritage, just enough for Christian Pierre to seize the opportunity. He found a loose fireplace poker, and with a swift, vicious jab, he drove the iron point into Monsieur's side. Monsieur Heritage let out a howl of agony, the pain breaking his focus. Christian used the moment to shove him off and quickly scramble to his feet. As Christian stood to his feet, Monsieur still clutching his dagger, sliced across Christian's thigh with deadly precision. The blade cut through his pants and left a deep diagonal cut across his thigh. Christian staggered away as a raw scream escape him while blood poured down his leg. "Why?!" he yelled through gritted teeth, his voice laced with both fury and confusion. He pressed his hand against the wound, trying to slow the bleeding. "Why are you here?!" Christian repeated, as the two moved around in a circular defense stance. A glare of sunlight impeded Christian vison as he moved around the room, Monsieur, seeing an opportunity lunged towards him again with his dagger raised in hand. Christian, despite his searing pain, grabbed a statue from a nearby table and with all his strength, swung it upward in a wide arc motion, which struck Monsieur across his face. The force of the blow sent him crashing backward, shattering the long window behind him as he tumbled out onto the veranda. Breathing heavily, drenched in blood and rage, Christian limping toward the broken window, grabbed his flintlock musket from its perch on the wall. Its long barrel gleaming ominously in the dim light. He leapt through the broken frame, glass crunching beneath his boots as he stormed the veranda. Raising the musket, he aimed its deadly barrel at Monsieur, who was struggling to rise from the debris that surrounded him. He knelt on one knee while trying to rise, as Christian shouted, "I will ask you once more why are you here! What business do you have with me?" Christian growled, his voice cold and laced with danger. Monsieur still unsteady remained silent, "Answer me, or with this one shot, I'll put a bullet straight through your heart." Monsieur Heritage, still trying to rise with his face bloodied and his breathing labored, let out a sinister laugh mixed with pain, "My daughter! you've stolen my daughter, and I want her back. She is no man's slave!" he snarled. Christian's grip tightened on the musket as fury burned hotter in his chest. "Your daughter?" now glancing at Gem Marie who bore no resemblance to the infuriated man, Christian Pierre retorted, "Your daughter sir was a captive in that wretched school. I saved her from a man who would have made her play until her dying day for his own twisted gain and pleasure!" Monsieur sneered, his eyes flashing with malice. "Wretched school maybe but know that man, now lies at the bottom of the Atlantic, inside the belly of a great white. Where you, too, will soon meet your fate. You have stolen her, release her and I may spare your life." Christian's temper snapped at the threat, his eyes blazed in disbelief and rage as he pressed the musket firmly against Monsieur's chest. "You dare come to my land, a land of peace, and wreak havoc on my soil and Before your child you destroy everything in your path. Then with your blind rage you dare speak of my fate with a musket in my hand. Are you truly her father!" "Yes I am!," Monsieur screamed. "You lose her to the wolves of the world! Well she is my wife now!" Christian retorted. Monsieur Heritage with desperation creeping into his eyes, made a sudden attempt to reach for the dagger hidden in his boot. Christian with faster reflexes shifted his aimed towards Monsieur's leg. "I wouldn't try that if I were you sir," Christian warned, his voice low, sincere and dangerous. "This musket's put more men in the ground than I care to count. I always carry three bullets as a part of my wardrobe, and I've got enough to divide them between your head, heart, and leg if you make another move. You know that dagger of yours is no threat to me. So I would leave it alone unless you want to lose that leg." Monsieur froze, his hand hovering inches from the dagger in his boot. He locked eyes with Christian, the weight of the musket barrel pressing into his leg he knelt on. The tension between them reaching a deadly peak, "You dare defile my daughter for your own sick pleasure for growth of your plantation!" Monsieur roared his voice trembling with a mix of fury and grief. "Gem Marie was young, innocent unaware of the darkness in this world. Perhaps I'm to blame for sheltering her, but you, sir, you are nothing but a hunter thirsting for virgin blood. "Christian Pierre, clutching his bleeding leg, let out a painful, mocking laugh. His eyes darkened with contempt as he faced his accuser. "A child? You fool have you no eyes," he spat. "I have not laid a single hand on your daughter! That child belongs to one of my slaves, not Gem Marie." With that, Christian lifted his musket, first aiming it squarely at Monsieur Heritage's face then lowering it toward his leg, where his dagger gleamed menacingly. Gem Marie now standing in the doorway distraught cradling Lilac pleaded. " Monsieur this is not my baby I have never." Christian's eyes burned with rage as he recalled the destruction of his home. he sneered, his voice now dripping with malice. "You locked her away and taught her nothing, Gem Marie caring for that child, you can consider it practice. For once I consummate our marriage, she'll be caring for her own child soon enough." The taunting words were like venom, which struck Monsieur like a fatal blow. Without warning he snapped, in a flash he reached into his boot, pulled free the dagger, and hurled it with deadly precision. The blade sunk deep into Christian's chest, lodging itself above his heart. Christian staggered, the sudden blow forced his finger to pull the trigger a deafening shot echoed through the veranda as the bullet struck Monsieur Heritage in the chest, instantly sending him crashing backwards to the ground. A chilling scream pierced the air. From Gem Marie, cradling baby Lilac that too let out a piercing scream. She carefully placed the baby in a basket of flowers seated on the veranda. Horror etched into her delicate features as the echo of the gunshot rippled through the plantation, summoning a surge of slaves toward the big house. Margaret the first to arrive, her heart pounding arms filled with flowers as she stumbled upon the gruesome scene. Her eyes widened in terror, with no time for shock. she rushed to Christian's side, her hands trembling as she snatched the dagger out, pressing her hand against the gaping wound in his chest, she quickly removed the head scarf from her head and tied it around him and pressed on the wound. She called out for Cook and McCoy but received no answer. Blood soaked through her fingers as she removed her apron, to apply on the wound. fighting panic as his breathing grew more shallow. Margret whispered, "Master Pierre, hold on, it's not that bad." She quickly turn to Gem Marie and scream, "What did you do!" Gem Marie now caring for Monsieur Heritage pulled his body off the broken glass and placed his head on her lap as she sat on the debris filled veranda and softly spoke, " I am sorry I ran away to the world." Monsieur whose eyes were closing slowly smiled and replied, "Mon Petite Gem Marie." His eyes now opening and closing more frequently were coaxed open by Gem Marie's tears that fell upon his face. "You must not sleep Monsieur you will sleep on the ship back to the Scotney not now." Margret in a panic yelled again, "McCoy!" There were now slaves gathering around the big house all too frighten to take a step on the veranda. Some turned away from the sight others ran for fresh water. "Cook!" Margret screamed out again crying uncontrollably. Her voice breaking in the air, Christian's eyes fluttered open, and with a voice barely more than a breath, he uttered some words, a ghost of defiance on his lips: "Where is she?" In that moment, Gem Marie who had been caring for Monsieur paused and spoke," I am here my love." her presence commanding. Margret now staring at Gem Marie mind swirled with a series of thoughts, trying to speak realizing that Christian had finally fell in love, was only able to gave Gem Marie a pleading stare. Gem Marie sensing her mental anguish and query stated, "She is in the basket." Margret carefully adjusted Christian and placed his head on her hand and leg, then picked up Lilac who had drifted to sleep. Gem Marie staring down onto her lap looked from left to right at the two men she had loved and who had loved her in return, witnessing their lives slowly slipping away. Their shallow breaths a testament to their drifts in and out of consciousness, she spoke to them softly, her words tinged with an aching sorrow. The weight of grief and guilt bore down on her heart, intensifying with each fading breath they took. As tears welled in her eyes, her voice remained steady she began to softly speak. " I will explain everything so you two will not fight. I found the article about you," she whispered to Christian," and I ran away from home just to find you." Monsieur breath becoming shallow listened while Christian's eyes fluttered open, a faint smile breaking through the pain. "I know," he whispered. Silence enveloped Honey Water as the two men lay still, their breaths mingling with the melancholy that filled the air. The two men now both experiencing flashbacks of their moments spent with Gem Marie. Her voice now growing soft and distant, began speaking in French, her words flowing like a haunting melody as she spoke to both Christian and Monsieur. She told them of the nights she spent hiding beneath her bed, and of her escape under the wagon, each word a thread weaving her story with theirs. Switched effortlessly between French and English, her voice a quiet, determined force. The veranda and steps now filled with all slaves and servants gathered around listening attentively as she continued to tell her story. The air was still, with only the sound of Gem Marie's voice carrying through the air. Her tone was steady yet tender, weaving a warmth that enveloped everyone around her. Each word was measured, laced with a calming assurance that softened even the hardest edges of the moment. The two men lying on the veranda floor each resting in one of Gem Marie's arms and legs their breaths shallow and strained as they listened intently as she told her story. It was as though her voice alone could soothe their suffering, offering a sense of peace to whatever lay ahead. Then rising through the silence from the distance, the thunderous sound of horses' hooves approaching, growing louder and louder with every passing moment. The crowd's focus now on the cloud of dust erupting on the rich soil that was once known for its harmony. Amongst the rumbling noise, a young voice broke through the tension a lone slave, breathless and wide-eyed, shouted one word that resonated like a bell tolling in the stillness: "Pirates!"

Made in the USA
Columbia, SC
05 January 2025

49320308R00172